P9-DTE-343

Literary Lives
Founding Editor: **Richard Dutton**, Professor of English, Lancaster University

This series offers stimulating accounts of the literary careers of the most admired and influential English-language authors. Volumes follow the outline of the writers' working lives, not in the spirit of traditional biography, but aiming to trace the professional, publishing and social contexts which shaped their writing.

Published titles include:

Clinton Machann
MATTHEW ARNOLD

Jan Fergus
JANE AUSTEN

John Beer
WILLIAM BLAKE

Tom Winnifrith and Edward Chitham
CHARLOTTE AND EMILY BRONTË

Sarah Wood
ROBERT BROWNING

Janice Farrar Thaddeus
FRANCES BURNEY

Caroline Franklin
BYRON

Sarah Gamble
ANGELA CARTER

Nancy A. Walker
KATE CHOPIN

Roger Sales
JOHN CLARE

William Christie
SAMUEL TAYLOR COLERIDGE

Graham Law and Andrew Maunder
WILKIE COLLINS

Cedric Watts
JOSEPH CONRAD

Grahame Smith
CHARLES DICKENS

George Parfitt
JOHN DONNE

Paul Hammond
JOHN DRYDEN

Kerry McSweeney
GEORGE ELIOT

Tony Sharpe
T. S. ELIOT

David Rampton
WILLIAM FAULKNER

Harold Pagliaro
HENRY FIELDING

Andrew Hook
F. SCOTT FITZGERALD

Mary Lago
E. M. FORSTER

Shirley Foster
ELIZABETH GASKELL

Neil Sinyard
GRAHAM GREENE

James Gibson
THOMAS HARDY

Linda Wagner-Martin
ERNEST HEMINGWAY

Cristina Malcolmson
GEORGE HERBERT

Gerald Roberts
GERARD MANLEY HOPKINS

Neil Roberts
TED HUGHES

Kenneth Graham
HENRY JAMES

W. David Kaye
BEN JONSON

R. S. White
JOHN KEATS

Phillip Mallett
RUDYARD KIPLING

Literary Lives
Series Standing Order ISBN 978–0–333–71486–7 hardcover
Series Standing Order ISBN 978–0–333–80334–9 paperback
(*outside North America only*)

You can receive future titles in this series as they are published by placing a standing order. Please contact your bookseller or, in case of difficulty, write to us at the address below with your name and address, the title of the series and one of the ISBNs quoted above.

Customer Services Department, Macmillan Distribution Ltd, Houndmills, Basingstoke, Hampshire RG21 6XS, England

Tennessee Williams

A Literary Life

John S. Bak
Professor, Université de Lorraine, France

© John S. Bak 2013

All rights reserved. No reproduction, copy or transmission of this publication may be made without written permission.

No portion of this publication may be reproduced, copied or transmitted save with written permission or in accordance with the provisions of the Copyright, Designs and Patents Act 1988, or under the terms of any licence permitting limited copying issued by the Copyright Licensing Agency, Saffron House, 6–10 Kirby Street, London EC1N 8TS.

Any person who does any unauthorized act in relation to this publication may be liable to criminal prosecution and civil claims for damages.

The author has asserted his right to be identified as the author of this work in accordance with the Copyright, Designs and Patents Act 1988.

First published 2013 by
PALGRAVE MACMILLAN

Palgrave Macmillan in the UK is an imprint of Macmillan Publishers Limited, registered in England, company number 785998, of Houndmills, Basingstoke, Hampshire RG21 6XS.

Palgrave Macmillan in the US is a division of St Martin's Press LLC, 175 Fifth Avenue, New York, NY 10010.

Palgrave Macmillan is the global academic imprint of the above companies and has companies and representatives throughout the world.

Palgrave® and Macmillan® are registered trademarks in the United States, the United Kingdom, Europe and other countries.

ISBN 978–0–230–27352–8

This book is printed on paper suitable for recycling and made from fully managed and sustained forest sources. Logging, pulping and manufacturing processes are expected to conform to the environmental regulations of the country of origin.

A catalogue record for this book is available from the British Library.

A catalog record for this book is available from the Library of Congress.

10 9 8 7 6 5 4 3 2 1
22 21 20 19 18 17 16 15 14 13

Printed and bound in Great Britain by
CPI Antony Rowe, Chippenham and Eastbourne

For Margaux and James

Contents

Preface

Tennessee Williams's many lives, literary or otherwise, have been thoroughly documented over the last half century, so any new biography of the playwright is likely to tread on well-beaten ground. *Tennessee Williams: A Literary Life* thus revisits a playwright whom many readers already know. What I hope to add to the traditional narrative of his life are new perspectives on the old stories – new wine, as it were, in old bottles – ones that are in many ways abetted by Williams himself that have emerged in light of recent publications and archival research.

Among those biographies written about Williams, some are very good studies of the writer's tortured psyche, some average portrayals of his paradoxical life, and some downright self-aggrandizing memoirs by his many retainers. Williams's entourage, especially in the final decade of his life, fluctuated from the company of many to the companionship of one, and while his relationship with nearly all of those who went on to capture his life on paper was at best a give and take, he accepted their predatorial presences lest he face another morning of oblivion alone. Fighting together with a lover, a secretary, a travelling companion, an agent or a theatrical personality was largely more desirable for Williams during his later years than was the prospect of struggling alone with his creative blue demons. Consequently, there is a lot that we know about Williams, particularly later in his life, that is more apocrypha than fact. It is here that this biography will proffer its most original material.

Of these many studies, surely Lyle Leverich's biography *Tom: The Unknown Tennessee Williams* stands alone. It was the first biography of its day to make generous use of the extensive unpublished archives (letters and correspondences, college papers, private notebooks) and told the story of Williams's life through these personal sources rather than through the stories and tall tales perpetuated by Williams's friends, colleagues and hangers-on. Leverich was Williams's first and only authorized biographer (Williams had given him two letters of authorization, one just a month or so before he died, though both were squashed under the iron first of Lady St Just; only after her death was Leverich allowed to publish his biography), and his study delivered on most of its promises. It is the gold standard by which all biographies on Williams are, and should be, measured. Since the recent release of those many unpublished sources has made public what Leverich had examined in private, a new biography could complement Leverich's *Tom*, which takes readers only up to the year 1945, just after the success of *The Glass Menagerie*. Unfortunately, Leverich passed away before he completed his second volume, *Tenn*. Theatre critic and writer John Lahr, on whom the task to complete the project has been conferred, will soon publish this long-awaited second volume.

The other biographies, good in their ways, are also riddled with apocrypha or errors. Donald Spoto's hastily written study, *The Kindness of Strangers*, falls into this category, as do the ghost-written 'memoirs' of his mother Edwina and his brother Dakin. If Ronald Hayman's *Everyone Else Is an Audience* improved upon these biographies in accuracy, it did not advance them much in content. And I even hesitate to speak about Dotson Rader's *Cry of the Heart*, Donald Windham's *As If*, Harry Rasky's *Tennessee Williams: A Portrait in Laughter and Lamentation*, Gilbert Maxwell's *Tennessee Williams and Friends*, Bruce Smith's, *Costly Performances: Tennessee Williams: The Last Stage*, Mike Steen's *A Look at Tennessee Williams*, and Scott Kenan's *Walking on Glass: A Memoir of the Later Days of Tennessee Williams*, which were penned as much to celebrate their authors as they were to honour the playwright they toasted – or roasted. Many of the inaccuracies perpetuated by the earlier biographies have been corrected by Leverich, as well as by Allean Hale, Albert J. Devlin, and Kenneth Holditch in their biographical articles, and by William Jay Smith in his recent book *My Friend Tom: The Poet–Playwright Tennessee Williams*; all cover the younger Williams's life very well. Holditch has recently written an informative critique of Williams's many early biographers, and I hope to avoid committing the same errors in this book that he criticized them for in theirs.

Many of these biographies/memoirs, regardless of their (re)liabilities, have for the most part painted portraits of a troubled playwright: angry over his stormy adolescence; guilty over his having escaped his sister's mental illness; troubled at first by his homosexual desires. While all of these life stories did play a significant role in shaping Williams's experiences, to the degree that they preoccupied Williams throughout his life remains conjecture. There was enough pleasurable love, sex, and success in his life (e.g., travels, partners, theatrical awards) that also allowed him to laugh, and what a laugh that was – legendary to some, disarming to others. Mummers's director Willard Holland described that laugh in the following terms: 'He had the most inane laugh I ever heard. It was a high squeaky cackle, a shriek and a cackle'.[1] It is *that* Williams that I wish to capture more extensively in these pages.

There was not always reason for Williams to laugh later in his life and in his career, and when he did, it was frequently laced with a thick coat of irony or bitterness. Without neglecting the truth that dark clouds did often hover over St Louis, Provincetown, New Orleans, Rome, New York, and Key West, this biography ultimately wants to capture a gay Williams (in both senses of the word), for in life he rarely if ever wallowed in guilt over his sexual orientation. And even if those many 'dark clouds' did temporarily block out the sun for Williams – writer's block, Rose's lobotomy, life with his father, psychoanalysis, Frank Merlo's death, drug and alcohol addiction, *Time* magazine's theatre department – he never stayed in one place long enough to let their darkness oppress his own mercurial nature. Williams left behind as many ghosts as he did manuscripts in those cities that 'swept about [him] like dead leaves', recalling the nomadic amblings of his first great dramatic protagonist, Tom Wingfield. If this book had an epigraph, it would be that famous line from *The Glass Menagerie*.

Chapters in this book are thus titled after the many cities – and his voyages between them – that gave structure to his life, from the various productions his plays enjoyed in St Louis's Wednesday Club in 1936–37 to those in New York's Jean Cocteau Repertory in 1979 and Chicago's Goodman in 1982. What many of the previous biographies may have missed or glossed over in the decades or space separating these productions and their host cities, Williams had frequently supplied by himself: in his numerous letters and private notebooks, in his early or unpublished writing, in his middle or late interviews, and in his *Memoirs* and its dark spin-off, 'Mes Cahiers Noirs', a rather ignoble rant written during a particular 'cloudy' period of the late 1970s when revivals of *A Streetcar Named Desire* and *Cat on a Hot Tin Roof* were overshadowing the reception of his current plays in production. This biography does not attempt to displace or supersede any of these earlier works on Williams's life in (or already out of) print, but it does intend to offer an original angle to the discussion of Williams's life and work, and the times and the circumstances that helped produce them.

Drawing extensively from his correspondences, his notebooks and his archives in ways even Leverich could not have benefited from in his day, this biography offers a look not at Williams's life, but rather at his *literary* life. His notebooks, to which Leverich did have access, are particularly valuable as sources, but rarely do they weigh in during the important months of a given play's production. Williams was often so busy with rewrites during a production's try-out period that he left no time in the evening for his notebook entries. As such, the commentary missing here is frequently taken up in his letters and other sources of autobiographical documentation, as in his many published and unpublished essays and prose pieces. If his notebooks were a confessional, his letters and essays were a public meeting house. In the former, he jotted down his daily thoughts and professional activities, as well as his nightly quests. As he wrote in the 16 March 1947 entry: 'So I turn to my journal. I always do when things look bad. That's partly why I seem such a morbid guy in these journals'.[2] In the latter, he poured out his heart to its sole recipient or to its Sunday readers as clearly and as honestly as he had worn it on his sleeve with every play or story he wrote. Together, the notebooks, letters and essays provide the most accurate – and the most entertaining – biography on Williams ever written. I advise every reader interested in Williams's life to begin, or at least end, there.

But the notebooks begin late (1936) and end early (1958), and so much more to Williams's private life and creative thoughts exist before and after these dates. Though he would briefly take up his private journal in 1979, then again in 1981, the pages of his blue jay notebooks were filled half-heartedly and offer us little about Williams's later years. As for the letters, we have several collections to date: *Tennessee Williams' Letters to Donald Windham, 1940 to 1965*, *Five O'Clock Angel: Letters of Tennessee Williams to Marie St Just, 1948–1982*, and the invaluable volumes one (1920–45) and two (1946–57) of *The Selected Letters of Tennessee Williams* published by New Directions. Since a third volume from New Directions had not yet been published at the time of this biography's writing, Windham's and St Just's letters (and those read in the archives at the HNOC and at Columbia and Harvard universities) represented the only direct access to his life from 1957 onward. Spoto's autobiography for this period is sketchy at times or based solely on interviews with the people around him, many of whom were not even part of his inner circle.

Where this biography repeats least and complements most of the previously written life stories on him is in its recounting of Williams's later years. Much of his later life is directly captured in his *Memoirs* or indirectly documented in the prose fragments that went into the drafting of that work but which were later discarded or intentionally edited out by Doubleday. As such, the commentary on Williams's life not covered by his later letters or essays is frequently taken up in these unpublished fragments that fatten the many files of the Williams archives. Whereas the HRC's holdings are the largest, Harvard's and Columbia's are particularly rich in late Williams material that he either bequeathed them or that they acquired from his homes in Key West or New York after his death. These fragments, along with his abundant non-fiction sources (some recently gathered in the updated collection, *New Selected Essays: Where I Live*), show Williams in a different light.

As Williams repeatedly said throughout his career, if you want to get to know him and his life, read his plays. Better than any biography could do, they lay bare the playwright's heart, mind, and soul. (I intentionally avoid literary analysis as much as possible in this book, except when dealing with little-known or widely unappreciated works that could benefit from a few extra words.) To these plays, I would add the letters and the notebooks for, like the plays, they were written by a man who had no reason to think they would one day pad his celebrity or fill out his canon. Finally, I would say devour (do not dip into) his *Memoirs* and his essays, for they speak in a voice similar to that in the letters, though he was now aware he was addressing the world. Then, and perhaps only then, I would suggest that readers pick up this book, and those biographies like it. While it is certain that Williams's 'literary life' is best told through his plays and stories, there is a lot to be said about his 'non-literary life', and it is here that this biography hopes to advance fellow scholars' understanding of Williams the writer, while faithfully respecting his already-told life for a more general reader whom this book might attract.

John S. Bak
Nancy, 26 March 2012

Acknowledgements

Several of Williams's friends, scholars, and aficionados have at one time or another improved the contents of this book. I would especially like to thank William Jay Smith, Robert Bray, W. Kenneth Holditch, Allean Hale, George Crandell, Michael Paller, Annette Saddik, R. Barton Palmer, David Kaplan, Jacqueline O'Connor, Philip C. Kolin, Brian Parker, Nancy Tischler, Albert J. Devlin, Thomas P. Adler, Felicia Hardison Londré, Henry I. Schvey, David Savran, Catherine Fruchon-Toussaint, Ralph Voss, Fred Todd†, and especially Thomas Keith. I owe all of them a debt of gratitude. Any error that may have been inadvertently overlooked is, of course, my sole responsibility.

I would like to thank the staffs of the various Williams archives for their invaluable service. At the Rare Book and Manuscript Library, Columbia University, Director Michael T. Ryan and Jennifer B. Lee were instrumental in locating essays and Williams's passport picture used on the cover of this book. Siva Blake and Mark Cave of the Williams Research Center of the Historic New Orleans Collection were always available to answer my queries and respond to various requests for manuscripts. Richard Workman at the Harry Ransom Humanities Research Center provided copies of invaluable manuscripts and letters. Monique Duhaime and Theatre Collection curator Tom Horrocks at the Houghton Library were particularly helpful in locating and dating several of Williams's later manuscripts.

I would also like to thank New Directions, Kate Johnson, and the Tennessee Williams Estate, as well as The University of the South, for allowing me to reproduce portions of Williams's published and unpublished letters and manuscripts. At Palgrave Macmillan, I would like to thank my many editors and contacts: Steven Hall, Paula Kennedy, Linda Auld, Elaine Bingham, Sue Hunt, Christabel Scaife, and Catherine Mitchell.

Research for this book was made possible by the Rodney G. Dennis Fellowship in the Study of Manuscripts, Harvard University, and by funds provided by the Université de Lorraine and the research group I.D.E.A. (*Interdisciplinarité dans les études anglophones*).

Finally, I would like to thank my wife Nathalie, and my two children, Margaux and James, to whom I dedicate this book in the hope of one day passing onto them my passion for the trope.

List of Abbreviations

c. = circa.

CP = *Collected Poems*. Eds. Nicholas Moshchovakis and David Roessel. New York: New Directions, 2007.

CS = *Collected Stories*. New York: New Directions, 1989.

CTW = *Conversations with Tennessee Williams*. Ed. Albert J. Devlin. Jackson: University of Mississippi Press, 1986.

CTS = *Candles to the Sun*. Ed. Dan Isaac. New York: New Directions, 2004.

DLB = *Dictionary of Literary Biography, Documentary Series, An Illustrated Chronicle*. Vol. 4: *Tennessee Williams*. Eds. Margaret A. Van Antwerp and Sally Johns. Detroit: Gale, 1982–84.

FTTW = The Fred W. Todd Tennessee Williams Collection, Williams Research Center, Historic New Orleans Collection.

FK = *Fugitive Kind*. Ed. Allean Hale. New York: New Directions, 2001.

FOA = *Five O'Clock Angel: Letters of Tennessee Williams to Maria St Just, 1948–1982*. Ed. Maria St Just. New York: Knopf, 1990.

HNMS = *A House Not Meant to Stand*. Ed. Thomas Keith. New York: New Directions, 2008.

HRC = Harry Ransom Humanities Research Center, University of Texas at Austin.

IB = Dakin Williams and Shepherd Mead, *Tennessee Williams: An Intimate Biography*. New York: Arbor, 1983.

IHDSR = *It Happened the Day the Sun Rose*. Los Angeles: Sylvester & Orphanos, 1981.

KS = Donald Spoto, *The Kindness of Strangers: The Life of Tennessee Williams*. New York: Ballantine, 1986.

L I and *L II* = *The Selected Letters of Tennessee Williams*, Vol. I: *1920–1945*. Eds. Albert J. Devlin and Nancy M. Tischler. New York: New Directions, 2000; and Vol. II: *1945–1957*. Eds. Albert J. Devlin and Nancy M. Tischler. New York: New Directions, 2004.

LDW = *Tennessee Williams' Letters to Donald Windham, 1940–1965*. Ed. Donald Windham. New York: Holt, Rinehart and Winston, 1977.

M = *Memoirs*. 1975. New York: New Directions, 2006.

MP = *Mister Paradise and Other One-Act Plays*. Eds. Nicholas Moshchovakis and David Roessel. New York: New Directions, 2005.

MT = *The Magic Tower and Other One-Act Plays*. Ed. Thomas Keith. New York: New Directions, 2011.

MWR = *Moise and the World of Reason*. New York: Simon and Shuster, 1975.

N = *Notebooks by Tennessee Williams*. Ed. Margaret Bradham Thornton. New Haven and London: Yale University Press, 2006.

NN = *Not about Nightingales*. Ed. Allean Hale. New York: New Directions, 1998.

n.pag. = No page number assigned, no pagination given.

RMT = Edwina Dakin Williams and Lucy Freeman, *Remember Me to Tom*. St Louis: Sunrise, 1963.

NSE = *New Selected Essays: Where I Live*. Ed. John S. Bak. New York: New Directions, 2009.

SR = *Stairs to the Roof*. Ed. Allean Hale. New York: New Directions, 2000.

SS = *Spring Storm*. Ed. Dan Issac. New York: New Directions, 1999.

T = Lyle Leverich, *Tom: The Unknown Tennessee Williams*. London: Hodder & Stoughton, 1995.

TC = *The Traveling Companion & Other Plays*. Ed. Annette Saddik. New York: New Directions, 2008.

TWCD = Tennessee Williams Collection, Special Collections Department, University of Delaware Library.

TWPC = Tennessee Williams Papers, Rare Book and Manuscript Library, Columbia University.

TWPHL = Tennessee Williams Papers, Houghton Library, Harvard University.

TTW = *The Theatre of Tennessee Williams*. 8 vols. New York: New Directions, 1971–1992.

1
Columbus to Columbia (via St Louis): Separating Fact from Fiction

It is unorthodox, and perhaps even unethical, to begin a biography of a writer's life *in medias res*. Where are the early years that formed him? Where are the faces and places of his childhood? Surely, a historical biography on Tennessee Williams *should* begin in Columbus, Mississippi, and not in Columbia, Missouri. Such a biography, like Lyle Leverich's classic *Tom: The Unknown Tennessee Williams* (1995), would cover Williams's childhood from his birth in Columbus on 26 March 1911 (and not 1914, as he would later tell the Group Theatre and early interviewers) to the months he lived with his grandfather, Walter Edwin Dakin, and his beloved grandmother, Rosina Otte 'Grand' Dakin, in their rectory in Clarksdale, Mississippi, or in Memphis. As Leverich notes, Tommy Williams, during these early years, was 'growing up more a minister's son than the son of a traveling salesman, whom he scarcely recognized as a father'.[1] Then, the biography would follow the Dakin/ Williams family north (briefly) to Nashville, then back south to Canton and then Clarksdale, all the while in the company of the playwright's mother, sister, and grandparents, since his father, Cornelius Coffin, or C.C. for short, had spent his time on the road drumming first men's clothing and then men's shoes. The biography's introductory chapters would eventually terminate with his mother Edwina and his sister Rose following his father north again, this time to St Louis, where C.C. accepted a promotion to assistant sales manager at the International Shoe Company. Such would be the opening chapters of that historical biography, similar to those chapters we can already find in Leverich's *Tom*, as well as in the biographies written by his mother Edwina and his brother Dakin, just to name a few.

This is not that biography.

Instead, it begins in St Louis in the summer of 1918, when Williams was already seven years old, for that is arguably when and where Williams's 'literary life' began. One could argue the case, as indeed many have, that Williams's youth in the South formed him much more as a writer than St Louis ever did. Surely his serious illnesses at age five – diphtheria and then Bright's disease – had a significant impact on his literary affections; first bedridden then confined to the house for nearly two years, Tommy had turned from 'a little boy with a robust, aggressive bullying nature' into a 'decided hybrid', whose imaginative games and stories and aesthetic sentiments were honed during a time of relative isolation.[2] After all, he considered himself to be a southern writer, and the South is his locale of choice in his plays and in many of his stories.

I do not wish to debate that point. Arguably, though, St Louis and the Midwest had shaped Williams, too, more than he had himself considered or at least had imagined, in particular his early political and artistic credos. It is my contention in the opening of this literary biography to confirm that St Pollution – as Williams would later refer to St Louis – had at least as strong, if not a stronger than previously considered, role in transforming Thomas Lanier Williams III, the distant cousin of Civil War poet Sidney Lanier, into Tennessee Williams, the poet–playwright who championed the lowly, disenfranchised flotsam of American society.[3]

Because of that childhood illness and those frequent uprootings that ultimately landed his family in the industrial city of St Louis and its many (first unfashionable, then later highly bourgeois) suburbs, Tom Williams was a shy, unassuming boy who would sooner take to his books than to his fellow classmates. His world in the South, inhabited by his sister Rose, their black nurse Ozzie, and all of the characters in his grandfather's library, was one built on stories and playacting. His world in St Louis for the next ten years – one dominated by nearly a dozen social-climbing removals from boarding houses to apartments to rented then purchased houses in increasingly upscale districts of St Louis and stymied by the conservative ideals and gaping divides between the city's haves and have-nots – was built instead on escapism and on social activism. This chapter will explore these two themes in the early writings of Tom Williams.

Finding it difficult at first to make friends with local boys his own age at the Eugene Field Public School, or Stix School later (returning to St Louis after a brief respite in Clarksdale in 1920), Williams sought companionship in the escapist protagonists of his writings. Williams would later fantasize about fleeing to exotic climes aboard a Merchant steamer; he would actualize certain escapes to summer camp in the Ozarks and, eventually, to college in Columbia, Missouri. This need to escape – be it the oppressive conservatism of St Louis, the volatile reproaches of a drunken and disillusioned father, or the choking repression of a puritanical mother – stayed with Williams throughout his life. Even before he had the financial freedom to drift between cities and over continents, Williams was the perennial vagabond, the archetypal poet-gypsy. And when he finally left St Louis for New Orleans in December 1938, he fled more than his father's suffocating house to which he would make brief returns *always* on the way to somewhere else. Williams, it would seem, was ultimately fleeing from himself. But that Jamesian doppelganger he left behind in his parents' attic, where cigarettes and black coffee fuelled his nightly production of poems and stories – duly submitted and duly rejected – pursued him throughout the remainder of his life. Though Tommy Williams, then Thomas Lanier III or simply Tom, became Tennessee Williams en route to New Orleans, he had begun the transformation much earlier. Having escaped one past, he never really stopped looking for a future and sought it out in nearly every corner of the world.

One of those corners, which he would later celebrate in *The Glass Menagerie*, was wherever Rose happened to be at the time, be it in their bedroom in Nashville (to where the Williams family had moved when Walter Dakin accepted the ministry of the Church of the Advent in December 1913[4]) or in Clarksdale (after his childhood illness in the summer of 1916) or in Rose's white room in their 'dismal over-crowded flat'[5] on 6554 Enright Avenue in University City (a middle-class suburb in western St Louis that, with its 'vast hive-like conglomerations of cellular-living units', was more the setting for *The Glass Menagerie* than was the fashionable Westminster Place address where they had first lived on arriving in the city). Rose was not only Williams's muse, now as forever; she was also his security blanket, his small craft harbour, his God so suddenly. As Williams later described in his essay 'The Author Tells Why It Is Called *The Glass Menagerie*' (1945):

The apartment we lived in was about as cheerful as an Arctic winter. There were outside windows only in the front room and kitchen. The rooms between had windows that opened upon a narrow areaway that was virtually sunless and which we grimly named 'Death Valley' for a reason which is amusing only in retrospect.

[...] Something had to be done to relieve this gloom. So my sister and I painted all her furniture white; she put white curtains at the window and on the shelves around the room she collected a large assortment of little glass articles, of which she was particularly fond. Eventually, the room took on a light and delicate appearance, in spite of the lack of outside illumination, and it became the only room in the house that I found pleasant to enter.[6]

These were the years of brother-sister bonding which would see them throughout their lives. As Williams recalled from his earlier days in Clarksdale:

My sister and I were gloriously happy. We sailed paper boats in wash-tubs of water, cut lovely dolls out of huge mail-order catalogs, kept two white rabbits under the back porch, baked mud pies in the sun upon the front walk, climbed up and slid down the big wood pile, collected from neighboring alleys and trash-piles bits of colored glass that were diamonds and rubies and sapphires and emeralds. And in the evening, when the moonlight streamed over our bed, before we were asleep, our Negro nurse Ozzie, as warm and black as a moonless Mississippi night, would lean over our bed, telling in a low, rich voice her amazing tales about foxes and bears and rabbits and wolves that behaved like human beings.[7]

But, as Leverich points out, war hit the nation and the Williams family, and that peace which Tom and Rose and the rest of the Williamses-Dakins knew in the South was about to be upended.[8] With so many men being sent to Europe to fill the military ranks for the Great War, workers became scarce,[9] and Williams's father, who throughout the young Tom's formative years was frequently on the road, could not refuse the position offered to him at the Friedman-Shelby branch of the International Shoe Company (which bought out the local company in 1912), and the family followed him to St Louis. From that summer of 1918 until the winter of 1938, Williams lived on and off in the city he would grow to detest (and would ultimately be interred), and life would never be the same, despite the several respites he would enjoy on returning to his grandparents' home in the South.

Another of those lugubrious corners was his grandfather's Episcopalian rectory on 106 Sharkey Avenue in Clarksdale, Mississippi. While Grand frequently came north to St Louis to help Edwina out with the house, Williams, now in the fourth grade, returned alone to Clarksdale in the spring and autumn terms of 1920 to live with his grandfather. Even back in the South, Williams was so tormented at school that he had found sanctuary more in his art than in his grandfather's rectory. Williams describes in a May–June 1920 letter to his sister how he had sketched a 'Ranbow' [*sic*] comic paper for her and planned to write about the wedding of a character named Jane H. Rothchild, a suffragette who is frightened that 'Wido' Rose L. Williams will 'paint up so much' that she will attract all the potential 'million' suitors.[10] These early artistic endeavours carry with them much of what would preoccupy Williams's many later plays and stories, namely a young woman's struggle to stave off loneliness.

One final corner into which the young Williams sought refuge was the Ben Blewett Junior High School, an experimental school that a few years later instilled in him so profoundly his love of the trope that he began writing – and publishing – his work at a tender age. Williams had become an avid reader since his stay in Clarksdale, where he had the run of his grandfather's impressive library, and St Louis's famed educational system only fuelled that desire for stories. Recognized for his reading skills and literary talents, Williams was placed in an advanced reading group at Blewett, which he entered on 31 March 1924, and his mother rewarded his literary efforts with a second-hand typewriter. Williams also discovered an audience beyond himself and Rose. In November 1924, Williams published his first piece of writing, 'Isolated', in Blewett's biweekly newspaper, *The Junior Life*. It is a short prose piece of 251 words (Philip Kolin calls it a short story[11]) that established early that signature theme of loneliness. 'No wonder', he wrote in it, 'that I felt like Robinson Crusoe doomed to a lifetime of isolation'.[12]

In 'Isolated', the thirteen-year-old Williams proved himself a wordsmith and a dramatist. The piece ignores exposition and rushes headlong toward climax, for the narrator describes being drawn to White Fan Island 'on that fateful Friday'. Why it was to be 'fateful' we are not told at first, but the narrator constructs a dramatic situation from which he later emerges unscathed but not unaffected. He rows a boat against the current toward the island in the middle of the river with the intention of going fishing. More Huck Finn (or Rip van Winkle) than Crusoe here, the narrator soon falls asleep on the warm sand and is awakened by the rising flood waters – of what, we do not learn. During those two hours, waters rushed through the river at a rapid pace, wreaking havoc along the shores. It was not a storm, as that would have woken the narrator. He speaks instead about a 'thaw in the far North', but no thaw in the space of two hours would have created such a flood, despite the signs the narrator saw beforehand in the river's strong current. Perhaps a dam broke upstream; perhaps it was, as it would often be later in Williams's work, an act of divine intervention not unlike the deluge described in Genesis and his later play *Kingdom of Earth* (1968). At any rate, the narrator is stranded (presumably his own rowing boat that took him to the island was washed away by the flood) and awakes to see 'from shore to shore [...] the torches of searching parties who were reclaiming the dead bodies'. Drama is heightened when he is rescued just as the flood waters 'washed over the last hillock of my erstwhile refuge'.[13]

It is unclear if the piece was even remotely autobiographical. Williams scholars like Philip Kolin and Allean Hale find that assertion dubious. As Hale writes in a letter to Kolin: 'Tom might have recalled an island in the Meramec River or in a place in the Ozarks where he went to camp in the summers. Or it could have been a memory of Clarksdale, Mississippi or from summers near Knoxville. Too many possibilities. He probably just invented it'.[14] Whatever its history and its genre, 'Isolated' contains many of the themes and images of later Williams work (in particular water or a refuge that proves later to be a trap, as Kolin points out) save one: the happy ending. Perhaps still optimistic as an eighth grader, Williams drew victory from the clutches of tragedy, though the narrator has no doubt been traumatized by the sight of dead and bloated bodies flowing past him on his receding hillock. Endeavours such as these earned Williams the nickname 'Tom Williams – Our literary boy' from his peers, and 'mah writin' son' from his mother Edwina.[15]

Despite his forays into prose fiction, the young Williams was first and foremost a poet whose 'sympathies were with the Romantics'.[16] In his early hand at poetry, Williams found kinship with John Keats, Edna St Vincent Millay, Sara Teasdale, and later Hart Crane.[17] This can be seen in his first published poems in *The Junior Life*, 'Nature's Thanksgiving' (25 November 1925) and 'Old Things' (22 January 1926), both written when he was fourteen.[18] While 'Old Things' is lyrical in its nostalgic depiction of an old man sitting alone in 'the silence of the garret, midst things of long ago',[19] 'Nature's Thanksgiving', which speaks of the 'Bob-White [...] whirring' and the 'wood-brook [...] singing / And happily sobbing', has much in common, stylistically speaking, with his 'Sonnets for the Spring', written eleven years later in March 1936 when he turned twenty-five:

> [...] (Singer of darkness, Oh, be silent now!
> Raise no defense, dare to erect no wall,
> But let the living fire, the bright storm fall
> With lyric paeans of victory once more
> Against your own blindly surrendered shore!)[20]

Williams's future as a writer, much to the dismay of his father, was already taking shape. As Hale rightly notes, 'At fourteen, he had found his vocation'.[21]

By sixteen, Williams had learned one important lesson about writing: that his imagination could earn him money. The older he became, the more Williams needed a way to escape the nightmare that was the Williams house during the 1920s and particularly the 1930s. Writing, certainly more so than a college education (Williams would later declare higher education a stumbling block more than a stepping stone to his desired career as a writer), was to be his ticket out of that tortured familial relation. Though the more he ran from them, the more he would return to these troubling years in St Louis as the basis of his literary production. Given this fact, it would not be incorrect to situate his essay 'Can a Good Wife Be a Good Sport?' at the centre of his corpus, the nucleus from which his literary fission exploded in subsequent years. The essay not only taught him that writing pays, but it also showed him how he could use his troubled family life in St Louis as a source of literary inspiration. At one time, he would revisit the devils of the past in a wayward attempt to put them to rest, and at another time he would discover within those haunting memories the bliss that he rarely enjoyed after that 'sea gull' of fame and fortune shat 'a pot of gold on' his head.[22]

As horrific as he depicts his early years in St Louis, then, Williams was not altogether entirely despondent because he was still the idealistic Tom Williams. Tennessee Williams would change all of that, and not entirely for the better. As a wealthy and successful playwright, Williams would struggle with the idea that he betrayed the socialist themes that later dominated his early work. As a lonely, romantic heart, he would later hate his many retainers though he could not send them away. As a brother whose near 'twin' Rose left him to face the world alone when she was diagnosed with schizophrenia in 1937 and lobotomized in 1943, his life-long devotion to his sister was fuelled as much by guilt for having failed to protect her from her life sentence in an asylum as it was for having escaped a similar fate. Even the most casual dip into Williams's private notebook entries or essays reveals a writer nostalgic for the simpler days of his life, no matter how horrid those days may have been or seemed. This, and much more, is what we find in 'Can a Good Wife Be a Good Sport?'

Published in *Smart Set*, May 1927, 'Can a Good Wife Be a Good Sport?' opens with the following provocative question: 'Can a woman after marriage maintain the same attitude towards other men as she held before marriage?'[23] The male narrative voice (not Williams's, since the narrator presents himself as a married man, and Williams was only sixteen at the time he wrote this) recounts his own 'unhappy marital experiences' in order to 'present convincing answers' to the contrary. The persona here, a travelling salesman not unlike Williams's father C.C., describes 'modern married life' and how he proposed marriage to 'the flapper type' Bernice across a 'glass-topped cafeteria table', the unromantic surroundings lending proof of her true love for him. As if narrating an early F. Scott Fitzgerald story, the male protagonist then relates how he was emasculated by his flapper wife, who was bent on 'drinking, smoking, and petting', and how he caught her in the arms of another man after returning home earlier from a business trip. Now divorced, the narrator concludes on the sour note: 'No, I don't think that a wife can be that kind of "good sport"'.[24]

Williams drew his inspiration for the essay partly from his own parents' marital strife, but, strangely, he reversed the roles. The narrator was based on his travelling salesman father, who ironically was the hard-drinking philanderer in the couple, and not the frigid Edwina, who was turned into the petting flapper, Bernice. Edwina was no flapper type, but she was 'an unusually attractive girl' who possessed the 'gift of a quick tongue' with Cornelius and who 'had been a popular girl' in the South but who, now, in the barbaric city of St Louis, 'was naturally dissatisfied to sit at home "darning socks"'.[25] Why Williams would adopt his father's point of view and make him the victim of his wife's extramarital affair at a time when he did not get along with his father is anyone's guess. Perhaps it was because, deep down, Williams wanted to understand his father better (he voluntarily underwent psychoanalysis the year following his father's death and produced from it one of his best essays, 'The Man in the Overstuffed Chair', a sympathetic portrait of his father that appears as a short story in *Collected Stories* and as an essay in *New Selected Essays: Where I Live*). Or perhaps we were seeing signs of his growing antipathy toward his doting and suffocating mother, whom he would later refashion into Amanda Wingfield in *The Glass Menagerie*. Whatever the reason, the essay demonstrates a lot about the young writer's budding talents and confused state of mind about his family.

The essay won Williams a third-prize award of five dollars, as well as a warning from his grandfather in a letter of 12 April not to publish in pulp magazines or at least to use a 'nom-de-plume' instead of his real name.[26] But it also won him much more: bragging rights with high school friends, a rejoinder to his father who thought the boy was wasting his time sitting hours behind a second-hand typewriter, and self-confidence that he could reach a wider audience and make them *believe* his stories. Not only were the editors convinced of the essay's veracity, but so was the reading public, which demonstrates the historical changes taking place in America per gender roles of the 1920s, as well as Williams's precocious ability to recognize those changes based on his experiences at home. As the magazine's editors wrote, 'Thomas Lanier Williams, of St. Louis, gave a rather dreary picture of the man's side of the problem [...]'.[27] Williams had demonstrated his affinity even at a tender age for writing in a persona entirely different from his own.

Williams at this time had reason to feel depressed. Rose was away in Vicksburg, where her parents had placed her at All Saints College, ostensibly to ease some of the social and psychological torment she was experiencing. Dakin, who was spending more time with their Boston bulldog Jiggs that Cornelius bought with his poker winnings after one of his many weekend drinking and gambling parties than with him, was currying most of his father's affections. Dakin and C.C., in fact, would listen to the Cardinals baseball games for hours on the radio, which irritated his older brother. Edwina underwent a serious operation at this time as well (probably a hysterectomy), which was a cause for concern in the family. Grand was brought up from Memphis to help out with the household chores, for Edwina recalls in her memoirs that she 'lingered between life and death for five days'.[28] By November 1927, Rose's socialite Aunt Isabel ('Belle') Williams Brownlow, her father's younger sister, was preparing the young girl's debut. In a long letter to Rose dated 19 November, Williams wrote about the events at home, which included references to their charity work to bring Thanksgiving dinner to the needy (a detail we find later in *Fugitive Kind*) and his incessant 'type-writer clicking', a writing frenzy no doubt fuelled by his *Smart Set* essay.[29]

The fact/fiction divide in Williams's earlier prose pieces took a decidedly imaginative turn the following year when he published his first (long) short story. He wrote a lot during these last years of high school (first at Soldan, then at University City High School following the family's move to Enright Avenue in September 1926). It was mostly poetry, but also short stories and essays for contests, such as one 'on why Pillsbury flour was the best of all' or why 'Demon Smoke' and city smog 'Must Go'.[30] 'The Vengeance of Nitocris', the story he wrote during his junior year at University City High School and which appeared in the national magazine *Weird Tales* in August 1928, seemingly set the young writer down a path toward violence in his work from which he rarely strayed. It is about an Egyptian princess who avenges her brother's murder by inviting all who participated in the Pharaoh's death to a banquet in a newly constructed temple dedicated to him. The story reaches its sensationalized climax when the princess, Nitocris, opens a sluice gate and floods the temple (recalling the rising tide of 'Isolated'), the 'black water' hurling its 'victims, now face to face with their harrowing doom, into a hysteria of terror'.[31] Being a nationally published fiction writer at the age of seventeen gave Williams a certain cachet while in high school, and he had by now certainly considered writing to be more than just a hobby or a passion.

Like many budding authors, however, Williams thought it prudent to become a journalist first, which would open potential doors to the literary world, just as it had done for Mark Twain, Stephen Crane, and Ernest Hemingway. From 6 July to early September 1928 before the start of his senior year, Williams accompanied his maternal grandfather, Walter Dakin, on a European tour for parishioners of the pastor's Episcopal church in Clarksdale. Williams documented his trip through a series of vivid letters he sent home to his family and to his girlfriend, Hazel Kramer, as well as through a travelogue he kept of the tour, which he published in instalments the following academic year in his high school newspaper, *U. City Pep*, from October 1928 to April 1929. As Williams wrote to his grandfather on 31 January 1929, 'The editor of the school-paper, who is in my Latin class, wants me to continue my writing for the paper. I have just completed an article on Pompeii this evening which I will send to you as soon as it is published'.[32] He was supposed to have graduated in January 1928, but certain unfilled credits pushed his graduation to June. Negligence on his part (another trait that would stay with him throughout his life) made him miss the graduation ceremony altogether.[33]

These travel essays, which represent the final published writing of his youth, reveal the young man's fascination with the continent's various people, cultures, and histories. When Williams returned to Europe on 30 December 1947 after the war and an eighteen-year hiatus, his renewed interests in post-war France and Italy altered the course of his life and his literary aesthetics forever. 'Europe?' he wrote in his notebook for January 1948 while retracing his and his grandfather's earlier steps from Paris to Rome, 'I have not yet organized my impressions'.[34]

The travel pieces, which do not appear in the order of the tour, describe the young Williams's journalistic impressions about Paris on Bastille Day, as well as on the battlefields of Belleau Wood. From Paris, they voyaged to the south of France: Marseilles, Monte Carlo, and Nice. From there, they continued south to Rome and Naples, a path Williams would repeatedly follow years later, before heading back north to Venice, Milan, Montreux, Cologne, Amsterdam, and finally London.[35] The essays are important in Williams's life for essentially two reasons: one, they provide insight into the observational skills (and passion for travel) found in the mature Williams writings; and second, they reveal historical details and the daily life of post-war Europe.

The first piece, 'A Day at the Olympics', chronologically covers the penultimate city he and his grandfather visited, Amsterdam. They arrived at the end of the Games of the IX Olympiad and only saw the equestrian events, which ran from 8 to 12 August, with showjumping being the final event. Williams first describes, with journalistic precision, the 'enormous magnitude' of the city's infrastructure and all the stadiums built or modified to accommodate 'the immense multitude of people, assembled from all parts of the world'.[36] The detail in itself is not significant, nor is Williams's comment about the 'greatness of their cost' during construction; yet when we consider that only ten years had passed between these games and the endgame of World War I, we begin to understand a bit more Williams's fascination with what he was experiencing.[37] With the 1920 Games having been held in Belgium, and the 1924 Games in France, there was a visible effort to invest money not only in the countries most torn apart by the war, but also in their people. This reassembling of people from various nations previously at war had no doubt taken the young Williams by surprise.

Williams suggests as much in the following paragraph, when he describes the various nationalities sitting around him and their verbal disagreements about the event they were watching:

> The diversity of the nations represented among the spectators of the games on this day was indicated to us by the great variety of languages we heard spoken. Behind us were Germans, in front of us French. The motley of languages was such as to bring one in mind of the tower of Babel. We had programs with us but we were in some confusion as to the point in them at which we had entered. The French to the front of us and the Germans behind us both endeavored to clear our perplexity. Both of them, however, disagreed and fell into violent argument which was settled only when an Englishman, annoyed by their shouting, showed that both of them were wrong and pointed out the right place to us all.[38]

It is unclear if the hostilities vented during this argument were emblematic of nations still at war, and the sports venue simply replaced the erstwhile battlefield, or if they were meant to show how quickly warring nations could sit side by side in relative peace, or if indeed they were not an invention of the author all together (one wonders, for instance, what language the three parties spoke and, if it were not English – hardly the international lingua franca that it has since become – how Williams was able to understand them). Whatever the case, the irony of jingoistic nationalists, be they at war or at sport, was not entirely lost on the seventeen-year-old boy, who certainly understood the dynamics of their conversation and the travesties of the war that tore them apart long before ever stepping foot in Europe. His final anecdote in this piece about the horse named Miss America, who was 'showing' her 'contempt for royalty' by 'stubbornly refus[ing] to stand before the royal box and present salutations to the queen', confirms to a certain extent that Williams was not entirely jejune to political commentary.[39]

If Williams could only partly ingest Europe's intricate political machinery, he was at least capable of discerning the complexities of its human intercourse, a trait that would serve him well later in his career. In a letter to his parents dated 10 August, he speaks glowingly of the Germans and the Swiss as being more 'good-natured and kindly than the people of the other nations' that they have come into contact with.[40] Unconsciously, Williams was already defending those deemed public enemy number one, which the Germans still largely were to the French and to the English a few months shy of the Armistice's tenth anniversary. Though the young Williams would soon grow politically radical in the coming years, he never devalued personal integrity in the balance of human nature, where individual acts of kindness always outweighed gross indecencies toward the masses, and the scales of Williams's literary justice forever tipped in favour of those disenfranchised few or many.

If the general theme of death and raised spirits permeates his second piece, 'The Tomb of the Capuchins', the theme of war returns in his third piece, 'A Flight over London'. No doubt the novelty of flying for the young man overshadowed his interests in London's landmarks; he had, after all, already visited countless historical sites throughout Europe, recalling later in his *Memoirs* how he found 'the endless walking about art galleries to be interesting for only a few minutes now and then'.[41] So like any boy being forced to swallow history one museum at a time, including Shakespeare's grave and 'various other reliquary things',[42] it is understandable that he should not write much about how London rose up phoenix-like from its ashes, a metaphor he makes use of later in his homage to D. H. Lawrence. At any rate, this piece is more about seeing London from above than from ground level, giving the young boy the impression of flying over London as the Luftstreitkräfte had done the previous decade. For this reason, he begins the essay not in London but in one of its southern boroughs, Croydon, with its 'famous Croydon Field'.[43]

Though inaugurated in name in 1920, Croydon Aerodome had served during World War I as the airfield from which planes were dispatched to protect London from attacking Zeppelins. A decade later, Williams found himself among the spirits of the Royal Flying Corps:

> Scattered about the field were a great number of yellow hangars and before them were lined the planes flashing in the sun and filling the field with a terrific roar. It was during that exciting period when London was testing her air defenses by a series of mock bombard-ments and making the disturbing discovery that it was possible for her to be completely annihilated within a few nights. The planes upon the field were those which were to participate in the attack that night and were now undergoing a mechanical inspection.[44]

On 29 April 1929, *Time* magazine contained the following article on Croydon, 'Airports', which describes this aerodrome in terms similar to those in Williams's essay:

> Aviation still does not know what it requires in fields. Bad example is England's Croydon field. It was remodeled and enlarged just a year ago. Now it must be altered again at great cost. [...] Croydon's chief merit is that planes have a 1,400-yd runway in any direction. Practically all the field is grass-covered. That permits comfortable landings and takeoffs, except in rainy weather. Then the planes tear up the sod. To remedy that fault Croydon officials are considering putting a paved strip all around the field, as at the Rotterdam field. [...].[45]

The young Williams's description, though surely less technical, is nonethe-less journalistically significant in terms of the airfield's documentation.

As for the plane itself, the details Williams provides are also acute and historically relevant, not just to the physical design of this early passenger plane, with its fourteen 'wicker chairs', 'seven on each side of the aisle', but also with its metaphysical impact on people not yet accus-tomed to flying:

> As we walked toward it, we saw another equally large plane com-ing to the ground. It was a trans-channel plane. When we saw the

passengers stepping to earth, with such relief upon their faces as might be expected of lost souls who had been wandering in the regions of Erebus, we felt grateful that our flight was a short one and that we were not to be committed simultaneously to the perils of both sea and air.[46]

Fear soon gives way to fascination, however, and Williams's account of experiencing flight in 1928 surely complements other historical accounts of being airborne for the first time:

Half-way across the great field it speeds, and then there comes a slight bump, a barely perceptible tilt. You look down and you see the earth skimming lower and lower beneath you. Your breath leaves you for a moment in a gasp of exultation. You are UP! For the first time in your life the earth has released you from its grip. The trees, the yellow-roofed hangars, the tall, iron fences scud beneath us; then the gleaming concrete road and the open fields. We look down and marvel at the dwindling objects.[47]

Williams's experiences with the War are evident in one other piece that he wrote, 'A Tour of the Battle-fields of France'. While visiting Versailles, Williams comments in a letter to his mother, dated 19 'Juillet', that they saw the room 'in which the peace treaty of the Great War was signed'.[48] The tour group had earlier visited the city of Rheims, which they had expected to find 'grim with blackened ruins' but were surprised to find 'bright and richly colored'. The countryside, a once barren waste-land shorn of its trees and stripped of its poppy fields from constant bombardment, is here, only a decade later, 'patched gaily with fields of variant yellow and green':

It seemed scarcely conceivable that this land just ten years before had been ravaged by war; that these fields of golden grain, sprinkled with the night crimson of poppies, were then a barren waste, over which desperate conflicts were waged. Here and there we see a shattered wall, the ruins of a farm house, or a clump of rusted wire. These things, which we would not have noticed had they not been pointed out by the guide, are the only scars of war left upon the land which a decade ago was in a state of almost complete devastation.[49]

When they reach Belleau Wood, the battle for which took place from 1 to 26 June 1918 and which was one of the bloodiest battles the American

Marines fought in World War I (the Aisne-Marne American Cemetery contains the graves of 2289 American soldiers killed in the battle), the 'traces of the war [become] most distinct' to the young writer:

> The holes which the soldiers dug in the ground remain clearly visible. If one has any imaginativeness in his nature, he is sure to find it a rather thrilling sensation to step down into one of these deep, grass-grown holes, realizing that ten years ago the chill, aching body of a soldier crouched there through some long torturing night, clasping with stiff fingers the handle of his bayonet and waiting tensely for the enemy's attack. It is hard to imagine that these serene, verdant woods, silent except for the chirping of birds, were once filled with the thunder of a terrific battle and that bursting shells scattered fire over the tops of the trees; that this ground over which we walk, now carpeted with soft grass and many colored flowers, was deeply stained with the blood of dead and wounded soldiers. Nature seems to forget even more quickly than men.[50]

With a journalistic eye that might not have escaped literary journalists Albert Londres or Ernest Hemingway, who had that previous spring just left Paris and the Café de Paix that Williams visits in 'A Festival Night in Paris', the young writer sees at once his immediate surroundings and sagaciously gleans their underlying meanings.

While the sights, sounds, and smells of a reconstructed Europe fill most of the pages of this travelogue, Williams also pays close attention to the people he meets, and frequently those he describes are European types that we encounter later in his plays. The combative Germans in Amsterdam were later incarnated as Herr and Frau Fahrenkopf in *The Night of the Iguana*, who 'tuned in to the crackle and guttural voices of a German broadcast reporting the Battle of Britain'.[51] The 'small [Gypsy] boys [who] pursued our bus, holding out their hands for coins' in 'A Trip to Monte Carlo' resemble the Spanish 'flock of black plucked little birds' who pursue Sebastian Venable 'halfway up the white hill' before devouring parts of him in *Suddenly Last Summer*.[52] Even the very 'stout woman, dressed with gaudy splendor of a circus queen' who steps out of the 'sumptuous lavender, Hispano-Suiza limousine' could be any number of Williams's faded starlets, from Alexandra Del Lago to Flora 'Sissy' Goforth.[53] Many of Williams's European figures had already found life here in these juvenile travel pieces.

Among the ten pieces he wrote for the *U. City Pep*, however, one experience that haunted the young Williams forever failed to appear among them – his trip to Cologne on an open-decked boat travelling along the Rhine River. Years later in his *Memoirs*, Williams recounted this detail of his trip that he avoided revealing in his letters home and in these short essays – 'the most dreadful, the most nearly psychotic, crisis' that had convinced him he was growing 'quite mad'. He describes having experienced a 'phobia' attack in Paris 'about the process of thought' and its 'complex mystery of human life', and two more in Cologne and Amsterdam, where 'a truly phenomenal thing happened': '[...] the hand of our Lord Jesus had touched my head with mercy and had exorcized from it the phobia that was driving me into madness'.[54] Whether Williams is recalling a factual or an invented experience, we cannot know for certain; he had not yet begun documenting his daily thoughts and events in his notebooks, so we have no complementary evidence to confirm or deny the story's accuracy. Regardless, his impending struggle with a madness that would later hold his sister hostage took place early in his life. Spiritual or not, as he claims to have become from this transcendental moment, Williams once again demonstrated his ability to negotiate madness through his words, an outlet denied to Rose.

Williams also recalls in his *Memoirs* that

> the high-school paper, at the suggestion of my English teacher, invited me to narrate my European travels, which I did in a series of sketches, none containing a reference to the miracles of Cologne and Amsterdam nor the crisis, but nevertheless giving me a certain position among the student body, not only as the most bashful boy in school but as the only one who had traveled abroad.[55]

As with the fact/fiction divide in his earlier prose pieces, Williams evinces here a personal/public divide: he talks about the countries and the people of Europe in his travelogue but only about himself in his *Memoirs* and, to a lesser extent, in his letters and notebooks. On 19 March 1936, for example, he writes in his private notebook: 'Oh my, what a blissful exhaustion! I haven't felt quite like this since that night in Cologne or Amsterdam – when the crowds on the street were like cool snow to the cinder of my individual "woe". Over seven years ago'.[56]

In addition to the red shawl that he bought for his mother, Williams brought back from Europe the memories, fears and impressions that would preoccupy him for the rest of his career, if not his life. These ten short high school newspaper pieces that recount Williams's 1928 European tour with his grandfather exemplify his skills at observation, analysis and engaging narrative, three skills he had hoped would serve him well when he left St Louis the following year to attend the celebrated journalism school at the University of Missouri in Columbia. This one summer trip, then, did more to awaken the writer in Williams than did his collective experiences as a boy growing up in the South.

Williams entered the University of Missouri in the fall of 1928. Earlier plans for him to attend Washington University in St Louis were foiled by his father, probably because he wanted his son out of the house and knew that it would be foolish to pay for housing when the family lived so close to the Washington campus. Hazel Kramer was supposed to join Williams at Columbia the following autumn, though she was already going steady with another boy, unbeknownst to Williams. It is uncertain who had the final say in the matter, Cornelius or Hazel's manipulative grandfather, but Hazel eventually enrolled at the University of Wisconsin, where she would meet, and later marry, Terrence McCabe, whom Williams would immortalize in name and in evil deed in the play *Battle of Angels* a little over a decade later.

Williams's three years at Mizzou also helped his writing career in ways he could not have foreseen at the time. He planned on entering the School of Journalism there – the oldest in the country – by his junior year, after completing general education courses his first two years. Though he left the university in 1932 without taking a degree (his father dragged him out for having failed miserably in his third year, in particular his Reserve Officers' Training Corps [ROTC] course, which C.C. felt brought shame upon the Williams family known for its exploits against the Indians in Tennessee the previous century), Williams's writing experiences there taught him that his passion and his abilities lay in creative and not in expository writing, academic or otherwise.

No doubt his greatest literary achievement at Mizzou was winning honourable mention in a college writing contest in his freshman year. He had arrived on campus bearing the promise of a great career. Even the local newspaper had run a story about him, 'Shy Freshman Writes Romantic Love Tales for Many Magazines'. That literary career was shaped in part by Professor Robert Lee Ramsey, who ran a modern drama course that first year which Williams audited and which was patterned on the celebrated 47 Workshop at Harvard designed by George Baker Pierce. Through the advice of Ramsey, Williams submitted a play, *Beauty Is the Word*, to the university's Dramatic Arts Contest during his second semester. His play, as reported by the *Daily Missourian*, had placed sixth, the first ever achievement for a college freshman.[57]

Beauty Is the Word (1930) is Williams's fascination with the atheist Percy Bysshe Shelley, manifested in the conflicting views of God between traditional Christianity and the pagan belief that divine power lives in the beautiful, colourful and primitive things of this world. Written when Williams was just nineteen, the play (which was first published years later in the *Missouri Review*) is an open affront to his mother's choking Puritanism. In it, the newlywed Esther pursues 'a life of carnal pleasure!' and makes love to her husband in the open fields to the consternation of her Aunt Mabel, who helped raise her. Mabel and her husband Abelard, two older missionaries, harbour the staunch, puritanical notion that God should be feared, while physical adornments and sexual pleasures should be shunned. Mabel reprimands Esther, her young niece who 'is too proud of her body', for her and her newlywed husband's blatant disregard for the missionary's Puritan ways. Mabel feels that wearing colourful clothing, dancing with the natives, and making love in the open fields are counterpuntal to her and Abelard's work in preaching God's word. In dramatizing Esther's retaliation – calling her aunt and uncle prisoners 'shut up in this mission house' and teaching Ruth, a native girl, the pagan meaning of the word 'Beauty' – the young Tom Williams voiced an early opposition to revealed religion and repressive dogma and carved out of their marble statues of saints a carnal spirituality which had made a church of the flesh.[58] *Beauty Is the Word* is also Williams's paean to then recently deceased D. H. Lawrence, in whose novels and short stories he was also discovering the sexual/spiritual dialectic that would become his artistic signature from *A Streetcar Named Desire* (1947) to *Something Cloudy, Something Clear* (1981).

Williams was enjoying life for the first time since moving north to St Louis. With the help of his father's cousins, he was approached by, and later rushed, the Alpha Tau Omega fraternity and left the little boarding house that Edwina had placed him in. He had taken up golf with clubs that his father had sent him and horseback riding for an Equitation Physical Education course. He attended college basketball games and dances and road-tripped with room-mates to Kansas City to listen to music. He frequented juke joints regularly, at times drinking too much. In short, he had the freedom now to explore life in ways Rose never really had, and that may have had all the difference on his well-being and her eventual decline. In spite of these extra-curricular activities, he had a fairly successful first semester, earning 'superior' grades in English composition, French translation with Mr Austen, and citizenship, a 'medium' grade in geology, and an 'inferior' grade in ROTC.

The fun, however, was not to last for very long, as America was verging on a Stock Market collapse and the Depression that resulted from it. Despite his curmudgeon father's attitude toward spending money on his ne'er-do-well son, Williams's education was not immediately threatened by the time's financial austerity; in fact, the Williamses, though hardly rich, were not touched by the Depression as other families in St Louis had been. As she would repeatedly do for her grandson, Grand found the money necessary to keep his college dreams alive, and her magnanimity helped pay his tuition fees for another year, much to his father's chagrin. As an interesting aside, though never gifted in financial matters, before or even after he became a millionaire, Williams had presciently alluded to the Depression almost a year before that fateful October. In a 22 November 1928 letter to his grandfather, Williams wrote:

> Have any of your investments been affected by these fluctuations on the stock market? My economics teacher was saying yesterday that periods of great 'inflation' were often followed by panics and that people should invest very cautiously. I suppose, however, that you have got your fortune invested just as securely as possible. It's generally wise, though, to investigate now and then.[59]

A rather spooky piece of advice from a boy of seventeen less than a year from Black Tuesday.

By May of his freshman year, Williams had won respect with his play and even had his short story 'A Lady's Beaded Bag' published in the university's literary magazine, *The Columns*, for which he had briefly joined its advisory committee. But such writing had taken its toll on his academic record. He had numerous unexcused absences from his classes, and he managed by the end of his first year to achieve a slightly better than average grade point average. Upon returning home for the summer of 1930, his father forced him to find work to help pay for his second year. As he sold subscriptions to a woman's magazine, *Pictorial Review*, for $21 per week, breadlines were increasing in St Louis, a sign that would eventually alter his political views. Rose, during this time, was becoming increasingly agitated, suffering from a stomach ailment related to her nervous condition, and she often warred openly with their father. She was medically examined several times, most recently at the Barnes Hospital that Williams himself would experience first-hand in the late 1960s. Most of the young men that Rose was dating after her return from Vicksburg rarely called a second time, which probably was one of the causes of her illness, a decline Williams often recounted in detail in the letters he wrote to his grandparents. While Williams's 'star' was rising, hers was already setting, though her brother did not yet know just how far it would fall.

By the start of his second year at Missouri, he became closer to one of Hazel's best friends, Esmeralda Mayes, who was a freshman and who, like him, had entered Missouri with the hopes of a future career in journalism. Williams was still stung by his recent break-up with Hazel, and Esme and he became literary companions. It is possible that she (along with Ursula Genung, whom Williams briefly dated at Missouri) was his model for Homer Stallcup's love interest, Myra, in the story 'The Field of Blue Children' (1939), or even the girl Flora in 'The Important Thing' (1945), a story about repressed desire. Williams continued writing poetry and short fiction, often for contests or for magazine submissions. He would again receive honourable mention for his short story, 'Something by Tolstoi' (1930–31), about a young Russian Jew, 'timid and spiritual and contemplative', and his young wife Lila, 'something of a hoyden – full of animal spirits, life, and enthusiasm', who find that they cannot reconcile 'the conflict between their temperaments'.[60] This spiritual agon was to become another of the young writer's signature themes for years to come.

As Lyle Leverich notes, 'Tom, in fact, showed little interest in playwriting that spring, but he was listed among fifty contestants in the First Annual Mahan University Essay Contest'.[61] It is possible that Williams's essay, 'The Wounds of Vanity', dated 'Dec. 2, 1930' in the top right-hand corner of the first manuscript page, was a potential submission to the essay contest, for the handwritten words 'contest possibility', along with the grade 'M' (meaning 'within the median of the class'), appear at the end of the three typewritten pages, probably in the hand of his teacher. The essay begins: 'Our chief trouble is that we are all so tremendously important to ourselves and so tremendously unimportant to everyone else'.[62] The short essay, echoing another piece he wrote at this time, 'Thinking Our Own Thoughts', bemoans the state of the human condition as egocentric because we let vanity control our every humour and 'distort our thinking'. The example that Williams, or his persona here (by now he was deft at separating writer from narrator and making fictional situations seem real), supplies is the error in judgement he makes toward another whom he thinks has insulted him. Now, he is obsessed that every comment this person makes 'contained some veiled sarcasm', forcing the narrator to retreat into 'a clam-like shell of silence'. But the narrator soon discovers his misjudgement and, 'as wind breaks a fog',[63] he dispels the rancour surrounding his vanity and soon counts the former enemy among his best friends. Since there is nothing in Williams's biography that suggests the essay is autobiographical – he may be referring to Harold Mitchell here, his best friend during his second year at Missouri – it is likely to be just another example of Williams's fact/fiction writing divide.

Following a brief summer stint working as a clerk for the Continental Shoemakers (a division of his father's International Shoe Company) at the demand of his father to help defray tuition costs for his third year, Williams returned to the University of Missouri for what should have been his final year. There is little doubt that his seasonal escapes gave him all the advantages that were denied Rose, whose run-ins with Cornelius were growing increasingly more violent and more frequent.

On campus that third year, however, it was the literary circles, and not the journalistic assignments, that drew Williams's attention. Eugene O'Neill was all the rave with the national success of the Theatre Guild's production of *Mourning Becomes Electra*, starring the Russian actress Alla Nazimova as Christine. In the company of William Jay Smith, Williams would later see her perform on tour as Mrs Alving in Ibsen's *Ghosts* at the American Theater in St Louis in February 1936, a performance he often attributed to his decision to become a playwright.[64] Perhaps he was erroneously giving more attention to the player than the play, for O'Neill was certainly a major factor in shaping Williams's dramatic voice. Williams's short play *Hot Milk at Three in the Morning* was obviously influenced by O'Neill's naturalist one-act plays *Before Breakfast* and *The Dreamy Kid*.

Hot Milk – the only pre-1940 work to appear in the 1948 collection *American Blues* – was reworked years later into the one-act play *Moony's Kid Don't Cry*. It portrays a workingman's struggle to leave his family and find room outside his cramped apartment to swing an axe and cut 'his own ways through the woods'. Moony (called Paul in the earlier version) is suffering not from spiritual anxiety but from claustrophobia. Moony feels himself a caged animal: 'Live an' die [...] that's all there is to it!' The life force is so strong in him that when he tells his wife Jane to 'Chuck it all', and she thinks he means life, he corrects her: 'I don't wanta die! I wanta live!' When Jane refuses to accept his leaving the suffocating town to go North with his axe, he tells her that he is leaving her anyway, since he feels like 'an escaped animal at a cage'.[65] While Paul/Moony feels restricted in his marriage and family obligations and desires to be free, Jane wants her husband to acknowledge that she and their infant come first. Like her counterpart Mabel in *Hot Milk*, Jane represents the harsh realities of married life and parenthood, whereas Paul/Moony romanticizes a life that glorifies the individual devoid of societal or familial duties. The wife recognizes the apartment as a cage she lives in with a newborn to care for; the husband dreams foolishly of hobby horses and virgin woods waiting to be felled. Perhaps an early sign of his growing dedication to his sister, Williams brought Paul/Moony back to reality once his child is placed in his hands. Both men return to their cages and accept life with Mabel/Jane and their baby.

In a 15 May 1932 letter to his mother, Williams wrote about *Hot Milk* as a 'domestic satire' that 'was given honorable mention [thirteenth place], with the criticism that it contained no stage diagram and that the speeches were too long'.[66] Again undiscouraged by failing to win the Dramatic Arts Club One-Act Play Contest, Williams submitted the short story 'Big Black: A Mississippi Idyll' (1931–32) to another contest, for which it won fifth place. A story about an escaped chain-ganger who contemplates raping a young white girl before turning against his own ugliness in relation to her immaculate beauty, 'Big Black' examines the strong drives of the flesh that cannot be controlled by the spirit alone. His flesh is denied him, as he deems it should be, but his spirit flies free in the 'savage, booming cry' of his spirituals.[67]

If Williams's literary achievements were noteworthy during this third year at college, his academic exploits were, well, 'relatively colorless'.[68] Now enrolled in the School of Journalism, Williams failed to raise his grades any better than in the previous two years. In all honesty, he was not ready for the discipline necessary to learn the trade, which included classes in writing, editing, and production. In one reporting course, he was given the 'beat' of covering 'the daily reporting of prices in local produce';[69] another beat included writing obituaries. One of Williams's obituaries around this time is a typed, two-page assignment (handwritten at the top of the first page is 'corr. in class') which begins: 'Yesterday morning the city of Midland suffered a bitter and irreplaceable loss in the death of one of its oldest and most honored citizens, Dr. Robert Jansen, who had been a distinguished resident of this city for more than half a century'.[70] The piece goes on to list Dr Jensen's life achievements, which earned Williams sharp criticism from his teacher/commentator for his 'editorialization' in using phrases such as 'a most unhappy attack' or 'one of Midland's less principled newspapers'.[71] Again, while Dr Jansen was a real person, and Williams describes having gone to the house to cover the death (which was actually the doctor's wife, and not his, an error that cost Williams dearly in his class[72]), the extent of the details Williams provides in the obituary reflect his interests in literary creations at the time.

In another piece potentially written for the same class, titled 'Somewhere a Voice...', Williams received some of his harshest criticism yet from his teacher. The piece, whether a journalistic feature story or another attempt at a short story remains uncertain (but the corrector's handwriting is the same as in the obituary above), is about Fred Welte, a sixty-four–year-old 'hobo or wandering minstrel' who is arrested for vagrancy for having broken into the local Episcopal church to play its new expensive organ. Fred is sentenced to ten days in jail, but the sentence carries a silver lining as it will give the complainant, the Reverend Mr Stauffer, time enough to convince his vestryman to hire the hobo as an assistant janitor. All that Williams's teacher could muster in ways of constructive criticism was this rather myopic comment: 'A fair piece of writing. Too drawn out, however, and hardly worth the effort because it isn't much of a story to begin with'.[73] No longer the literary boy wonder Tommy, whose published poems, stories and essays would repeatedly earn him praise, the older student Tom was discovering that harsh criticism awaited serious writers. He would have to swallow more of this medicine for the next fifty years.

In January 1932, Williams joined the Missouri Chapter of the College Poetry Society, becoming its treasurer.[74] A few years later, William Jay Smith would join the Society which was 'held at the house of Professor Alexander "Sandy" Buchan of the English Department'.[75] Later that summer, after his father had forbidden him from returning to Columbia, Williams expressed in a letter to grandfather his 'disappointment' with the journalism programme at Missouri, and how he was now considering applying to Columbia University's School of Journalism, this time in New York City, perhaps more for its proximity to Broadway than for its academic reputation. '[B]ut that may be hitching my wagon to too high a star', he admitted. Williams simply found journalistic writing 'not very edifying': 'I was somewhat disappointed in the Missouri School of Journalism. They do not give the student a chance to do the type of writing he is best fitted for, but stick him with whatever job suits them'. Even now, the literary Williams could not be kept out of the text, even those as banal in tone and in style as obituaries. For Williams, it was clear that he was not cut out for journalism, for even in this letter he complains about not having time for 'personal writing' to 'type off a few short stories' or produce a few poems.[76]

In the end, his low grades for his third year – two 'mediums', three 'inferiors' and another failing grade in ROTC – prompted his father to pull him out of college permanently and put him to work full time to help out the family during the Depression. His nearly three subsequent years earning $65 a month as a clerk-typist for the Continental Shoemakers were eventually erased from his life all together, when he began telling contest organizers and newspaper interviewers that he was born in 1914. Arguably, though, it was these three years at this St Louis company that shaped much of his literary production for the next decade to come, in terms of his anti-capitalist leanings and his sympathies with the working class.

2
University City to Clayton
(via Memphis): Looking for
a Publisher in Spring

With America still reeling from the effects of the Stock Market crash, Williams was soon to experience the pain of his own personal Black Monday – the day his father told him he was not going back to college and put his son to work full-time as a clerk/typist at the Continental Shoemakers. As Williams's mother recalled in her memoir, 'Tom entered a world of dusting shoes, typing out factory orders and hauling around packing cases stuffed with sample shoes, the world of his father', when all he really wanted to do was 'get a degree, to keep learning, [and] to be able to write more effectively'.[1] The job was obviously tedious and demeaning for the young man, so much so that he shaved these three years off his life's record, claiming for a long time to have been born in 1914 instead of 1911. Initially, the loss of three years was to help Williams enter the under-twenty-five playwriting contest sponsored by the Group Theatre in the winter of 1938–39, when he was already twenty-seven. When asked later why he committed the fib, Williams said he felt justified in not counting those three years of his life lost at the Continental. The false birth year would follow him for a long time.

As difficult as those years at Continental were for Williams, they were also instrumental in shaping his outlook on life. While being homosexual and perhaps only now just discovering what that meant for him, Williams also began understanding what constituted his 'fugitive kind' – that social flotsam whose cause he would champion for the rest of his career. As he said, he now had 'first-hand knowledge of what it meant to be a small-wage earner in a hopeless routine job'.[2] Though never considered wealthy by American standards, the Williamses and the Dakins were better off than most families during the Depression. Cornelius, after all, still had a well-paying job, and, what is more, he had enough clout in the company to find work for his son. Williams, however, did not fully appreciate the opportunity his father afforded him. Sure, it gave him some pocket money for the movies at the Fox or the St Louis cinemas, or plays in the cheap seats at the American or the Little theatres downtown which he frequented so often on his free time; but the work also reduced his time to write. And writing for Williams was more than a leisure activity or even a form of escapism from the tedium of his job or the tumult of his family home. Simply put, writing was his *raison d'être*, his therapy, his ticket out of his father's house on Enright Avenue in University City.

Typing orders and dusting off shoe boxes in the warehouse also opened Williams up to a world of people destined to fill the flophouses, to queue up in soup lines, and to squirm under the heel of bosses who exploited them. Romanticism was still Williams's literary aesthetic, but it was a romantic vision steeped in turgid social realism. His literary productions at this time, from poems to stories to eventually plays, were about escapes from these dehumanizing situations, but his social commentary was frequently sophomoric or derivative of the work of the day produced by writers like Jack Conroy. It was this mixture of high Romanticism and social realism that now infused his work and would continue to do so up to the last play he wrote during these apprentice years, *Stairs to the Roof*, which, begun as a story in October 1936 and developed more fully in 1940, was completed in January 1942, though Williams no doubt tinkered with it before and even after its March 1945 premiere at the Pasadena Playbox.[3]

But these three years – between 1932 when he left Missouri and 1935 when he went back to night school at Washington University College to obtain credits that would allow him to enter his senior year at Washington University the following autumn of 1936 – were not about writing plays but poems and short stories and, moreover, finding a magazine to publish them. Like his semi-autobiographical namesake in *The Glass Menagerie*, Tom Wingfield, Williams was obsessed with leaving St Louis, and writing, not journalism as he had once thought, was going to be that ticket out. His romantic thoughts about exotic places, fuelled no doubt by his many trips to the Jewel Box conservatory in Forest Park with Hazel Kramer and her mother Florence, who exerted an important influence over the young man, spilled over into his Romantic verse and prose. He had also met Clark Mills as early as 1933, when he was still working in the shoe factory, but the younger poet's influence on Williams would not yet achieve the effects that it would a few years later.

While Williams was not fired for writing poems on the lids of shoe-boxes as Tom Wingfield was, he did often use his father's International Shoe stationery to ink his poetic thoughts. On one extant leaf of Friedman-Shelby 'Red Goose Shoes' stationery (c. 1933), the young Williams wrote a Keatsean apostrophe to Psyche on how summer flowers lose neither their fragrance nor their colour. The persona dedicates a song to this notion and sings of a 'love without effort':

> word by word as it comes to my mind not looking for distant symbols or difficult rhymes. It is not a song. It is my own heart spelt out. Will you hear? [...] Ah, Psyche, Do you remember those days. Each part of you was sweet to me and utterly fresh. It would not have been spoiled. Not by many years. And so you were wrong in going. Or at least from my point of view. But there are always two people, two decisions. And roads going different ways.[4]

Much of Williams's published and unpublished poetry and short fiction recall this same theme – evanescence. The 'enemy: time' would become another staple theme of Williams's, drawn at first from his exposure to the various Romantic writers from England, the Continent, and the US. While still in his youth, Williams equated the loss of time with the loss of innocence; only when he grew older and more experienced did he associate the loss of time with loneliness. As an older gay man in love with youthful beauty, Williams would come to understand time's effect on beauty and attraction much differently than he did here. But the question lingers: how much was Williams aware of his truer romantic notions in his writing? Was he really interested in such themes, or did he feel that such poems and stories won contests and appeared in magazines? Was he not simply writing toward a market as opposed to writing toward his heart? In a notebook entry for 7 March 1936, Williams suggests it was more the latter than the former: 'Wrote story "Cut Out" – pretty cheap but well-done – feel rather guilty writing such stuff – so far from what I really want to do – '.[5] This chapter will examine this question of artistic commitment in Williams, who appears in these interim years as a Romantic writer-for-hire more than an artist looking for his voice.

Spring. If one theme dominates Williams's work during the 1930s, it would have to be the season of rebirth and of his birth. Nearly every poem, story and play written during this decade seems to have some connection to spring time, either in terms of its seasonal setting or the time of year in which the work was composed. He wrote his 'Sonnets for the Spring' in 1935, set his story 'Cut Out' in 'early spring days', and even began his private notebooks on 6 March 1936 addressing 'the first robin today – two in fact'.[6] Williams's fascination with spring is no doubt linked to his March birthday. With each passing year lost, he felt the renewed pangs to write and to finish his work before it finished him. As such, its message of rebirth is tainted by the truth that Williams was growing older and did not achieve the real literary success he had longed for and began seeing other writers his age or even younger than him experience on a national level.

If this dark period of Williams's life ends with the successes (and the failures) of the spring of 1936, it surely begins with the summer of 1932 when Williams learned that he would not return to the University of Missouri in the fall and when Hazel was conspicuously absent from his life. Williams had heard once from Esme Mayes, back in the summer of 1930, that Hazel was already seeing another boy, Ed Meisenbach. In February 1935, Williams heard that his story 'Stella for Star' won the St Louis Writers Guild's ten dollar first prize among seventy-six entries, but there was little joy in the news: Williams had simultaneously learned while attending one of Miss Florence Kramer's recitals that Hazel was already engaged to be married.[7] During those five interim years, Williams had never entirely given up hope that one day he and Hazel would be together. In his 'Madrigal' (1932) to Anna Jean O'Donnell, his friend at Missouri, Williams wrote,

> Hand in hand with Spring you came –
> Her's your sweetness, her's your flame!
> Her beauty with yours indivisibly blent,
> Hand in hand with the Spring you went![8]

The references to 'her' here are for Hazel, with whom Williams still very much felt in love, despite the fact that she was with another young man.

With little other entertainment available to him (the movies depleted his $65 a month salary and his swimming was interrupted by a diving accident which left his mouth in need of serious dental work), writing became Williams's sole passion and getting published his one obsession. He began submitting poems and stories more frequently now to various little presses and major literary magazines, including 'verse' that he had sent in March 1933 to Harriet Monroe, who edited the celebrated *Poetry* magazine. As Devlin and Tischler note, Williams published 'forty-odd lyrics from 1933 to 1938, nearly all in collegiate and little magazines, but he did not appear in *Poetry* until 1937'.[9] All in all, he had sent out his work in the space of just over a year to *Poetry, Manuscript, Neophyte, Inspiration, Counterpoint, L'Alouhette, A Year Magazine, Voices, Literary Digest, American Prefaces, Story,* and *The Anvil,* as well as to a host of local and national literary contests. Knowing that poetry was not going to help him escape his father's house, he began sending out short fiction, too.

Williams's prior essays into short fiction, 'The Vengeance of Nitocris' and the 'essay' 'Can a Good Wife Be a Good Sport?', showed him that his words could earn him money, though not enough to live on. Now, he was going to try and convince Whit Burnett at *Story* magazine to publish his work. Perhaps the public exposure there would open up literary doors for him. Having already tried once (and failing) to get a story published in *Story,* Williams sent Burnett in January 1935 the story 'Stella for Star' (1934), which he describes as shedding a 'highly fanciful light upon what an old English professor of mine once described as "one of the greatest enigmas in the biography of English literature"' – namely, Jonathan Swift's unconsummated love affair with Esther Johnson.[10] After winning first prize for the story the following month, Williams wrote a letter to Guild member, Josephine Winslow Johnson, adding this bit of self-criticism: 'This story about Jonathan and Stella is a good cross-section of my writing, as it shows my best and worst characteristics. It is full of bombastic irrelevancies, the characters aren't logically developed, and the romantic spirit, like Stella's garden, is almost unbearably sweet'.[11]

Williams had introduced himself this time to Burnett as a writer 'having contributed verse to a number of small journals, without doing the name or the journal a great deal of good'. And if his earlier stories were bent toward the flame of vengeance, this story, and many that followed it, carried 'a rather sentimental treatment' that he had hoped would 'still be tolerated' in American letters heavily influenced by darker political pieces steeped in social realism.[12] Though life for many in America was still downtrodden, and Williams would begin to turn his sentimentalist eye toward their cause (one quarter of the country was out of work), he still enjoyed many of the benefits his father had garnered for him with his clerical job. Williams was able to buy his own second-hand roadster, which he called 'Scatterbolt', and he regularly drove himself, Rose, and Dakin out to the Westborough Country Club in Webster Groves during the summer evenings to swim, play tennis, and go golfing, as he told his grandfather in a letter of 19 June 1934. All the while, he kept writing and 'sending a good many stories out', hoping 'to have some acceptances before long'.[13] Along with his forty-something poems, Williams sent out 'two-dozen so stories' between 1933 and 1938, with only one, 'Twenty-seven Wagons Full of Cotton' (1936), having been accepted for publication in Jack Conroy's *The Anvil*.

Normality returned, as it often would with Williams, only after a nervous breakdown. First, he had lost Hazel for good with her engagement to Terrence McCabe. Williams recounts his pain at hearing this news in the autobiographical story 'The Accent of a Coming Foot' (1935). Then, after suffering from a real heart break – what he presumed on the eve of his twenty-fourth birthday in March 1935 was a heart attack, which was later determined to have been nervous exhaustion – Williams broke down, and spent a week at St Luke's Hospital. Rose broke down, too, unable to handle her brother's crack up. It was true that both Williams and his sister Rose were gradually declining in health, ostensibly for similar reasons. Rose's doctor had told Edwina that the girl was overly frightened of sex, owning in many ways to her own depiction of it as dirty (whether from Edwina's Puritan background and her withholding sexual intercourse from her husband, or Cornelius's several extramarital affairs, or both, as the second often was related to the first). He suggested that Rose find a release for this anxiety, a prescription that shocked Edwina and later prompted Williams to write of Laura's gentleman callers in *The Glass Menagerie*. At twenty-four and still a virgin (as was Williams at twenty-two), Rose had had only a few prior brushes with sexuality. Though Dakin suggests in his biography of his brother that Williams had already discovered his homosexuality by this time, it is very likely that Williams was still struggling with his own notions of desire. Whatever the case, brother and sister together broke down, though only Williams was given the opportunity to convalesce effectively, which his writing helped him to do.

Williams was subsequently released permanently from his job at Continental and headed south to 1917 Snowden Avenue in Memphis for a rejuvenating stay with his beloved grandparents. While there, Williams learned of Josephine Winslow Johnson's own recent literary success at the age of twenty-four: her first novel, *Now in November* (1934), written in the attic of her mother's house, won the 1935 Pulitzer Prize for literature. Only nine months her junior, Williams was both impressed and jealous of her success, which perhaps motivated him even more to write his 'head off'. (A year later, he would have a dream that she was killed and convinces himself that it was 'not a wish fulfillment' borne from any jealousy.[14]) The fruit of this writing spur of his was an early one-act comedy, *Cairo, Shanghai, Bombay!* The play is about two sailors on shore leave in an unnamed seaport who proposition two girls, one 'a coarse affable girl of the Mae West type'.[15] One of the sailors falls for Aileen, and the two dream of travelling to faraway lands together. The comedy turns melodramatic in the end when his shore leave ends, and he jilts her at the altar. The play was performed on 12 July 1935 by The Garden Players, a small theatre company in Memphis, in Mrs Rosebrough's backyard in collaboration with a neighbour of the Dakins, Bernice Dorothy Shapiro (she wrote the prologue and the epilogue), who was a member of the Rose Arbor Players.

By the following fall of 1935, a rejuvenated Williams pursued his writing ambitions and returned to university, auditing evening classes at Washington University College to prepare to enter his senior year the following autumn. The family had moved again (though still in the unfashionable suburb of University City), this time out of an apartment and into a rented Colonial-style house close to the university on Pershing Avenue, complete with grape arbour and rose garden. Williams's night classes that autumn included 'Contemporary British and American Literature' with Professor George Bruner Parks, which he took to earn credits for his failed courses at Missouri. During his second year at Washington University, he enrolled as a degree-taking student, where he hoped to finish his undergraduate studies once and for all.

Two important events had an impact on Williams during this time: his meeting Clark Mills McBurney (and later William Jay Smith) and his initiation into the activist world of St Louis's socialists. If the first encounter opened Williams up to a literary community similar to the one he enjoyed at university in Columbia, the second one helped give dramatic content to his evolving aesthetics.

Williams first met Mills in 1933, but it was not until they were students together at Washington University from 1935–37 that their friendship really blossomed. Two years Mills's senior, Williams nonetheless held him in high esteem because Mills was already a recognized poet and because he, more than any of Williams's university professors past or present, had convinced him of the necessary literary changes in Modernism. Enrolled in postgraduate courses in French at the start of the 1935 academic year at Washington University, Mills introduced his older friend to Arthur Rimbaud, Rainer Marie Rilke, and, more importantly, Hart Crane. Mills also introduced Williams to various little magazines similar to *Neophyte: A Journal of Poetry*, a bi-monthly magazine run by George Cardinal Le Gros, a St Louis poet.[16] Le Gros had published an earlier Williams poem 'October Song' (1932) in its third issue, a traditional sonnet that seemed out of step with literary times. The poem concludes thus:

> Think you love is writ on my soul with chalk,
> To be washed off by a few parting tears?
> Then you know not with what slow step I walk
> The barren way of these hibernal years,
> My life a vanished interlude, a shell,
> Whose walls are your first kiss and last farewell![17]

Arguably, Williams wisely abandoned his career as a poet and undertook to writing plays instead when he recognized that Mills's poems, more than his own Romantic ones, were the future of modern poetry in America.

With Mills, Williams soon joined The League of St Louis Artists and Writers, where they met weekly 'down at the old Courthouse on Broadway'[18] and planned on producing a progressive magazine called 'Span'. Among Williams's League friends, there were several artists who influenced his work. Joe Jones, a social realist painter and a Communist activist who left the Midwest for New York in 1935 and later worked with Thomas Hart Benton, who would paint the celebrated poker scene of *A Streetcar Named Desire*. Orrick Glenday Johns, a St Louis poet of renown a generation before Williams, had recently published his autobiography, *Time of our Lives: The Story of my Father and Myself* (1937), an important lesson for Williams in the importance of life stories. Jack Conroy, editor of the radical magazine *The Anvil*, wrote the novel *The Disinherited* (1933), which influenced Williams's play *Candles to the Sun*, a social drama about a coal mine disaster in Alabama. J. S. Balch, a writer and a poet who was assistant director of the Works Progress Administration (WPA)-sponsored Missouri Writers' Project, and Willie W. Wharton, a St Louis poet and one of Williams's friends, rounded out the social gallery.

Just how much these social realist artists directly influenced Williams's writing during the 1930s – beyond that of those socially informed Hollywood films that he saw during this period – remains conjecture. What is known is that, despite his activist leanings, Williams only read poems at the meetings that fell largely outside the social parameters of the group. Williams did eventually inject his stories and plays with a socialist message, but did he really believe in their message or did he simply shift his aesthetics in order to get a story published or a play performed? Williams's years at the Continental Shoemakers tarnished his views of capitalism, and Dakin notes that in 1932, when his brother had turned twenty-one and became of voting age, Williams voted for Norman Thomas, the six-time Socialist Party of America candidate for President, whom he had seen give a speech in St Louis in September 1936 – 'the only time he ever voted in any election. He said he had become a Socialist'.[19]

Williams later recalled in a 1940 interview with Mark Barron that his 'interest in social problems is as great as my interest in the theater and traveling. I try to write all my plays so that they carry some social message along with the story':

> 'I've changed to the full length play form of three acts now,' Williams said, 'but when I first started I did only one-act plays because I was even more social minded then and found it easier to get across a message and with more impact if I made it brief. All of my one-act plays are about such social groups I ran across in my wanderings'.[20]

True, many of his one-act plays written around this time do carry socialist agendas, but what serious artist's work in the 1930s did not? If social realism was a legitimate movement aimed at improving life through its candid, gritty exposure, it was also a meal ticket or, in Williams's case at least, a bus ticket. Williams did try for a grant from the WPA Writers' Project – first in Chicago and then again in New Orleans. Was his motivation to produce socialist art or to free him from his father's control?

Either way, Williams was denied the grant in Chicago, and again in New Orleans in 1939, partly because of his family's financial stability and partly because the Project was already on its way out by that June. Perhaps tellingly, when the grant opportunities shrivelled up, so did Williams's socialist leanings. Though he did experience poverty first-hand in New Orleans that winter and continued writing stories and one-act plays that evoke economic plight, Williams became more interested in the fugitive lives of Bohemians resulting from the Depression than in the inherent dangers of capitalism. Romanticism, more out of place than ever in the American 1930s, was winning back the artistic ground that it had lost to Mills's Modernism in Williams's evolving literary aesthetics. Raffish Quarter rats were more hip precisely because of their fugitive status, even if many of whom Williams met, such as the prostitute artist Irene, had suffered under their financial strain. The moneyed few were no longer Williams's chief bugbear; the philistines were.

But that was 1939, and this was still 1936, and the St Louis League still exercised some control over Williams's work. Evidence of such influence can be detected in his prose piece 'The Darkling Plain (For Bruno Hauptmann Who Dies Tonight)', written on or about the spring night of 31 March 1936, the night that Bruno Richard Hauptmann, a German immigrant, was meant to be executed for the abduction and murder of Charles Lindbergh's baby on 1 March 1932 (he was granted a stay until 3 April). 'We do not die separately. We die together'.[21] Such are the opening words of this short, unpublished piece, whose title refers to the final lines of Matthew Arnold's 'Dover Beach' (1867). Given Lindbergh's celebrity status in America following his solo, non-stop transatlantic flight in *The Spirit of St Louis*, Hauptmann's trial was being called 'The Trial of the Century', and its impact on Williams is palpable in this piece.[22] Hauptmann maintained his innocence up to the moment of his execution, which is why the young, socialist-minded Williams indentified with him as a hero. Williams wrote in his notebook on 31 March 1936, 'Dreamed I saw Hauptmann being electrocuted last night – he was extraordinarily calm about it – The real execution is tonight – a horrible thing'.[23] Williams also wrote a poem about Hauptmann, titled 'Ask the Man Who Died in the Electric Chair'.

And yet, a few months later in the year, Williams would type the following repudiation of socialist ideologies in his college essay, 'The Literary Mind by Max Eastman':

> For sincere proletarian propagandists I have all the respect that I have for any sincere worker but I know of a good many writers who profess to be ardently revolutionary who have never advertently read a single line of Karl Marx and would find him intolerably dull if they did. They really don't give a hand for social justice, the Scottsboro boys, the Sacco-Vanzetti 'outrage' or anything else but their own personal achievement. However they are just cutting off their noses, because a political preoccupation is a bad thing for any art. Political truths are about the most evanescent kind while artistic truths are the most perennial.[24]

Where Williams finally stood on the proletarian question thus remains problematic. In less than a decade, he would become the wealthiest writer of this St Louis League, and never fully regret the lifestyle that his new-found money would bring him. Nor, however, would he ever abandon his fugitive kind, who were more often than not products of a proletarian revolution, private or otherwise.

Williams's flirtation with socialism would continue over the next few years in the plays he penned – or rather typed – for Willard Holland's Mummers; but even in them, the message was much more about personal freedoms than it was about social conscience. Despite his wavering attitudes toward the movement, Williams remained close to Clark Mills (he was, after all, a serious artist more than an ardent socialist). And together they supported each others' literary efforts. Outside of the Williams household, Williams was able to find like literary companions, which no doubt helped him survive at home during these difficult years as an adult male still living under the weight of his father's roof and his mother's Puritanical mores. Inside his parents' walls, however, was another issue entirely. With the declining Rose no longer serving as his confidante and buffer, Williams began writing almost daily in his notebooks, which he would faithfully do for more than a quarter of a decade. The notebooks provide an additional portrait of the playwright not found in his already literary letters. And in them, he recorded not only his actions and experiences, which have helped establish and correct much of his early biographical details, but also his inner thoughts and emotions.

The notebooks open, appropriately enough, in the days leading up to spring, on 6 March 1936, with an entry that captures best the Williams of the 1930s – observant and hypochondriacal, perseverant and poor, desiring both the recognition that comes with literary awards and the occasional prize money:

> Saw first robin today – two in fact – pains in chest all morning but okay tonight – Went swimming – mailed verse to liberty amateur contest at Miss Flo's suggestion – Now have 4 manuscripts in the mail not counting plays & poems in St Louis contest – Returned case of empty bottles – collected $1.00 – felt rather stupid all day but will write tomorrow.[25]

Written when he was not yet twenty-five, this first entry could have seemingly been penned during any given year prior to his death. Only the reference to his working for a dollar is a dead giveaway that it refers to his years of post-Continental financial strain, when any spending money he was to acquire came not from the stingy Cornelius but rather from the few windfalls of literary contests or the generosity of his grandparents. But the rest of the entry describes Williams fairly accurately from age twenty-five to sixty-five: his obsession with bird symbolism, his fear of dying, his passion for swimming, his desire for literary awards, and his struggle to write daily. That was hallmark Williams, and here it was, laid out so clearly for him and for us, back in 1936.

During the spring, Williams did begin reaping the rewards of those literary contests he mentions in this first notebook entry. In a 12 March 1936 letter to his grandparents, Williams writes ecstatically of the changing season: 'It is quite spring-like here. Our elm trees are budding. We also discovered yesterday that we have a pussy-willow. It is blooming in the backyard. A pleasant surprise'.[26] And as the city began to shake off its winter doldrums, so did the writer welcome in his twenty-fifth year, which he told his grandparents would be the year he would finish his studies. If earlier that month Williams felt 'stupid' and 'fool[s] [him]self about [his] writing',[27] now he was looking forward to spring, and fortune was indeed turning his way.

Two literary achievements helped propel him into returning to his secondary studies the following fall to complete (or so he had thought) his bachelor's degree at Washington University. The first was his being awarded second-place from over four hundred entries and more than a hundred participants in the Wednesday Club's poetry contest begun by Sara Teasdale the previous decade.[28] The $25 award, and a write up in the local papers, was eagerly received, especially since he was out of work and out of pocket – and the contest paid much better than returning recyclable bottles. His entry was titled, appropriately, 'Sonnets for the Spring (A Sequence)'. Describing a 'sudden war' between the seasons of death and rebirth, the first sonnet, titled 'Singer of Darkness', opens, 'I feel the onward rush of spring once more'.[29] The second sonnet, 'The Radiant Guest', personifies the arrival of spring as a welcome companion who will help the narrator rid his house and his maddened mind of 'uncongenial' guests: thoughts. And 'A Branch for Birds', the third sonnet, has the narrator, now long since dead, reawaken in spring through the form of a tree whose branches will provide shelter for singing birds.

In addition to this literary triumph, celebrated by his beloved Aunt Isabel (whom he later immortalized in his autobiographical story about Rose's entrance into puberty, 'The Resemblance between a Violin Case and a Coffin' [1949]), Williams finally published a poem, 'My Love Was Light', in the renowned journal, *Poetry*. Williams had earlier pleaded in a letter of March 1933 to Monroe to publish one of his poems: 'Will you do a total stranger the kindness of reading his verse? Thank you! Thomas Lanier Williams'.[30] Four years later, she finally did, publishing 'My Love Was Light', which Williams recognized as being old-fashioned and sentimental: 'It is the kind of poem which I write most naturally but am always afraid editors will find too much in the traditional style'.[31] One particularly 'traditional' stanza reads:

> My love drank wine the old wives said
> And danced her empty days away;
> She baked no bread, she spun no thread,
> She shaped no vessels out of clay... .[32]

Nonetheless, Monroe accepted the poem, along with another one of his, 'This Hour' (retitled 'The Shuttle' in manuscript form, perhaps by Monroe herself). If the first poem echoes E. A. Robinson, this second one, an extended sonnet in form, resembles Emily Dickinson:

> This is the hour that imparts
> A special nudity to hearts,
> When every secret thing is known
> Inward to the very bone.[33]

Both poems would appear side-by-side in the June 1937 issue.

If spring infused his poetic muse at this time, it also influenced his prose as well, for Williams wrote several stories connected to the spring of 1936, the *mensis mirabilis* of his early writing career. The first one, 'Cut Out', was written in early March and reflects Williams's growing fascination with the gangster types he saw on screen or read about in the St Louis papers, such as those he would use a year later in other plays, such as the incomplete 'American Gothic' (1937) and *Fugitive Kind* (1937). The story, a first-person vernacular account of the struggle between the Kid and Rags, opens, 'It was one of them early spring days, the sun out bright and pretty, and me being off duty at the yards, I come on across the street to Bud's place for a couple of drinks and maybe a little game of pinochle. The Kid was there. He had on his watermelon shirt. You know. A green one with lots of pink stripes'.[34] Despite Williams's success throughout his career creating varied speech, replicating gangster vernacular would never be one of his artistic strengths.

A few days later, he would type out the following story, 'This Spring', about a woman whose terminal illness falls out of remission. Sensing that her end is near, she empties her bank account, heads south to a seaport town, and seduces a man, then asks him to leave her alone. This was not her first visit to this town, as she went there 'the time before when there had seemed to be so little chance of escape': 'This was again spring as it had been the last time'.[35] Williams had submitted the story to his 'Short Story' course at Washington University College, taught by Frank Webster. 'Only one girl liked it', Williams wrote in his notebook, 'and she didn't get the point – Prof. Webster seemed pleased with it however and told me to write more soon – But I was disappointed in story [*sic*] and feel discouraged about my whole prospect as a writer – '.[36] He picked it up a few days later and 'Rewrote it stream-of-consciousness style'.[37]

What would become typical of Williams later in his career, he would judge his success as a writer only on what he had just completed. All previous awards were seemingly forgotten, and those March 1936 victories were all but lost to him now. Williams's lack of confidence in his writing soon became an obsession of his later that spring. He felt all that he was writing was 'a lot of trash': 'How I fool myself about my writing! In some ways – if not all – I am a perfect idiot! [...] Gosh! What a lot of nature-faking I have done in my stories. – I am anxious to learn all I can about nature this spring'.[38] The only story he had liked was 'Gift of an Apple', which was sent to Burnett's *Story* magazine. He had sent the magazine twenty stories between 1933 and 1936; none was accepted for publication.[39] But the 'Gift of an Apple', about an older woman who attempts to seduce a young hitchhiker until she discovers him to be the same age as her son, was not accepted, prompting him to send it to Wilbur Schramm's *American Prefaces* at the University of Iowa. Schramm, who would become a mentor to Williams in the coming years, also rejected 'Gift of an Apple', but not without giving the young Williams some encouragement: 'Some of these days you are going to burst out and write some fine stuff'.[40]

Another story, 'The Bottle of Brass', written in March 1936, was quickly mailed off to *American Prefaces*. It was an expanded version of Williams's 1931–32 story, 'Big Black: A Mississippi Idyll'. In this version, the 'huge and ugly and black' protagonist who looked as though 'he had just escaped from a bottle of brass after being sealed up thousands of years for disobedience to Solomon', does rape the white girl, a reference to the 1931 Scottsboro trial in which nine black teenagers were accused of having raped two white women in a freight car in Alabama. Margaret Bradham Thornton notes that the revised version was influenced by John Henry and *The Arabian Nights' Entertainments* since 'Williams includes an excerpt from one of the tales, "The City of Brass," at the beginning of the story'.[41] The journal again rejected the story, explaining to its author that the story was ' "told rather than lived"', a criticism that Williams did not entirely agree with.[42]

Perseverance paid off for Williams, though, and a second literary achievement greeted him in the months ahead. Prodded by his mother to submit a one-act play to a contest sponsored by the Webster Groves Theatre Guild (located in a wealthy suburb of St Louis), Williams wrote *The Magic Tower* (1936). He had just experienced theatrical magic: first, Alla Nazimova in Ibsen's *Ghost* at the American Theater, and then Chekhov's *The Cherry Orchard* at the Little Theatre. He quickly became interested in the theatre of Ibsen, Strindberg, Shakespeare, and O'Neill. Now he wanted to put that passion to work to finally get his own play produced. Williams had just completed revising *Hot Milk at Three in the Morning* into *Moony's Kid Don't Cry* for Webster's short story class that he was taking at Washington University College. Williams found the rewrite a 'little too windy' but also thought it would be 'effective on the stage'.[43] And now, by April, he dashed off in record time the romantic play, *The Magic Tower*.

The Magic Tower, originally titled 'State of Enchantment', portrays a rather sardonic view of romance and marriage and the struggle between art and artist, both representing dramatic situations and literary themes that Williams would develop throughout his career. The play addresses a couple's struggle between their love for each other and the art and financial straits that eventually separates them. Linda, an ex-vaudeville actress, and Jim, a young artist five years her junior, live in a garret-studio – their magic tower – until Jim becomes disenchanted with his starlet and Linda disillusioned with love. While Jim lies down to sleep, Linda offers her poetic farewell, then slips of her wedding ring and leaves: 'There's a funny slice of moon coming out. Right over the Fixit Garage. It looks like a yellow dancing slipper – Jim, tomorrow's going to be an awfully swell day! Almost like spring, I imagine'.[44] The Webster Groves Theatre Guild judges were unanimous that spring, and Williams was awarded first prize – a silver plate and the promise of a production the following autumn, when it premiered 13 October in the presence of Edwina and, unexpectedly, Grand. At last, he was going to see a professional production of one of his plays, a little more than a year after his first play was performed in the backyard of his grandparents' neighbour's house in Memphis. Some glowing reviews in the local press no doubt boosted his ego but had little effect on his growing despair with his writing. His mood was echoed in his unpublished story 'Nirvana', which he finished at the end of April: 'Things were bound to pick up in the spring. But they didn't'.[45]

In June 1936, instead of enrolling in a summer course in the techniques of drama at Washington, Williams accompanied Clark Mills and Willie Wharton to the Mid-Western Writers Conference led by Meridel Le Sueur. While in Chicago, they would also pay a visit to Harriet Monroe's

Poetry office. Williams's time spent with Mills was growing increasingly significant to his literary redirection, which Williams later acknowledged in his September 1938 essay on Mills, 'Return to Dust (Via the Sorbonne and Cornell Universities)'.[46] In the essay, Williams describes his initial jealousy of Mills's success, having been a successful poet at a relatively young age, and rounds out the piece with descriptions of the various drunken parties they threw with their literary friends from the new chapter of the College Poetry Society of America that he and Mills organized in January 1936.[47]

In the following summer of 1937, Mills and Williams formed their 'literary factory' in the basement of Mills's house on Westmoreland Avenue in Clayton: 'in the basement because it was cooler down there and it offered a minimum of distraction'.[48] Together, they would write for eight hours a day 'at old kitchen tables' and seated on broken kitchen chairs which offered 'no temptation to lean back and "relax"';[49] Mills wrote poetry, and Williams drafted his play *Fugitive Kind*. Williams speaks nostalgically in 'Return to Dust' about how they were motivated by a bit of verse they had tacked above their writing tables:

> For lack of food some writers died,
> while some committed suicide
> and all though great and small of fame
> returned to dust from whence they came![50]

Williams felt that this 'grim little verse about the fate of all writers' no longer applied to Mills, and instead took it off the wall and considered 'stick[ing] it on mine'.[51] In the fall of 1937, when Williams left Washington University to complete his bachelor's degree at the University of Iowa, Mills left for Paris to complete his study on Jules Romains at the Sorbonne (the previous summer he had won a scholarship to study with Romains for six weeks at Mills College, California). When he returned the following autumn, he took a position as French instructor at Cornell University, where he enrolled for his doctorate, and would remain a close friend of Williams's for the next few years. Mills later drove Williams to New York in September 1939 to meet with a lady who had just contacted him about the possibility of becoming his literary agent. Her name was Audrey Wood, and she would become a near permanent fixture in Williams's life for the next thirty-two years.

Spring 1936 soon turned to summer 1936, and those careless days at camp in the Ozarks or in his parents' attic were filled with the composition of domesticated poems and stories, like 'Middle West', 'Sand',

'Ten Minute Stop' and 'Jonquils 10¢ a Dozen' that describe moments of human compassion that break the loneliness of our days, and those exotic ones, like 'Grenada to West Plains' and 'Las Palamos', and 'Las Muchachas', which spoke of the young writer's desire to pitch out on his own. To a certain extent, the summer of 1936 announced the trouble ahead for Williams, who would return to the stagnant environment of university classrooms and his 'single cramped unhappy place',[52] that smoke-filled garret on 6634 Pershing Avenue, University City, his own 'magic tower'.

If Williams's literary life outside of school was extremely active, thanks in a large part to literary friends like Mills and William Jay Smith, his life inside of school was equally bustling, though not fully to his liking. Once he entered Washington University for his senior year in the fall of 1936, he was wide-eyed and eager to return to the world of intellectuals. Or so he thought. Washington University was not Mizzou, if only for the reason that there were no longer the 126 miles separating him from his parents' home on Pershing Avenue but less than a city block. He had not escaped anything yet by enrolling in Washington. One more year to finish his degree and he would be gone. One more year.

3
University City to New Orleans (via Iowa City): Academic Blues versus 'American Blues'

In an entry in his notebook for 26 May 1936, Williams entered his thoughts about reading Hart Crane:

> I feel plumb stupid tonight. I've been reading a lot of Hart Crane's poetry – like it but hardly understand a single line – of course the individual lines aren't supposed to be intelligible. The message, if there actually is one, comes from the total effect – much of it has at least the atmosphere of great poetry – it is a lot of raw material, all significant and moving but not chiselled into any communicative shape.[1]

The poet and the year are significant here for several reasons. The most obvious one is the life-long influence that Hart Crane had on Williams, begun here in 1936, the year that his own literary aesthetics, under the watchful eye of Clark Mills, began taking shape. But if he was now, on the doorstep of discovering a whole new literary world at Washington University, moving away from the Romantics and toward the Modernists in theory, in practice his aesthetics were still a century in the past. Critics, scholars, and theatre historians of Williams over the years have, of course, shed extensive light on Crane's importance to Williams's literary life, and there is no reason to doubt that here.

Williams's poetry, short fiction, and plays written prior to the fall of 1936 are unflagging in their neo-Romanticism, whereas his literary production after this date reproduce either the era's social realism or its Expressionism, as seen in the plays by Eugene O'Neill, Elmer Rice, John Howard Lawson, and Sophie Treadwell. *Headlines* (1936), *Candles to the Sun* (1937), *Me, Vashya* (1937), *Fugitive Kind* (1937), and *Not about Nightingales* (1938) all have little in common, in fact, with earlier plays like *Beauty Is the Word, Moony's Kid Don't Cry*, and *The Magic Tower*. *Candles to the Sun*, for instance, is a social drama about a coal mine disaster in Alabama influenced by Jack Conroy's *The Disinherited* (1933) that theatre critic Colvin McPherson described in the St Louis *Post-Dispatch* (18 March 1937) as having been written by a playwright of 'unusual promise' and 'considerable technical skill'.[2] *Headlines*, a collage of newspapers headlines that Williams arranged dramatically, was an agitprop written as a curtain-raiser for Irwin Shaw's antiwar play, *Bury the Dead* (1936).[3] *Spring Storm* (1937), and its poetic struggle between sexual desire and social (and artistic) propriety,[4] does briefly diverge from the living newspaper sketches that Williams was asked to write in college (first at Washington University, then at the University of Iowa); but again, it was brutally attacked by his professor as being essentially a painted nude, that is, the naive eroticism of a playwright trying to shock the Puritan nature of his viewers. In all of these plays, though, 'lyricism won out over ideology [...]'.[5] If Williams's theatrical productions during the second half of the 1930s are essentially agitprops, most are still sugar-coated to a certain extent with the Romantic idealism from which Williams never entirely escaped.

Influences from other writers at this time, however, have also been given a lot of attention. D. H. Lawrence is probably the most significant after, or perhaps even before, Hart Crane. By 1936, the Lawrentian Williams was already cutting his teeth. Not only did Williams title his first notebook 'Dead Planet, The Moon' after a line in a 1927 Lawrence letter that Williams had come across, but he was reading everything of Lawrence that he could get his hands on, which was no easy task given the censorship laws in America that policed decency and morality in the arts, with Lawrence being one of its poster children of degeneracy, James Joyce another.[6] A few years later in July 1939, while visiting Lawrence's wife Frieda in Taos, New Mexico, and doing research on the author at the Harwood Foundation,[7] Williams noted this about the novelist in this first notebook: 'Today I read from D. H. Lawrence's letters and conceived a strong impulse to write a play about him – his life in America – feel so much understanding & sympathy for him – though his brilliance makes me feel very humble & inadequate'.[8] By the summer of 1936, Lawrence had become a staple in Williams's literary diet, as Lyle Leverich notes:

> Among the writers who especially shaped his interest during this period was D. H. Lawrence. Steeped as he was in Lawrence's novels, Tom could not have failed to identify with the mother-fixated

Paul Morel in *Sons and Lovers*, nor, for that matter, to recognize counterparts in Edwina and Cornelius to Morel's mother and father. Chekhov may have been a 'dramaturgic mentor,' as Tennessee Williams would come to idealize the Russian playwright, but now it was Lawrence's depiction of the isolation and loneliness of the artist as well as his passionate belief in sensual freedom that fascinated and challenged Tom.[9]

Like Crane, Lawrence would influence Williams for the rest of his career.

What all of this suggests is that Williams was willing to acquire new literary aesthetics from his literary friends and academic mentors, but his stubborn Romantic streak is evidence that his personal literary and dramatic voice was also forming at this time. Nearly every play that Williams wrote from *Battle of Angels* (1940) onward combines the lyricism of his Romantic poets, the social activism of his St Louis education (including his discovery of Chekhov), and the metaphysical dialectics of D. H. Lawrence. Williams's voice was indeed emerging, but there were many attempts by his teachers to silence it, and by other writers to liberate it even more. The years 1936–39 are thus a watershed in the playwright's artistic direction. He took the advice of friends like Clark Mills and Willard Holland and balanced it against that of his professional mentors, university teachers who also served as his editors in the little literary magazines they published, such as Wilbur Schramm at Iowa's *American Prefaces* to which Williams continually submitted his work. Taking the best advice he received and discarding the worst, Williams left St Louis in the winter of 1938–39 en route for New Orleans, and along the way the sonnet writer Thomas Lanier Williams became the playwright Tennessee.

In mid-September 1936, thanks to the $125 tuition money that his grandparents sent him, Williams matriculated at Washington University with the hope of completing his final year of undergraduate studies. Despite his intentions, he was admitted as a 'Student Not Candidate for a Degree', with sixteen hours of courses in English, Greek, French, political science, and physical education.[10] During his year there, he was required to read an enormous amount of literature, from the plays of Ibsen and Chekhov to the imagist poets, and from the Greek philosophers to the French Symbolists and British modernists. In addition to Chekhov, Williams had to write seminar papers on Sophocles, Molière, Joseph Conrad, John M. Synge, Bernard Shaw, Max Eastman, Clive Bell, and James Joyce, to name but a few.[11]

During the winter of 1936 and the following spring, Williams wrote two longer college term papers on the contemporary theatre for Otto Heller's 'General Literature III' course, 'Principal and Problems of Literature', the quality of which reflected his gradual decline at Washington. The first, 'Some Representative Plays of O'Neill and a Discussion of his Art', was a sixteen-page examination of O'Neill, who had just been awarded the Nobel Prize for literature. In a letter to his grandparents, dated around 15 November 1936, Williams wrote, 'All my mornings, including Saturday are taken up at the University and I have three courses which require a tremendous amount of outside reading. For one course I am having to read all of O'Neill's plays to make a term paper on his work'.[12] In his spiral notebook, in which he took notes for his courses and penned the occasional poem or play dialogue, Williams listed 'O'Neill plays [to?] read': 'In The Zone, Moon Of The Carribbees (Smitty a love lorn Englishman) The Hairy Ape, Anna Christie, Beyond The Horizon, Electra, Strange Interlude'.[13]

If the school year had begun on a promising note, it did not take long for that spirit in Williams to fade into academic blues. In his notebook for 25 September 1936, he wrote, 'I love school – Especially Heller and [Harcourt] Brown'.[14] By 7 October, Williams's impressions of Heller had completely soured: 'Dr. Heller bores me with all his erudite discussion of literature. Writing is just <u>writing</u>! Why all the fuss about it?'[15] His term paper on O'Neill bore the weight of that growing disillusionment. There are several corrections and marginal notes in Heller's hand. In one comment, following Williams's analysis of the 'ludicrously incongruent' speech of the farm boy in *Beyond the Horizon*, Heller wrote, 'You are right about the dialogue'.[16] At the end of the term paper, Heller provided the following commentary: 'Not quite in accord with your earlier estimate. Your style is a bit too truculent'.[17] He gave him the grade 'AB' nonetheless, and an 'A' in the course.

At the end of the first semester at Washington, Williams's grades were respectable to good, despite the disruptions that home life was having upon his studies. But his second semester would not live up to his expectations, and he once again grew disillusioned with academics. School work was cutting into his writing time, and when he could combine the two and write a story or a play for a class assignment, his teacher's lack of appreciation of his work embittered the young artist. Undoubtedly, Williams's grades were slipping because, as he had done at Missouri, he concentrated more on his literary efforts. If he had started his coal-miner play, *Candles to the Sun* (still called 'Red and Star'), for a contest sponsored by St Louis's Little Theatre in the fall semester, by the spring semester, he began devoting much of his attention to its revisions, since Holland had repeatedly rejected it, claiming it was not ready for production.

The second term paper, 'Birth of an Art (Anton Chekhov and the New Theatre)', showed how quickly Williams's interests in academe declined. This twenty-three-page essay was also written for Heller during the spring of 1937. On the title page of this lightly corrected essay, Heller had these two comments: 'Page numbers? This paper in no way fulfills the requirements of a term paper as indicated repeatedly. O.H.'; and 'All of this, or nearly all, was written without reference or relation to literary standards and criteria as studied in the course. O.H.'[18] Williams now 'despised' Dr Heller, for having given him a 'D' for his course.[19]

Throughout the academic year, Williams wrote no less than ten play reports in addition to his term papers. Some were based on live performances that he had attended, including S. N. Behrman's *Rain from Heaven* at the Little Theatre. At other times, he produced seminar papers on plays or books of literary criticism that he had to read. One incomplete, three-page typescript was written in late December 1936 or early winter 1937, either for William G. B. 'Pop' Carson's 'English 16' course, 'Technique of Modern Drama', or, more probably (since Williams read the play in its original language) for his French 16 'Origins of the Philosophical Movement' with Harcourt Brown. In the report titled 'Candide, ou L'Optimisme', Williams references 'our own recent best-seller, <u>Anthony Adverse</u>'. While the novel was written in 1933, its film version, starring Olivia de Havilland, was only recently released in late August 1936. In all likelihood, Williams had just seen the film and had not read the novel, which he ironically calls that 'masterful modern piece [...] designed for the delectation of middle-aged American club-women of the sort that are now going into ecstasies over "Gone With the Wind", the sort that wheezes into bookshops and asks the clerk to please give them the book that everybody will be talking about all this winter'.[20]

In his college spiral notebook, Williams lists some of his specific assignments. For an essay on Voltaire, for instance, he jotted down the directions from Brown that he had to follow: ' "Merope" [*sic*] by Voltaire for next report', noting later the form these subsequent reports were to take: 'Report on "Mérope" – Monday[.] briefest possible outline of plot – background – ~~Voltaire's~~ theatrical value of play – Voltaire's plays did impress audiences'.[21] Citing Joseph Wood Krutch's *The Modern Temper* in this essay, Williams exposes some of his budding prejudices against tragedy in the modern world: 'Something has destroyed our belief in fundamental human greatness and without that belief as a premises tragedy in its traditional sense is impossible. Even our kings are divested of their atmospheric grandeur: they fall in love with pretty divorcées, abdicate their thrones and concentrate on golf'.[22]

The reference to tragedy and to Edward VIII's abdication to marry Wallis Simpson are appropriate here since, as Williams was writing this essay, he was battling with his own tragedy at home. His father was in the hospital recuperating from an injury to his ear that occurred during a violent poker party (the result of the partially bitten-off ear would ruin Cornelius's chances for promotion to executive and begin his gradual decline). Rose's condition, while staying briefly in Knoxville for the Christmas season with C.C.'s sisters, Ella and Isabel, was degrading quickly, too, and Williams himself was experiencing his blue devils once again. Hoping to continue his work with Willard Holland and the Mummers to produce *Candles to the Sun*, Williams became distraught himself. He was reading Van Gogh's letters, and thought the two of them would have been friends: 'We would have understood each other. He went mad & killed himself'.[23]

When Rose came home in mid-January, she was soon institutionalized, and Williams intuited that his own descent was not far off. Consequently, he plunged himself further into his writing, academic and dramatic alike, which removed her from his daily thoughts. On 25 January 1937, he wrote in his notebook, echoing or presaging his comments in his essay on *Mérope*:

> Tragedy. I write that word knowing the full meaning of it. We have had no deaths in our family but slowly by degrees something was happening much uglier and more terrible than death. Now we are forced to see it, know it. The thought is an aching numbness – a horror. I am having final exams but can't study. Her presence in the house is a – Now I must stop and study Greek. Oh, yes, Greek is so <u>important</u> just now.[24]

Three other college papers that Williams wrote around this time also help to demonstrate the playwright's evolving aesthetics. While the first two were written for courses (probably Heller's 'General Literature III' course), the last one, 'Is Fives', was apparently Williams's personal efforts to establish a poetic manifesto. The first of these college papers, titled 'The Literary Mind by Max Eastman', is a critical review of the 1931 essay *The Literary Mind: Its Place in an Age of Science*. Williams begins the essay with a telling (if not blusterous) comment that predicts his later arguments with his critics: 'I usually attack literary criticism in a grim but determined manner, much as I would enter the front line trenches to defend the flag'. But in Eastman, he found a critic as entertaining as he was insightful. 'Anybody who reads critical journals', Williams writes, 'knows that there is a great deal of loose talk flying around the literary front these days, and if he continues to read he learns to discount about fifty percent of what he is reading as pure affectation'. Eastman is not spared this criticism either at times, but in general Williams finds him accurately capturing the inconsistency of Modernist writers: 'Complete consistency indicates an unhealthily static state of mind in an artist'.[25] Williams is wary, however, of Eastman's argument that the advances of science were threatening the world of letters, adding, 'I can see no fundamental conflict between science and literary thanbetween [sic] science and religion. The scientific truth is one thing. The poetic truth is another'.[26]

Williams took Eastman to task for attacking the imagist poets, a poetical school that Clark Mills had recently introduced Williams to. In one undated fragment draft titled 'Imagism Old and New' (c. 1936), Williams explains his growing interest with Modernist American poetry. He would develop this fascination with another essay that studies the poetical truths of what he defines as the 'is five' poets. An earlier version of this essay appears handwritten in his college spiral notebook for that year, already showing the cracks in his commitment to his academic assignments. The final six-page typescript, signed and dated 'Dec. 1936' at the end, was Williams's defence of E. E. Cummings's collection of poems, *Is 5* (1926).[27] Its aim, 'to give a definition of pure poetry in necessarily indirect fashion',[28] was Williams's attempt to negotiate his Romantic ideals about poetry with his increasing (or informed) appreciation of Modernist aesthetics. As he writes, 'I do not mean that no romantic poets are "Is Fives" or that all moderns are. That would be far from true. The "Is Fives" are a human type and not a period or literary type'.[29] They have a 'direct view of reality' and an intuition that often transgresses the literary tastes of their times:

> Arriving at this direct view is, then, an apocalyptic experience analogous to that of religious conversion – only it is not in most cases a sudden, inspired, instantaneous thing. It is a thing which may – and usually does – grow very slowly, almost imperceptibly, like a mental disease, only that it grows in the opposite direction, until all at once the individual awakes and looks about him and discovers that he has wandered as if by accident into quite a new and different world.[30]

The reference to Rose, here in Knoxville, is not lost in Williams's description, nor to his abandoned novella, 'The Apocalypse', that he was planning to write for a contest sponsored by Little, Brown publishers.[31] Though 'Is Fives' represents the ruminating of a still immature artist, it is also astute in its literary observations and weighs up well against the continued perception that Williams was only a Romanticist at the time. While it is true that his literary productions imitated the various British and American poets who adhered to Romantic ideals, his aesthetical writings at least demonstrate that he was aware of his literary times.

Nowhere is this recognition more evident that in his senior-year term paper on James Joyce's *Ulysses* that he wrote in the fall of 1936 for Heller's 'Principles and Problems of Literature' course. As Williams later confirmed in a 1972 interview with Jim Gaines:

> I remember I took a course in contemporary literature under a German teacher – wonderful old man. The first semester he taught me something I dug – I think it was Joyce – and the second semester he put us on to Goethe [...]. The professor gave me an A-plus the first semester and a D-minus the second.[32]

In a fragment draft to his *Memoirs* written decades later, entitled 'Some Random Additions to my Memoirs' (c. 1972), Williams recalls his reactions to the novel in more detail:

> I recall a German professor of English literature in Saint Louis' Washington University, a stout and powerful old scholar. The first term was devoted to the read ing and a nalysis of Joyce's <u>Ulysses</u>. At the term's conclusion we, the students, were required to w rite lengthy term papers on the work. The Professor was very pleased with my pa per which showed my great a ppreciation of the modern Irish classic: he gave me an A plus for that term.[33]

In this essay, Williams demonstrates yet another Modernist writer's influence on his developing aesthetic, perhaps more curiously since Williams had not yet recognized the influence as quickly or as consciously as he had with the other writers noted earlier:

> Speaking of <u>Ulysses</u>, there is, in the first place, much of it. There are 768 pages of small, close type with an almost maximum economy of punctuation and indentation. Obviously Mr. Joyce set out to produce a monumental piece of work and was determined that it should be monumental in every sense of the word. It is the most deliberately pretentious work of art I have [page break] ever come across. It would

seem doomed at the start to be either a colossal failure of a colossal success but somehow or other it doesn't seem to be exactly either. Mr. Joyce does not quite accomplish his object, in my opinion. He has made a tremendous effort and yet fallen short of his mark. [...] A great deal of dullness. Then some dirt. Then more dullness. Then a great deal more dirt and a great deal more dullness. That is my impression of most of Ulysses. The dullness and the dirt both reach a climax in the dramatized section of the book (Pages 422–593) which evidently is a symbolical interpretation of a drunken brawl at a bawdy house with young Dedalus and Bloom (whose paths crossed in a maternity hospital or saloon, I am not certain which) [page break] as the main participants.[34]

This term paper was later complemented by a handwritten final exam for the course (for which Williams received an 'A' grade), where Williams adds this commentary to his prior assessment of *Ulysses*:

No character comes more promptly to my mind, in this connection [that is, according to Joseph Wood Krutch, contemporary authors no longer made their leading characters ideal or heroic figures], than Mr. Bloom, the 'Ulysses' of James Joyce. This Hebraic wanderer is a real travesty of his Trojan predecessor. Throughout his wanderings (a single day and night) the gross, mean and pitiable characteristics of his nature are brought as methodically to light as were ~~those of~~ the heroic qualities of Odysseus in Virgil's Aeneid. He also comes home, in the end, to find that his wife has been a little more than domestically preoccupied during his absence but instead of making a magnificent hash of the lovers he forgivingly (or rather abjectly) kisses the offending spouse in a manner which is the crowning obscenity of the whole obscene story.[35]

Later in the exam paper, Williams returns to Joyce's novel and concludes: 'Ulysses is the great 'stream of consciousness' novel by James Joyce. It is a record of thought processes, principally in the minds of a middle aged Jew named Bloom, his wife and a young man, Stephen Dedalus. Most of the thought processes, however, seem to be Mr. Joyce's. The book is written in an unnecessarily difficult style and is full of superfluous coarseness'.[36]

While Williams's lack of appreciation for *Ulysses* can partly be attributed to his conservative background and to his youth (though, at twenty-five, he was older and far better read than most of his fellow undergraduates), the reasons for his consternation with the novel were only tangentially related to its literary complexities and its 'pornographic' nature. Williams's diatribes against the novel in 1936 were in accord with those of a nation still feeling the pressure from morality leagues such as the New York Society for the Prevention of Vice. Like other censored works in America at the time, Joyce's novel was deemed an affront to the nation's conservative mores, even long after US District Judge John M. Woolsey's pronounced it free of 'dirt for dirt's sake' on 6 December 1933.[37] To have put such an incendiary novel on an undergraduate course reading list at all – let alone at a private, non-sectarian university located in the conservative Midwestern city of St Louis – is testament to the enlightenment of Heller. Although the young Williams's 'love' for Heller in September 1936 had soured to 'bore[dom]' by early October, his dissatisfaction with the German professor was based more on pedagogy than on philology or aestheticism.[38]

Also by the end of 1936, it is clear that Williams had still not entirely freed himself from his mother Edwina's (if not St Louis's in general) choking conservative hold on him, though he was well on his way to establishing an identity contrary to her wishes. As such, echoes of Edwina's Episcopalian objections to 'lurid' literary filth are recognizable in Williams's final commentary on the novel:[39]

> Mr. Joyce puzzles, bores and finally exhausts the reader [...] [but] has created a magnificent tour de force in his Ulysses. His work impresses you as being much more labored, studied and ambitious. [...] Mr. Joyce places too much emphasis upon the sordid side of character.[40]

That Williams was also devouring the sexually explicit and literarily complex novels of D. H. Lawrence, and had even tried his own hand at writing about sexual liberation in *The Magic Tower* for the Webster Groves Theatre in St Louis, should be proof enough that Williams was not a prude about 'the sordid side' of human nature, or an anti-modernist, not even in these early years of his writing career.

Whatever led Williams to criticize Joyce at Washington University, it was not due to Williams's lack of experience with literature, experimental or otherwise. And though he did not like all of what he read, he was surely trained by Otto Heller, George Bruner Parks (Williams's 'Contemporary British and American Literature' professor at Washington University), and his earlier professors at the University of Missouri (1929–32) to appreciate Modernist aesthetics. In his notebook for 17 September 1936, Williams lists reading Marcel Proust's 'The Sweet

Cheat Gone', the translation of part six of *A la recherche du temps perdu*, *Albertine disparue* (1927), finding it 'nice but very slow': 'I admire his art above all others of the modern school'.[41] Even in his reading of *Ulysses*, there is a sense of Williams's earnest efforts to understand the novel's literary complexities. Among the eighteen type-written pages of the two-part essay (the second part compares Ernest Hemingway's *The Green Hills of Africa* and Sherwood Anderson's *Winesburg, Ohio*), Williams devotes over four pages to the description and analysis of *Ulysses*, by far the longest treatment of the four novels in the essay.

As an undergraduate at Washington University, Williams already had had enough exposure to literature and philosophy to appreciate Joyce's experimental techniques in *Ulysses*; his judgement against the novel should not be dismissed as simply the result of literary ignorance. Nor should his conservative upbringing be cited as the reason for his hostility toward the novel, since he frequently sought out and devoured the poetry, short fiction, and novels of writers who notoriously transgressed the frontiers of American social decorum. Though Williams was raised southern Episcopalian before moving to St Louis at the age of seven, by the time he had enrolled in college in 1929 at the University of Missouri, he was well on his way to dismantling certain religious values instilled in him at home. Among these was the discovery of writers whose flirtation with social and sexual transgressions greatly influenced him.

These college papers exhibit not only the breadth and depth of Williams's literary and dramatic education, but also his understated exasperation with having had to spend precious energy concentrating on the works of other writers when, as his notebooks inform us, he was in full stride writing and submitting poems, stories, and plays to various magazines and contests. Reports such as the one on Voltaire's *Mérope* (1743) or Max Eastman's *The Literary Mind* (1931) guard their value not only in what they have to say about the young Williams's perception of the literary world but also in the figures of that literary world to whom he was exposed and in whom he later took interest or rejected. And, more importantly, what these papers suggest, particularly the one on Joyce, is that Williams's literary appreciation was changing, and those changes become evident in the creative work he produced alongside of these academic essays.

As noted in the previous chapter, the anti-puritanical play *Beauty Is the Word* was the young Tom Williams's paean to the Romantic poet Shelley, but Williams no doubt saw affinities between the play and Lawrence's novels and short stories of sexual liberation that he was currently immersed in. If scholars have, for the most part, exhausted the Lawrence connection in Williams's work over the last thirty years or so, they have also neglected to explain why Williams chose a Lawrentian modernism over a Joycean one.[42] For example, after meeting Frieda Lawrence during a trip to Taos, Williams penned the lyric poem, 'Cried the Fox; For D.H.L.' (1939), and three one-act plays, the sexual farce 'A Panic Renaissance in the Lobos Mountains' (n.d.), *Adam and Eve on a Ferry* (c. 1939) and *I Rise in Flame, Cried the Phoenix* (1941). Famous now is the exchange between Tom and Amanda in *The Glass Menagerie*, when Amanda (based on Williams's mother, Edwina) orders Tom to get rid of his books on Lawrence:

TOM.   Yesterday you confiscated my books. You had the nerve to –
AMANDA.   I took that horrible novel back to the library – yes! That hideous book by that insane Mr. Lawrence. [...] I cannot control the output of diseased minds or people who cater to them – [...] BUT I WON'T ALLOW SUCH FILTH BROUGHT INTO MY HOUSE![43]

Edwina's version which appears in her own memoirs does little to counter Williams's recollections:

Tom also enjoyed reading, for he spent endless hours[,] when he wasn't studying, in the library. [...] One afternoon he walked in with a copy of *Lady Chatterley's Lover*. I picked it up for a look [...] and was shocked by the candor of the love scenes. I promptly marched Tom and the book to the library, where I gave the librarian a piece of my mind. 'The idea of allowing a fifteen-year-old boy to read this!' I told her.[44]

Traces of Lawrence can be found in nearly everything Williams wrote between 1936 and 1944 (and later), but the same could not be said for Joyce, at least not the 'Modernist' Joyce most recognizable to Williams, the Washington University student. Yet, paradoxically, Joyce *is* present in Williams's early writings, if only in the one-dimensional image Williams had of Joyce and of his literary experiments in *Ulysses*.

To Tom Williams, Lawrence's work, and not Joyce's, was 'the greatest modern monument to the dark roots of creation'.[45] Presumably, this was the case because Williams perceived Lawrence as affixing Joyce's 'sordid side of character'[46] to some higher, unconscious, and even spiritual drive in man, along the lines of Henri Bergson's *élan vital*. Williams had studied the theory of the *élan vital* in Heller's class at Washington in 1936–37, and no doubt its physiopsychological theory of sexuality had appealed to the not-yet-outed gay poet-playwright more than Joyce's psychopathological one, as it is rendered in several of Bloom's stream of consciousness passages in *Ulysses*. As Williams would later note in another college paper, 'Comments on the Nature of Artists with a few Specific References to the Case of Edgar Allan Poe', which he wrote the following year in October 1937 for Professor Wilbur Schramm at the University of Iowa:

> There are certain members of the human family cursed or blessed, as the case may be, with what I have seen defined more sharply in French than in English as 'la volonté de puîssance [*sic*]'. This means a fund of uncontrolled energy that exceeds the demands of ordinary living. Dr. Heller has defined the same things as 'L'élan vital'. But I think that leaves too much unsaid. The energy of an artist is something that possesses him rather than something that he possesses. It is a 'volonté': an unleashed force.[47]

Lawrence's belief in the transcendental truth of blood knowledge – that is, one did not engage in sexual intercourse principally to satisfy a carnal appetite alone but also, if not more so, to complete the natural order of things – was a more effective weapon against Puritanical tyranny than Leopold Bloom's sybaritic sex as self-gratification. Arguably, the blood knowledge-satyriasis dialectic that would dominate Williams's literary production for the next forty years emerged from the playwright's own struggle to comprehend his sexual urges at this time. For Williams to accept Joyce now as a literary influence over Lawrence was to prove Edwina right in thinking that Modernists only preached 'dirt'. In other words, lose Joyce to save Lawrence.

In Lawrence's writing, the young Williams could point to human nature transcended by sexuality, whereas in Joyce's *Ulysses* sex was merely democratized, part and parcel of our daily diets. Williams was not put off by sexuality in literature as Edwina was, but rather by the Joycean 'obscenities', those passages of 'dullness' and 'dirt' in the novel that celebrate human ordinariness – flatulence, urination, and masturbation – rather than its extraordinariness. If in their depictions of sexuality, Lawrence and Joyce shared gutters, as Edwina believed and Williams openly acknowledged, at least Lawrence's face was pointing skyward.[48] In Lawrence's lyrical blood knowledge, Williams discovered a career-defining theme; in Joyce he had merely encountered the 'sordid' descriptions of bodily functions and other details intended, he felt, for shock value alone, 'dirt for dirt's sake', as he labelled it. Lawrence was his champion of neo-Romanticism; Joyce, his smutty iconoclast.

Williams's perceptions of Joyce and of *Ulysses* become understandable when set alongside of his own developing literary aesthetics at the time, as found in the numerous poems, short stories, and plays he had written and published prior to 1936 and just after. Williams was, as he himself repeatedly declared, first and foremost a poet whose 'sympathies were with the Romantics'.[49] In his published and non-published poetry discussed in the previous chapter, Williams wrote essentially lyrics, heavily imitative of John Keats, Edna St Vincent Millay, Sara Teasdale, and later Hart Crane. In these early forays into poetry, we find more traditional forms of writing that Joyce had rejected years earlier.

Once enrolled at Washington University, Williams also began publishing poems more frequently, contributing twenty poems to the university's literary magazine, *The Eliot*, between November 1936 and February 1938. What his writing and publication history concerning his poetry prior to 1936 tells us is that Williams knew his literary aesthetics were outmoded months before he discovered Joyce. Yet, even if he could appreciate the Modernists, his aesthetics remained profoundly neo-romantic, and this surely played a role in his rejecting Joyce in his college essay. Unlike his friend Mills, Williams simply could not write that 'crazy modern verse'.[50]

In terms of his short fiction written during this period, Williams clearly demonstrated his neo-romantic bent, both in theme and in character type. Similar to the romantic tragedy of Jacob and Lila in a story discussed earlier, 'Something by Tolstoi' (1930–31), 'The Field of Blue Children' (1939) encapsulates all that preoccupied Williams for the next three years. It is not just a neo-romantic and sentimental tale of failed love, a story entirely lacking in sympathy to anything Joycean. Rather, it is also reminiscent of the *Märchen* stories of writers from *Die romantische Schule* like Novalis, Ludwig Tieck and E. T. A. Hoffmann, who mixed the magical with the prosaic in their characters' longing for the ideal and bemoaning the *ubi sunt*.[51] 'The Field of Blue Children' – whose potential sources are Hodgson Burnett's *The Land of the Blue Flower* (1909), Maurice Baring's 'The Blue Rose' (1910), or Rudyard Kipling's 'Blue Roses' (1891)[52] – describes the restless yearnings of Myra, a young college student who falls briefly in love with an idealized poet, Homer Stallcup, whom she cannot marry for social reasons. The story evolved to a certain extent from the short story Williams wrote in 1935, titled 'The Blue Rose', which was later reworked into the two-part story 'Blue Roses and the Polar Star' (1941) and 'Bobo' (1941), which contain material directly related to *The Glass Menagerie* and 'The Yellow Bird' (1947).

Typical of the *Romantiker* tradition, the blue flower (here, sexuality more than immutability) remains elusive for Myra. Led by nature to the field of blue flowers to consummate their unconscious desire for one another, Myra and Homer hesitate just before Myra leaves him, choosing to privilege social decorum over blood knowledge. Though the sexual content of this story is written into its margins, that was due more to Williams's desire to see it published in *Story* magazine than to his fear or loathing to reproduce sexual content in his fiction. In two earlier 'love' stories, for example – 'In Spain There Was Revolution' (1936) and 'Twenty-seven Wagons Full of Cotton' (1936) – Williams reveals his will more clearly to tackle love in a much more earthy, though still not 'dirty', manner. Written and submitted to *Story* in late August or early September 1936, 'In Spain There Was Revolution' captures Williams's early attempt at erotic writing. Here, a lifeguard named Steve seduces an unnamed girl in a blue silk bathing suit, who is a counsellor at the Idle Wild Camp in the Ozarks:

> As soon as the willow shade had closed over them he caught the shoulder strap nearest him and jerked it down. His hand cupped her breast. She looked at him with eyes half frightened and lips falling apart. It was always that way. She let things go until they had gone too far to be stopped. Then she felt herself absolved of the responsibility. [...] Now she sat up and straightened her blue silk suit. The lovely white parts of her [tanned] body disappeared.[53]

Noticeable in Williams's style here is Lawrence's stylistic handling of sexual content, different from what Williams would identify later as Joyce's 'gift for analyzing obscenity'.

Williams had submitted around two dozen stories like this one to literary magazines from 1933 to 1938, but only one, 'Twenty-seven Wagons Full of Cotton', was ever accepted for publication.[54] This story, from which the one-act play of the same title and the 1956 Elia Kazan film *Baby Doll* were to be later adapted, is a Gothic tale set on a southern plantation and recounts the sexual initiation of Mrs Jake Meighan (she is not given a first name) with the unnamed syndicate plantation manager, who seduces her while her husband gins his cotton. Mrs Jake Meighan is at first 'shocked [...] a little' but 'not unpleasantly' so, when the manager begins 'licking his lips' and sexually devouring her with his eyes.[55] The rape that becomes the climax of the 1946 one-act version of this story is here represented more as a scene of mutual seduction, blood knowledge cum violent sexplay: 'The little man has started twisting her wrist. Now he laughed and struck her smartly with the riding crop. "You play too rough", she groaned. [...] His hands cascaded leisurely down the front of her dress and came to rest on her lap'.[56]

Williams's sexual coming of age coincided with America's for the most part, with many seeing Williams as being partly responsible for that fact. Williams learned soon after 1936 that mores were thawing in his country that gradually accepted both Joyce's and Lawrence's handling of sexuality. Williams would even play a major role in the coming decade to speed that pace along. What Williams saw as the literary equivalent to 'dullness' and 'dirt' in 1936, would become by 1939, the year he wrote his sexual encomium, *Battle of Angels* (like *Ulysses*, based on a Greek myth), his *modus operandi*, if not his *modus vivendi*.[57] What all of this helps to establish is not just what Williams's literary aesthetics were at the time but what middle America's were as well. And while Williams's aesthetics would not drastically change for the next ten years or more following *The Glass Menagerie* and up to the supremely experimental *Camino Real* (1953) – his plays still wavered between neo-romantic expressionism and gritty realism; his poetry remained lyric in form until his death; his short fiction rarely evolved toward anything like Joyce's prose experiments, even in the free association novel *Moise and the World of Reason* – his appreciation for Joyce would. Though time was needed for these Modernist aesthetics to fully take hold of Williams as a writer, the seeds were sewn here in Washington University. It was St Louis, and not the South, that introduced Williams to Chekhov, Strindberg, Crane, Hemingway, Joyce, and Lawrence.

During the academic year 1936–37, then, Williams had achieved some necessary critical distance not only from his family but also from himself. Though his literary aesthetics were slowly taking form, his dramatic production was still heavily influenced by the socialism his friends at The League of St Louis Artists and Writers preached and by the naturalism Hollywood delivered monthly to the cinemas he frequented. Both were significant elements in his next six plays.

Buoyed by positive critical reception of *The Magic Tower* the previous May, Williams began turning to theatre more as his medium of choice. Now having made a reputation as a local playwright, Williams was asked by Willard Holland in the fall to write a curtain-raiser for Irwin Shaw's caustic war play, *Bury the Dead,* which was to be performed by the Mummers that Armistice Day, 11 November 1936, at the Wednesday Club Auditorium. The anonymous play, *Headlines* (1936), is a pacifist sketch that interpolates a senator's address with antiwar scenes in America. After a sleepless night, Williams wrote in his notebook:

> My prologue 'Headlines' will be given this evening. Holland has made something clever out of it. He's a genius I think – a real genius – though I can't say I like him especially as a person. He's too slipper. I enjoy working with 'The Mummers'. A delightful bunch of young people. Nothing snotty or St. Louis 'Social' about them.[58]

Typical of the self-effacing attitude he took toward his work (predicting failure was Williams's natural defence as an artist), Williams felt that the production of his play was 'rather botched' but did not care much because it was a 'stupid, pointless thing anyway – a piece of hack work'.[59]

Williams was also growing a little disillusioned at this time with the socialist movement he had wholly supported the year before, and his next play, *Candles to the Sun*, although ostensibly about socialist issues, is more about the individual's struggle to negotiate his or her ideals with those of society than they are about society's inherent superiority to the individual. Williams had, in fact, begun distancing himself, if not entirely from the ideals of socialism, then at least from its pragmatism. When both Conroy and Balch attended the Mummers's production of *Bury the Dead*, Williams had found them 'quite rude' and '[un]civil': 'There's just a natural uncongeniality between me and that bunch. They are professional "againsters". I don't believe in that stuff. It's not necessary to be against everything else in order to be for Communism'.[60]

During the spring of 1937, Williams was hard at work with Holland in getting *Candles to the Sun* ready for its 18 March production. *Candles to the Sun*, Williams described to the journalist from the *St Louis Times* who interviewed him, was about individuals and group consciousness, with the candles representing the individuals as people and the sun their society on the whole. The individuals discover that happiness is not achieved at the expense of what is best for the 'common good'.[61] In the play, John, who attempts to flee the mine's slow but certain death, is trapped in marriage and fatherhood and is socially pressured to work in the mines that eventually kill him. His wife Fern and son Luke subsequently move in with his parents and wait for the Depression to destroy everyone's spirits, just as the mines invariably do their loved ones. The question Williams addresses here, as Chris Bigsby asserts, would become a familiar one: 'What is the nature of the individual's responsibility?'[62] As Williams later told Mark Barron in 1940, 'I try to write all my plays so that they carry some social message along with the story'.[63] It was the 1930s, after all, and Williams, undoubtedly familiar with the socio-political plays of Clifford Odets, Lillian Hellman, Sidney Kingsley, Robert E. Sherwood, Maxell Anderson, John Howard Lawson, and William Saroyan, wanted to join the WPA Federal Writers' Project, as discussed in the previous chapter; and since social plays were a strong vehicle for acceptance into these federally funded programmes, they became Williams's mouthpiece as well. Later, he and his fellow experimental theatre students at Iowa, Thomas Pawley informs us, were assigned to write the then-popular living newspaper sketches, short social dramas that were based on the students' readings from current newspapers.[64]

In addition to getting *Candles to the Sun* ready for the stage, Williams was also working on *Me, Vashya* for William Carson's 'English 16' playwriting contest. Like *Headlines*, *Me, Vashya* was, on the surface, an anti-war treatise, a polemic against a wartime munitions magnate. Originally a one-act play titled 'Death is a Drummer', *Me, Vashya* addresses the political responsibilities that Sir Vashya Shontine neglects when he sells arms to both sides of a war. He is called, Bigsby notes in his *Critical Introduction to Twentieth-Century American Drama*, 'a sort of monstrous abstraction – the personification of – war and destruction or – death'.[65] And yet, the play cannot entirely avoid Williams's Romanticist inklings, or his increased fascination with Hollywood's gangster's films. Vashya's wife, Lady Lillian Shontine, is smitten with a young revolutionary poet and shoots Vashya to free herself from his control and, as a result, expiates the death with which she has had to live all her life because of his lack of a social conscience: 'Yes, he's gone! He's gone with the others! You can tell them all that Vashya's gone to the front!'[66] No irony is lost, however, when Vashya, like the killing of Jean-Paul Sartre's political leader, Hoederer, a decade later in *Les mains sales* (1948), is assassinated for jealous revenge and not for having committed crimes against humanity.[67]

As per tradition, three plays were selected by a jury in Carson's class (which was ostensibly him alone) to be produced the following year by the university's drama club, Thyrsus. When Carson did not select *Me, Vashya* among the winners of the 'English 16' playwriting contest, Williams felt it was an 'ignominious failure',[68] became entirely disenchanted with Washington University, and left the university before completing his degree. All of this may have prompted him to publish the anonymous essay 'What College Has Not Done for Me' in the June issue of *The Eliot*. He was now in a position no better than when he left

Missouri five years earlier. A year of Grand's tuition money now wasted, Williams would spend the summer writing *Fugitive Kind*, watching his sister's mental state worsen, and transferring all his credits to the University of Iowa for the following fall.

The summer of 1937, then, was about struggles, Williams with writing *Fugitive Kind*, and Rose with staving off madness. Williams felt later that he had selfishly plunged himself into his writing and consequently ignored his sister's condition. Ever since May 1937, in fact, Williams was eager to write another full-length play for Holland's Mummers, and Williams hoped that *Fugitive Kind* would be ready for production the following fall in St Louis. Troubled all summer long by his recurrent 'blue devils' and preoccupied with Rose's worsening condition (she would finally be institutionalized that July for *dementia praecox*), Williams would encounter repeated difficulties in writing his play. One trouble that he faced was finding that right blend of Romanticist individualism with social commitment, a melodramatic cocktail he had served up in his previous plays, at times with a twist. Another sticky point in particular was making his antihero Terry Meighan, a gangster hiding out in a flophouse in a Midwestern city not unlike St Louis, appear both real *and* sympathetic to the middle-class Christian audiences that patronized the Wednesday Club where the Mummers performed.

In her introduction to the New Direction edition of *Fugitive Kind* (2001), Allean Hale sums up the struggle Williams was having:

> His journal first mentions it [*Fugitive Kind*] on June 5 [1937]: '... [a]fter reading new play – laid in flophouse – felt thoroughly disgusted – will I ever produce another full length play that's worth producing?'
>
> June 12: '... play goes badly.'
>
> June [2]0: 'Wrote some good stuff – all but last scene of draft finished.'
>
> July 4: 'Saw Holland. ... He read play [and] seemed fairly pleased though much rewriting is necessary.'
>
> July 6: '[P]lay smooths [*sic*] out but does not develop[–]'
>
> July 7: 'I want to finish this new play – visit Memphis or the Ozarks. ... I will read Pulit[zer] plays and then try to sleep[–]'.[69]

Williams's notebook throughout the month of July portrays the young writer as being tormented by neuroses (he feared he was ending up like his sister) and looking for opportunities to escape his parents' home and the 'deadly middle-west' and flee to Spain to 'enlist in the Loyalist

Army'.[70] Despite his depression and fear of encroaching madness, which was exacerbated by his visits that summer to see Rose (who was first placed in St Vincent's Sanitarium before being transferred to the State Hospital in Farmington), Williams found a brief period of respite in early August when he returned to the summer camps in the Ozarks for a week. By 8 August, Williams had again taken up *Fugitive Kind*, reassured in his writing but finding the play 'still too melodramatic'.[71] He would continue working on the play for the rest of the month, but its problems, and his eventual decision to transfer to the University of Iowa later that month, redirected his attention to another writing project, 'American Gothic', a one-act play whose sole extent manuscript has missing pages.

Williams had personally known the editor of *American Prefaces*, Wilbur Schramm, since 1936, when Schramm served as his *ad hoc* literary mentor; only later did Schramm actually become his English professor when Williams completed his senior year at Iowa. Throughout the spring and summer of 1936, Williams frequently submitted his poems and his stories to Schramm at *American Prefaces*, though most were rejected. As Williams wrote in his notebook for 14 March of that year, 'This afternoon Am. Prefaces ret'd "bottle of Brass" with letter saying story was "told" rather than "lived". I quite agree – in part.... "Gift Of An Apple" gone to Amer. Pref. Hope it will stick'.[72] Later that August, Williams received promising news from David Ash, founding member of *American Prefaces* who served on its editorial board from the spring of 1935 to October 1937: 'Also had a letter this afternoon from David Ash of American Prefaces saying he was holding "Ten Minute Stop" and hoped the other editors would accept it [...]. So my hopes are high – It is extremely encouraging. Besides I just love that story & it would delight me to have it in *Amer. Pref'*.[73] It was not to be, however: 'The damned "American Prefaces" returned my story ['Ten Minute Stop'] with suggestions I *revise* it completely – made some preposterous suggestions – The story seems sort of rotten now that I read it over – but good enough for that bunch'.[74] As it had been just a week since his decision to enrol at the University of Iowa, where regionalist painter Grant Wood taught, the painting *American Gothic* was probably on Williams's mind that Monday, 30 August 1937, when he sat down and typed out the play: 'Wrote a new one-act this P.M. – "American Gothic"'.[75]

Set on a 'bone dry' Midwestern farm in late summer or early autumn, Williams's 'American Gothic' dramatizes the destruction of a family whose pious mother, Nonnie, refuses to heed her husband Alf's pleas not to hand their wayward son Amadee and his companion Mabel over to federal agents for the robberies they have committed.[76] Like many of Williams's apprentice plays of the period, 'American Gothic' wraps themes of social injustice in Christian garbs and challenges us to distinguish between his characters' acts of rectitude and those of dissolution. In the gospel according to Tom, the fugitive kind – those pariahs, prostitutes, and degenerates that society casts away as flotsam – invariably practise a humanism more magnanimous than the Christian zealots (mis)guided by their religious principles.

Williams must have imagined Wood's two figures in the painting as representing the hypocrisy of a Midwestern piety he confronted daily at home or in his city's Welfare Leagues (which many critics feel Wood was satirizing as well). As such, Nonnie, who is based on the woman in Wood's painting, chooses dogma over compassion in evicting Amadee from the family farm for his having sent her and Alf tainted money. We are not told in the extant pages why the money is tainted but, given Williams's reference to the 'Three Federal Officers' in the dramatis personae, we assume that it was stolen and that Amadee sent it home to help his parents pay the farm's back taxes and mortgage. Supportive of his son's generous act – perhaps more for selfish than paternal reasons, as Alf knows they will lose the farm without the money – Alf calls Nonnie 'a hard woman' for having turned out her own 'flesh'n blood'.[77]

The story of *Fugitive Kind*, with its lavish use of idiomatic language, follows closely that of Williams's 'American Gothic', where Terry Meighan, on the lam following a recent botched bank heist, seeks refuge in a riverfront flophouse managed by the proprietor's nineteen-year-old adopted daughter Glory. The play, like the one-act, is laden with Christian symbolism and repeatedly, if not rhetorically, espouses a revolutionary dictum that glorifies socialism and vilifies society's fat-cats for their derelict neglect of the city's underprivileged. As Leverich writes, *Fugitive Kind* was Williams's attempt to add 'his protest to the clamor of many 1930s intellectuals, saying that society's evils, carefully disguised behind the cosmetics of hypocrisy, were being maintained by capitalist greed'.[78] Terry, like all of Williams's fugitive kind, was cheated out of his rightful future by an unwavering and unsympathetic capitalist system. Meighan, like Amadee, strikes back at that capitalist machine by robbing banks.

But he, too, is no Robin Hood, entertaining no desire to share the money he steals with the other fugitives, and his selfishness (something that troubles this play as much as it does 'American Gothic') makes him an unlikely hero in a play ostensibly about community service and religious self-sacrifice. As Williams had done with Nonnie's zealotry in the one-act, here he tempers Terry's unlikable nature by introducing loathsome Christians in the play who are on a mission that outweighs, or at least balances out, all of Terry's indignities (save, perhaps, his accessory to murder). Nonnie is thus morphed into a gaggle of self-aggrandizing, Progressivist Junior Welfare Leaguers, '*a bevy of dazzling socialites on a charitable mission*'[79] who arrive at the flophouse in limousines and distribute Christmas gifts of soap and neckties to the homeless men 'only as a photo opportunity that will insure their good deeds go noticed by the local newspapers'.[80] No doubt, finding the right balance in *Fugitive Kind* between its conspicuous religious message that God lives in the human heart (and not in canonical dogma or 'Christian duty') and its gangster credo that life's for the taking proved difficult for Williams. 'American Gothic', which sketches out a similar dialectic, apparently helped Williams navigate his way through the material of *Fugitive Kind* without damaging the work he had already done on the larger and more significant play.

Whether readers and viewers finally judge *Fugitive Kind* successful or not in its attempts to balance crime against determinist theories of (r)evolution and religion, neither can charge the young playwright with negligence toward the development of his play's several themes. As he did in all of his dramatic writings, Williams worked exceptionally hard on making *Fugitive Kind* both a thoughtful and a theatrical play. Written at the end of a very long and onerous summer, 'American Gothic' helped Williams resolve his thematic and dramatic dilemmas surrounding the completion of *Fugitive Kind*, for presumably he never returned to the one-act, and *Fugitive Kind*, whose production by the Mummers would 'be announced in Sunday's paper' was 'practically finished' a week later on 8 September:

> Holding my thumbs for Iowa. It is almost definitely settled that I will get to go up there – play will be announced in Sunday's paper – Good thing I got it practically finished because I'm having one of my difficult periods with writing – First scene between Glory and Terry will not come to suit Holland – I think it is O.K. but he objects to interrupted sequence and references to Leo.[81]

The news for the University of Iowa was good in the end, and an ecstatic Williams set off for Iowa City on a bus, writing Clark Mills en route: 'I am seated in a coach bound for Iowa City – it is 11:45 P.M. – and I feel such a prodigious excitement – in spite of a double sedative – that I must communicate my feelings to someone or else <u>blow up</u>'.[82] Though the year itself was not much better, academically speaking, than his previous years at Missouri and Washington, two important results were achieved: Williams worked more exclusively in theatre, and he was awarded his bachelor's degree that August 1938. Being so far from the St Louis theatre scene that he had enjoyed the previous year now made producing his work that much more difficult, and Williams really did not know what to do with himself throughout most of that year. He had followed through with *Fugitive Kind*, though highly perturbed by the outcome. Its realistic set, one he had opted against (as he would throughout his career), irked him so much that he was ready to jump out the window in a feigned (and overzealous) suicide attempt. He had even hoped the Mummers would produce *Spring Storm* in 1938, the play he wrote for Professor E. C. Mabie, but the company disbanded when Holland left for Hollywood to act, much to Williams's chagrin.[83] But Iowa did offer Williams theatrical opportunities that Holland could not. Iowa's experimental theatre programme, directed by Mabie, was nationally recognized, and in it the young Williams could immeasurably reshape his dramatic skills and draw to him the ear of influential people in the theatre business.

Spring Storm, the title Williams finally settled on for a play originally called 'April Is the Cruelest Month' (Williams wrote out some preliminary dialogue in his college spiral notebook, among his American civics notes, the previous year at Washington) is a 'study of Sex – a blind animal urge or force', a 'tragedy of sex relations' that leads two couples 'into a tangle of cruel and ugly relations'.[84] As would be typical in Williams's work, the stronger, more violent of the forces drawing two people together (as much as it repels them) remains ignorant of its contribution to a divine project, where the weak and febrile creatures interpret their collision as part of God's greater plan. If healthy, consensual (though often violent) sex is Williams's truest expression of that plan, then the forced, stolen or misappropriated sexuality of rape systematically 'corrects' its celibate aberration, which in Williams is inevitably the result of ascetic Christian doctrine. As Hertha Neilson tells Arthur Shannon in the play, '[...] fornication was the straight line upwards [...]'.[85] When Arthur molests Hertha, as Mitch would later do Blanche, she *at first* resists his efforts to kiss her with phrases such as 'No! Don't touch me!', 'Let go of me, Arthur' and 'No, no, please let me go' – phrases that Glory utters in *Fugitive Kind* when the fugitive bank-robber Terry grabs and *'kisses her violently'*.[86] Then, after Arthur succeeds in kissing her, *'She struggles and then is limp in his arms. [...] She touches her lips wonderingly'* and wishes him to continue (just as Glory does).[87] Lawrentian blood knowledge or Bersonian *élan vital* win the day once again.

Believing in earnest that he had written a play of greater scope than his previous gangster efforts (plays that include *Curtains for the Gentleman* in January 1936 to *In our Profession* in 1938), Williams read *Spring Storm* to his class, hoping for external acknowledgements of his genius. Williams's efforts were not rewarded, however, as he recalled in his notebook for 2 August:

> Read final version of my second act and it was finally, quite, quite finally, rejected by the class because of Heavenly's weakness as a character. Of course it is very frightening & discouraging to work so hard on a thing and then have it fall flat. There is still a chance they may be wrong – all of them – I have to cling to that chance. Or do I? Why can't I be brave and admit this defeat? – Because it means the defeat of everything? Perhaps. I haven't the slightest notion what comes after this summer. Holland is about my last resource. If he likes it and will produce that would at least give me a spar to hang onto for a few months. I would do better to come back here but how? Mabie won't get me a scholarship.[88]

Mabie's only response was the now infamous line: 'Well, we all have to paint our nudes'. Mabie's lacklustre response to the poetic play perhaps turned Williams off to returning to Iowa the following year to start the master's programme that several of his fellow students did, such as Marian Gallaway, who became Mabie's graduate assistant and for whom Williams would later write a foreword to her 1950 book, *Constructing a Play*.[89]

With his bachelor's degree finally in hand, Williams petered about St Louis for the rest of the summer, hoping to land radio work at KXOK, for whom he had penned a 'spook radio drama' titled 'Men Who March', which was an adaption of *Me, Vashya*.[90] He even travelled up north to Chicago to try and find work on the WPA Theatre and Writers' projects there, but to no avail. Over the next few months, itching to leave St Louis and his father's house again, Williams started working on a new play, *Not about Nightingales*, a psychological agitprop of the imprisoned spirit, with the cage of the real prison cell metaphorically impeding human desire to transcend the physical world. As 'Canary' Jim Allison says,

> There's a wall like that around ev'ry man in here an' outside of here, Ollie [...]. Ev'ry man living is walking around in a cage. He carries it with him wherever he goes and don't let it go till he's dead. Then the

walls come to pieces and he stops being lonesome [...]. Cause he's part of something bigger than him.[91]

'Canary' Jim, a forerunner of Val Xavier who is trapped in solitary confinement in his own skin, here represents the spiritual longing for a life devoid of physical taint. The sensual side of human nature only really enters the play with Eva, prison warden Boss Whalen's guileless secretary. Recalling her biblical counterpart, Eva tempts Jim into finding a way out of his prison, both his barred cell and his misanthropic iso-lationism. Eva chooses to side with the convicts during a hunger strike that ensues after Boss places several inmates in the Klondike, 'a small, steam-heated room with little ventilation and no water', for protesting his reselling of prison food for personal gain. The warden is eventually beaten to death, and Jim, the convict Eva abets, flees into the river, presumably to safety.

By the autumn of 1938, Williams was also working hard on a collec-tion of long and short plays that he was calling 'American Blues'. As Thomas Keith points out, Williams enlarged the collection from 1937 to 1943 that had begun with two lists of plays:

Both are carefully typewritten to resemble playbills or title pages for a bound manuscript of completed plays. One reads as follows: 'AMERICAN BLUES / (A program of one-act plays designed to approximate in dramaturgy / the mood, atmosphere and meaning of American Blues music) / 1. American Gothic / 2. Hello From Bertha / 3. Escape / 4. The Fat Man's Wife / 5. The Big Game / 6. Moony's Kid Don't Cry.[92]

The second list adds *The Long Goodbye, Summer at the Lake, Every Twenty Minutes, In our Profession*, 'Manana Es Otro Dio', and 'Death in the Movies'.

Summer at the Lake, which Nick Moschovakis dates around 1939, deals with a young boy's longing to escape from his family and his adolescent angst. Donald Fenway, sixteen, is obsessed with fire escapes and the 'hideous trap'[93] of their city apartment and chooses to commit suicide by drowning rather than returning to the city with his mother from their summer home. The connections to Tom Wingfield's desire to escape his family and the boredom of his city life in *The Glass Menagerie* or even Shannon's threat to swim to China in *The Night of the Iguana* are unmistakable. As noted earlier, most of Williams's later themes and images can be found in these early one-acts and full-length plays.

But Williams was also experimenting greatly at the time, both in content and in voice. He typed out several slice-of-life plays, some inspired by his or Rose's troubled home-life, including plays like *Why Do You Smoke So Much, Lily?* (1935) or *The Big Game* (c. 1937). Many were influenced by the cinema that Williams continued to frequent. Several of these one-acts, in fact, such as the chain-gang story *Escape* (c. 1939) or *The Palooka* (c. 1939/1940) – about a 'worn-out boxer',[94] Galveston Joe, who is as disillusioned about his life's failures as is Mrs Hardwicke-Moore in *The Lady of Larkspur Lotion* (c. 1941) or Jane in *I Never Get Dressed Till after Dark on Sundays* (1973) about their Brazilian business contacts – evince Williams's continued fascination with Hollywood idiom and argot. Their dialogue, like that found in 'American Gothic' or *Fugitive Kind*, reflects Williams's efforts to replicate Eugene O'Neill's success with dialect, though most of it appears a bit shop-worn or out of place with respect to their Romantic themes of a failed life or an abandoned dream. *The Fat Man's Wife* (c. 1937) attempts to mix several of these play's characteristics: the boorish, two-timing Joe Cartwright; the young, day-dreaming playwright Dennis Merriwether, whose brief fling that New Year's Eve with Joe's wife Vera convinces him he is in love with her and wants her to flee with him aboard a tramp steamer; and the middle-aged, 'Lynn Fontaine [*sic*]'[95] type Vera, whose ego is flattered by the young man's advances but who chooses not to leave and instead say 'unimportant things' to her husband 'for the rest of [their] lives'.[96]

Williams's own anxiety, like that of Dennis Merriwether or Donald Fenway, to flee was growing since he moved back home from Iowa. He wrote repeatedly in his notebook about trying to gather up the courage to set out on his own, desiring '<u>vital</u> contact' with the world which he was 'too cowardly – so far – to make'.[97] With his father pestering him again about finding a 'real' job, and Williams hoping to burst out of St Louis all together, he first considered leaving for New York. Like one of his many characters, in particularly the penniless Blanche living off the favours of her family, Williams felt caught in 'a terrible trap' and only wanted 'to live, live, <u>live</u>!!'[98] Grand once again came to the rescue and promised Williams in November that she would finance his trip out east where he could put his theatre skills to the test. He was questioning *Nightingales*'s worth, as he eventually did all of his plays, but he was hoping that it would be his ticket out of local celebrity and onto the national stage. No doubt his visits to Rose at the sanatorium in Farmington, where she was 'like a person half-asleep now, quiet, gentle and thank God – not in any way revolting like so many of the others', prodded him to run from madness and preserve his sanity, but he also needed to experience new, *lived* material for his plays.[99]

In December 1938, Williams had once again changed his plans, though he was still bent on heading out toward a 'new' city, New Orleans. Williams changed his mind in favour of New Orleans because it would be cheaper to live and write there than in New York. Edwina eventually financed his trip south. If Williams had only felt 'a prodigious excitement' about life when he left for the University of Iowa back in September 1937, that excitement would now fully be realised when he boarded a bus bound for Memphis then New Orleans, a place he 'was surely *made* for', as he wrote in his notebook upon arrival.[100] By the 28th of the month he was 'here [...] in a completely new scene – New Orleans – the Vieux Carré'.[101]

Williams had heard of the Group Theatre drama contest for playwrights under the age of twenty-five. As he was already twenty-seven, he shaved off nearly three years from his birth to enter the contest. Before arriving in New Orleans, he stopped at his grandparents' home in Memphis and mailed all, or a portion, of his one-act plays titled 'American Blues' (*Moony's Kid Don't Cry*, *Hello from Bertha*, *The Dark Room*, and *The Long Goodbye*, which Theatre Guild member John Gassner did not consider as good as the other, O'Neill-like one-acts), along with two full-length plays, *Fugitive Kind* and *Spring Storm*, to the Group Theatre, signing them 'Tennessee Williams'.[102] It would be this collection that would earn him a letter from Molly Day Thatcher in March 1939 informing him of the special award of $100 he had won for the one-acts. That one letter effectively launched his career.

4
New Orleans to Hollywood (via Acapulco): *Mañana Es Otro Día*

Somewhere between St Louis and Memphis in late December 1938, Thomas Lanier Williams III became Tennessee Williams. Perhaps he had already become 'Tennessee' years before, but the changing of his name, a frequent issue in Williams scholarship, remains curious. Why create a nom de plume when he was already a published poet and a performed playwright? Few writers would risk obscurity after having gained some local fame, and Williams was by then something of a celebrity in St Louis. And yet, when he left Iowa City and Chicago and St Louis and headed by bus to New Orleans via Memphis, he did just that: he turned his back on Thomas Lanier and welcomed Tennessee.

In a 1940 interview with Mark Barron, Williams said that he acquired the name during his senior year at the University of Iowa from classmates (William Inge's account says fraternity brothers) who knew he was from a southern state with a long name, but 'when they couldn't think of Mississippi, they settled on Tennessee'.[1] Seven years later, talking with R. C. Lewis, Williams said he gave himself the name in honour of his Tennessee ancestors, among them Civil War poet Sidney Lanier from Macon, Georgia (a city he would soon visit).[2] Still another account has Williams believing that his original triptych name only suited 'an author of sonnets to spring', which he in fact was, having won $25 from the Wednesday Club of St Louis's poetry contest in 1936 for a sonnet series of the same title.[3] Donald Spoto offers another possibility: Williams remembered fondly his convalescence at his maternal grandparents' home in Memphis after he left the Continental Shoemakers in the summer of 1935, so the name was synonymous with happier times. It was there, after all, that he wrote his first play, *Cairo, Shanghai, Bombay!*

Another possibility is that Williams, who had just submitted plays to the Group Theatre for a contest for writers under the age of twenty-five but who was already approaching twenty-eight, feared exposure by his college professors in St Louis or Iowa. He had managed to irritate both theatre professors of his, W. G. B. Carson and E. C. Mabie, whom he felt left him SOL at WU and the U of I. Despite the setbacks of his university experiences, his 'luck' would soon change, as he wrote to his mother on 21 March 1939:

> Some good news at last. Mr. 'Tennessee' Williams got a telegram last night from the 'Group Theatre' saying they were happy to make a special award of $100.00 for my group of one-act plays 'American Blues'! [...] Do not spread this around till the cheque has arrived, as some of my 'friends' in St. Louis such as Carson might feel morally obliged to inform the Group that I am over 25 – probably that wouldn't make any difference, but I'd rather play safe.[4]

Perhaps Williams simply knew that he needed a fresh start in everything, including in name, when he left his father's home and his despised St Louis. As Albert Devlin asserts, Williams loved to perpetuate the myth of himself. As a rule, Williams's words were 'not attended with academic pomp or even with Williams's own peculiar brand of precision' and were therefore filled with 'contradictions, self-promotion, and more than a little misleading information'.[5] Whatever the reason, the poet Tom was now the playwright Tennessee.

But that transition was not an easy one. Among all of the obstacles, which in hindsight is probably what gave the playwright the experiences he needed to grind out his poetic tragedies later, three are most notable during the next four years. The first hurdle was his constant poverty, assuaged periodically by the theatre fellowships he won and the 'loans' or 'advances' for future plays he was accorded; by the continued generosity of his grandmother and his mother; and by the beneficence of friends, acquaintances, and even total strangers. And yet, Thoreau-like, he learned the benefits of an economical life: a physical hunger that fuelled a spiritual and a professional hunger in him. He would go for days having just 'Salad for supper. Milk for lunch. Coffee for breakfast'.[6] Other meals included cigarettes or stolen avocados or, when money did arrive or was 'lent', a sandwich at local eateries like the Pig'n Whistle in Macon.

His second preoccupation was the war, or more specifically his lack of participation and, at times, interest in it. There exists very little in Williams's written work about his thoughts on the war. In his letters, it comes when he is watching his brother Dakin enter his military service.

Dakin, who was studying law at Washington University, reported for basic training at Jefferson Barracks in St Louis in March 1942 and was drafted into the Air Force later that November. In December 1943, Williams returned to St Louis to visit with his dying grandmother and to see off his brother, who was 'home on final leave before sailing with a convoy for some place where he will need mosquito netting'.[7] For some inexplicable reason, his father refused to pay for Dakin's schooling at Harvard University, which would have made him a commissioned officer; but seeing his brother serve during the war just added another reason among the many why his father C.C. favoured his little brother over him.

The third obsession, for which he repeatedly berates himself in his notebooks, involves his having forgotten or ignored the increasing madness and eventual pre-frontal lobotomy of his sister Rose and the gradual and painful death of his beloved Grand. Famous now is the fact that Williams dated the lobotomy during 1937, when Rose was first placed in St Vincent's Sanitarium, and then Farmington State Hospital, when Williams was preparing to leave for Iowa to finish his undergraduate studies. Lyle Leverich questions Williams's inaccuracies behind – and more importantly potential reasons for – predating the surgery by six years. Williams had not seen his sister much between 1939 and 1943, so he could have easily forgotten when it took place. It was also probably more convenient to ease a guilty conscience if he remembered having already left the family – and Rose – *after* the lobotomy was performed, hence the 1937 date when he left for Iowa, and not the 1943 date, which would essentially suggest that he selfishly left her behind to suffer the fate that she did.

By December 1939, he, too, began detecting in himself the attitude toward Rose that he had previously only attributed to his parents: 'Visited Rose at sanitarium – horrible, horrible! Her talk was so obscene – she laughed and talked continual obscenities. Mother insisted I go in, though I dreaded it and wanted to out, stay outside. [...] It was a horrible ordeal. Especially since I fear that end for myself'.[8] In retrospect, Williams probably *did* save himself from madness by fleeing the family home and allowing himself to explore the limits of his sexual desire, something Edwina had denied Rose. Rose's medical report from the previous August could easily have been Williams's, save the first item: 'Does no work. Manifests delusions of persecution. Smiles and laughs when telling of person plotting to kill her. Talk free and irrelevant. Admits auditory hallucinations. Quiet on the ward. Masturbates frequently. Also expresses various somatic delusions, all of which she explains on a sexual basis [...]'.[9] And because Williams did work daily, he staved off madness for a time and gave the world over the next decade the plays *Battle of Angels, The Glass Menagerie, Summer and Smoke,* and *A Streetcar Named Desire.*

This chapter will examine these three obsessions of Williams from when he finally left home for New Orleans that December 1938 to when he tried his hand as a playwright in New York City, only to return home five years later to witness first-hand what the lobotomy had done to his beloved sister.

Williams left St Louis on 26 December 1938 and arrived in New Orleans two days later (having spent one night with his grandparents in Memphis) with a bad cold. He first had trouble finding a room as the city was hosting that year's Sugar Bowl game, but he found a room in the French Quarter on St Peters Street, before relocating to a hotel on 431 Royal Street for $4 a week. Life was a stark contrast to what he had come to know in St Louis, Columbia, or Iowa City, or had known years before in Clarksdale or Memphis. At first, the Quarter shocked him, though not unagreeably so. He wrote in his notebook that first night, 'Here surely is the place that I was <u>made</u> for if any place on the funny old world'.[10] Armed with a letter of introduction from Alice Lippmann, a family friend in St Louis, Williams met Swedish painter Knute Heldner, who invited the young playwright to spend New Year's Eve with his family. After a *nuit blanche* of house-hopping, Williams recalled the next day in his notebook as having been introduced that evening to the 'artistic and Bohemian life of the Quarter with a bang!',[11] something he would later recount in interviews (perhaps erroneously) as his first homosexual encounter with a paratrooper stationed in New Orleans. If 'Tennessee' had just been a name only a few days before, he was now becoming flesh and blood, and Williams began exploring freely the limits of his sexual and social nature, searching for it in nearly every bar, curio or pawn shop of the Quarter.

He was also looking for 'Tennessee' the writer. As he had done in Chicago early that year, Williams attempted to find work at the WPA Theatre Project in New Orleans, headed by Herbert Ashton, Jr, but the governmental programme was already being dismantled, and Williams would once again find only rejection. He told his mother that he was hoping they would eventual produce a revised version of *Fugitive Kind.* Another literary connection of his upon arrival, Lyle Saxon, offered Williams little more than advice on where to send his work to be published. He dutifully sent off his poems, though a bit ashamed of their poor quality.

After a week at his Royal Street address, Williams moved into 722 Toulouse Street and occupied the skylighted room on the third floor, opposite an artist/professor from Northwestern University. The other tenants were 'musicians, artists, and salesmen – all quite respectable', and the social life was 'very gay', but Williams insisted (no doubt lying) to his mother that he was 'not participating very much in that'.[12] The building's owner, Mrs E. O. Anderson, took kindly to Williams, and, as poor as he was, he needed to find work quickly. He convinced his landlady to turn the ground floor into a café, where he invented the phrase 'Meals for a Quarter in the Quarter'. The adventure lasted only a week, and Williams eventually found himself in court providing evidence in a case that involved Mrs Anderson's having poured boiling water through the slats of her floor onto a wild party hosted by a 'Jewish society photographer'.[13] The incident, which earned her a fifteen dollars fine, is told in Williams's 1977 play, *Vieux Carré*, the same title he had given to a poem dedicated to Andrew Jackson and life in the Quarter and then to a 'Long Play' (alternatively titled 'Dead Planet, the Moon') about Mother O'Neill's boarding house that he began writing around this time, as he told Edwina in a January 1939 letter.

Williams met a lot of new artist friends, some perhaps more wanna-be than real artists, and he bonded easily with them. Many of Williams's colourful characters in fact have their sources in these French Quarter 'rats' that he met during the early months of his stay there. One was an artist–prostitute named Irene, whose contrastive situation in life had made such a strong impression on him that Williams returned to her repeatedly for material for a play, story, or poem. In his essay *'Amor Perdido*, Or, How it Feels to Become a Professional Playwright', Williams refers to Irene as a New Orleans prostitute 'who painted the marvelous pictures and disappeared'.[14] She also becomes the protagonist of his story 'In Memory of an Aristocrat' (c. winter 1939–40) and figures centrally in Williams's many litanies on 'the destructive impact of society on the sensitive, non-conformist individual'.[15] In a series of fragments titled 'A Letter to Irene' written in Boston on the opening night of *Battle of Angels* (c. December 1940), Williams recalls having testified on behalf of the Irish prostitute Irene who was arrested for having thrown 'green snowballs [made] out of the mint sherbet' at her critics (at other times, it is Williams who is confined in the House of Detention for having thrown with her 'red snowballs [made] out of raspberry sherbet into the faces of various high priests' of the art world who demanded that her work be removed due to its indecency).[16] In each version, Williams attempts to capture the dignity of the fallen woman who would eventually become the model for Blanche DuBois.

After a brief, but eye-popping stay in the French Quarter (he was perhaps skipping town because of debts he had accrued[17]), Williams left New Orleans on 20 February 1939 with only a tent and two army cots. He had arranged a ride with 'a swell young fellow', Jim Parrott, a clarinet player and high school English teacher. They arrived in Los Angeles (via San Antonio, a dusty and dull El Paso, Mexico, Phoenix, San Bernardino, and Palm Springs) on 7 March, where he spent some lonely nights at a Los Angeles YMCA.[18] Williams told his mother that he was picking up a lot of good writing material along the way. Parrott was looking for work in Los Angeles as an actor, and Williams, who was eventually denied work in New Orleans at the WPA, joined him to find work in the Hollywood studios as a screenwriter. Instead, he wound up setting pins in a bowling alley, selling shoes, and picking squabs.[19] At the pigeon ranch of Parrott's uncle in Hawthorne, California, he and his friend would kill from fifty to one hundred squabs a day, putting a feather in a milk bottle for each one they plucked. Williams felt terribly lonely at this time, having regretted leaving his Bohemian circle of friends in New Orleans. With Parrot frequently away at work at an airplane factory, Williams occupied himself by chauffeuring around his friend's drunken uncle Fred and painting with his aunt Adelaide, a WPA art instructor.

Though it has been repeatedly stated that the men were just friends during the trip, it is more likely that their friendship went beyond being platonic. Writing in his *Notebooks* in a tone similar to one we encounter later in the book with Williams pining after the departure of a lover, Williams describes in detail his mounting anxiety at Parrott's leaving him from time to time. Perhaps still uneasy about his active homosexual lifestyle, Williams never disclosed his love affairs in the notebooks – not even privately to himself – until well into the early 1940s; and when he did, he often mentioned his partners only by their initials. With Parrott, the most Williams could admit at this time was that they were not happy together anymore because Williams 'demand[s] so much' and '<u>give</u>[s] so much in a relationship'.[20] In a fragment titled 'Final Materiel' [*sic*] (c. 1972) that Williams intended to include in his *Memoirs*, he writes of Parrott: 'And that night we slept together and hugged each other so closely, and how do I know that he shared my wild excitement in his bare body clasping mine, the sleepless night through?'[21] It is very possible that Parrott, and not Kip Kiernan, was Williams's first love, though how much of that love was reciprocated remains conjecture.

Through connections from his father, Williams began selling shoes at Clark's Bootery in Culver City. He was still banking his future on the Group Theatre contest, but a series of self-pitying notebook entries, which were a 'succession of such apparent finales which turn out to be continued in the next issue',[22] attest to his dejected state at the time. Things then drastically changed in his favour at the eleventh hour, as they would often do in the first half of Williams's career: he received a telegram from Molly Day Thatcher, Elia Kazan's wife, of the Group Theatre in New York, informing him that he won a special prize of $100 for his one-act plays (the first prize of $500 dollars went to Ramon Naya for his play *Mexican Mural*, which was produced in 1942 starring Montgomery Clift and Kevin McCarthy). Thatcher congratulated Williams and informed him that she had sent his plays to a potential literary agent, Audrey Wood.

Wood contacted Williams on 1 April 1939, calling him 'the kind of author whom I might help'.[23] Williams wrote back on 10 April, informing Wood that he had an offer from another agent and was considering his options. Williams then wrote his mother on 4 May 1939 that Wood 'has gotten Rockefeller fellowships (of $1000 each) for four of her clients and she has advised me to apply for one which I am going to do'.[24] Wood soon helped get Williams's story 'The Field of Blue Children' published in Whit Burnett's *Story* magazine (finally!), the first published work of his to bear the name 'Tennessee Williams'. Wary of his continued good fortune, Williams was still waiting for that proverbial other shoebox to fall from his father's International company. The notebook entries of this period testify to his nervousness about his future as a writer and his obsession with guilt over having left his 'little sister' Rose behind to suffer in her sanatorium. The character of Laura, about whom he had already written in Iowa, blowing out her candles, soon filled the void in the young playwright's lonely nights when Parrott was away.

Williams and Parrott celebrated the news from New York by riding their bicycles down to Tijuana, then back up to Laguna Beach, before Williams hitched a ride to San Francisco to visit the World's Fair. Essentially broke and waiting for the $25 cheque from Audrey Wood for the *Story* piece, he hitched out to Taos to meet D. H. Lawrence's fiery widow, Frieda. Once there, he fell under the Lawrence influence more fully and began several writing projects about Lawrence's life, beginning with the final act when Lawrence dies: first a poem, then a story titled 'Why Did Desdemona Love the Moor?' (about David's affair with a married woman from Texas), then a one-act play, and finally an uncompleted full-length play. At Wood's request, he did not continue working on the full-length play (perhaps she thought it dangerous material for the yet-unknown playwright in America), though in the autumn of 1941 he completed and later published the one-act, *I Rise in Flame, Cried the Phoenix*, a fictional account of Lawrence's final days in Saint-Paul de Vence, France. In the author's note to the play, Williams writes in celebration of a Lawrentian 'mystery and power of sex, as the primal life urge' and praises him as a 'life-long adversary of those who wanted to keep the subject locked away in the cellars of prudery'.[25] Along with *Steps Must Be Gentle* (1980), a non-realistic play about the death of Hart Crane that may have been written as early as 1947 just after Grace Crane's death,[26] *I Rise in Flame* would be one of the few plays he wrote about one of his literary influences. In addition to the several other one-acts Williams wrote about Lawrence was 'She Walks in Beauty', a play about Lord Byron that he wrote in 1938 while at Iowa, of which only fragments exist.

Anxious to pursue his writing career, Williams left California for New York, passing through St Louis and hitching a ride with Clark Mills, who was heading back to Cornell University to begin his second year of teaching there. In late September, he went to see Audrey Wood at her Radio Corporation of America (RCA) office in the Rockefeller Center and to meet the theatre world head on. After having met several actors and theatre personalities, Williams desired to live in New York, but he did not have the funds to stay long. Despite Wood's and Molly Day Thatcher's efforts to find him work, less than a month later, he returned home to St Louis. He had applied for the Rockefeller fellowship at Wood's request and, by early December 1939, was growing impatient for news from the Rockefeller Fellowship Committee. He was again doubting his talent, perhaps now more than he had ever done. As he wrote in his notebook for 11 December:

P.S. Today I wrote one very good line – 'Time keeps getting bigger and bigger at the future's expense [from *At Liberty*[27]].' – Too good to be good in a play. The tragedy of a poet writing drama is that when he writes well – from the dramaturgic, technical pt. of view he is often writing badly – one must learn – (that is the craft, I suppose) – to fuse lyricism and realism into a congruous unit – I guess my chief trouble is that I don't. I make the most frightful faux pas. I feared today that I may have taken a distinctly wrong turn in turning to drama – But, oh, I do feel drama so intensely sometimes! Again – Good night. I'm going to read some Lawrence or Joyce before sleep. Mailman – be good tomorrow![28]

This fusion of lyricism and realism was something Williams learned from Joyce, not from Lawrence. In his 'Preface to My Poems', which he published in 1944 in New Directions's *Five Young American Poets*, Williams finally cites Joyce's *Ulysses* in his 'Serious' attempt to explain his artistic vision.[29] A year later, in a 6 July 1945 letter to Robert Penn Warren, he even begins referring to Joyce's work, 'which is really a treasure'.[30] By 1949, after Williams had learned to accept that 'crazy modern verse' of the Modernists, he wrote to Frederic 'Fritz' Prokosch about his poetry, finding that it has 'a feeling of freedom from usual form such as I remember finding only in Kafka or Joyce [...]'.[31] And finally, more than a decade later, Williams would add the following entry into his notebook on 2 January 1954: '[...] I may just lie there watching TV or reading James Joyce, "The Dubliners" which is truly superb and which I somehow had missed till now. A lyric talent which is controlled by intellect, the rarest of happy accidents in the world of letters. Lyric, intellectual and "noble". probably [*sic*] the greatest writer since Shakespeare'.[32] That one word – *lyric* – isolates all that finally made Joyce appealing to Williams: the lyrical Joyce, the one of 'Penelope' which he had singled out for praise in his college essay back in 1936. Fused with the reality of waiting for the postman to deliver him from St Louis indefinitely, the lyricism of Williams's notebook entries that November and December suggest that Williams was not stepping in the wrong directions; he just needed a few more days to find fortune shining down on him once again.

Williams was currently at work on a play titled 'Opus V' or 'Shadow of my Passion' (early versions of *Battle of Angels*). He imagined at this time producing a trilogy of southern plays: *Spring Storm*, *Battle of Angels*, and 'The Aristocrats', which was based on the artist–prostitute Irene he had met in New Orleans the previous December. The good news finally arrived on 21 December. The Rockefeller fellowship came through, and he received $1000 in ten equal monthly instalments, some of which went to costs related to getting his work professionally typed:

Thursday – Wow! Received fellowship! – Was awakened this A.M. by arrival of congratulatory telegram from Audrey. Mother literally wept with joy – I felt numb – [...] Happy? Yes, yes, yes!!! – It still seems like a dream – trite statement but, oh, how true – Freedom – the one desire – now possible – for ten months![33]

The Dramatists Guild brought him back to New York in early January. At the request of theatre critic John Gassner, Williams, along with Arthur Miller, attended his playwriting seminar at the New School for Social Research, where Williams worked on revising *Battle of Angels*. With Gassner's help, the play was recommended to Lawrence Langner and Theresa Helburn of the Theatre Guild, which put an option on it in early June. It seemed as if his career was finally off to the start that he had fretted over in his notebooks for the last four years.

While in New York in early 1940, Williams immersed himself in the theatre world, attending as many Broadway plays as he could afford, and even taking in a show or two at the Apollo Theatre in Harlem. He watched the build up and eventual collapse of Clifford Odets's experimental play *Night Music* with the Group Theatre, which was a warning to him that his budding theory of the plastic theatre was not potentially commercial enough for Broadway. Despite this lesson in Broadway politics, Williams continued working on his own experimental play, *Stairs to the Roof*, which partly evolved out of the one-act play 'Fate and the Fishpools' and the January 1940 story 'The Earth is a Wheel in the Great Big Gambling Casino', which Wood failed to get placed in *Story* (*Esquire* also rejected several of his stories at this time). Williams told Lawrence Langner later that July that 'Seeing "Night Music" all through rehearsal was a marvellous object lesson [...] since that experience, I would never release a play – however profound in subject matter – till I felt it had sufficient theatricality to make it commercial. Any play that is not "commercial" – that is, "good theatre" – is necessarily still-born, isn't it?'[34]

Williams had already understood the theatric economy of Broadway, a paradigm of success that he would repeatedly challenge throughout his career. There is a medical prescription made out to Williams for a Fleet's enema (c. 1974), and at the top of the prescription Williams provided commentary about his recurrent rectal problems: 'Here I live down the indignities of my former profession. Whoring'.[35] Whoring was a charge that several of Williams's theatre critics, most notably George Jean Nathan and Robert Brustein, later pinned on him. Often failing to look beyond their own prejudices, they labelled Williams a playwright of sensationalism who shamelessly exchanged titillation for box office receipts. Though Williams did desire success in the 1940s and 1950s and dearly wanted another Broadway success in the 1960s and 1970s, he always did his own thing and never prostituted his muse or compromised his commitment to the truth. *Battle of Angels* would become his first test. During Gassner's seminar later that April, it was suggested that Williams harmonize the play's starkly contrastive moods between the

second and third acts, to which Williams responded: 'To me the sharp
division of atmosphere seemed a good thing [...] God knows, however,
I am not going to be obstinate about a thing like this with a possible
production by the Theatre Guild impinging upon it'.[36] He was learning
all too quickly that the St Louis Mummers were not the Group Theatre,
nor was the Wednesday Club Auditorium a Broadway playhouse.

By the end of January, he had sent to Wood a list detailing all of his
literary work currently in her possession:

Short Stories (6)
'The Red Part of a Flag'
'The Lost Girl'
'The Dark Room'
'A Tale of Two Writers'
'Something About Him'
'In Memory of an Aristocrat'

Short Plays (not bound with American Blues)
At Liberty
This Property Is Condemned
Once In a Life-time
The Lullabye or Something Special for Special People

Long Plays
Battle of Angels
Spring Storm (Did this one get back from the Guild?)
Fugitive Kind
Not About Nightingales.[37]

It was a considerable (if hardly exhaustive) list of literary properties,
certainly enough to justify the Guild's and Wood's faith in his future.
Unmitigated success, however, was still four years away for the young
playwright, and his vision of the plastic theatre was sharply at odds
with the direction American theatre was taking.

Another ill omen hit in early February when Williams saw one of
his plays, *The Long Goodbye* (c. 1938), produced by the New School in
a student production. He wrote in his notebook about the 'Miserable'
rehearsal that 'made [him] quite disgusted', but then later admitted that
he was 'pleased' to hear his lines spoken.[38] Also in February, Williams
attended a reading given by W. H. Auden, who was teaching poetry at
the New School. Williams's rather neutral impressions about Auden
in his letter to Alice Lippmann, founder of the St Louis poetry circle
that included Clark Mills and William Jay Smith, became darker in his

1975 tribute to the poet, 'W. H. Auden: A Few Reminiscences', where he describes their encounter as 'rather chilling'.[39] By March, Williams completed work on the one-act play *Portrait of a Madonna*, which would significantly influence *A Streetcar Named Desire* six years later.

Attending performances, corresponding with budding (Arthur Miller) and established (William Saroyan and Clifford Odets) playwrights, honing his craft at the New School, Williams was finally opening himself up to New York's literary world, and nothing else would soon matter, including the imminent war in Europe: 'Tonight Germany seized Denmark and war was declared by Norway – but infinitely more important is the fact that my play will be discussed and perhaps a decision rendered by the Theatre Guild'.[40] The previous year, Williams admitted in a notebook entry that the world was 'on the point of explosion – war, war, war! – And I write fanciful introspective stories & precious verse'. Several months later he added commented upon the same entry: 'How rarely I seem to notice events in the outside world!'[41]

Williams was equally opening himself up to New York's gay world and more actively sought partners to get his 'ashes hauled', a sexual metaphor popular in blues music of the day.[42] Though he had been sexually active in New Orleans, only now did he begin to be more open about it, both to the established gay community in New York as well as to himself. If prior to January 1940, Williams wrote endlessly in his notebooks about his art and his desire for success and for freedom from his father's control, after this date his notebooks become filled with his sexual predilections. For the first time, he began expressing in private words his fears about growing old and ugly and no longer being attractive to younger men. Like many of his fears, this one was unfounded, for he was always surrounded by good-looking young men, attracted more to his money than to his looks, yes, but attracted nonetheless. Through *Voices* editor Harold Vinal, Williams met and befriended the young Donald Windham and his lover Fred Melton around the time, with whom he would frequently live while in New York.

Alternating between joy and sorrow over his wild and free nights bingeing on sex and alcohol with his new gay friends, Williams feared that his work was suffering. He needed to break away, and Mexico seemed like the best place to run and hide. But the Guild's 'sudden, unexpected interest'[43] in *Battle of Angels* brought him back to New York when he had gotten as far as, first, his parents' home at 42 Aberdeen Place in Clayton (by the fall, they would again move, this time to the 53 Arundel Place house that C.C. would eventual cede to Edwina in their legal separation in 1946), and then his grandparents' in Clarksdale. Once the Guild had officially optioned *Battle of Angels* for the following season, Williams felt obliged to stay close at hand to complete the demanded revisions. He was growing (over)confident with *Battle of Angels* at this time, setting himself up for an enormous fall when his predictions were not realized: 'I do think this play is Commercial! – Capital "C" as in CASH! [...] – I suppose, to be consistent, Shakespeare should have written the play!'[44] Audrey Wood saw that he was growing increasingly distracted among his gay friends and suggested that he move out to Provincetown that summer of 1940 to complete the play there. Perhaps that was not the best place to send the sex-obsessed young man. There was a lot of summer theatre there, sure, and the sand dunes might inspire him as they had done when he and Jim Parrott lived on Laguna Beach the previous summer.[45] But there was also a lot of sex, and Williams was all for the taking.

The Cape's summer theatre stock *did* leave its mark on the young playwright. In the winter of 1939, Williams had seen Tallulah Bankhead perform Regina Giddens in Lillian Hellman's *The Little Foxes* and, like Miriam Hopkins, she was sent a script for *Battle of Angels* the following summer, and Williams had hoped now to meet her face to face.[46] She was touring in summer stock when Williams bicycled down in July 1940 to Dennis Port to see her perform in *The Second Mrs Tanqueray* at the Cape Playhouse. Williams described this encounter in his 1963 essay, 'T. Williams's View of T. Bankhead', where he explains how she informed him that his play was just too 'impossible' to do:

> I went backstage after the play that night and she received me in her dressing room with that graciousness that has nothing to do with her Southern origin and genteel breeding but with her instinctive kindness to a person in whom she senses a vulnerability that is kin to her own. I suppose I simply mean that she saw or sensed immediately that I was meeting, for the first time in my life, a great star, and that I was more than just properly awed. I was virtually dumb-struck. I can't quote accurately the conversation between us. I think she asked who I was and then I think she said something like, 'Oh, so it's you, the play is impossible, darling, but sit down and have a drink with me.' Which I did.[47]

Williams also met several plastic artists, including the abstract painter Jackson Pollock, whom he would meet there again in the summer of 1944, and Anaïs Nin.[48] The following summer of 1941, Williams met New Orleans artist Fritz Bultman and the German-born American abstract expressionist Hans Hofmann, who had established art schools in New York City and on the Cape, and who would later influence Williams's notion of the plastic theatre. Williams later wrote an appreciation of Hofmann, in whose work

> there is understanding of fundamental concepts of space and matter and of the dynamic forces, identified but not explained by science, from which matter springs. He is a painter of physical laws with a spiritual intuition; his art is a system of co-ordinates in which is suggested the infinite and a causality beyond the operation of chance. [...] Hans Hofmann paints as if he could look into those infinitesimal particles of violence that could split the earth like an orange.[49]

No doubt, his exposure to the artist community in Provincetown influenced what he would later call his 'sculptural drama' or plastic theatre.

Yet it was Provincetown's sex, or at least *love*, that left its most lasting impression on Williams. It was here, at Captain Jack's Wharf, that Williams met his first 'real' love (if we do not count Jim Parrott): Kip Kiernan, a Canadian draft-dodging dance student at the Hanya Holm school who had studied ballet with Joe Hazan in New York.[50] Williams, Hazan, and Kiernan shared a two-floor shack that summer on the Cape. In his notebook entries written at this time, Williams expounds at length about his genuine love (after a season of one-night encounters in New York) for the younger man, whom he compares to a Greek statue come to life. His relationship with Kiernan quickly turned intense, and for a while Williams was the happiest he had ever been. Actively writing during the day, Williams turned his attention to Kiernan at night, and together with Hazan they would cruise P-town's gay bars. Playfully describing in a letter to Windham his experiences with drag queens that August, Williams wrote, 'The belles are jingling gaily all over town and I am still in love [...]. They had a "drag" at the "White Whale" night club last night. Most of the boys went as girls but Froufrou [Williams] thought it would be more of a masquerade if she went as a *man*, so she *did*'.[51] Williams would later dramatize the events of this summer, including its sorrowful end, first in his one-act play *Parade* (begun that summer 1940 but completed in 1962), and then in the full-length play *Something Cloudy, Something Clear* (1981): for some reason – Williams attributes it to the intrusion of Shirley Brimberg Clarke in the couple – the relationship with Kiernan ended abruptly, and a distraught Williams fled the Cape mid-August with Melton via a boat from Boston bound for New York City.

Williams soon left for Mexico, where he had wanted to go since April, via 'a Cuban mail ship' organized by the New School.[52] As he describes in his *Memoirs*, Williams contacted the Share-a-Ride travel service that connects travellers heading to a common destination, and he soon joined a carpool (paying $25 for the trip) with a young Mexican, who had come to New York for the World's Fair, and his American prostitute 'bride'.[53] There in Mexico, Williams would find solace in his loneliness, mend his broken heart, and discover a new muse.

This second trip to Mexico, in fact his first prolonged stay there, is documented extensively in Williams's several letters to Joe Hazan and in his essays 'The History of a Play (With Parentheses)', 'A Summer of Discovery', and '*Amor Perdido*, Or, How It Feels to Become a Professional Playwright'. Written not long after Williams's stay in Mexico City, then in Acapulco at the Hotel Costa Verde,[54] this last essay recounts rather anachronistically the playwright's last pleasurable months of obscurity and poverty before *The Glass Menagerie* (the unexpected failure of *Battle of Angels'* Boston opening the following seasons would set his career back several years). Mexico in 1940 offered Williams a place to stretch his $100 option cheque from the Guild (his Rockefeller fellowship had already been spent), though he recalls later, amusingly, how that cheque was delayed when it was sent to the wrong destination: Williams had forgotten to forewarn Audrey Wood of his wanderlust and left Mexico City unbeknownst to his agent. Just prior to his Mexico jaunt, Williams had written Theresa Helburn a letter on 20 April 1940, explaining why he 'bolted' from New York so quickly after receiving his first cheque: 'I seem to be constitutionally unable to stay [in] one place more than three months [...]'.[55] His creative juices simply could not flow when his feet were planted. For the rest of her years as Williams's agent, Wood would have a difficult time keeping tabs on where her client was at any given moment.

These were bittersweet times for Williams, lovelorn in his break-up with Kiernan but energized by the tropical beaches of Acapulco, where he stayed at Todd's Place, a resort run by a 'Georgia cracker' and his 'fat Mexican' wife, before moving on to the Hotel Costa Verde.[56] It was as if his time in this foreign country formed in him a compass, and *Battle of Angels* was his North. Whenever he felt lost in the theatre world, worried that another play of his would not be received favourably by the press or by the public, Williams would steer himself in his essays and letters via the needle that guided him safely back to the security of a past just prior to fortune and fame. Strangely (or purposefully) absent from both essays is Kiernan and their Provincetown affair. Instead, we encounter Andrew Gunn, the son of a railway tycoon whose name barely figures in any of Williams's writing (though it appears years later on a brass plaque in his Key West gazebo[57]). Their experiences together formed the backdrop to Williams's short story 'The Night of the Iguana' and the 1961 play of the same name (but of few similarities). Perhaps Williams focuses on Gunn, or even Paul Bowles, because both men influenced Williams's aesthetics at an impressionable time in his life, whereas Kiernan and Provincetown were more matters of the heart. Gunn's lecture one night to him on 'Cupidity' and 'Stupidity' about capitalism, Communism, and Fascism's roles in the present war had a peculiar effect on Williams's writing at the time.

Still stinging from his break-up with Kiernan while in Acapulco (though not so much that he refused a trick if it came his way), Williams awaited news about the Guild's production of *Battle of Angels* and, amid the silence, continued working on *Stairs to the Roof*, which bore the subtitle, *A Prayer for the Wild of Heart that Are Kept in Cages*. In his essay 'Random Observations', written in New Orleans the following year in December 1941 and published as a foreword to the New Direction edition of the play in 2000, Williams describes, with signature inaccuracies, how the play was written as a 'katharsis' for the years he spent at the Continental Shoemakers in St Louis: 'This eighteen months' interlude, my season in hell, came at a time when I was just out of high school and the world appeared to be a place of infinite and exciting possibilities. I discovered how badly mistaken it is possible for a young man to be'.[58] Though the play, which contains a disconcerting amount of 'didactic material', was written when America entered World War II, Williams describes how he decided against writing 'something light and frothy' and chose instead to pursue a play whose 'problems are universal and everlasting':

> At the bottom of our social architecture, which is now describing such perilous gyrations in mid-air, are the unimportant little Benjamin Murphys and their problems ... and if there is something at the bottom that started the trouble on top, what could be more appropriate at this moment than inspecting the bottom.[59]

His earlier interest in writing lyrically laced agitprop drama was now turning more steadily toward the plastic theatre, despite his claim to Mark Barron in 1940 that he always tried to write plays 'that carry some social message along with the story'.[60] Several years later, Williams would confide to drama critic Burton Rascoe that he believed art such as the theatre was not 'a weapon' but 'a powerful instrument' to improve society.[61] He would further define his political ideologies about the theatre in his essay 'On the Art of Being a True Non-conformist', writing, 'In my opinion art is a kind of anarchy, and the theater is a province of art'.[62] Noteworthy here are several of the play's anti-realistic elements: it is written in nineteen, film-like scenes, and not traditional acts like his previous plays; it is dominated by the voice and haunting laugh of a certain omnipotent Mr E, who looms over the play extra-dramatically as Tom Wingfield would do a few years later in *The Glass Menagerie*; and it contains a mimed/read, metatheatrical play-within-a-play called 'The Carnival – Beauty and the Beast'.

Social progress is achieved in the play only through the turbulent clashing of opposing worlds, be they social, sexual, or both. That doctrine is dramatized in the Beauty and the Beast pantomime. Like the eponymous Big Black in Williams's 1931–32 story who 'seiz[es] upon Beauty',[63] the Beast stalks Beauty, 'treading on the grass / So lightly that his victim heard no sound / Until he *plunged* – and pressed her to the ground!':

> How long she lay with cold, averted face,
> Beneath the Beast, enduring his embrace,
> I cannot say – but when his lust was spent
> And from his veins the scorching fever went – [...]
> He rose above her and was cold as she.
> Then, shivering in equal nudity,
> One faced the other with a speechless look,
> The sky had darkened, now the branches shook – [...]
> She took his hand and whispered – [...]
> Do not grieve –
> I owned no beauty till it felt thy need,
> Which, being answered, makes thee no more Beast,
> But One with Beauty![64]

The 'rape' here does not debase Beauty at all, whose face remains as 'holy as a nun's at church',[65] and instead removes all evil taint from the Beast: together, they have produced a 'child' of sorts – 'One' who is their union of opposites. This was a theme Williams would rework again and again during the 1940s, where we encounter it in *Portrait of a Madonna*, *Summer and Smoke*, and ultimately *A Streetcar Named Desire*.

Allean Hale notes that Williams's pantomime resembles Jean Cocteau's film *Beauty and the Beast* (1946), 'which Williams, the movie-goer, probably saw, with its surreal ending of the lovers floating into space'.[66]

Williams had in fact seen the film, but it was produced several years *after* Williams wrote *Stairs to the Roof*. Though Williams would later borrow material from Cocteau for his plays *The Milk Train Doesn't Stop Here Anymore* (1963) and *The Pronoun 'I'* (c. 1975), in this case it is Cocteau's work which resembles Williams's. Williams, who would eventually meet Cocteau and his lover Jean Marais in Paris in 1948 (Cocteau was preparing to mount the French production of *Un tramway nommé Désir*), later wrote a critique of Cocteau's *Diary* of the filming of *La Belle et la Bête* for the *New York Times*, which is not only similar to his own version but perhaps expresses most succinctly his unique view of this rape/desire dialectic: 'Beauty, who represents purity of heart, releases the Beast from his evil enchantment: the brutal and arrogant forces are brought to shame: the Beast, resuming his original form of Prince Charming, ascends to some unearthly kingdom with the lovely instrument of his release'.[67]

Production for *Battle of Angels* was progressing rapidly in New York, much to the playwright's dismay, as he felt the play was not yet finished. The scheduled opening was for 30 December in Boston, barely enough time to return to New York from Mexico via Clayton, Missouri, and polish the dialogue. Williams's fears would prove prophetic as the opening was a disaster (in part because the play was not ready, but largely because the try-outs were rushed). In his essay 'The History of a Play (With Parentheses)', which he wrote in March 1944 as a preface to the published version the following year in Jay Laughlin's short-lived magazine, *Pharos*, Williams would document these summer weeks in great detail, from his 'Vie Horizontale' lying in a hammock and drinking rum-cocos, through to the play's doomed rehearsals, and up until the final 'Wagnerian' fire that climaxes the play and sent patrons gasping for the theatre doors, a 'pandemonium' that William Jay Smith, who was present at the premiere, said Williams later wildly exaggerated.[68] Though Williams was devastated by the problems that the play brought him (and not those incurred by the Guild), he was able in the essay to treat the failure rather light-heartedly: 'I am not a good writer. Sometimes I am a very bad writer indeed. There is hardly a successful writer in the field who cannot write circles around me and I am the first to admit it. But I think of writing as something more organic than words, something closer to being and action'.[69] He was not yet done with the play and would return to it in *Orpheus Descending* seventeen years later.

When *Battle of Angels* closed disastrously in Boston on 11 January 1941, Williams was doled out remittances by Audrey Wood of his advanced royalty payment 'loan' by the Theatre Guild to rewrite the play for a possible New York premiere the following season, which it was never given (Williams submitted the revisions in May 1941, but Lawrence Langner rejected the revised script the following summer). In January, following the closing, Williams headed south, holding true to word to Barron that 'I'm getting out of town the minute my play opens and maybe sooner. Where I'll go I don't know. Just wherever my feet take me'.[70] It was a tradition he would hold to all his life. His feet here first took him to New York, where he underwent an eye operation – something he would do following the opening of *The Glass Menagerie* in 1945.

In February 1941, Williams was classified as IV-F by his draft board due to his poor eyesight. He had already experienced problems with the board dating back to late 1940, and he would later encounter run-ins with the local police when he failed to produce his draft card upon request.[71] Williams's lifelong problem began when he received a sharp blow to his left eye while playing 'Indians and early white settlers' when he was a child.[72] From New York, he took a train to Miami, Florida, where he was met by Parrott, whose family owned a winter home there. Williams had hoped the warm southern weather would inspire his visions on the play. Unable to concentrate on the play's rewrite, however, Williams confessed in a 13 February letter to Donald Windham: 'I am not even trying to write till I get more rested. I seriously doubt that my ideas for revision will correspond with the Theatre Guild's so after these two months are up I may be in a very uncomfortable situation'.[73]

After a brief visit with the Parrott family in Miami in February, Williams and Parrott travelled down the Florida coast to Key West, staying at The Trade Winds. On 12 February, Williams wrote his parents, 'I am stopping in the 125-year-old house [The Trade Winds] you see on the envelope. It belongs to an Episcopal clergyman's widow, Mrs. Black [...]. I am to complete my re-write on "Angels"'.[74] As Williams noted in his 1973 essay 'Homage to Key West', 'my attachment to the island of Key West dates back to 1941 when I sought solace there from the first important disaster in my profession [...]. It was still a mecca for painters and writers in 1941. I met the poet Elizabeth Bishop and artist Grant Wood there that winter, and Arnold Blanch and his wife'.[75] In his *Memoirs*, Williams expands upon the details of that encounter:

In those days in Key West there was a wonderful colony of artists. There was Arnold Blanch, and there was his lady friend Doris Lee. Then there was the wife of the Japanese artist Kuniyoshi. And Grant Wood, the man who painted *American Gothic*, was there. It was the last year of his life. He was a rather dumpy little man with a white shock of hair and very, very friendly. Quite flushed in the face, and not from embarrassment either.[76]

During his stay in Key West, Williams befriended Cora Black and her daughter Marion Vaccaro Black, the wife of a drunken fruit-trading magnate. Vaccaro is the model for the sex-starved Cora in Williams's 1951–52 short story 'Two on a Party', with the gay character Billy personifying Williams's poet–professor friend, Oliver Evans. With his new friend, who would remain one of his closest until her death in 1970, Williams cruised the Keys for his 'nightingales', a personal code word he used frequently in his notebooks to describe his homosexual encounters. In spite of the many distractions, Williams worked on the revisions of *Battle of Angels* and alternated between it and other literary pieces. He was concentrating on writing more dramatic action into the first half of the play, adding the trumped-up rape charges against Val by the woman from Waco, Texas. That February, he also wrote the story 'Portrait of a Girl in Glass', which greatly influenced *The Glass Menagerie*, and in March *The Case of the Crushed Petunias*, a one-act 'fantasy' dedicated to Helen Hayes that he told Audrey Wood might be sold as a radio play, which Devlin and Tischler call a 'seedbed for future plays' and 'an echo chamber for recent ones'.[77] He also penned poems like 'Moon Song: Key West', 'Heavenly Grass', and 'Minstrel Jack'.

Around his thirtieth birthday, Williams spent time again with Parrott, who had enrolled for flight training courses at the University of Miami in Coral Gables to avoid being drafted into the army. His 'nightingale' encounters were becoming numerous, and at times they did not turn out so well. At the end of the month, Williams had asked Wood to stop payment on a $25 cheque she had sent him from Margaret Mayorga for the inclusion of *Moony's Kid Don't Cry* in her anthology *The Best One-Act Plays of 1940*; the cheque was probably stolen from his wallet by one of his trade. Williams remained constantly on the move. During his sojourns, Wood informed him in April that the Dramatists Guild had awarded him an additional $500 Rockefeller fellowship (to the $1000 he had received from them in December 1939) to 'write a new play'.[78] He considered using the money to write a play titled 'A Woman's Love for a Drunkard', an early version of Maggie and Brick Pollitt inspired by Vaccaro's love for her husband Regis.[79]

By late April 1941, the restless and near-penniless Williams hitchhiked north just outside Brunswick, Georgia, to stay at the Vaccaro-Black home, Marsh Haven, to finish his revisions. At the start of May, Williams was back at his parents' house, now on 53 Arundel Place in Clayton, and by early June he had a new draft of *Battle of Angels* ready to bring with him to New York. Around this time, Williams may have written his essay 'Te Moraturi [*sic*] Salutamus' ('Those who are about to die salute you', in reference to what the gladiators purportedly said to the Roman Emperor just before doing battle). At the top of the manuscript Williams wrote, probably to Audrey Wood, 'Keep this on ice for me – I intend to deliver it before the next production 10'.[80] Since it was addressed to a 'First Night Audience' of *Battle of Angels*, the essay's recollection of the play's inauspicious opening in Boston implies that Williams was confident of another Guild production based on the revised script he delivered to Langner, who ultimately rejected it later that August.

With little to do in New York now that a new production of *Battle of Angels* was lost, Williams returned to Provincetown in the summer of 1941 with the memoirs of Kip no doubt still fresh in his memory. There, he stayed again with Joe Hazan and others at the wild 'Cogan House', but the sex and orgies at Provincetown proved little respite for him, and Williams soon moved back to New York for a short time, again revising *Battle of Angels* and working on *Stairs to the Roof, I Rise in Flame, Cried the Phoenix*, and several short stories, including 'The Malediction' (1945), which Whit Burnett later rejected for *Story* the following month. In August, Williams headed south to Sea Island, Georgia, to visit Jordan Massee, Jr (Paul Bigelow's lover), and then on to St Simons Island, where he ran out of money. He wired Audrey Wood, asking that Luise Sillcox, the Guild's executive secretary, forward him a cheque. Wood had a $25 cheque sent to Williams, informing him that it was the first payment of a new $200 option that Hume Cronyn had taken out on several of his plays. Before arriving back in New York via Charleston (where he penned 'Poem for Paul'), his train made an extended stop-over in Washington, DC, where some sightseeing, and a casual fling, made Williams miss his train back to New York, on which he had left his luggage and typewriter.[81]

In late August 1941, William informed Wood about a one-act play that he was working on, 'The Front Porch Girl', or 'If You Breathe, It Breaks', a forerunner to *The Glass Menagerie*. He decided against mailing it to her because it 'seemed good enough to justify longer attention'.[82] By September and until December, he was again in war-changed New Orleans. His notebooks are filled mostly with his sexual exploits at this time (nearly one or two per day, before he caught crabs[83]), his self-doubts concerning his writing, and his financial problems: 'O I want to have <u>money</u> again. I love the pleasures, the sensual pleasures so much. And how I loathe the squalor, the awkwardness, the indignity of being broke.

I suppose I am too much body, not enough soul'.[84] He was sent an additional $25 for the Cronyn option and continued writing, noting that he could live on $1.10 a day, with meals costing 30¢. He was now completing work on the one-act *I Rise in Flame, Cried the Phoenix*, despite Wood's objections to it, but was not sure of its merits. Williams also wrote at this time the story 'Bobo', a precursor to 'The Yellow Bird', and the one-act plays *The Lady of Larkspur Lotion* (based in part on his experiences in 1939 while living at the 722 Toulouse Street boarding house whose newest proprietor, Mrs Louise Wire, was nothing like the previous landlady, Mrs Anderson; Larkspur lotion was a common treatment for crabs) and *Thank You, Kind Spirit* (c. October 1941), about a spiritualist who is exposed as a fraud. In a 27 October letter to Audrey Wood, Williams expressed an interest in grouping this play with two other New Orleans plays of his into a programme called 'Vieux Carré'. To fill in his time between plays and stories, he continued writing poetry: 'Blood on the Snow', 'Ice and Roses', 'Warning', 'The Stonecutter's Angels', and 'Which Is He?', lines that appear in 'The Spinning Song' and later reused in the poem 'Little Horse' about his relationship with Frank Merlo.

Also in New Orleans that autumn, Williams renewed his friendship with Oliver Evans, the poet-professor whom he had met previously in Provincetown, and began an affair with Eloi Bordelon. In a letter to Paul Bigelow, dated 25 September 1941, Williams wrote:

> I got reckless and invested half of my current checque [*sic*] in a membership at this rather exclusive Club [New Orleans Athletic Club], but it is worth it as there is a marvelous salt water pool, Turkish bath, Etc., and the prettiest Creole belles in town. I am already well-established in their circles and my particular intimate is a [Eloi] Bordelon one of the oldest families in the city. Such delicate belles you have never seen, utterly different from the northern species. Everybody is 'Cher!' – I actually pass for 'butch' in comparison and am regarded as an innovation – 'The Out-door Type'! – and am consequently enjoying a considerable succés [*sic*].[85]

Though attracted at times to the *belles*, Williams could not sustain any relation with them, as he told Bigelow on 2 November:

> I had a violent and rather bloody matrimonial break-up with the Bordelon, and as she is the queen bee of the bitch society there, it would be unpleasant for me to remain during her displeasure which I must admit was somewhat unjustly provoked – Marriage is not

for me! [...] I am quite fed up with piss-elegant bitches (don't you love that phrase?) of the New Orleans variety, and wish to get back to nature.[86]

Following his late coming out, Williams first became fascinated with transvestitism and drag queen culture, but later found it an obstacle to gay liberation in the way that drag and camp and 'swish', as he called it in his *Memoirs*, fuelled stereotypes about gay men and contributed to their self-mockery.[87] Williams had already written about the 'transvestite queen with accuracy and compassion'[88] in his 1938 play *Not about Nightingales*, but she appears more as a caricature in comparison to the queens in plays such as *And Tell Sad Stories of the Death of Queens ...*, written initially in 1957, then revised, and completed in 1962.

With his grandmother gravely ill from cancer, Williams decided in early November to return briefly to St Louis for two weeks, a trip his mother paid for. Yet trouble with his father forced him to leave again, but not before he finished and mailed to Wood the one-act play *Lord Byron's Love Letter*. He left for St Petersburg after spending Thanksgiving with his family, then hitch-hiked with great difficulty down the Florida coast. He returned briefly to New Orleans by early December, and by New Year was back in St Louis, where he completed work on *Stairs to the Roof* and published two one-act plays in William Kozlenko's collection, *American Scenes*: *This Property Is Condemned*, about a delusional young girl, Willie, who dresses up in her dead sister's clothes, and *At Liberty* (c. 1939) about a faded young actress, Gloria, who returns home to Blue Mountain. Williams began moving further and further away from imitating other playwrights (such as O'Neill, Anderson, Rice, and Odets) for his St Louis agitprop theatre and closer to finding that southern voice which would become his trademark.

In early January 1942, the famed German theatre director, Erwin Piscator, who had worked with Bertolt Brecht in forming the epic theatre before emigrating to the United States, sent Williams a telegram to return to New York. Apparently, after the Guild renounced *Battle of Angels*, Audrey Wood convinced the New School for Social Research to option it, and Piscator wanted to produce it. On his return to New York, Williams underwent his second (22 January) and third (9 February) eye operations. While in New York, he stayed with the New Orleans artist Fritz Bultman, whom he met in Provincetown the previous summer, and worked at the Beggar's Bar, a bistro on Morton Street in New York run by Valeska Gert, another German émigré. Together with Bultman, he renewed his friendship with members of the art community who seasonally commuted between Provincetown and New York. Williams describes this adventure in his *Memoirs*, as well as in an early version of the autobiography, 'Some Memoirs of a Con-Man' (c. 1971), detailing how he wore an eye patch with an eye painted on it, and recited poems while waiting tables. The first 'Item' of 'Some Memoirs of a Con-Man' recounts how he was 'unexpectedly evicted from a fickle friend's apartment in the warehouse district of the West Village of Manhattan': 'This friend was, nervously speaking, a basket-case: I mean he was very nervous'.[89] He had reason to be: Williams brought home one night trade of 'a roguish nature',[90] who apparently stole some of the artist's paintings and his electric razor, which was the reason for Williams's having later been evicted (a detail he left out of *Memoirs*).

By March 1942, Williams began reworking *Battle of Angels* for Piscator and his assistant Herbert Berghof, who were preparing the play for the experimental Studio Theatre of the New School. It was also around this time that Williams began contemplating his 'sculptural drama', a non-realistic drama based not on acts but on 'short cumulative scenes', similar to Ramon Naya's 'panels' in his experimental play, *Mexican Mural*, which had won first prize in the Group Theatre contest that awarded Williams its special prize back in 1939.[91] Williams had expressed to himself in his notebook that he 'must be able to be a post-war artist'[92] and recognized how he could change American theatre:

The experimental dramatist must find a method of presenting his passion and the world's in an articulate manner. Apocalypse without delirium.

In considering this problem while at work on new scripts, I have evolved a new method which in my own particular case may turn out to be a solution. I call it the 'sculptural drama'. Because my form is poetic.

The usual mistake that is made in the presentation of intensified reality on the state is that of realistic action. If the scenes are not underwritten, the acting must compensate by an unusual restraint. We will find it increasingly necessary to write our emotions out. Correspondingly restraint in acting and directing must increase. A new form, non-realistic, must be chosen. This necessity suggests what I have labelled as 'the sculptural drama'. Obviously it is not for the conventional three-act play which is probably on its way out anyhow. This form, this method, is for the play of short cumulative scenes which I think is on its way in. I visualize it as a reduced mobility on the stage, the forming of statuesque attitudes or tableaux, something resembling a restrained type of dance, with motions honed down to only the essential or significant.[93]

Williams expressed similar ideas in an incomplete essay titled 'The Sculptural Play (a method)' (c. 1942), in which he handwrites (a rarity for him) the following extended definition of what would soon become his plastic theatre:

> The turgid and violent emotions growing out of world war two must have their katharsis, or purification, in art. America in World War I was barely touched by violence. ~~This [imm] relative im-munity will not~~ Consequently we did not have here the radical new forms or emotional release in art which occured for instance in the Germany of post War I and which created such significant new forms as the later expressionism and the epic drama. This relative immunity will not be our privilege again. Already we are intensely involved in the psychological changes of warfare. We will undoubtedly be involved still more. Behind us, now, is the time for placid drama. Before us is the need for expressing, for giving a satisfactory vent, to the passion of life and the passion of death, the epic conflict of the bright and dark angels, which, which are concommittant with a world in flames.
>
> The artist of tomorrow is the passionate man, the man who is capable of containing battlefields and marshalling their action in his work. Passion alone is not, of course, sufficient. In art there must be unified art, which is the completion of partialities.[94]

Williams's 'sculptural drama', a precursor to his plastic theatre, had its roots in Richard Wagner's *Gesamtkunswerk* and Jean Cocteau's 1921 declaration, 'Je veux substituer la poésie du théâtre à la poésie au théâtre'.[95] Along with his 'Production Notes' to *The Glass Menagerie*, there is no better early expression of the *Gesamtkunstwerk* of Williams's plastic theatre, and his emerging dramatic theory, than these two examples.

Despite the auspicious turn of events, *Battle of Angels* was never produced at the New School because Williams detested Piscator having '"rewritten" the play with scissors'.[96] Williams felt Piscator, who had called it a Fascist play, had turned it from a religio-poetic encomium to individual liberty into a socialist vehicle damning the selfish pursuits of characters for 'their little personal ends and aims in life with a ruthless disregard for the wrongs and sufferings of the world around them'.[97] As Williams wrote to his parents on 6 March, '[...] and while I haven't satisfied Piscator's absurd demands with "Angels", he is going to have a trial reading of the play by actors before an invited audience which may result in attracting other producers'.[98] If not in 1941 before delivering his revisions of *Battle* to Langner, Williams may have drafted his essay 'Te Moraturi [*sic*] Salutamus' for this Piscator production of the play, which seems more likely. In one notebook entry, dated 25 August 1942, Williams wrote: 'And I am very much "Mortaturi" today'.[99]

After Bultman had kicked him out of his apartment, Williams stayed briefly in the penthouse of his music friend Carley Mills, whose famous song 'If I Cared a Little Bit Less (and You Cared a Little Bit More)', recorded for Decca records by the Ink Spots in 1943, was written for Williams, who could not finally see what love was for Mills. It was also around that spring that Williams and Windham agreed to collaborate on *You Touched Me!*, a play based on a D. H. Lawrence story. As Williams recalled,

> I was very tired when he gave me the book. I went to bed with it. But in spite of exhaustion I didn't sleep that night. Something kept saying 'you touched me, you touched me' like those skinny wood pyramids that music teachers have [i.e., metronomes]. All of a sudden, about 2 or 3 A.M., I sat upright and turned on the light. The play was born. I woke up Windham and said, 'It's all of life this story. You and me and the Touch. It's all of life'.[100]

As Leverich notes, Williams saw the direction his plays needed to take if they were ever to make it to Broadway, and experimental plays were not the direction to take. Odets's *Night Music* taught him that. 'At the Theatre Guild', Leverich writes, 'Langner and Helburn were staging comedies, revivals, and imported vehicles, preferring these to the work of new experimental playwrights like Saroyan and Williams. Everything was a commercial endeavour, and except for Piscator's polemical workshop [at the New School], there was no other theatre that a poet-playwright could work toward'.[101] Audiences, particularly war-time audiences, wanted light entertainment, whereas playwrights wanted truth, and somehow that gap had to be narrowed. Williams no doubt thought *You Touched Me!*, which he gradually took over from Windham, would provide that compromise: sentimental enough for Broadway audiences, yet Lawrentian enough for his plastic theatre of dramatic symbols.

The war, in fact, began to preoccupy Williams more and more. Perhaps it was the result of guilt seeing Dakin prepare to head off to Asia; perhaps it was because, despite his perennial poverty, Williams was having a ball when he should not have been. In his notebooks, references to the war are often tempered with a self-conscious, if not selfish, attitude, that he was only directly concerned in the effects that war would have on the theatre. Nearly two years earlier, on 30 May 1940, Williams had written: 'Holocaust in Europe – it really does sicken me, I am glad to say. Of course my reactions are primarily selfish. I fear that it may kill the theatre'.[102] In his copy of *The Collected Poems of Hart Crane*, Williams wrote at length about World War II and the bombing of Europe's great cities but admitted that his life 'goes on very little concerned with all this'.[103] Then a year later in April 1941, he noted that Germany had victories in the Balkans; and in late October, Moscow: 'Moscow is being seiged. A footnote to all this trivial chatter. Typical bitch Tennessee'.[104]

By early December 1941, Williams's casual tone changed slightly. In his flip-book journal, he wrote: 'World news improved with Germans pushed back at Rostov and Libya'.[105] Then, following the attack on Pearl Harbor, Williams began to feel a bit more involved, recognizing that some of his past lovers might have died in the raid: 'America entered the war yesterday, against Japan. Dirty business. I knew some boys on the SS Oklahoma reported afire in Pearl Harbor'.[106] Apart from this, and despite the fact that Dakin was soon sent to the Pacific theatre, Williams paid little attention to the war and only when it affected him personally. Williams did write a letter to Paul Bigelow in early January 1942, where he explained that he was going to write a series of seven or nine short stories on Bohemian life in the Vieux Carré, 'ending on December 7, 1941': 'Our fin du monde, as everyone feels too distinctly'.[107] Now, on 6 January 1942, he admitted to himself:

> I am frightened of the changes or rather the increased vicissitudes the war may create in my life. I suppose if it did not affect me person-ally my feelings about it would be only abstractly regretful. [...] No, I feel no desire to participate in war work. O, I ~~might~~ would be glad to be a Florence Nightingale if I could but – incompetent and lazy me. Thank god I don't have to go to camp or fight.[108]

By February 1942, Williams was noting that 'Singapore has fallen': 'Everyone in our little group is cynical and hopeless and without an ounce of patriotic feeling. We expect an air raid soon. We expect social disaster'.[109]

It is possible that Williams pursued writing *You Touched Me!* as a *sine qua non* for not having contributed to, or even cared about, the war effort. The play would be a sort of Lawrentian salve applied to the nation's wounds, and he its materteral administrator. More likely is the fact that Williams's growing interest in the play dealt less with healing or even with spreading the word of a totemic writer and more with the fact that 'war' plays were big business for Broadway theatres and patriotic audiences: Maxwell Anderson's *The Eve of St Mark*, Emlyn Williams's *The Morning Star*, Clifford Odets's *The Russian People*, D. L. James's *Winter Soldiers*, and Irving Berlin's *Winter Soldiers*. The fact that *You Touched Me!* dealt with war (originally World War I, but they advanced time to the present war) in a nostalgic way might simply fill the theatre's seats and his (and Windham's) pockets.

Unfortunately, the play did not reach Broadway until the fall of 1945, and then only on the coattails of *The Glass Menagerie*. Williams suspected that *The Glass Menagerie* was a better play and feared that 'a production of the first would hurt the Caller' because of 'similarities between Matilda & Laura'.[110] That prediction may have played out in reverse since *You Touched Me!* was delayed for over a year until after *The Glass Menagerie* opened in New York in March 1945. By the fall, though, the war was over, and the play already seemed passé, in spite of its similarities to *The Glass Menagerie*: 'the war had ended and so had the play's contrived relevancy'.[111]

Most of Williams's war updates came via the radio or his reading of *Time* magazine: 'Read "Time" – news appalling – what a world, what times confront us! Russia, Egypt crumbling – I cannot see ahead nor can anyone. But I suspect it will be hard for us who are not made to be warriors. Our little works may be lost'.[112] Perhaps his 'little works' included his taking a job later that summer as a teletype operator for the War Department in the US Engineer's office in Jacksonville, Florida. On 18 August, he jotted down in his notebook: 'Ah, well, I am not in the army. I supposed this [his loneliness in St Augustine] is better than that would be'.[113] There were no yellow Stars of David or pink triangles in America to designate someone IV-F. Wherever Williams went, he felt the stinging glances of people who wondered why an able-bodied man was not going off to fight the Axis powers. While working at the Strand Theatre in New York in 1943, Williams even felt the physical sting of contempt when an old woman slapped him and asked, 'why aren't you in the army?'[114]

In the downtime that he had from his menial, albeit socially signifying job, Williams penned poems like 'The Angel of Fructification' and typed out stories on his Underwood and worked continually on various plays: 'The Spinning Song', about his sister Rose; 'Dos Ranchos', a verse play about brother-sister incest that would become *The Purification*; and *Stairs to the Roof*. In June 1942, he headed down from New York to Macon at the request of Paul Bigelow and spent the sweltering summer in his attic. Here, he began a brief affair with Andrew Lyndon. In early July, Williams was picked up by the police on Cherry Street in Macon and taken to jail because he 'did not have [his] draft card'.[115] In his notebook, he describes how a crowd had gathered to look at the arrest of these 'suspicious characters': 'Shows the change of our world – personal freedom is gone, even the illusion of it'.[116] The war was affecting Williams more than he was letting on, and more than before, with the crackdown in New York on gay bars and the growing paranoia in America of suspicious-looking people (Williams had to wear sun glasses, even at night, because of his recent eye surgeries), his 'fugitive kind' were forming in his literary limekiln. One was Emily Jelkes (of his story 'Miss Jelkes' Recital'), whose slight handicap on a failed date prepares the way for Laura Wingfield's encounter with Jim O'Connor. Another was the Chaplinesque Lucio of the story 'The Malediction' (written the previous summer) who enters an unknown town in search of a room and companionship, which he finds in the form of a homeless cat named Nitchevo. Williams was dramatizing the story into a four-scene play, first titled 'The Beetle of the Sun', then *The Strangest Kind of Romance*.

He continued work on *You Touched Me!* and wrote the short story 'Dragon Country', about a Jewish librarian, Bertha Shapiro, who is ill-treated in a small southern town. He worked on dramatizing the story and ended up envisioning it as part of a group of short plays about the South, called 'Dragon Country', which would become the title of his 1970 collection of late plays. Williams tried at this time to get Robert Lewis, director of *Mexican Mural* and one of the founding members of the Group Theatre (which disbanded in 1941 and reformed, with Elia Kazan and Cheryl Crawford, as the Actors Studio in 1947), to produce some of his one-act plays. Lewis, who loaned Williams money at this time, could not fund the productions, as one-act plays were not attractive enough to financial angels on Broadway. Instead, one-acts were the stuff of student productions, such as *This Property Is Condemned*, which was given a performance that August at the New School.

Williams was living too much on others' generosity and needed to make money himself so that he could continue to write. He tried turning to Key West in mid-August 1942, getting only as far as St Augustine.

In his notebook for 25 August, he wrote, 'As usual I use this journal mostly for distress-signals and do not often bother to note the little and decently impersonal things which sometimes have my attention'.[117] His depression and loneliness, not to mention his poverty, were palpable, but so was his guilt over complaining about his situation: 'Such is the "basis of Zero." Simple endurance. There are worse things than this. The physical agonies of men at war, this existence would appear lovely to them. I think, however, it is all about on the same level – a diseased will and a sick mind – a life at the battlefront'.[118] Desperate, he had once again asked his mother for bus fare back to St Louis. Haunted, though, by the thought of seeing his father, Williams decided instead to move onto Jacksonville, where he worked the night shift as a teletype operator for the War Department in the US Engineer's office until November, earning $120 a month. He took the job out of necessity, of course, but it may also have been out of some sense of honour to his father and brother and of duty to the nation's war effort.

By November of 1942, Williams was back in New York for the eighth time, this time at Audrey Wood's request to rewrite *You Touched Me!* He found temporary work as a teletype operator for the British Purchasing Commission (he lasted only two days there), as an elevator operator at a hotel, and, in early 1943, as an usher at the 'swanky' Strand movie theatre on Broadway, where he was at least able to entertain one of his passions, films – third only to writing and cruising. He spent more than five months in the city, trying to drum up support for any of his plays, whether a production with producer Carley Wharton for *You Touched Me!*, an option on his one-acts with esteemed director Guthrie McClintic, or the publication of his poems with literary-angel James (Jay) Laughlin, publisher of New Directions and heir to a Pittsburgh steel fortune whose long-term friendship had just begun.

But Williams was not having much luck getting his plays optioned or performed. He kept meeting artists, though, who would continue to shape his plastic theatre at the time: Tony Smith (who had studied with Fritz Bultman at the New Bauhaus in Chicago) and Olive Leonhardt, who would reappear later as Moise in Williams's 1975 novel, *Moise and the World of Reason*. He met Margo Jones, the 'Texas Tornado', at Audrey's Liebling-Wood office in late 1942, and she would become instrumental in getting several of Williams's plays performed, including *You Touched Me!*, which she helped try out in Cleveland in October 1943 and then at the small Playbox of the Pasadena Playhouse in California a month later. Williams was hoping good press notices would help procure a Broadway producer for the play but to no avail. Laughlin came out to see it, accompanied by Tony Smith and his newlywed wife Jane Lanier Smith, a distant cousin of Williams's. Williams also experienced his first recorded act of physical homophobia after being beaten up by a sailor he invited to his room and robbed by his 'trade turned "dirt"': 'Why do they strike us? What is our offense? We offer them a truth which they cannot bear to confess except in privacy and the dark – a truth which is inherently as bright as the morning sun'.[119]

No physical pain he suffered would ever compare to the psychological trauma that awaited him that new year. On 20 January 1943, Edwina wrote her son, informing him of Rose's lobotomy, one of the first performed in America: 'Now that it is over [...] I can tell you about Rose who has successfully come through a head operation'.[120] Williams replied a few days later on 25 January: 'I did not at all understand the news about Rose. What kind of operation was it and what was it for? [...] Please let me know exactly what was done with Rose [...]'.[121] He wrote nothing about the operation in his notebook that same day, however. This pregnant silence to himself is perhaps the best extant proof in Williams's long life about the struggle he had with himself over abandoning Rose to avoid his own onset of madness and to fulfil himself artistically and sexually. He knew he had to leave her, as Tom does Laura in *The Glass Menagerie*, but the guilt never quite left either of them. As early as October 1941, he had confessed in his notebook about his solipsism: 'No word from home lately but I am too hard to worry. Love Grand but don't think of her except casually – say, for a moment or two once a day. – I'm sorry I'm so selfish'.[122]

In January, after Rose's operation, Williams wrote in his notebook: 'I will probably return to Clayton and live on the folks for a while. Worse things are possible, since I have been away so long I'm really longing for home a bit. Excepting, of course, the old man'.[123] But he recognized his egotism, which suggests it played on his conscious as well: 'It is Jan. 10 [1943] and I haven't mailed the Xmas presents home. Or written Auntie [Ella Williams]. Self, self self – How wearisome and ugly. I think it poisons my work. I must purify it somehow before the end'.[124]

By spring, Williams was back in St Louis, at 53 Arundel Place, where his grandmother was dying of cancer. When he did go back to St Louis, he always had a triple motive: to see Grand before she died, to eat a decent meal for a change, and not to worry where his next bed would be. Rose was in Farmington by now, which certainly prompted Williams to return to his story 'Portrait of a Girl in Glass' and begin dramatizing it as 'The Gentleman Caller'. He had also completed work on the dramatization of the story 'Twenty-seven Wagons Full of Cotton', but thought it 'a little nasty perhaps': 'I am afraid,' he wrote Mary Hunter in mid-April, 'that plays of sadism are a symptom of emotional exhaustion, the sort of thing that artists with exacerbated nerves are peculiarly subject to'.[125]

By the end of April, Audrey Wood had informed him that he had been sold to MGM for a short-term contract of six months to work on film scripts. He was ecstatic to escape his father again, though wary that this would perhaps be the last time he saw Grand alive and scared about who would look after Rose now that she was lobotomized. One life was beginning, while another was coming to an end and another fixed forever in time. But he needed to write, needed to publish. What else could he do for either of them? Williams was already a published writer and a performed playwright, that was certain. As Ronald Hayman notes, 'To protect his copyright control over the writing he had already completed, [Wood] sent the studio a list of his works, which included 10 full-length plays,12 "long-short" plays, 17 one-act plays, 19 stories, and over 250 poems'.[126] Yet he returned from Hollywood a fully fledged playwright, ready to take Broadway by storm with *The Glass Menagerie*. That, alas, was still a year away. He still had Los Angeles, New York, and Provincetown again to contend with. Williams was on his way up; he was just not certain yet where 'up' actually was – and what it would mean to his life, if and when he got there.

Throughout these past few years, Williams remained faithful to his signature line, *En avant!*, or 'Forward, March'. Yet he frequently filled his notebook entries or his letters at this time with the phrase '*Mañana es otro día*' (he was never very good at Spanish): '<u>En Avant</u>! <u>Manana es otro dio</u>! Hasta <u>Manana</u>!'[127] The line, a poor Spanish translation of Scarlett O'Hara's 'Tomorrow is another day', was an appropriate catch-phrase since Williams often fled St Louis with the wind. About his past, he had summed it up nicely in his notebook:

> Reminiscent. I looked back through my life – starting with the summer of 1938 that I graduated from Iowa. – Chicago – New Orleans – California – and all the shuttling times since – the travels, the people – the anxieties, hardships, affairs, events, disappointments, fevers, kaleidoscopic shifts and changes – What a four years it has been! A lifetime in itself – not one moment of rest, hardly a bit of real peace in it all. But good! And terrible – a liberation. a [*sic*] fight. Well, here I am, still living – and going on. Not young anymore. If one dared to face it, what a thing he would see! – this life.[128]

About his future, he was uncertain, but he always looked to tomorrow, perhaps because he now knew that Rose could not, and he had to live for the both of them. Perhaps he would write better than he did today. Perhaps the Guild, or the Group Theatre or the New School, or some Broadway producer or publisher would take an interest in his work. Perhaps a cheque will arrive in the mail tomorrow. Perhaps he will give up his daily cruising and find that one love who has escaped him. Perhaps.

5
Hollywood to Rome (via Chicago): The 'Catastrophe' of his Success

On 30 April 1943, Audrey Wood sent Williams a Western Union cable, informing him that she had been successful in securing him a 'writing deal' for the 'pictures' where he would earn $250 a week.[1] Williams, who had dreamed for years of making big money from his writing, at first felt 'Excitement and some pleasure' at the announcement that he had been 'sold to Hollywood'.[2] He had been working hard on 'The Gentleman Caller' and imagined selling MGM the play, which was already adapted for the screen in its 'sculptural' style of 'short cumulative scenes'. Yet after two weeks in his two-room apartment in Santa Monica, he was lonely, suffering from what he believed to be TB (for years he had been coughing up blood), and bored with his movie assignment.

He was hired initially to dramatize Marguerite Steen's novel, *The Sun Is my Undoing*, but that project was 'shelved until Clark Gable return[ed] from service'.[3] He was then asked to write a script for Lana Turner, *Marriage Is a Private Affair*, what he referred to in a 29 May letter to Jay Laughlin as her 'celluloid brassiere'.[4] He had confided to Audrey Wood a week earlier that he was ill-fit for the project, much like an 'obstetrician required to successfully deliver a mastodon from a beaver'.[5] The failed contract with MGM was probably a Godsend for Williams, not only because it would have stifled his creative genius, as it had so many writers before him, but it would have tied him down to one city for the rest of his career. Footloose as he was, Williams could never have stayed put long enough to see a film through from concept to editing – even when it was one of his own.

The catastrophe that was Hollywood would soon become a 'catastrophe' of another sort, as the product of Williams's time there would eventually become *The Glass Menagerie*, whose immediate success plunged Williams into a level of despair that he was not ready to handle.

He had known success before, through his college writing awards, his semi-professional productions with the Mummers in St Louis, and his Group Theatre award and Rockefeller fellowships. But once *The Glass Menagerie* successfully left Chicago bound for Broadway, thanks in part to the support of that city's theatre critics – Ashton Stevens of the *Chicago Herald American* and Claudia Cassidy of the *Chicago Daily Tribune* – Williams's name was finally inscribed in the annals of American theatre. The success of *A Streetcar Named Desire* that followed retraced that name's etching in indelible ink.

The word 'success' can be found in most of Williams's writing during this decade, from his letters to his notebooks to his essays, as this chapter will demonstrate. In many of his pre-opening pieces for the *New York Times*, Williams would refer to it by looking nostalgically upon his salad years, from when he discovered New Orleans in the winter of 1938 to his several summers in Provincetown and Mexico. They were difficult times for the poor and starving artist, but it was that hunger for success which fuelled his creative energies. Now, with his financial freedom secured, would he still find the desire to write? The rest of the decade ahead of him would provide clear answers to that question, though each 'success' had brought him renewed encounters with 'catastrophe'.

Williams worked at MGM from May to October 1943. His contract had stipulated a seven-year deal with a six-month option to break the contract,[6] which MGM exercised by laying him off for six weeks in mid-August without pay. Though his work on the Turner film (and on material for a film based on Billy the Kid) was not entirely unsatisfactory, Williams was obviously more interested in *his* writing than in the studio's. Becoming a well-paid Hollywood hack writer frightened him: he would be comfortable, materialistically speaking, but it would cost him his theatrical idealism. 'Unlike playwriting', R. Barton Palmer and Robert Bray write,

> working on scripts for the commercial cinemas was a collaborative activity [...] but it could hold little appeal for a romantic individualist like Williams, who believed that writing was, at its best, the most sincere and honest form of self-expression, the communication of hard-won inner truths.[7]

It is probable that he willed his eventual firing the following October.

Williams was 'back on the pay-roll at Metro' on 24 September, though the six-month contract option was not renewed.[8] This free time allowed him to focus on the 'Provisional Film Story Treatment of "The Gentleman Caller"', a twenty-page screenplay, brad-bound in a blue 'Liebling-Wood' folder that developed from the rough stage version of the same material, which was itself a dramatic rendering of his short story 'Portrait of a Girl in Glass'. Faced daily (when he was not laid off) with a photo of Rose sitting on his MGM office desk, as someone would a picture of his wife or girlfriend, Williams thought of her often, and he began considering the possibilities of turning his story and play into a film. The treatment is

> primarily a character portrait of an American mother. Amanda Wingfield. It covers a period of time from about 1915 up to the present. It begins and ends in a small town in the Mississippi Delta country, which we will call Blue Mountain. It begins with the entrance into Amanda's life of the gentleman caller whom she came to marry, the telephone man (who fell in love with long-distance) from Tennessee.[9]

He understood that it was powerful material but tried repeatedly to turn it into the comedy 'The Pretty Trap' with a 'considerably lighter, almost happy' ending.[10] In the play, which 'corresponds to the last act' of 'The Gentleman Caller', Jim Delaney kisses Laura Wingfield and the two lovers leave to take a long walk, much to the delight of a giggling Amanda.[11]

Williams struggled intensively that summer with the storyline, no doubt haunted by his sister's lobotomy earlier in the year. With strong black coffee and cigarettes no longer keeping at bay his 'blue devils' – those 'periodic neuroses', as he called them in a 28 July 1943 letter to Donald Windham, that were like 'wild-cats under [his] skin' that he felt were also responsible for Rose's madness[12] – Williams turned to barbiturates like Phenobarbital: 'I wonder if anyone has ever dealt more skillfully with a more vicious and deadly opponent than have I with the beast in my nerves? I cannot kill him, nor ever <u>entirely</u> escape – I can only dodge him, evade him, put him off'.[13]

Williams felt that the film dealt with a theme as 'big in scope' as *Gone With the Wind* and believed earnestly in its potential success on the screen. He had told New York producer Mary Hunter in April 1943 that 'The Gentleman Caller' was becoming a long play that needed more serious treatment, and he believed he was adding that content through the cinematic medium.[14] What he would bring to them during this period were Joyce's stream of consciousness and the silent film era's placards, which became Williams's screen device and magic lantern projections.

He would later try silent film sequences in *Summer and Smoke* to present material that he could not capture in language, only to eliminate them in subsequent drafts.[15] Williams repeatedly worked alternatively on the stage and the film version of 'The Gentleman Caller', never knowing which medium was appropriate for the story.

After consulting his agent Audrey Wood, Williams offered the film treatment to Lille Messinger, an executive at MGM, but the studio unconditionally rejected it. MGM later claimed that the successful play from which the screenplay partly evolved was rightly its property since Williams had worked on it while under contract, but in his 31 May letter to Wood, Williams shrewdly noted that he had begun the stage version before signing his contract with MGM, thus the rights were still entirely his.[16] By late October, he had abandoned the film version and concentrated on the 'rough' play he had started before leaving for Hollywood:

> Just read over the one fairly long thing I've done out here, the 1-act version of Gentleman Caller ['The Pretty Trap']. It is appalling. Something has definitely gone wrong – that I was able to write such shit. Hysterical and empty [...]. I went on writing this past week. Returned to Gentleman Caller limiting my efforts to Cautious patchwork [...].[17]

MGM's loss was Broadway's gain, and Williams would continue working on the play for the next twelve months.

Also in 1943, Williams was preparing a collection of twenty-nine poems titled 'The Summer Belvedere' for New Directions' *Five Young American Poets* series that would be published the following year and to which he was to write two prefaces: a 'Frivolous' and a 'Serious' one.[18] Laughlin could not decide which one to publish, nor could Williams, as he explained in his 29 May letter to him:

> I could not decide between the two prefaces either. There is a paragraph about Joyce at which point the two could be joined – or if you like the serious and the frivolous angle – that would do just as well, I think. Certainly I would be pleased to have them both printed if you can give me that much space in the volume.[19]

Reviews of the collection were vituperative, in particular of Williams's contribution. As Williams later admitted to Laughlin in a letter dated 15 December 1944: 'I have seen only one review of my poems, in the

Herald Tribune. It was pretty condescending but not really evil. – as the View would have been. But I think the View has killed their review – for lack of space in the Christmas issue'.[20] Albert Devlin and Nancy Tischler note that the '"evil" notice of *Five Young American Poets* was not "killed" but delayed until the March 1945 number of *View*. In it, Philip Lamantia deemed the anthology to be "of hardly any consequence" and Williams none at all. Both versions of Williams's preface were 'inane', Lamantia thought, and his poetry showed an 'obvious lack of talent'.[21]

Later that October 1943, Williams also began working on a collection of short stories for Laughlin. He asked Wood to mail carbons of two or three of his best stories, including 'The Vine', 'The Red Part of a Flag', 'In Memory of an Aristocrat', 'Miss Rose and the Grocery Clerk', 'The Lost Girl', and 'A Tale of Two Writers': 'Something very, very good may come of it [...]'.[22] In his notebook, he wrote that he was '[s]haping some stories' for the collection, and added 'Portrait of a Girl in Glass', 'The Mattress by the Tomato Patch', 'Blue Roses and the Polar Star', and 'The Malediction'.[23] Aside from the obvious influence Rose was having on Williams at this time, he drew support and inspiration from his present surroundings, as well as his recent encounters. His landlady in the Palisades of Santa Monica, Zola Godina, provided the material for the story 'The Mattress by the Tomato Patch', which he would rewrite in the summer of 1953 and publish the following year in *Hard Candy*. The British writer Christopher Isherwood, whom he met that May through a letter of introduction from Lincoln Kirstein, also fascinated him, and they remained good friends and occasional lovers.[24] In the autumn, Williams read his novel *Goodbye to Berlin* (1939), which was adapted for the stage in 1966 as *Cabaret*, and Williams felt that the Sally Bowles story was 'a brilliant study'.[25]

Williams soon finished 'The Angel in the Alcove', about his grandmother and his first homosexual experiences in the French Quarter in 1938/39, and continued working on the story 'One Arm', which he began in May 1942 and completed three years later in Mexico.[26] Williams feared that the story, about the one-armed hustler, Oliver Winemiller, who is executed, despite the interventions of a latently gay minister, for having killed a Miami broker, would get confiscated by US Customs officers given its homosexual content. Windham later reported that Williams had just misplaced it beneath 'a pile of dirty sheets'.[27] Williams also tried working again on 'The Spinning Song', a verse play alternately titled 'The Columns of Revelry' that dealt with the decline of a southern family through 'adultery, incest, murder and mental fragility'.[28] It was another early incarnation of *The Glass Menagerie* with its Narrator character, but its storyline was preparing Williams to write *A Streetcar Named Desire*.

In addition to these several stories and poems, like 'Goofer Song', Williams continued working on 'The Gentleman Caller':

> Today for the first time in a month or so I wrote pretty nicely. On the last scene of 'The Gentleman Caller'. I have returned to the original version of it. It won't be a total loss after all. But it is very, very sentimental. Ah, well, I am not Dostoevsky nor even Strindberg. I must work within my limits.[29]

Dated 16 November 1943, this last notebook entry was written around the time that Williams was discovering James Joyce's *A Portrait of the Artist as a Young Man*, which was a significant contribution to his understanding of how expressionism could work in his play. Joyce made structural use of the epiphany, where memory-based passages did not serve the narrative thread alone but provided entry points into the narrator's thought processes. Given the play's cinematic treatment, Williams's previous experiences with Erwin Piscator at the New School, and his own theories behind the 'sculptural drama', Williams began infusing *The Glass Menagerie* with non-realistic elements that would hallmark his plastic theatre and extend the artistic reach of expressionist theatre.

Edwina wrote to her son while he was still in California, telling him to come home because Grand 'was fading fast'.[30] On 29 November, he was still in Hollywood, attending the Pasadena opening of *You Touched Me!* that Margo Jones had brought out to California from its recent Cleveland run.[31] Cornelius was also in California on business and attended the play. But Williams knew it was time to head back and face the imminent death of his beloved grandmother, just one year after suffering from the news of his sister's operation. By 20 December, he was only in Taos, New Mexico, ostensibly dragging his feet to thwart confronting the inevitable in St Louis. He wrote to Laughlin from Taos, explaining that his Hollywood experience made him feel like a 'worm – prostrate – crawling'.[32] Williams did not return to St Louis until later that month. When he arrived in St Louis late at night, only Grand was awake to greet him. Williams recalls the touching reunion in his 1960 essay 'The Man in the Overstuffed Chair' and the 1953 piece 'Grand' (published in 1964). As if waiting to say goodbye to her grandson, Grand would die just a couple weeks later on 6 January of a violent lung haemorrhage.

Williams stayed on in St Louis a few more weeks, though he did not attend Grand's burial. He underwent instead another eye operation, paid for, curiously, by his father C.C., who was growing increasingly drunk but strangely affectionate to all of the family members save his father-in-law, the Reverend Walter Dakin.[33] During this three-month stay, Williams wrote the story 'Oriflamme' (based on an earlier story he wrote in 1937 titled 'The Red Part of a Flag') and continued work on 'The Gentleman Caller' and new verse play, a romantic tragedy titled 'A Balcony in Ferrara' (also called 'Cock Crow' in his letters) after Robert Browning's dramatic monologue, 'My Last Duchess' (1842).

He returned to the West Side YMCA in New York in mid-March 1944 for what he had hoped would be the start of rehearsals for *You Touched Me!*, which Mary Hunter was trying to produce; but his play (budgeted at $35,000, which they could not yet raise) was shelved in favour of a restaging of Horton Foote's 1944 play, *Only the Heart*, a decision Williams greatly resented.[34] At Laughlin's request, Williams received another financial blessing that March in the form of a $1000 grant from the American Academy of Arts and Letters, which he promptly put into the bank after the 19 May ceremony and avoided drawing on it for several months. He was supporting himself financially from the money he earned in Hollywood the previous summer. Audrey Wood had opened up a savings account for him in New York when he took the MGM job, and he had managed by October 1943 to save an additional $800 by himself in his Culver City account, and another $75 in an account his mother opened in St Louis from the money he was mailing her. But money always had a way of slipping through his fingers.

With the American Arts and Letters money, he rented a cottage on Fire Island and began concentrating on 'The Gentleman Caller', now calling it 'The Fiddle in the Wings' or 'The Caller'.[35] He was shuttling back and forth between the cottage and New York City. While there, he visited Kip Kiernan in the hospital. He was suffering from an inoperable brain tumour and died on 21 May at the age of twenty-six, a death that would crush Williams as much as Frank Merlo's nearly two decades later. Williams returned to Provincetown in June, when the war was reaching its climax in Europe. Laughlin was preparing the publication of *Battle of Angels* for the first issue of his *Pharos* literary magazine (1945–47), which was distributed by New Directions and edited by his wife, Margaret Ellen Keyser. Laughlin wanted to print *Battle of Angels* in its first volume, which was scheduled for July 1944, but publication was postponed almost an entire year because Laughlin's Mormon printer in Utah found *Battle of Angels* to be a 'sinful text'.[36] In the summer of

1944, Williams was off yet again to Captain Jack's Wharf on the Cape, Provincetown being where he put the final touches on 'The Gentleman Caller'. As he confessed to Margo Jones, writing the play was 'an act of <u>compulsion</u>, not love. Just some weird necessity to get my sister on paper'.[37]

By September, Williams returned to New York, where he would stay for the next six weeks. The play had now become *The Glass Menagerie*, and Williams, in a September letter to Jones, praised its 'interesting new techniques': 'That is, when I consider the terrible, compulsive struggle it was to do the thing and what a frightful, sentimental mess it might well have been, and was at some stages [...]. I think it contains my sister, and that was the object'.[38] He was once again pursuing work at the New School, and Piscator told him he would have hired him had Williams stayed in one place long enough to be on the faculty. By mid-October, Williams had sold the play to Eddie Dowling, who was to direct it and perform the role of Tom Wingfield. His career as a playwright was finally sealed.

All told, Williams worked on *The Glass Menagerie* for more than eight years, more time than he had devoted to any of his major plays save *Battle of Angels/Orpheus Descending*. He began by reading vignettes about a mother and sister in William G. B. Carson's 'English 16' course at Washington University in 1936–37, and his fellow students were surprised when he turned in *Me, Vashya* instead for the contest.[39] His many stories and play treatments, including 'Portrait of a Girl in Glass' and 'Blue Roses and the Polar Star', written during the summer in Hollywood, and 'If You Breathe, It Breaks', and 'The Pretty Trap (A Comedy in One Act)' were essentially steps in the achievement of his first masterpiece.

As history has informed us, the play was not at first a success. Dowling's wife, who read the script, passed it on to her husband, who contacted a co-producer, Louis B. Singer, and the theatre critic George Jean Nathan, who would become one of Williams's greatest nemeses in the theatre. Nathan questioned the play's merits but saw an opportunity to place his girlfriend, Julie Haydon, in the role of Laura. Together, Dowling and Nathan would alter the script slightly, adding a drunken scene that Williams did not like and a concluding line that he downright despised.[40] Instead of Williams's original line, where Tom tells Laura to blow out her candles, they added this one, which Tom says directly to the audience: 'Here's where my memory stops and your imagination begins'.[41] With or without the final line, the play was the toast of Broadway when it arrived there via Chicago.

In an essay written on 9 April 1945, 'A Reply to Mr. Nathan', Williams laid out most of his complaints against the embittered critic.[42] The response, which Williams wisely chose not to publish so early in his career, is a rejoinder to Nathan's review of *The Glass Menagerie* in the *New York Journal-American* (4 April 1945), where he claimed that the 'wooden' role of Tom Wingfield was entirely 'rewritten' by Dowling in order to add 'some living plausibility' to the play. Whatever praise Nathan attributed to the play was directed toward its production, which he says outright hides the faults in the play's structure. Nathan added that the play was 'a freakish experiment and replete with such delicatessen as moving picture titles of silent drama days thrown intermittently on the scenery, it has been metamorphosed under Dowling's guidance into the unaffected and warming simplicity that it should have had in the first place' and that it was '[d]eficient in any touches of humor'.[43] In his 'Reply', Williams defends, among other things, his acceptance of removing the use of the play's screen device, which greatly altered its 'sculptural' design.

When the play finally opened for its try-out in Chicago at the Civic Theatre on 26 December 1944, two local critics, Claudia Cassidy and Ashton Stevens, liked it so much that they championed its cause, which many theatre historians today believe saved the play from its half-filled houses and pushed it on towards it success on Broadway. Even Chicago's mayor offered a fifty per cent ticket subsidy to keep *The Glass Menagerie* from an early closing.[44] After much legal wrangling between the play's producers and MGM over ownership rights, the play had its Broadway premier on Holy Saturday, 31 March 1945, at the Playhouse Theatre. It was an instant success, earning Williams not only a considerable sum of money and making him forever financially independent (and his mother as well, to whom he signed over half of the royalties), but also the literary recognition he so long sought after.

The Glass Menagerie remains the quintessential Williams play of the post-war theatre. While it resembles in theme and in character the neo-romantic stories and plays Williams wrote during the 1930s, in literary technique it comes closer to Joyce than Chekhov. Oddly enough, though Williams repeatedly shied away from employing the stream of consciousness in his fiction, in this play we find him experimenting with it in a way that would alter the course of American theatre forever. As part of what he described in his 'Production Notes' to *The Glass Menagerie* as the 'plastic theatre' – one that 'must take the place of the exhausted theatre of realistic conventions'[45] – Williams mixed Modernist theatrical expressionism with neo-romantic storylines and characters to produce a self-proclaimed 'memory play' – perhaps 'epiphany play' would have been more accurate.

To the extent that Williams understood the complex workings of the stream of consciousness as a way of 'presenting reality exactly as it presents itself to the mind',[46] which is how he defined it in his college essay on James Joyce, is conjecture. Williams had recognized Eugene O'Neill's attempt to achieve something similar in *Strange Interludes*. Writing to his grandfather on 31 January 1929, Williams reminded him of O'Neill's play, which was playing 'in New York while we were there': 'Its unusual feature is that all the actors speak their thoughts, showing decided difference between what people <u>say</u> to others and what they <u>think</u> in reality'.[47]

In terms of the stream of consciousness, Williams attempted in *The Glass Menagerie* to do on the stage what Joyce had accomplished on the page: to find 'a more penetrating and vivid expression of things as they are' to the perceiver.[48] Certainly, his experiment was a challenging one since the modern stage frowns upon lengthy speeches and soliloquies, especially ones that reproduce, as the stream of consciousness does in fiction, anti-linear thought processes similar to Molly's in the 'Penelope' section of *Ulysses* that Williams had singled out in his college essay as being the novel's 'best portion'.[49] Theatrical production simply does not share the same principles of arresting signification with the reading act, and Williams knew that any attempt to reproduce a character's private thought processes on stage had to be done through an extra-literary language. To achieve his aim, Williams made use of numerous devices outside of speech to help disrupt the linear representation of human thought patterns – e.g., music, art, transparent scrims, and magic lantern slides, all of which reveal a character's thoughts or words as placards did in the silent movies that Williams knew so well.[50] This was to become the staple of his imagined plastic theatre.

Explaining his reasoning behind the visionary use of the screen device, Williams writes in his 'Production Notes':

This device was the use of a screen on which were projected magic-lantern slides bearing images or titles. [...] These images and legends, projected from behind, were cast on a section of wall between the front-room and dining-room areas, which should be indistinguishable from the rest when not in use.

[...] In an episodic play, such as this, the basic structure or narrative line may be obscured from the audience; the effect may seem fragmentary rather than architectural. This may not be the fault of the play so much as a lack of attention in the audience. The legend or image upon the screen will *strengthen the effect of what is merely allusion in the writing* and allow the primary point to be made more simply and lightly than if the entire responsibility were on the spoken lines.[51]

Williams elaborated in a letter of 9 April 1945 that the 'magic lantern slides' were meant to provide 'satirical and sometimes poetic counterpoint to the dialogue' and maintain the narrator's point of view 'even when he was not present on stage, for these slides were the narrator's own commentary on what was taking place'.[52] Rarely used in stage productions of the play since its 1944 try-out, the forty-three screen legends and images nonetheless allow us expressionistic access to a character's thought processes in concert with or in counterpoint to their actions on the stage.[53] What makes Williams's expressionistic device move beyond the theatrical and into the psychological realms of the stream of consciousness is the fact that the entire play is a re-enactment of Tom Wingfield's memory. Thus all the screen legends and images are those which his mind has conjured up in the reconstruction of the words and actions of an emotionally wrenching time of his not-too-distant past.

The screen legends, then, connect several of Tom's thoughts – spread throughout time and space as he stands before those perfume bottles in a foreign city – that reflect both his celebration of his sister and his guilt at leaving her behind. Though some critics viewed the screen legends, like the music and lighting techniques, as stage trickery, Williams repeatedly took to the stump to defend his vision of the plastic theatre. Later, in a 12 July 1948 letter to Eric Bentley, Williams cozened the august theatre critic for his 'lack of respect for the extra-verbal or non-literary elements of the theatre' such as 'light and movement and color and design': 'Actually all of these plastic things are as valid instruments of expression in the theatre as words [...]'.[54] Again, though not precisely Joycean in its usage, the screen device does show how Williams attempted to adapt the stream of consciousness for his plastic theatre on the American stage. And though he would never again use the screen device in any of his plays, Williams continually looked for ways to render intense thought processes in dramatic form, and this formed the basis of his plastic theatre.[55] That several contemporary productions of the play, one even in France in 2011, have restored these screen devices suggests that Williams's 'plastic' vision of the play was clearly ahead of its times.

The Glass Menagerie ran for 563 performances, won the New York Drama Critics' Circle, the Sidney Howard Memorial, and the Donaldson awards, and made Tennessee Williams the darling of Broadway, if not almost a household name. It would have won that year's Pulitzer Prize instead of Mary Chase's sentimental *Harvey* (1944) had it not been for the Machiavellian interventions of Nathan, who had championed the cause of Eugene O'Neill as America's greatest playwright and did not want that title challenged. Bennett Cerf at Random House, and not Jay Laughlin at New Directions, quickly published the play in July. Williams had signed and honoured a contract with Cerf dating back to 1940, promising publishing rights to his 'next work' after *Battle of Angels* in exchange for a needed $100 advance.[56] With the production earning him over a thousand dollars a day from the play's daily receipts *prior* to its Broadway appearance and with the publication bringing in untold amounts of money, Williams would never again know hunger or poverty. So soon did success hit him that he called it a 'catastrophe of success'.

Williams's response to his wealth was swift and predictable: he hid from it. Like Joyce, Williams's eye problems intensified with age. He had already undergone the first of four eye operations in January 1941 at St Luke's Hospital[57] and a second operation in 1942, even wearing a black eye patch while working at The Beggar's Bar in Greenwich Village.[58] Williams then had a third eye operation in 1944, and a fourth in 1945, just after the opening of *The Glass Menagerie* on Broadway. In his essay 'The Catastrophe of Success', which he included as a preface to the play, Williams discusses how being bandaged for four days had enabled him to hide from his success and ponder its detrimental effects:

> [...] I decided to have another eye operation mainly because of the excuse it gave me to withdraw from the world behind a gauze mask. It was my fourth eye operation, and perhaps I should explain that I had been affected for about five years with a cataract on my left eye which required a series of needling operations and finally an operation on the muscle of the eye. (The eye is still in my head. So much for that). Well that gauze mask served a purpose.[59]

Success was not bittersweet, just bitter. Williams certainly enjoyed the financial security. It allowed him to travel first class and pay for those who accompanied him, for he hated being and travelling alone. But he was not entirely ostentatious in his tastes. His homes were always modest, and he preferred staying in hotels that catered to his Bohemian lifestyle than those that promised unfettered luxury. Yes, he had finally achieved the fame and the fortune, and above all the recognition of his talent, that he had struggled for more than a decade to attain. But at what cost?

Reaching the summit provoked two fundamental problems for Williams: the pressure to remain there, and the loss of the careless days in Bohemian anonymity. How could he be sure now that those who professed their love and admiration for him were genuine? If Williams were plagued by an unfounded persecution complex these past years (the generosity alone of many people, from family to good friends to even casual acquaintances, should have convinced him of the general goodwill the world had toward him), his growing paranoia over peoples' intentions around him was legitimate. Perhaps Williams's greatest error laid in failing at times to distinguish between those who were out to use him and those who remained loyal from the very beginning. Success for Williams would forever come with a hefty price tag, one often paid in credit with overextended moral funds.

While the question of loyalty was an important one for Williams, and would remain so throughout his life, his most pressing concern was that of staying on the Broadway summit. If Williams did want to make a claim to O'Neill's crown, he had to write another play that would confirm his genius. Immediately. Williams returned to material he had begun years earlier with the southern prostitute–artist Irene and found ways to blend it with the verse play 'The Columns of Revelry' (or 'The Spinning Song') that he had been working on just before the start of the new year. The play would have obvious links to the one-act play *Dos Ranchos, or The Purification*, dedicated to Margo Jones and published by Laughlin that year. On 23 March 1945, a week before *The Glass Menagerie* opened in New York, he wrote a letter to Audrey Wood, detailing the plot for a play about 'two sisters' and 'the remains of a fallen southern family':

> I have been buried deep in work the last week or so and am about 55 or 60 pages into the first draft of a play that I am trying to design for [Katherine] Cornell. At the moment, it has four different titles, The Moth, The Poker Night, The Primary Colors, or Blanche's Chair in the Moon. [...] There is a violent scene at the end of which he takes her by force.
>
> There are at least three possible ends.
>
> One, Blanche simply leaves – with no destination.
>
> Two, goes mad.
>
> Three, throws herself in front of a train in the freight-yards, the roar of which has been an ominous under-tone throughout the play.[60]

Three years later, that play would be *A Streetcar Named Desire*.

At the end of May, Williams booked a private berth on a train and headed south for Mexico City (via Dallas), which he felt would be the Lost Generation Paris of World War II. Among the glitterati he met there included composer-conductor Leonard Bernstein, ballet master George Balanchine, and silent film star Delores Del Rio. Williams also attended several bull fights, which upset him at first, and operas that he found fascinating. He worked well and moved north to Lake Chapala in Guadalajara, where he took a guest house to work on 'The Passion of a Moth', which he was now calling 'Blanche's Chair in the Moon' (the title 'The Poker Night' was resuscitated in later drafts). While there, he wrote the poem 'Recuerdo' in memory of his recently deceased Grand and the interned Rose, and the essay 'A Playwright's Statement', which he sent to Jones in early July.[61]

He had received from Jones an urgent telegram: 'Desperately need short article on playwright's attitude toward Dallas theatre to show Dallas and the country what we are trying to do. Wire when I can expect it. Love, Margo'.[62] Supported by a Rockefeller grant, Jones hoped to contribute to the decentralization of American theatre from its New York stronghold. The 'Project' was her vision of a non-commercial, poetic theatre that perfectly aligned with Williams's plastic theatre. Their friendship began in 1942, a year before she staged *You Touched Me!* at the Cleveland Play House, and was confirmed with her production of *The Purification* in July 1944 in Pasadena. She had championed Williams's cause before he was famous, and now she had hoped to use their connection to revolutionize that national theatre.

Though lauding Jones's Theatre '45 in his essay for the *Dallas Morning News*, Williams had confessed to Guthrie McClintic in a 23 May letter that he did not like Dallas at all and was 'trying to hide' from Jones the fact that he did 'not feel the atmosphere here in which anything really progressive is likely to happen', in theatre or in anything else.[63] For Williams, Dallas was 'a creative booby-trap', and 'the real power in artistic circles here is John Rosenfield of the Dallas News – Jones's chief supporter – and in discussing Martha Graham he says "I don't care for that kind of showmanship"'.[64] McClintic, husband of the actress Katherine Cornell, for whom Williams was presently creating the role of Blanche,[65] had originally turned down the direction of *Battle of Angels* but had finally accepted to direct *You Touched Me!*, which was to open at the Booth Theatre in New York on 25 September. As was typical of the mercurial Williams, a week later he had changed his mind, writing to Eddie Dowling that he felt the 'outlook' for Jones's Dallas Theatre 'is really wonderful' and will be 'valuable to theatre all over the country'.[66]

Williams did not want to return to Broadway, owing to the fact that producing a play took time away from writing one, and he saw the Dallas Theatre as 'a place to experiment and clarify' and 'to remain in touch with [the] stage while at the same time escaping the exhausting responsibilities of Broadway'.[67]

Williams returned to New York (again via Dallas) in August and then moved onto Boston for the try-outs of *You Touched Me!* Its opening was a disappointment, though Williams was not entirely bothered by it, since he shared the criticism, just as he had the box office receipts, 50/50 with Donald Windham, despite Wood's attempt to renegotiate the original contract in Williams's favour.[68] He stayed at the Shelton Hotel (which would later evict him for his brothel-like parties), stopped work on 'Blanche's Chair in the Moon', and began drafting a new play, 'A Chart of Anatomy', an early version of *Summer and Smoke*, which combined elements of his stories 'Oriflamme' and 'The Yellow Bird'. He was also at work on a one-act play that autumn 1945, 'Camino Real, or The Rich and Eventful Death of Oliver Winemiller', the logical next step in his plastic theatre since *The Glass Menagerie*. But the one-act was giving him trouble:

> Assembled and read the l-act – another fiasco, weak as picnic punch – has a few faintly pleasant touches – plastic details – but is trite and gutless – bloodless – had depended on it to revive my confidence so I could tackle a major project but it is just another in the fairly unbroken succession of diminuendos.[69]

By 28 November, the one-act play had developed 'into a full length play' to which he 'attached [his] hopes' in getting it performed.[70] Williams later planned on sending Jay Laughlin a '30 or 35 p. Ms of a "work for the Plastic Theatre" with Mexican backgrd. & characters' within the week following his 25 January 1946 letter to him.[71] And by 12 March, he wrote Wood that he had 'read over Camino Real' and did not 'think it ought to be typed up in its present form'.[72] He was now calling the play 'Cabeza de Lobo', a Mexican myth about a girl, Esmeralda, who turns into a werewolf.

Williams returned to New Orleans that December 1945 and stayed at the swanky Pontchartrain Hotel outside the Quarter (some of the drafts of *Streetcar* were written on the hotel stationery). He was met with good news when New Directions just released the collection of his one-act plays, *27 Wagons Full of Cotton and Other One-act Plays*. By the new year 1946, he was living in a four-room apartment at 710 Orleans, just behind St Louis Cathedral, and in full view of the Christ statue, 'arms outstretched as if to invite the suffering world'.[73] He traded (or almost) his nightly quests for a live-in lover, Amado 'Pancho' Rodriguez y Gonzales, who would remain his longest partner before Frank Merlo. Rodriguez and Williams had a volatile relationship (something Williams would have with a lot of later partners, such as Robert Carroll), with Rodriguez's outbursts helping Williams to rethink his character Ralph Stanley, an early version of Stanley Kowalski. Williams soon completed his 'Mexican fantasy' for the plastic theatre, *Ten Blocks on the Camino Real*, and alternated his attention between 'A Chart of Anatomy' and 'A Street-car Named Desire', as he told Wood he was now calling his play, though he would repeatedly return to earlier titles at this stage of the writing.[74] At the end of the month, he attended a 'command perform-ance' of *The Glass Menagerie* in Washington, DC.[75]

By April Williams had completed the story 'Night of the Iguana' and the religio-gothic tale 'Desire and the Black Masseur', one of his dark-est prose pieces about a middle-aged, milquetoast white man, Anthony Burns (the namesake of the last slave caught under the Fugitive Slave Act of 1850), who discovers a fetish for masochism dished out by a sadistic black masseur, who eventually eats him when their sessions end in Burns's death. The year 1946 would indeed prove to be one of his most productive, if not darkest, in terms of his classic works.

Williams apparently sent Rodriguez onto Taos after returning briefly himself to St Louis (via Memphis) to buffer his grandfather and mother from his recently retired father, whose free time was filled with binge drinking and slamming doors. Worried about his family's reaction to his homosexuality, Williams asked Rodriguez to 'be extremely careful' in 'any communication addressed here'. He would later ask Laughlin to sell his collection of stories titled *One Arm* (1948) only through subscription out of fear that his mother would buy a copy in a St Louis book store.[76] While in St Louis, Williams spent time again with Williams Inge, whom he met previously in 1944 when Inge interviewed him for the *St Louis Star-Times*. Time with his father, however, was not the only thing giving Williams pain. He was suffering from acute pain in his abdomen, but he continued on with his trip as planned, driving his black 1937 Packard convertible toward New Mexico. On his way to Taos, he complained of stomach ailments and was to have a minor operation in Wichita for a misdiagnosed diverticulitis. He refused the surgery and continued by bus on to Taos (his car's bearings had burned out, and he left it in Alva,

Oklahoma, and returned a month later to retrieve it[77]), where he suffered from an inflamed appendix, Meckel's diverticulum.[78]

Following his visit to Taos, and 'after weeks of exhausting travel',[79] Williams decided to spend the rest of the summer that year on the island of Nantucket, sitting opposite a worktable with Carson McCullers, whom he had invited to stay with him and Rodriguez. The three of them lived in a rented lopsided frame house at 31 Pine Street, where they both set about to write, McCullers on dramatizing her successful novel, *The Member of the Wedding*,[80] and Williams on *Summer and Smoke*. They worked at 'opposite ends of a table' and would 'read each other our day's work over our after-dinner drinks, and she gave me the heart to continue a play that I feared was hopeless'.[81] It must have reminded Williams of his 'literary factory' with Clark Mills back in St Louis during the summer of 1937. Though they had never before met, McCullers would become one of Williams's most cherished friends. Rodriguez fell again into one of his violent rages and packed up his trunk to leave, but Williams cozened him back, explaining that their relationship was identical to that of a married husband and wife. Rodriguez, like Merlo and the many paid secretaries/travelling companions after him, had to settle on being the traditional wife with all that implied in post-war America.[82]

A few years later in 1949, while living in Rome, Williams wrote an introduction to McCullers's novel *Reflections in a Golden Eye*, in which he describes his and her interests in the '"morbid"' side of human nature as being akin to the Southern Gothic tradition of William Faulkner. The Southern Gothic, that 'spiritual intuition of something almost too incredible and shocking to talk about, which underlies the whole so-called [...] uncommunicable [*sic*] something',[83] is similar to Jean-Paul Sartre's existentialism in its 'anxiety of the incommunicable sublime, the nothingness that feeds the *pour-soi*'s epistemological encounters with the Other'.[84] The only difference for Williams between the two schools of existential thought was that 'the motor impulse of the French school is intellectual and philosophic while that of the American is more of an emotional and romantic nature'.[85]

By the autumn of 1946, Williams was back in New Orleans, staying at 632½ St Peter Street in the French Quarter, and continued work on *Summer and Smoke*, which he now saw as a Gothic play and a promising vehicle for Katherine Cornell (he had turned away from Blanche's story for the moment). Over the summer, he began working into the play bits of his plastic theatre, such as the use of a silent film sequence to accompany the stage action, but he eventually scrapped the idea, finding that the film sequences upset the poetic unity of the play.[86] Later, in his programme notes to the play, 'The History of *Summer and Smoke*', Williams would clarify the confused timeline of his writing at this time that found him working on three plays at once:

> First: 'The Glass Menagerie,' begun Winter 1942, finished Summer 1944.
>
> Second: 'Streetcar,' begun January 1945 at the Sherman Hotel in Chicago while I was there with Laurette Taylor Company. Abandoned as hopeless one month later.
>
> Third: 'Summer and Smoke,' begun Autumn 1945 in Shelton Hotel in New York when I was there for the opening of 'You Touched Me.' Abandoned as hopeless about two months later.
>
> In Winter of 1946 I was working on a Mexican fantasy, finished but never produced, called 'Ten Blocks on the Camino Real.'
>
> In Summer of 1946 I returned to 'Summer and Smoke' and continued to work on it till January 1947, when I abandoned it once more as hopeless, although Margo Jones read it and loved it in that first draft, which she accepted for Dallas Theatre.
>
> In late January of 1947 I decided 'Streetcar' was not hopeless and went back to work on it. Finished it Spring of 1947 and it was produced in December 1947 in New York.
>
> Summer of 1948 I returned to 'Summer and Smoke' and completed my own final version of it, the one produced Autumn of 1948: in New York.[87]

On 1 November, Williams wrote an 'Envoi' to accompany the script of *Summer and Smoke*, wherein he describes the metaphysical war between John and Alma in terms similar to those he was using to mitigate Blanche and Stanley's struggle in *A Streetcar Named Desire*: 'It is impossible to say who won the argument in the play. Neither of them did and both of them did, and that is how it has seemed to me. Perhaps I could have made it clearer. That can be said of almost all my work. But to be clearer is not necessarily to be more truthful. Enveloped as all of us are in the inscrutable....'.[88]

By the end of December, just before his grandfather had come down to New Orleans for a visit, Williams turned his attention once again to 'The Poker Night', as *Streetcar* was once again being called. After a rough period with Rodriguez, who could not stand Williams's frequent infidelities, and with Edwina, who could not accept Rodriguez, the presence of his liberal-minded grandfather calmed him. The Reverend had fully accepted his grandson's homosexuality and would soon become a near-permanent fixture in his household. Williams was having trouble with the ending of the play, looking for Blanche's endgame: departure, insanity or suicide. On Christmas Eve, he wrote in his notebook, 'The ending is not yet right. May continue working on that tomorrow'.[89] He worked on the play for the next few months at La Concha Hotel in Key West, to where he and his grandfather drove out in Williams's new Pontiac. He wrote Rodriguez at this time, informing him about their trip and about his recent 'pledge' with other playwrights not to perform their plays in Washington, DC, while 'negros are being kept out of Washington theatres' – one of the few references in Williams's letters to Civil Rights issues.[90] While in Key West, they met Hemingway's ex-wife, Pauline, and, by mid-March, 'The Poker Night' was finished: 'A relative success, not pleasant but well done. I think it will make good theatre, though its success is far from assured'.[91] So busy was he with preparation for *A Streetcar Named Desire* and writing letters to the interested parties in that production that Williams did not write a single entry in his notebook from the end of April until October 1947.

Preparations for *A Streetcar Named Desire*, as it was now being called, were soon underway. Audrey Wood managed to convince Williams to join her in Charleston to seal their contact with a potential producer. On 8 April, Williams sent Wood a telegram from New Orleans prior to his departure for Charleston: "MY TRAIN LEAVES 5:30 WEDNESDAY EVENING ARRIVES 8:15 THURSDAY EVENING. THIS WOMAN HAD BETTER BE GOOD'.[92] That woman was Irene Mayer Selznick, daughter of Hollywood mogul Louis B. Mayer and wife of David O. Selznick, another movie magnate. Wood then convinced Elia Kazan, who had just made Arthur Miller's *All My Sons* a Broadway sensation, to direct the play. Now all they needed were the actors.

In May, Williams saw *All My Sons* again and, writing Kazan from Provincetown, he agreed that '[Karl] Malden was right for Mitch'.[93] On Wood's sound advice, Williams travelled with Rodriguez that July from Provincetown, where he was still tinkering with *Summer and Smoke* before its Dallas premiere at the Gulf Oil Playhouse on 8 July, to California to see Jessica Tandy perform in *Portrait of a Madonna*, which Hume Cronyn had been staging at the Actors' Lab in Los Angeles since January. Williams knew that the success of the play hinged upon the perfect casting of Blanche, and Williams was so uncertain that he would find the right actress that he advised his mother to hold off investing her money in the play.[94] After the performance, Williams thought it 'instantly apparent' that Tandy was Blanche DuBois, and she was cast in the role.[95]

Williams left California after spending nearly a month there, a guest at each of Selznick's three Beverly Hills or Malibu homes. On his way back East, Williams passed through Dallas to see Jones's production of *Summer and Smoke* at her Theatre '47. From there, he and Rodriguez headed on to Provincetown, where they spent the rest of the summer. A month later, Williams met for the first time a New Jersey-born Sicilian, Frank Merlo, at the Atlantic House Bar in P-town. Both Merlo, whom Williams would refer to affectionately as Little Horse or just Horse (more for his equine jaw than for his prodigious genitalia), and Williams were on the verge of ending souring relationships, but they were still a while away from beginning theirs, which would be Williams's longest, though hardly monogamous, relationship with any one partner.

A young twenty-three-year-old Marlon Brando was sent to Province-town to read the part of Stanley Kowalski, after hiring John Garfield proved too much of a complication. Williams had written to Audrey Wood in late March, asking her if she thought Tallulah Bankhead was right for the role of Blanche: 'My fear is that Bankhead would not be sympathetic enough in the softer aspects of the character'.[96] Williams's fears would be justified ten years later when Bankhead did camp up the role of Blanche in a 1956 revival of the play, which caused quite a stir in theatre circles and put a strain on the pair's relationship. As serendip-ity would have it, Bankhead was performing in Cocteau's *L'aigle à deux têtes* that winter of 1946–47. Williams, who fled New England, and then New York, in October 1946 for the warmer climes of New Orleans, had just missed by a couple of months the Boston try-out of the first English adaptation of the play, *The Eagle Has Two Heads*, which starred a young Brando as Stanislas playing opposite Bankhead's Queen.

The Eagle would prove an eventual disaster for several reasons, not the least of which included Brando's efforts to upstage Bankhead by urinat-ing, farting, or scratching his crotch onstage during her important mon-ologues.[97] Bankhead, to whom Williams had sent a draft of 'The Poker Night' in the hopes that she would accept the role of Blanche, informed the playwright of Brando's antics in her subsequent rejection letter:

My Dear Mr. Williams: Thank you for showing me your latest little play [...]. Regretfully, I must turn down the role of Blanche DuBois in The Poker Night. [...] I do have one suggestion for the casting. I know of an actor who can appear as this brutish Stanley Kowalski character. I mean, a total pig of a man without sensitivity or grace of any kind. Marlon Brando would be perfect as Stanley. I have just fired the cad from my play, *The Eagle Has Two Heads*, and I know for a fact that he is looking for work.[98]

Now out of work, Brando arrived in Provincetown at the end of August. Williams wrote to Wood that he was 'very anxious to see and hear him', though he was still hoping that Garfield could be signed.[99] After fixing Williams's plumbing and fitting a copper penny for a temporary fuse, Brando read the part and instantly won over Williams. As Williams wrote to Wood, 'I can't tell you what a relief it is that we have found such a God-sent Stanley in the person of Brando. [...] I don't want to focus guilt or blame particularly on any one character but to have it a tragedy of misunderstandings and insensitivity to others. A new value came out of Brando's reading which was by far the best reading I have ever heard'.[100] Brando was immediately cast in the role of Stanley Kowalski.[101]

By October, rehearsals were underway on the roof of the New Amsterdam Theatre, and a New Haven try-out was fast approaching. The play was scheduled to open that December. When *A Streetcar Named Desire* premiered at the Ethel Barrymore Theatre on 3 December 1947 – amid blizzards that ranked as the worst snowstorm in New York City's history – it stirred up controversy overnight. The play met with rave reviews in the following morning's papers, like that from Brooks Atkinson who called it 'a quietly woven study of intangibles' and Tennessee Williams 'a genuinely poetic playwright whose knowledge of people is honest and thorough'.[102] In the days ahead, Joseph Wood Krutch in *Nation*, Kappo Phelan in *Commonweal*, John Chapman in the *New York Daily News*, John Mason Brown in *The Saturday Review*, and Irwin Shaw in *The New Republic* all sounded similar praise for Williams and for *Streetcar*.

The play was not impervious to negative reviews, however. As would be expected, George Jean Nathan panned it, calling it 'The Glands Menagerie', and Mary McCarthy, satirized Williams's use of symbolism and flowery rhetoric, saying Williams would have been better off writing 'a wonderful little comic epic, The Struggle for the Bathroom'.[103] As Thomas Adler points out in his monograph *The Moth and the Lantern*:

> What criticisms the early reviewers did register centered on three issues: the potentially shocking nature of Williams's material, the seemingly loose way in which he structured it, and the apparently pessimistic stance he took toward human existence.[104]

For the most part, though, Williams and *Streetcar* were both critically acclaimed and commercially successful: Williams won the New York Drama Critics' Circle Award in March, the Donaldson Award, and the

Pulitzer Prize in May for that year's most outstanding drama. *Streetcar* ran for two years (855 performances) on Broadway before bringing most of its cast to the Hollywood screen in 1951, again under the direction of Elia Kazan.

Half a century's academic criticism on *Streetcar* has perpetuated the debate begun by the drama critics in 1947, which now centres on essentially two issues. The first evolved from a question that has been raised time and time again: with whom are we supposed to sympathize at the end? The second issue resulted directly from the difficulty in answering the first: is this ambiguity an artistic failure on Williams's part? In other words, is *Streetcar* a social or a psychological drama? If it is a social play, what do both Blanche and Stanley represent and who is victorious by the end? And if it is a psychological play, with what is Blanche struggling: past and present, illusion and reality, death and desire, or flesh and spirit? The answer to any or all of these questions are parried by Williams's 'inscrutable' comment in his 'Envoi' analysis of *Summer and Smoke* and in his 'tragedy of misunderstandings' plea to Wood about the need not to take sides in the struggle.

Many critics today believe Williams sided with the delicate Blanche from the beginning, her being one of his many fugitive kind. But Williams was also attracted to the explosive types like Stanley or Rodriguez or even his father, whom he would finally come to understand a decade later with the help of psychotherapy. Joseph Wood Krutch reported that the playwright had once summarized *Streetcar*'s message in the following terms: 'You had better look out or the apes will take over'.[105] 'Despite all the violence of his plays,' Krutch explained, and

> despite what sometimes looks very much like nihilism, [Williams] is really on the side of what modernists would call the Past rather than the Future – which means, of course, on the side of those who believe that the future, if there is to be any civilized future, will be less new than most modern dramatists from Ibsen on have professed to believe [...]. That is, a break with the past as radical as that which much modern thought and much modern drama seems to advocate unintentionally prepares the way for the apes to take over. A civilized man is likely to find it increasingly difficult to live in either the physical or the spiritual world which has *gradually been evolving*.[106]

Williams unintentionally corroborated this theory back in a 12 January 1943 entry in his notebook: '(I saw 4 middle aged-men moving heavily and dully across the lobby in their dark clothes and I thought how little they were unlike 4 apes. It hasn't happened yet, the human race, it has not yet been created.)'[107]

Ape or moth, 'humankind cannot bear very much reality', to quote a line in T. S. Eliot's 'Burnt Norton', the first poem of his *Four Quartets* that Williams had used at one point as the epigraph to *Streetcar*. What was important in the play was not the stranger's kindness, or Stanley's brutality, or even Stella's forgiveness. Instead, it was the Kowalski's baby and the promise of new life in the Quarter. In a manuscript draft titled 'What is "Success" in the Theatre?' (c. 1977), Williams had this to say about *Streetcar*: '[...] the final line of "Streetcar" is not "I have always depended upon the kindness of strangers" but the dealer's choice of the next game at the poker party, "This game is seven card stud", meaning that the hand of life which is dealt us has an important number of its cards face down on the table'.[108] Whatever Williams 'meant' in the play, *Streetcar* is undeniably powerful, and it remains one of the best plays, if not *the* best play, yet produced by an American playwright.

As he would repeatedly do after his play's Broadway premiere, whether or not it was a success, Williams fled Manhattan. And since he had spoken so much about wanting to travel to a post-war Europe now that the war had ended, Williams boarded a ship on 30 December 1947 and set sail for Cherbourg, before taking a train to Paris. Onboard, he took a single cabin and enjoyed the solitude that he often dreaded. His relationship with Rodriguez, and the *Streetcar* production, had taken its toll on his nerves, and he was ready for some peace and quiet. He described to Audrey Wood having met 'a very good and influential friend',[109] Hélène Gordon Lazareff, who had founded *Elle* magazine in 1945 and who promised Williams that she would introduce him to the celebrated French actor-director, Louis Jouvet, concerning the French production of *Streetcar* that ultimately Jean Cocteau would produce.

In Paris, he first stayed at the chic Hôtel Georges V, but then moved to a raffish hotel on the Left Bank more to his liking. In his *Memoirs*, he recounts spending two undesirable weeks upon arrival being treated for hepatitis and mononucleosis at the American Hospital in Neuilly, a suburb of Paris.[110] Years later, in the 30 December 1953 entry of his notebook, Williams would write, 'But then, remember the panicky night at the American hospital in Paris, I said (wrote on a fly leaf of Crane's 'Bridge') – 'the jig is up"'.[111] His renewed interests in post-war France and Italy altered the course of his life and his literary aesthetics forever, and not long after Rome would become his second home. 'Europe?' he wrote in his notebook for January 1948 while retracing his and his grandfather's earlier steps from Paris to Nice, then from Rome to Sicily, Amalfi, Naples, and eventually on to London – 'I have not yet organized my impressions'.[112]

By the end of January, Williams was in Rome, ostensibly for the sun and swimming but also, perhaps, to flee France and the French. Though his reading tastes at the time were influenced by French dramatists like Camus (*Caligula*), Sartre (*Huis clos*) and Giraudoux (*La folle de Chaillot*), in addition to a growing fascination with Einstein's theory of relativity,[113] Williams was never a great fan of the country or of its people. The Italians, however, were his cup of *grappa*, this even before he had settled down with Merlo. Williams rented an apartment on 45 via Aurora in Rome, which he now found to be the Paris of the new Lost Generation of writers. He spent more time playing than working, however, enjoying the celebrity and the wealth that he had always sought but would soon regret. He longed for the time when physical hunger spelled creative desire. He thought, given his ill health, that he would never have the energy to work on another long play. Luckily, he had had these thoughts repeatedly throughout his life. Well into the 1970s, he thought a bad cold was the first sign of death, and each play he was working on inevitably going to be his last.

Between the nightly cruising – 'Sexually it's a bull market. I have never been so full of manly vigour'[114] – and the morning writing of short stories like 'Rubio y Morena' (a thinly disguised retelling of his life with Rodriguez), Williams occupied himself with revisions of *Summer and Smoke*, which was to have its Broadway debut the following theatre season. He found a new lover, Salvatore Moresca, a seventeen-year-old Roman whom he disguised as Raffaello in his *Memoirs* and about whom he wrote the 1982 poem 'The Blond Mediterranean (A Litany)'. Rome was still reeling from World War II, and many of inhabitants were poor, such as those Williams cruised. His wealth often made him self-conscious and uncomfortable among them. He was living, to a certain extent, the parable of Sebastian Venable that he would describe later in *Suddenly Last Summer* (1959), and sexually 'devouring' the poor young men like 'items on a menu': 'This one's delicious-looking, that one is appetizing' or 'that one is *not* appetizing [...]'.[115] Guilty or not, Williams was attracted to the 'dirty' trade available to him and never let an opportunity slip by.

While in Rome, Williams used his celebrity status to engage with some of the country's famed art set. One of those was Italian filmmaker Luchino Visconti. On 7 February 1948, Williams boarded a small plane from Rome to Sicily to visit the set of *La terra trema*, a neo-realist film based on the novel *I Malavoglia* (1881) by Giovanni Verga. As Williams recalls in the *Memoirs,*

> That winter Visconti was directing a film in Sicily called *La Terra Trema* ('The Earth Trembles'), which I think is still likely his greatest work for the screen, although it is perhaps the least known. The American journalist [Donald Downes] and I flew down to Catania near which Visconti was shooting – the location was a suburb called Acitrezza [Aci Trezza]. There I met both Visconti and Zeffirelli, who was at that time a very handsome blond Florentine youth. Although an aristocrat of great inherited wealth, Visconti was an owed Communist at this time.[116]

In June, Williams published the essay 'A Movie Named *La Terra Trema'* in the magazine *'48*, favourably describing his experiences,[117] as well as the film's having placed local inhabitants in principal roles to lend the film authenticity.[118] In his notebook, however, Williams recorded an entirely different impression: 'Catania, Sicily – A letdown – the place, the people seem dirty – the film-making tedious – an hour for a single shot – And I an outsider'.[119] Williams asked Wood to submit the essay to the *New York Times* or *Harper's Bazaar*.[120] Wood did submit it to several magazines, including the *New Yorker,* 'where it was rejected for being "mannered", "phoney", and "unbelievably bad"'.[121] Success for Williams still had its limits.

Throughout the spring, Williams spent much of his time with American novelist expats, including Fredric Prokosch and Gore Vidal, with whom he travelled around Italy to Sorrento and Amalfi in a mufflerless US army jeep that Williams had bought off a GI.[122] One encounter Williams had with Gore, which he describes in his notebook and his *Memoirs,* was meeting the serene philosopher George Santayana at the Convent of the Blue Nun.[123] For the most part, though, Williams's post-*Streetcar* spring was one of convalescence. While the sex was bountiful, the work was not. 'My work was more of my life than I knew and – now', he mournfully wrote in his notebook for 7 May, just days after he learned he had won the Pulitzer Prize for *Streetcar*.[124] Donald Windham and his lover Sandy Campbell soon arrived, but Williams was no longer good company for anyone, not even Moresca. By the end of May, Margo Jones had joined them, hoping to finalize the script for the Broadway run of *Summer and Smoke*. After a brief tour of Capri, Ischia, and Sorrento in the jeep, Jones was ready to accompany Williams to London, packing up his trunk and making all their travel arrangements.[125]

Williams attended rehearsals of the London production of *The Glass Menagerie* in mid-June and then the try-outs in Brighton in July.[126] Eddie Dowling had announced to the *New York Times* plans for a London production of *The Glass Menagerie* in August 1945, but problems over British rights to the play and contractual disputes between interested American and British parties delayed its West End premiere at the Haymarket Theatre until 28 July 1948. By 8 July, Williams wrote in his notebook about his disappointment with England and its 'Snobs and hypocrites', especially director John Gielgud and actress Helen Hayes, and with the London production in general.[127] Unaware of, or uninterested in, the plight of post-war London, Williams even complained to Wood about the Cumberland Hotel where he was staying: '[...] the barest and ugliest single room that I've ever seen outside of a YMCA'.[128] Wood made sure that he was moved to the upscale Savoy, an act of snobbish petulance that was in direct opposition to his downscaling of hotels in Paris when he first landed in Europe a few months previously. What was a further insult to Williams was that H. M. Tennent Ltd, the British production unit that would later produce *Summer and Smoke*, was not covering his expenses, and the current pound-to-dollar exchange rate was not at all favourable.

Money, now that he had it, started to become a real concern. Would he get bank statements to follow his expenses? Could he deduct financial gifts from his taxes if they were used for creative projects?[129] With a reported weekly take-home pay of around $7500, Williams could afford to pay back the financial and moral debts that he had accrued over the past ten years, which he felt he could not do back in 1945 or even in 1946 after the success of *The Glass Menagerie* because of the hefty taxes that he owed.[130] As such, Williams began spreading around his wealth to those who had before helped him: 'I want to help my indigent friends as much as possible now while I have a lot of money coming in'.[131] If part of that was now trying to get Cerf to give up Random House's rights to publishing *The Glass Menagerie* so that he could repay Laughlin for all that he had done for Williams in terms of publications and fellowships, it would later include giving money (such as cheques to his grandfather), or even manuscripts of his stories (to Maria Britneva for her to sell and keep the money) and plays to friends like Windham so that they could sell them like cashed-in insurance policies.[132]

If Williams had arrived in England 'late in the week of June 6', he was now 'escap[ing] from England' on 25 July and heading to Paris, missing opening night, just as he would years later the London premiere of *Camino Real*.[133] His apologetic letter to Hayes tried to account for his sudden flight with a fantastic story about his 'pixy behavior' and nervousness and black-outs and missed flights, but it was clear from the beginning of his stay there that he had no intention of suffering through the premiere.[134] In Paris, he took two rooms at the Hôtel de l'Université in the Saint-Germain des Près quarter in Paris. He was to meet Jean Cocteau, who wanted the French rights to *Streetcar*. Stanley, Cocteau thought, would be the perfect acting vehicle for his lover, Jean Marais.

Williams recalls in his *Memoirs* having met 'quite a lot of artists' in Paris that summer of 1948 but was 'most interested in meeting Jean-Paul Sartre, whose existential philosophy appealed to [him] strongly, as did his play *Huit* [*sic*] *Clos*'.[135] In a 1953 letter to Brooks Atkinson, Williams expounded upon this anecdote:

> Apparently he has no use for me. In the summer of 1948 I gave a cocktail party for theatrical friends in Paris and sent him a long wire, inviting him, to which he didn't respond, and during the party I heard he was in a bar nearby and dispatched a French writer to bring him over. He assured the writer he would come, but a short while later he strolled by my hotel without even looking up.[136]

Out of what can only be attributed to his bitterness for having been snubbed by Sartre in Paris, and for his rather lacklustre first meeting with him at the Hotel Nacional in Havana in October 1960, Williams said of Sartre in a 1965 interview with John Gruen: 'Perhaps we all understood existentialism before Sartre did'.[137]

By August, he boarded the *Queen Mary* with Truman Capote, with Williams recalling in his *Memoirs* their rather mischievous behaviour with a Bishop during the crossing.[138] Williams was heading back to New York for rehearsals of *Summer and Smoke*, which later opened at the Music Box Theatre on 6 October to a rather lukewarm reception. Williams instinctively knew that the play was not great in its present state. A few months later, while re-crossing the Atlantic to Europe, he wrote in his notebook,

> So far I have never failed to push a thing through to some kind of completion if I determined that I should. Not even 'Summer and Smoke' the whole history of which was fraught with the most abysmal discouragement: abandoned five or six times, I nevertheless picked it up again each time and went doggedly on with it, and the result is a play that is good enough to impress some people – not

myself, not many but <u>some</u> – as the best of the four long plays I've had presented. Someday, somewhere is the end.[139]

That 'end' came a few years later in the rewrite of *Summer and Smoke*, titled *The Eccentricities of a Nightingale*, the version he had hoped would open in London in August 1951 but which would have to wait another twenty-five years before its New York premiere.

If there was any consolation in Williams's life that autumn, it was stumbling again into Frank Merlo on East 58th Street in New York City. In Merlo, Williams discovered a partner with whom he could get 'those colored lights going inside my brain!'[140] Williams did not really want a long-term relationship at this time, evident in his arrangement with Moresca to stay every other night, so that he could cruise. But Merlo was a calming force in Williams's life, which he did need, providing a stable environment for Williams in which he could renew his creative energy. Over the next year, while again in Rome and Sicily, that energy would be responsible for the novel *The Roman Spring of Mrs. Stone* and the play *The Rose Tattoo*, his love-letter to the world. Back in May 1947, Williams had written to Irene Selznick, 'Love cannot be discounted, even in a hardboiled profession, as one of the magic factors in success'.[141] Love, and often its failures in life, would become another dominant theme of his work throughout the next decade, but it did not always guarantee him success. If Williams's prior success was not entirely tarnished in the years to come, it had certainly begun now to lose a bit of its lustre with the critics.

6
Rome to Rome (via Nearly Everywhere Else): 'Comfortable Little Mercies'

In early December 1948, Williams and Merlo boarded the *Vulcania* from New York headed for Gibraltar, and then Tangier, where they met Jane and Paul Bowles, before moving on to Marseilles and then to Rome. Ten months later, they returned to New York via Naples on the *Saturnia*, which represented Williams's longest stay outside of America to date. In northern Africa, they toured for three weeks: two weeks in Tangier, and then another one in Fez and Casablanca. In Rome, they stayed at the apartment on via Aurora that Williams had rented the previous year. In the notebook which he kept during the crossing, which he called his 'Log Book', Williams detailed his thoughts and feelings about his recent success and the company of retainers it drew to him. He wondered if he would ever write another great play, conscious now of the fact that he needed to conserve his money just in case the answer was no. He tried writing but was rarely satisfied with the results. Only life's 'comfortable little mercies'[1] were seeing him through from day to day. Ironically, it would be these creature comforts that would gradually take its toll on his creative energies.

The jet-set life began wearing on Williams, and a brief stay in March 1949 at the spas on the island of Ischia, where the 'Ischia shits'[2] Truman Capote, W. H. Auden, Chester Kallman, and 'various other of the spiteful sisterhood'[3] were also staying, soon depressed the playwright. He was working on several plays at once – *The Rose Tattoo*, *Camino Real*, and 'The Big Time Operators', his 'political play' about Huey Long that would eventual evolve into *Sweet Bird of Youth*[4] – as well as a novel, *The Roman Spring of Mrs. Stone*, which he referred to for the time being with the punning title 'Moon of Pause'. None of his writing, however, was going particularly well. He would later admit to Kazan in a 12 July 1949 letter that 'The simple truth is that I haven't known where to go since Streetcar'. None of his characters or his plays' ideas interested him enough to 'push [them] through to completion'.[5]

In April, he was in Paris, then in London for the English run of *Streetcar*, meeting Laurence Olivier and his wife Vivien Leigh, who would eventually be chosen over Jessica Tandy to reincarnate Blanche on screen. When major works were proving unproductive, Williams often turned to minor works, such as essays, poems, and stories. In addition to pieces like 'On the Art of Being a True Non-conformist' (1948), an 'Introduction' (1950) to Carson McCullers's *Reflections in a Golden Eye*, and 'A Writer's Quest for a Parnassus' (1950), he wrote poems such as 'Counsel', 'The Soft Cry', and 'The Eyes', published together as 'Three Poems' in *New Directions in Prose and Poetry Eleven* in December 1949. He also wrote stories and worked on a new comedy called 'The Eclipse of May 29, 1919', which would eventually become 'Stornello' and then *The Rose Tattoo*. By May, he was back in Rome. His growing addiction to barbiturates made him sluggish, and his work production waned. He had also admitted to Kazan in his 12 July letter that he felt his new writing was 'so much about the same thing' he had written before, and he was struggling to find a way out. The letter was in response to Kazan's refusal to direct *The Rose Tattoo*, which greatly troubled Williams.

The 1950s opened with difficulties for Williams on many fronts, and it would close with them as well. In between, he filled his time with writing, with love, with productions, and of course with travel. He would eventually complete *The Rose Tattoo*, which premiered on 3 February 1951 at the Martin Beck Theatre on Broadway, and then flesh out his 'Mexican fantasy' into the full-length play, *Camino Real*, which opened on Broadway at the National Theatre on 19 March 1953 but closed a failure on 9 May. In his pre-opening piece for *The Rose Tattoo*, 'The Timeless World of a Play', which Williams published in the *New York Times* on 14 January 1951, he wrote of his quest for a balance between life and immortality, a theme that had more to do with immortal figures who haunt *Camino Real* than with those 'Dionysian', 'quicksilver' characters who populate *The Rose Tattoo*:

> Whether or not we admit it to ourselves, we are all haunted by a truly awful sense of impermanence [...]. Snatching the eternal out of the desperately fleeting is the great magic trick of human existence. As far as we know, [...] there is no way to beat the game of *being* against *non-being*, in which non-being is the predestined victor on realistic levels.[6]

Any doubts about his lost talent were soon countered with the enormous success of *Cat on a Hot Tin Roof*, which won him his second
Pulitzer Prize in 1955. But the spectre of failure returned with *Orpheus
Descending* (1957) and *Sweet Bird of Youth* (1959), two plays he struggled
with collectively for over two decades.

All told, Williams would experience highs and lows in each new production, more extremely than he had in the previous decade, and this
chapter is dedicated to recounting those successes and failures in his
life and work. He would write some of his best stories and plays during
these years, but also some of his worst, and the inconsistency in his life
and his art would take an enormous toll on his physical and mental
health. If life's 'little mercies' were precious to him at the start of the
decade, he would need each one of them even more by the end. Though
he was not yet on the downward slide that he would experience in the
1960s, Williams knew success's peaks and troughs repeatedly, and only
love – or at least sex – seemed to pull him through it all.

In February or March 1949, McCullers had written to Williams, asking
him to write the preface to the New Directions's edition of her novel
Reflections in a Golden Eye, first published in 1941 by Houghton Mifflin.
McCullers was one of Williams's closest friends by now, partly because
she was a Southern writer of the Gothic strain like himself, but mostly
because she reminded him of Rose. He wrote at this time two long
prefaces to the novel, 'Praise for an Assenting Angel', the opening lines
of Rilke's Tenth *Duino Elegies*, and 'This Book'.[7] In a letter to McCullers
from Napoli on 23 March 1950, Williams wrote, 'I got the copies of
"Reflections" from both you and Laughlin. It seems absurd for me to
write a preface to a great work by such a completely established writer
and I should feel almost embarrassed to try, but I will try if you really
want me to [...]'.[8]

The introduction, and the many drafts that led to it, detail a Williams
who began using his essays about other writers to shore up the flanks
of his own literary reputation. Here, his discussion about McCullers's
'Sense of Dreadfulness' as being 'anything sensible or visible or even,
strictly, materially, *knowable*'[9] is a defence for his own glorification of
violence in his work, which critics would begin underlining in their
assessments of his work. The Sartrean '*mystery*' that he notes here would
serve him later in defending Brick's 'mystery', which was at the centre
of several attacks levelled against him, his famed 'bird' stage direction in
Cat on a Hot Tin Roof, as well as the 'mystery' of his own life documented
in *Memoirs*.[10] In 'Some Words of Introduction', another draft version of

the essay, Williams talks about the 'derivative talents that have flooded the literary scene in America', and in 'Praise for an Assenting Angel' he writes of 'the derivative talents that have boisterously flooded our literary scene', which is the phrase that appears in the final essay.[11] These were Williams's veiled attacks against Truman Capote and Gore Vidal, whom Williams told McCullers in March 1948 were 'infected with that awful competitive spirit and [seem] to be haunted over the successes or achievements of other writers [...]'.[12] The 'a book a year' comment echoes Williams's review of Paul Bowles's *The Sheltering Sky*, titled 'An Allegory of Man and his Sahara' (1949), which he wrote a couple of months later. In fact, in all of his other introductions to the book of fellow writers – 'Foreword' (1950) to Marian Gallaway's *Constructing a Play*; 'Foreword' (1950) to Oliver Evans's *Young Man with a Screwdriver*; 'Some Words Before' (1954) to Gilbert Maxwell's *Go Looking*;[13] and 'If the Writing Is Honest' (1958) to William Inge's *The Dark at the Top of the Stairs* – Williams talks as much about himself and his own developing troubles with audiences and critics as he does about the writer whose work he is apparently praising. Non-fiction prose was becoming his best line of defence against the mounting criticism against him and his work.

When Williams and Merlo returned to the States at the end of the summer of 1949, he was in the middle of two film negotiations, *The Glass Menagerie*, directed by Irving Rapper for Warner Brothers, and *Streetcar*, which would bring most of the major actors of the stage version to the screen, again under Kazan's direction. Williams had little desire to work on the script for *The Glass Menagerie*, seeing that Hollywood was rewriting the quiet tragedy to give it a happy ending – a strange twist given that Williams had already flirted with this denouement in 'The Pretty Trap'. Disgusted, he and Merlo left Los Angeles and headed for Key West via St Louis, collecting along the way the nearly blind and deaf Reverend Dakin, who was now his surrogate father. In Key West, the three of them lived at 1431 Duncan Street, a cottage Williams first rented and then purchased a year later, mostly for his grandfather, who loved the 'Conch' city. The winter there proved beneficial, despite the depressants Williams was taking more regularly, for he begun a darkly humorous novella, 'The Knightly Quest' (1966), which he would complete years later, and had finished the first draft of *The Rose Tattoo* in January 1950, which combined his new interest in Sicily with Frank and his continued obsession with Rose, whom he had moved the previous year out of Farmington and into private care.[14]

Cheryl Crawford announced that she would produce *The Rose Tattoo* for the following season. In a December letter to Donald Windham, Williams explained how writing the new play exhausted him:

> Ordinarily my ratio of concerns is something like this: 50% work and worry over work, 35% the perpetual struggle against lunacy (neuras-thenia, hypochondria, anxiety feelings, Etc.) 15% a very true and ten-der love for those who have been and are close to me as friends and as lover. But at a time like the recent time there is a great dislocation and the ratio changes to something like this: Work and worry over work, 89%: struggle against lunacy (partly absorbed in the first category) ten percent, very true and tender love for lover and friends, 1%.[15]

By 20 May 1950, he and Merlo were heading back to Europe on the *Ile de France* with Jane Lawrence. After arriving in Plymouth on 26 May, they quickly moved on to Paris, then to Rome and Vienna in July.

In Paris, they met Carson McCullers and dined with Anna Magnani, for whom Williams had written the role of Serafina delle Rose.[16] Williams began courting her to accept the role.[17] Magnani loved the play and the role but refused to accept it because she already had acting engagements for the year (she was to act in *Bellissima*) and was not at all confident in her English.[18] After months of negotiations, she finally pulled out of the role. Eventually, Maureen Stapleton would incarnate Serafina for the Broadway production.

In late June, he and Merlo headed south to Sicily, before taking up per-manent summer residence in Rome. The July publication of *The Roman Spring of Mrs. Stone*, whose affronts to Catholic morality would later get Williams into trouble with the posh Roman club Circolo de Golfo,[19] provoked their trip to Vienna, escaping the pursuit of Roman reporters seeking an interview. Back in Rome again, the results were not much better. In a 19 July 1950 entry in his notebook, Williams wrote,

> this Roman period has all the defects of the one before and very little of the occasional charm. I blame this on myself, my failure to lose myself in really satisfactory work, lack of accomplishment, dis-appointment in the play overshadowing the whole ambient of my present life.[20]

The play was *The Rose Tattoo*, and he was struggling to find its focus after having completed the first draft months earlier. Days later, he added, 'How infinitely <u>wrong</u> this Roman period has turned out!'[21]

It was during this time that he also wrote, with all of its irony, the essay 'A Writer's Quest for a Parnassus', published in the *New York Times Magazine* on 13 August 1950. In it, he describes the perfect place that writers choose in which to write. '[W]riting is actually a violent activity,' he explains, and 'writers, when they are not writing, must find some outer violence that is equivalent, or nearly, to the inner one they are used to'.[22] Williams said American writers like himself left the United States because their writing places became exhausted and, he added only half jokingly, because they needed to escape the House on UnAmerican Activities Committee (HUAC) hearings. In line with his view of Rome as the Paris of the Lost Generation 1920s (before he had thought it was to be Mexico City), Williams described the via Veneto like Montparnasse and the Jicky Club and the Caffè Notturno as the Roman versions of the Café de Flore and the Deux Magots. Alas, Rome – overrun by pilgrims responding to a papal bull by Pope Pius XII, declaring 1950 a Holy Year of pilgrimage to Rome, a tradition dating back 650 years – was not his Parnassus that summer, nor the previous one, nor the next.

An invitation by Charles Feldman, who was producing the film version of *Streetcar*, to come to Hollywood to see the project through was welcome news for the weary playwright. He was revising the screenplay of *A Streetcar Named Desire* to meet the censorship demands of the Production Code, then headed by Joseph Breen. He was also working on revisions for *The Rose Tattoo*, which would have its try-out in Chicago on 29 December 1950. In the notebook entry for 30 January 1951, he wrote, 'and again I wait for the opening of a new play "The Rose Tattoo". Anxiety over all these weeks has made me ill and sleepless'.[23] As he described in one of his rare interpretations of his plays, 'The Meaning of *The Rose Tattoo*', Williams wanted the play not to be 'a noose but a net with fairly wide meshes',[24] but it turned out to be a bit of both. A few days later, he confessed to Brooks Atkinson, 'Now that it is over, the waiting, I can tell you that I was scared out of my wits, as I knew that a sense of defeat at this point might have been altogether insurmountable'.[25] *The Rose Tattoo* received a rather lukewarm reception by the critics but was a moderate success on Broadway, winning the Tony Award.

In May 1951, Williams passed through New York and 'dropped by the Actors' [*sic*] Studio [where] Kazan was conducting an exercise with Eli Wallach and Barbara Baxley and some other student actors – and they were performing *Ten Blocks on the Camino Real*':

I realized that Audrey had been altogether mistaken [i.e., her telling him to shelve it], that it played remarkably well, and I said,

'Oh, Kazan, we must do this [...].' He was very excited about the idea and we exchanged letters about all that summer (when I was in Rome, and he was in New York).[26]

Later that month, Williams and Merlo were again en route for Europe. However, this third consecutive summer in Europe – London, Munich and Venice were added to the traditional itinerary, where all of Williams's *viae* led to Rome – was to be as unproductive as the previous two, and Williams's nerves quickly deteriorated. He was taking more depressants to help him fight his insomnia, but the effect was not working. If there was one bright spot, it came from the first draft of a short story he wrote while joining Merlo in Venice, 'Three Players of a Summer Game'. He would continue it the following summer, publish an expurgated version of it in *The New Yorker*, and dramatize it into a one-act play that would later become *Cat on a Hot Tin Roof*. The first ending of the story has Mary Louis and the narrator catching fireflies in a jar, an image he had used in *The Rose Tattoo*. The incident recalled his childhood summer nights with Rose in Mississippi, as described in his poem 'The Couple', published years later in the collection *Androgyne, Mon Amour* (1977).

Between the heat and the insomnia, Williams felt the need to escape Rome – again. His first attempt failed when he crashed his Jaguar on the outskirts of the city. He was heading toward the Costa Brava of Spain, as he told Audrey Wood (he told Maria Britneva that it was St Tropez), but a sudden panic struck him, and he wound up driving the car into a tree at seventy miles per hour to avoid hitting a truck.[27] He suffered only light causalities, which included his portable typewriter hitting him in the head. Poetic justice for writer's block, if there ever was one. He eventually did make his way out of Rome and went on to Paris. Life with Merlo was already growing intense, though. Merlo, who had wanted a stable and monogamous relationship, could not stand Williams's frequent infidelities. Williams would later express his feeling about these affairs in a July 1952 entry in his notebook: 'My attitude is that "romps in the hay" – "trade" – no matter how often – within reasonable limits – is fair and sensible in a homosexual alliance of long standing but that if one or the other starts cultivating close and extended intimacy with a third party, then it becomes a cheat, and someone is the "The Patsy"'.[28] Hypocritically, Williams grew increasingly angry at Merlo when he responded to Williams's infidelities in like kind. Earlier that summer, Merlo had fled to Vienna, leaving Williams to his despondency and insomnia in Venice. Eventually, Merlo returned to Rome, but Williams went north to Paris alone, staying at the Hôtel du Pont Royal instead of his preferred Hôtel de l'Université. He then continued on to London to see Maria Britneva and to get his typewriter repaired, before flying back to Paris that August. With a working typewriter and a dislodged writer's block, Williams again set about to work.

In Rome that summer of 1951, Williams worked steadily on an entirely new version of *Summer and Smoke*, which he later titled *The Eccentricities of a Nightingale*. He was hoping that the current London production would use this version, which he later felt was superior to the original. But the writing was still too fresh, and Williams rarely liked today what he wrote yesterday. He continued to be disappointed in his work that summer, writing in his notebook on 9 August: 'The experience of reading over the "New S. & S." was a staggering blow. Probably the worst job I've ever done. Quite pitiful'.[29] Nonetheless he submitted it to John Perry at H M Tennent in London, writing to Wood on 23 August: 'I completed a first draft of the new "Summer and Smoke" (it has a different title and is almost a completely new play) but I have an idea Tennent will prefer to do the old one'.[30] Williams then wrote in his notebook on 29 August that he feared Perry was not 'very serious about the new version (or old one) of "Summer"' and that he would not produce *The Rose Tattoo* either. On 16 September, he wrote to himself, 'Rome again, [...] although my work hasn't really revived, and although they didn't like the new version of "S. & S." and are doing the old one – still the world is tolerable, and even pleasant sometimes'.[31]

Williams's predictions were correct: Tennent did produce the old version of *Summer and Smoke* at the Lyric in Hammersmith on 22 November, not because they did not like *The Eccentricities of a Nightingale* but because rehearsal was already under way on *Summer and Smoke* and producing the new version would not only delay the opening but increase production costs. To a certain extent, Williams's own predictions about his new version were wrong. *The Eccentricities of a Nightingale* would have to wait a quarter of a century before its premiere, and, when it did see the lights of Broadway, it was quickly chased off the stage. A play's 'artistic purity' need not rest only within its words, plastic or otherwise, and Williams surely should have understood that.[32] For *Summer and Smoke*, though closer to a medieval morality play than to contemporary American melodrama, was 'purer' in the artistic sense than its rewrite. Although Margo Jones could not tap into its plastic beauty in her October 1948 production, José Quintero's 1952 revival certainly did. Quintero's production of *Summer and Smoke* at the Circle in the Square Theatre in Greenwich not only rewarded Williams with a success he was denied four years earlier, but it also gave birth to Off Broadway. Perhaps the more important lesson that Williams and others in the theatre world, namely producers and drama critics, discovered with *Summer and Smoke* was that a Broadway production should no longer provide the sole litmus test of a play's success.

By early September 1951, Williams was off to Scandinavia to view the various openings there of *The Rose Tattoo*, and Merlo accompanied him to Copenhagen. Williams described in a letter to Cheryl Crawford on 8 September that the play was very well done, though privately he wondered why he went there in the first place.[33] Williams returned to Rome by mid-September. At the end of the month, he flew up to Paris and met Maria Britneva for a shopping spree with his royalty francs from Cocteau's *Un tramway nommé Désir*. With Merlo arriving in tow (he was driving up from Rome, the Jaguar having been repaired), Williams cruised the Parisian streets and brought home one night a 'beautiful dancer' but was so 'intimidated' that he could do nothing with him.[34] Soon, Williams was distressed again, this time by the fact that the one story he wrote that unproductive summer, that 'one accomplishment' – 'Three Players' – was dull, dull!': 'And I hit the bottom! The old familiar rock bottom—'.[35]

They continued on to London at the beginning of October because Williams wanted to observe the Peter Glenville production of *Summer and Smoke*, which turned out to be a hit. He stayed first at the Montalembert hotel, before moving back into his suite at the Cavendish, where he had stayed the previous August. After spending nearly a month in England, Williams left just days before the London premiere.[36] Despite a rather dry summer, creatively speaking, he was able to write one good play, *Something Unspoken*, about the sublimated love between two women, in addition to 'Three Players of a Summer Game', which proved to be anything but dull.

Williams and Merlo sailed back to New York with Elia Kazan on the *Queen Elizabeth* on 7 November, and Williams continued working on *Camino Real*, trying to get Brando to accept the role of Kilroy. In October 1951, Williams wrote in his notebook: 'A letter from Kazan. He is really serious about doing "Camino Real" and that makes me feel much better about going back to America'.[37] Thanksgiving took place in St Louis in the presence of his brother, though his grandfather had already fled to Memphis. Williams then collected the Reverend there, and they, along with the Kazans, went south to Clarksdale, Williams's childhood home town. Kazan wanted to take in scenes of the Delta as he was preparing a film based on several of Williams's one-act plays.

Williams and his grandfather spent Christmas in New Orleans with Oliver Evans – Williams's first visit there in years. They stayed a few days at the Hotel Monteleone in the Quarter before continuing onto Key West. Merlo was to drive the Jaguar that was shipped from London to New York south and meet them at their 1431 Duncan bungalow. In addition to preparing poems for publication with New Directions at this time, Williams was working, as he told Cheryl Crawford and Maria Britneva in separate February letters, on a film script that combined several short plays of his, including *Twenty-seven Wagons Full of Cotton* and *The Long Stay Cut Short, or The Unsatisfactory Supper*.[38] When work was not going well (Williams pleaded with Kazan to send him a writer to help him with the script), Wood sent Paul Bigelow down to Key West. The 'incredible' Bigelow, as Williams often referred to him,[39] frequently served as Williams's amanuensis, typing up his spoken dialogue and helping him complete the script. The film would eventually become the scandalous *Baby Doll* (1956), which Kazan would not shoot that April as planned given his recent testimony before HUAC.

Like 1946, the year 1952 proved to be a banner year for Williams. The film version of *Streetcar* took home several honours at the 24th Academy Awards, including best actress (Vivien Leigh), best supporting actor (Karl Malden), and best supporting actress (Kim Hunter); it lost best picture and best screenplay to *An American in Paris* and best actor to Humphrey Bogart in *The African Queen*. *Summer and Smoke* was now the toast of New York theatre critics and audiences. And Williams, along with Carson McCullers and Eudora Welty, was elected into the American Academy of Arts and Letters. Still working on the film script for *Baby Doll* and the play *Camino Real*, Williams returned to the story 'Three Players of a Summer Game' that he had begun the previous summer in Venice, informing Wood in a 14 April letter that he thought he might publish it in a collection with New Directions.[40]

By early June, he and Merlo were again heading to Europe aboard the SS *Liberté*. They disembarked at Le Havre before heading south to Paris, where he met with the self-exiled Kazan to discuss *Camino Real* and with Magnani again to discuss her incarnating Serafina in the film version of *The Rose Tattoo*, which Audrey Wood had just sold to Hal Wallis at Paramount for $100,000. While in Paris, Williams visited McCullers and her husband Reeves at their 'Ancienne Presbyterre', located in the village of Bachvillers on the outskirts of the city. He and Merlo then proceeded to Rome to seal the film role with Magnani in *The Rose Tattoo*. The blistering summer heat there, however, sent him packing to Hamburg at the end of July for a week, and then later to Munich in August to see Kazan, who was directing *Man on a Tightrope* there. Whether it was the effects of the stifling clime on his muse or the promise of Bavarian trade on his insatiable sex drive, Williams was extremely restless this summer in Europe. The cooler weather and his '3 lays – none memorable' accounted for the 'pleasant' week in Hamburg that provided 'a good change';[41] both were part of Williams's needed 'little mercies' that got him through his depression at this time when work on *Camino Real* was not going well.

Williams worked hard on *Camino Real*, reading Casanova's memoirs, Alexandre Dumas's novel *Camille*, and Cervantes's *Don Quixote*. The play was finally taking shape, and, with Kazan now officially inked in as its director, Williams had little reason to be unhappy, though plagued he was by depression and insomnia. His notebook entries for the summer tell the story of a playwright of two of the nation's best plays of the century worrying about whether or not he was a good writer. The only other 'little' mercy he had was following the recent fallout from Kazan's testimony at the April HUAC hearings and reading Henry L. Luce's 'revoltingly interesting publication',[42] *Time* magazine, which made itself the official mouthpiece of the anticommunist league, whose knight errant was Senator Joseph McCarthy.

Despite Kazan's having named names that April about his former Communist activities, Williams did not spurn him as others had done and would do for years to come. Perhaps Williams empathized with Kazan's sudden 'fugitive' status in America, always having fought alongside those who society casts out; perhaps Williams just wanted to hitch his plays onto that Kazan wagon of success. Williams was not naive of the risks his association with Kazan might bring him – the Breen office was already making trouble for them with declaring the *Baby Doll* script as immoral for the screen – and he had always been politically minded without ever being politically active. But *Camino Real* was now becoming as much a veiled defence of Kazan (Williams's eventually dedicated the play to him) as it was an open attack against HUAC in particular and America's post-war anticommunist hysteria in general. Williams had indirectly prepared audiences for the play's political leanings in his 1948 essay 'On the Art of Being a True Non-conformist', republished as the introduction 'Something Wild ...' to the collection *27 Wagons Full of Cotton and Other One-act Plays* in 1953:

Today we are living in a world which is threatened by totalitarianism. The Fascist and the Communist states have thrown us into a panic of reaction. Reactionary opinion descends like a ton of bricks on the head of any artist who speaks out against the current of prescribed ideas. We are all under wraps of one kind or another, trembling before the spectre of investigating committees and even with Buchenwald in the back of our minds when we consider whether or not we dare to say we were for Henry Wallace. *Yes, it is as bad as that.*[43]

This was the political climate that Williams grafted onto the Mexican myth he had first envisioned with *Ten Blocks on the Camino Real* in 1945–46. Now six years later, in returning to the play, Williams's political aspersions against Whittaker Chamber (for his role in the Alger Hiss affair), Richard Nixon (for his role in HUAC), and Luce (for his increasing hostility to the American left) began fusing with his romantic idealism present in the play's fugitive heroes.

It seemed as if Williams were again living in the year 1936–37. The only difference now was that he finally did have the clout to make certain changes in society once expressed in his plays *Fugitive Kind, Candles to the Sun*, and *Not about Nightingales*. While it may be true, as W. H. Auden famously noted, that poetry never 'saved a single Jew', equally true is that statement's corollary: certain poetry did help expedite the Holocaust. One need only to think of Leni Riefenstalh's poetic images in her 1934 documentary *Triumph des Willens* (*Triumph of the Will*), or those in any of the propagandist literature that came out of the Third Reich before and during the war, to understand the power of the plastic word to move society, for good or for ill. Williams believed in earnest that *Camino Real* would have a similar affect upon a narcotized America, delivering it from its current obsession with what he saw as Fascism.

In late August 1952, Williams was reading Chamber's account of the trial, *Witness*, and was awed and disgusted with the general anti-left direction America had taken after the New Deal helped pull it out of the Depression. But the Cold War was underway, and its conservative backlash was strong, which prodded Williams to see *Camino Real* brought to the stage sooner more so than later.[44] In a 26 August entry in his notebook, Williams wrote, 'Intellectuals and liberals are more and more openly the real target of [the] Luce gang'.[45] A few days earlier, Williams had written to Kazan about his political thoughts and their relationship to the play:

Current issue of 'Time'. ... They are taking the gloves off. The Divine Nixon on the cover! He looks like the gradeschool bully that used to wait for me behind a broken fence and twist my ear to make me say obscene things. [...] What does 'left-wingism' mean to the Luce gang except a free and enlightened and humane and <u>articulate</u> voice of America? Finished 'Witness' with a feeling of awe. The episode of the microfilm in the pumpkin, the receptacle with lethal chemicals and damp-towel, somehow missing fire – couldn't read the directions because of bad eyesight, towel fell off in his sleep – is quite sufficient in itself to put the whole business in the 'Ritz Men ONLY.' Jesus, what's going on?! Nixon has also come out for McCarthy! Will support his candidacy without necessarily endorsing all his views, and says Eisenhower will, too. We must get to the States for this election, Brother ... [Postscript] Burn this letter, or hide it in a pumpkin![46]

The 'Ritz Men Only Hotel' in *Camino Real* was Williams's (and Kazan's) vision of the Fascist regime currently running America, and the play would be their equivalent to Arthur Miller's *The Crucible*, which also opened on Broadway at the start of the new year and to which *Camino Real* would inevitably be compared (often losing in the comparison). Kazan had little to gain beyond face in their play's political gambit, but Williams, always worried about his next production, had everything to lose. For whatever the reason, and it was surely a gamble on Williams's part, he stuck by Kazan, and they maintained a working relationship throughout the decade, bringing Williams another Pulitzer Prize with *Cat on a Hot Tin Roof* in 1955.

At the beginning of October, Williams returned to New York with Merlo via London on the *Queen Mary* and began working again on *Battle of Angels*, having written the poem 'Orpheus Descending' (1952) the previous year. Production for *Camino Real* was also now in full swing, once Kazan returned to New York that November. By Christmas, Williams was back in Key West with Merlo, Edwina, the Reverend Dakin, and a new English bulldog, Mr Moon. In February, Williams returned to New York to prepare for the premiere of *Camino Real*, which opened on 19 March to notices that spewed '[i]nvective[s] and ridicule', with John Chapman writing in the *New York Daily News* that it was 'an enormous jumble of five-cent philosophy, $3.98 words, ballet, music, symbolism, allegory, pretentiousness, portentousness, lackwit humor, existentialism and overall bushwah'.[47] Hardly the response Williams had wanted but rightly had predicted. The nation was still under the Fascist's thumb, be it in New York or Washington, DC.

Camino Real closed an utter failure on 9 May, and many well wishers, including Edith Sitwell, sent Williams letters of condolences. No one, including Williams's erstwhile supporters, understood the play. Even Walter Kerr admonished Williams not to head 'toward the cerebral': 'don't do it. What makes you an artist of the first rank is your intuitive gift for penetrating reality, without junking reality in the process'.[48] Not surprisingly, Williams fled New York, flying to Houston, where he directed (and apparently rewrote dialogue for) Donald Windham's play, *The Starless Air*, before spending quality time with his grandfather in Memphis. In his programme note to Windham's play, Williams called it an attempt to create a theatre 'of sensibility' on par with the 'novel of sensibility'.[49] He and Merlo then boarded the SS *United States* bound for Le Havre on 5 June, arriving there three days later.[50]

That summer of 1953, his and Merlo's relationship remained strained, as it had been the previous year in Rome. They often punished each other with frequent one-night stands. Now staying at a new residence in Rome at 11 via Firenze, near the Teatro dell'Opera, Merlo took up again with his lover of the previous summer, Alvaro, and Williams called Moresca back to his bed. Growing tired of 'this Roman period already',[51] Williams decided to head to Spain alone. He was at work on the revision of *Battle of Angels* and a play based on a story begun in 1942 (*Kingdom of Earth*), as well as on the film script for *Baby Doll*, now called 'Hide and Seek'. Before leaving for Barcelona (his first attempt via ship from Naples had to be scrapped due to the expiration of his car's papers), Williams had arranged to meet with Luchino Visconti, whose film *La terra trema* Williams had written about back in 1948 and who had directed the Italian premieres of Williams's *Zoo di vetro* and *Un tram che si chiama desiderio* in 1945 and 1949, respectively. Their meeting concerned English dialogue that Visconti wanted Williams to write for his film *Senso* (1954). Williams really wanted no part of the deal and privately told Paul Bowles in a 22 June letter that he would turn over directly to him his two weeks' salary of $1000 for the contracted dialogue.[52]

Williams flew to Barcelona in mid-July with Bowles's lover, Ahmed Yacoubi, a Moroccan painter (Yacoubi could not get a visa to drive through France[53]), leaving Merlo in Rome in what appeared to be another serious separation between them. As was his *modus operandi* without Merlo, Williams divided his time equally between writing, swimming, cruising – in that order – working on what would soon be called *Orpheus Descending*.[54] Like Sebastian Venable in *Suddenly Last Summer*, he was procuring young Spanish men on La Playa San Sebastián, a popular beach club on the outskirts of Barcelona. Conversing in his broken French, he met the young Spanish director, Antonio de Cabo, who managed the Teatro de Cámara that had produced *El zoo de cristal* and *Un tranvía llamado Deseo* (1947 and 1948). The sex was welcomed, but it did not ease his loneliness. Williams badly needed friends to fill the time between his work and his lovers. His on-again/off-again admiration for Maria Britneva soon occupied his mind. Since he had promised to bring her down to Spain, 'as it is cheap there', he wanted to get in touch with her, admitting to himself that, though generally fun to be around, she was 'really so expensive' to keep with him.[55] As he had often done in these early years, Williams travelled on letters of credit on which he could draw money. At one point during the summer, he claimed the letter was stolen, but in all likelihood he had simply lost it, or had misplaced it among his belongings, something he frequently did with his money.

By the end of July, he was back in Rome, joined there now by Britneva (who was not invited this time to Spain in the end[56]) and Paul Bowles and his entourage that included Yacoubi and their chauffeur.[57] He travelled with Britneva that August down to Naples, then to Positano, and then finally in September to Verona, where he continued work on *Orpheus Descending*. During this time, Williams also wrote the story 'Man Bring This Up Road', which would become *The Milk Train Doesn't Stop Here Anymore*; began preliminary work on *Cat on a Hot Tin Roof*; and was obliged to provide Visconti with dialogue for *Senso* since the director was dissatisfied with Bowles's writing.[58] At the end of October, he was to travel to Helsinki to see the Finnish productions of *The Rose Tattoo* and *The Glass Menagerie* and to give a talk at the university.[59] But the northern clime (with its blond young men) did not appeal to him at the moment, and he, Merlo and Bowles drove their Jaguars down south to Madrid, Grenada, and Malaga before crossing over to Tangier. During the two-week trip, Williams felt that the 'dried tortured country' personified his burned out self. He could no longer write and looked instead, as he had done a few years earlier, to 'the little animal comforts of simple existence'.[60]

Despite all of his past success, Williams remained a lonely and unconfident man and playwright this past summer. Six to eight hours' work done the previous day would be reread in horror and discarded. Repeatedly, he would disparage the writing, believing himself to be a washed up writer by the age of forty-two. 'What troubles me most,' he wrote in his notebook in October 1953, 'is not just the lifeless quality of the writing, its lack of distinction, but a real confusion that seems to exist, nothing carried through to completion but written over and over, as if a panicky hen running in circles'.[61] Though he was talking about an early draft of *Cat on a Hot Tin Roof*, these words could have applied to most everything he wrote after *Streetcar*. A month prior, he had confessed in his notebook, '(What fearful admission do I have to make, that after "Streetcar" I haven't been able to write anymore except by a terrible wrenching of the brain and nerves?)'.[62] In a 14 October letter to Audrey Wood, discussing his revisions to *Battle of Angels* for *Orpheus Descending*, he even admitted, 'Unfortunately in 1940 I was a younger and stronger and – curiously! – more confident writer that I am in the Fall of 1953'.[63]

Most of his notebook entries over the past few years document his continued ill-health, his dreams of Rose (one even semi-erotic), his loneliness and insatiable sexual appetite, his dependency on Seconals – or 'pinkies' as he often referred to them – his crotchety behaviour toward Merlo and other friends, and his creative exhaustion. His letter writing during the period was a bit more upbeat, however. He wrote mostly about his need for productions and publications, but he also wrote about his problems with Merlo. It was easier to see, during this dark period, why he longed for the simpler times of Acapulco or Laguna Beach or Provincetown before the celebrity, the money, and the many retainers (many of whom he asked to join him) began souring his disposition on life and on love. By late October/early November 1953, depression had taken its toll on Williams, and he returned to New York with Merlo on the *Andrea Doria*, feeling that he had not written anything of substance that summer to pave his triumphant return to Broadway.

Or to Hollywood, for that matter. Williams left New York with Mike Steen, a New Orleans friend he had met through Bill Gray. They moved around quite a bit – Philadelphia, Pittsburgh, and Columbus (OH) – before passing through St Louis to see his grandfather, who was now ninety-six years old. Rose had just been brought back to St Louis from Ossining because she was not doing well and stayed for several years on a farm run by an elderly Missouri couple and at St Vincent's Sanitarium until 1956, when she was transferred back East, first to the Institute for Living in Connecticut and then back to Stoney Lodge.[64] His mother Edwina was living in another home at 6360 Wydown Boulevard in Clayton, which she purchased with her half of the rights to *The Glass Menagerie*. By Christmas, he, Steen, and the Reverend were in New Orleans, where Williams ran again into Pancho Rodriguez and Oliver Evans. With Merlo still in New York, Williams continued his cruising, and now for the first time admitted in his notebook that the cost of his own 'epic fornications' was excessive:

> The nightingales were on key. though [*sic*] their tone has been sweeter on occasions. But those girls [Williams's term for male trade] are costing me plenty: $40 for the past two concerts. I always relieve my embarrassment by over paying perhaps – I mean probably – because the whole thing seems offensive to the inextinguishable Puritan in me still.[65]

He also admitted to himself that they were the kind of characters that filled his plays, and that their 'lingo' was his 'stock-in-trade'.[66] Given what Williams was already spending daily on the company he kept, and how much of the trade he cruised were paid male prostitutes, is there any wonder that he still felt concerned about money, hoping to strike it rich again with another hit play or film?[67]

Williams was again hard at work on the *Baby Doll* screenplay, and he would continue to hound Kazan to get him on board the production. His trip to Miami with Steen was postponed because of haemorrhoids, whose excruciating pain reminded him of his ruptured appendix and Meckel's diverticulum attack in the spring of 1946. He spent a few days in the Ochsner Clinic but asked a friend to move him to another clinic, the Touro Infirmary, because he was not allowed alcohol at Ochsner. He had complained repeatedly over the past year of excessive gastric and intestinal pain, haemorrhoids/piles, but this time he could not urinate. He felt very nostalgic and thought often of his friends, past and present, for he believed seriously (when did he not?) that he was dying of cancer. He sent for Merlo, who came down to New Orleans from New York to be with him.[68]

On the feast of the Epiphany in January 1954, Williams and his grandfather flew to Miami, leaving Frank and their dog Mr Moon in New Orleans. The dog's unexpected death that April would affect Williams and Merlo greatly; it was soon replaced by Signor Buffo, whose death in April 1956 troubled Merlo in particular, as he always looked after their dogs and found in them a faithful companion whenever he and Williams were estranged. Work improved for Williams when he finally reached his home in Key West. The new studio, with its skylight, no doubt reminded him of his earlier days working under the skylight at 722 Toulouse Street in 1938 or on *Streetcar* in 1946 while living in Dick Orme's apartment at 632½ St Peters Street, watching the clouds, or vapours off the Mississippi River, pass overhead.[69] He was still struggling with *Baby Doll* (called alternatively 'Hide and Seek' or 'Whipmaster'), *Orpheus Descending*, the screenplay for *The Rose Tattoo* (which premiered in December 1955 with Anna Magnani and Burt Lancaster, but not Brando as Williams had at first hoped), and work on a new play 'A Place of Stone'.

In preparation for his annual European summer excursion, Williams brought his grandfather back to the Gayoso Hotel in Memphis, fearing that the next time he would see him would be in Dakin's Corner, Ohio, where Grand was buried in 1944.[70] As Merlo was preparing their voyage, Williams received news that, due to his Communist sympathies, Arthur Miller had just been denied a passport to attend a production of *The Crucible* in Brussels. Williams wrote a letter to the State Department in Miller's defence, but he never mailed it, telling Brooks Atkinson that it was out of fear that it would 'antagonize the department'[71] and put his own passport in jeopardy. He travelled by train from Memphis to New York where, on 15 May, he and Merlo again set sail across the Atlantic, heading this time south for Tangier instead of Le Havre or Southampton. By June, they flew to Madrid and stayed at the Palace Hotel, taking in several bullfights.

A few days later they flew on to Rome. Williams's dependency on alcohol and Seconals and Nembutals was growing stronger, and his writing suffered as a consequence – a repeat performance of the previous summers. Audrey Wood and her husband Bill Liebling joined them in Rome to discuss *Orpheus Descending*. Williams was working on several projects simultaneously, allowing him to avoid writer's block when work on one play or story was not advancing well. Williams continued working on *Kingdom of Earth* and would complete its first draft by September. He liked it and, despite Wood's hesitations, imagined producing it in a double bill with 'A Place of Stone', the play that would eventually become *Cat on a Hot Tin Roof*. Williams exchanged several letters with Cheryl Crawford about his problems with writing, and she recommended that he see a psychiatrist. In June, Williams wrote to her: 'Dr. Kinsey, after a four and a half hour talk in 1949 or 50, told me that I needed analysis and that he would recommend a good man for me. He seemed to realize that I was facing an eventual impasse, at which I am now arriving'.[72]

Williams and Merlo moved on to Vienna in July, then to Venice and Zurich before returning to Spain. In another letter to Crawford dated August 1954, Williams wrote that he and Britneva, whom he had 'inherited [...] for the summer' since she was recently 'jilted' by Jay Laughlin,[73] met up with Oliver Evans 'and took a trip by car along the Costa Brava, two weeks in Barcelona in which we saw seven bull-fights',[74] this time armed with Hemingway's bullfighting book, *Death in the Afternoon*.[75] Merlo had stayed on in Rome, further signs that the relationship was breaking apart. This quick succession of cities once again attests to the fact that Williams's writing was not going well, and he hoped a change in scenery would inspire his muse. Missing Merlo terribly, he and Britneva flew back to Rome. Williams soon abandoned both for Taormina (she and Merlo were not getting along) and was not sorry he left Britneva in Rome because he 'could hardly afford' to bring her with him, 'the way [his] money's been going this summer'.[76] At the end of September, he and Merlo were again aboard the SS *Andrea Doria*, this time with Anna Magnani, heading back to Key West to shoot the film *The Rose Tattoo*. Exterior scenes were shot on location on an empty plot next to Williams's Duncan Street bungalow, which served as Magnani's and Burt Lancaster's dressing rooms.[77] From there, they went on to New Orleans just after Thanksgiving, before catching a connecting flight to Los Angeles (via Dallas and El Paso), where studio production was to continue.

The play version of *The Rose Tattoo* had caused quite a stir back in 1951, given its frank handling of sexual intercourse outside of marriage. Williams was even criticized by one reviewer for having a condom fall out of Alvaro's pocket onto the stage.[78] Williams had tried submitting a revised scene to Audrey Wood in 1951 to 'alleviate some of the "moral" antipathy'[79] that the play was causing. Now, he feared that the Code would require further changes that would ruin the film by taking out all of the poetry and turning it into 'a grade B picture'.[80] He already saw proof of that in Hal Kanter's hatchet-job on the script. Knowing full well that Hollywood was stricter than Broadway in terms of putting sensitive material on the screen, Williams attempted to pre-empt any objection to the film's sexual content by downplaying its lewdness and playing up its plastic poetry.

In a short, unpublished essay titled 'Notes on the Filming of "Rose Tattoo"' (1952)[81] that he wrote a couple years earlier in anticipation of the necessary negotiations for the film version of the play, Williams bowed to potential objections about the film's sex scenes, which he felt could be approached artistically, as it had been in *Streetcar*. This was a comedy, after all, and its sexual content, though important to the story's development, could be implied and even burlesqued. His principal concern involved the film's fulfilment of its promises as a plastic medium that the performed play did not fully realize on stage:

> Many of the audience and the critics had the mistaken idea that the community life, the Strega, the goat, and crowd scenes and the

activities of the children were meant only to fill in and distract the eye. Very few seemed to realize that all of these were an integral part of the artistic conception of the play, that this was a play built of movement and color, almost as much as an abstract painting is made of them. [...] 'The Rose Tattoo' should have been a riotous and radiant thing but the spatial limitations of the stage and the limits of time, etc, put it in a straight-jacket and only about two-thirds of its potential appeal came through. In transferring it to the screen, the producer should make sure that the full advantage of his medium is being used.[82]

Daniel Mann, who had mounted the Broadway production and who was now directing Magnani and Lancaster in the film, did tease out the story's Dionysian nature using Williams's 'poetic-plastic' elements, as Kazan had done in the film version of *Streetcar*, and for Williams this was more important than stonewalling the censors.[83]

In all, the summer of 1954 shaped up in many ways to the summers of 1952 and 1953. Williams wrote almost daily but was rarely happy with what he had written. To compensate for his apparent writer's block, Williams continued to travel, rarely staying in one place for more than a week. Travel, like sex, filled the void left between writing and swimming sessions. Unlike many of his contemporary expatriates, such as Truman Capote or Gore Vidal, Williams travelled to write and did not write to travel. And if his writing habits made some writers jealous, they were enough to make others downright angry. Williams was capable at times, for instance, of writing a poem in one afternoon, while sitting next to a pool and drinking a glass of wine, and then sending it off to his publisher Laughlin the next morning for possible inclusion in his collection *In the Winter of Cities* (1956); seasoned poets would spend hours or even days on a line or a signal word.[84] Williams could complete a short story in the time that it took him to travel by boat from New York to Le Havre,[85] or even by train from Paris to Rome, mailing it right after to Marie Britneva with the instructions that she try and sell it; polished fiction writers would spend months to complete a story.[86]

Work on his plays, though, underwent a gestation period of several months, years or even decades. This was certainly the case with his plays of the 1950s, from the months to compose *Cat on a Hot Tin Roof* to the years for *Sweet Bird of Youth* to the decades for *Orpheus Descending*. As each play's critical and commercial reception would evince, the more Williams spent writing a play, the less likely were its chances of success.

Given this trend, the seventeen years between *Battle of Angels,* the poem 'Orpheus Descending', and the play *Orpheus Descending* (1957) – the longest Williams ever spent on one play, though he would never quite leave any of his plays alone, even after they were published – would logically translate into a failure from beginning to end, which sadly was the case with both *Battle of Angels* and *Orpheus Descending.* Conversely, the seventeen months, give or take a few, between the publication of 'Three Players of a Summer Game' and the completion of *Cat on a Hot Tin Roof,* the play that the story gave life to, should translate into a hit. And it did.

The poems and stories that he did write during these difficult years – some dashed off in white heat, others laboured over intensely – not only broke through a given day's writer's block but also served as a pre-liminary treatment of what would be developed later into his full-length plays. Concerning the composition of *Cat on a Hot Tin Roof,* Williams described in a notebook entry dated 29 July 1951 his having completed a first draft of 'a brief little story'.[87] By April 1952, he completed that story, titled it 'Three Players of a Summer Game', and then published it the following November in *The New Yorker.* 'Three Players of Summer Game', which remains one of Williams's best short stories, would eventually find its larger treatment in *Cat,* which, Brian Parker informs us, Williams began drafting in 1953. His failed work on it that summer would throw Williams into a serious depression.[88] Several months later, Williams had broken through his block and wrote to Wood on 21 March 1954: 'I'm also pulling together a short-long play based on the charac-ters in "Three Players" which I started last summer in Rome [...]'.[89]

By April, he was back in New Orleans with the Reverend and mak-ing great advances in the work once titled 'A Place of Stone' that he was now calling 'A Cat on a Hot Tin Roof' (Williams later quipped that the title was inspired either by his father or by Jordan Massee, Sr[90]). He wrote in his notebook on 6 April, 'Work somewhat blocked today – but the design is clearer and seeing the play "Cat on a hot tin Roof" named in print [in that day's *New Orleans Times-Picayune*] made it seem realer to me. Why did I despair of it so in Madrid, in this same journal? When was I seeing it clearer, now or then?'[91] He still feared the play was 'low voltage' and imagined it appearing in a double bill with a 'curtain-raiser to make a full evening'.[92]

Typically cruel in his self-judgement about his work, Williams wrote another April entry in his notebook that describes his attempt to avoid making the play singularly about homosexuality: 'I wrote sort of messy today on "Place of Stone". The intrusion of the homosexual theme may be fucking it up again'.[93] Juggling work on *Orpheus Descending* with production demands for the film *The Rose Tattoo*, Williams soon recognized that he was onto something big with *Cat* and began devoting more attention to 'fill[ing] out these two acts [...] to a full evening without extending the story as I see it'.[94] By the fall of 1954, he was in the midst of responding to Kazan's frequent requests for various revisions in the script, particularly in the third act. And by the end of September, he and Kazan were seriously debating the revisions Kazan had demanded in the play, in particular the need to show that Brick has changed by the end. Williams was 'determined to get what [Kazan] want[ed] without losing what [he] wanted'.[95]

In another notebook entry, this one on 29 November, Williams expressed his main objections to Kazan:

> Got a 5 page letter from Gadg elucidating, not too lucidly, his remaining objection to the play. I do get his point but I'm afraid he doesn't quite get mine. Things are not always explained. Situations are not always resolved. Characters do not always 'progress'. But I shall, of course, try to arrive at another compromise with him.[96]

Williams saw no reason to bring Big Daddy back and felt Kazan only wanted to make the play 'softer or sweeter' than was originally planned. And concerning the drastic change in the ending, Williams feared that Kazan's version, where Brick comes to admire Maggie instead of questioning her motives, as he had done in the play's original ending, would appear affected. 'Do you think it contains an echo of "Tea and Sympathy"?', he wrote to Wood on 23 November. 'The other, harder, ending of it didn't. Here is another case of a woman giving a man back his manhood, while in the original conception it was about a vital, strong woman dominating a weak man and achieving her will'.[97]

A few days later, on 31 November, Williams sent his still unsigned director (they had only a verbal commitment by then[98]) the following letter, wherein he declares not only his perception of Brick's homosexual latency but also his rationale for not revealing it to the audience at the play's end:

> Here's the conclusion I've come to. Brick did love Skipper, 'the one great good thing in his life which was true'. He identified Skipper with sports, the romantic world of adolescence which he couldn't go past. Further: to reverse my original (somewhat tentative) premise, I now believe that, in the deeper sense, not the literal sense, Brick is

homosexual with a heterosexual adjustment: a thing I've suspected of several others, such as Brando, for instance.

[...] In a way, this is progress for Brick. He's faced the truth, I think, under Big Daddy's pressure, and maybe the block is broken. I just said maybe. I don't really think so. I think that Brick is doomed by the falsities and cruel prejudices of the world he comes out of, belongs to, the world of Big Daddy and Big Mama. Sucking a dick or two or fucking a reasonable facsimile of Skipper some day won't solve it for him, if he ever does such 'dirty things'! He's the living sacrifice, the victim, of the play, and I don't want to part with that 'Tragic elegance' about him. You know, paralysis in a character can be just as significant and just as dramatic as progress, and is also less shop-worn.[99]

Williams met all of Kazan's demands, including the insertion of the now-infamous 'Broadway version' of act three, but his acquiescence would cause much strife between them, with Williams believing that Kazan had overstepped the boundaries between playwright and director.

In mid-January 1955, Williams and Merlo were in New Orleans to view a production at Tulane University of *Twenty-seven Wagons Full of Cotton*, starring Maureen Stapleton, along with the operatic version of his one-act play, *Lord Byron's Love Letter*, which was scored by Raffaello de Banfield. By February 1955, *Cat* was in rehearsal, and his notebook entries were now few and far between. Something must have been going well for Williams, for the first time in nearly three years, to allow such a gap in his private writing. So much of his energy was being devoted to *Cat's* preparation for Broadway that he hardly even mentioned the death of his beloved grandfather. On 2 March 1955, he added in his notebook, nearly three weeks after the Reverend's passing, 'Why is luck so resolutely against me of late? Did it die with grandfather?'[100] He had written him for the last time the previous December, looking forward to spring to bringing the Reverend down from St Louis, where he had been staying since his stroke the previous year, to Key West. The shock of his death, though not unexpected, kept Williams from actualizing it on paper, just as he had been unable to record his thoughts about Rose's lobotomy before. Luck was surely against Williams now, or so it seemed.

Cat soon changed all of that. Riding into New York on the tide of strong notices in Philadelphia, *Cat*, Williams's self-avowed play of '[p]ersonal lyricism' to bring estranged people together and initiate dialogue between them, opened at the Morosco Theatre a day before his forty-fourth birthday on 24 March 1955.[101] It was an immediate success, ultimately winning Williams his second Pulitzer Prize and the New York Drama Critics' Circle Award the following May.

In spite of its success, the play did have its detractors, and the arguments that were to emerge would set Williams along a new course in the way he represented homosexuality on the stage. Walter Kerr reviewed *Cat* twice in the *New York Herald Tribune* (25 March and 3 April 1955). After the second review appeared, 'A Secret Is Half-Told in Fountains of Words', Williams wrote to Kerr (9 April 1955) and submitted a rejoinder that he wanted the paper to publish.[102] Kerr had charged Williams in both reviews for having never provided an adequate reason for the 'emotionally paralyzed' Brick. In his second review, Kerr boldly asks, 'Is he a homosexual? At one moment he is denouncing "queers", at another describing the way he clasps his friend's hand going to bed at night [...]. Listening, we work at the play in an earnest effort to unlock its ultimate dramatic meaning. But the key has been mislaid or deliberately hidden'.[103]

Williams immediately defended himself and his choices in characterizing Brick in an article for the *New York Herald Tribune*:

> I know full well the defenses and rationalizations of beleaguered writers, a defensive species, but I still feel that I deal unsparingly with what I feel is the truth of character. I would never evade it for the sake of evasion, because I was in any way reluctant to reveal what I know of the truth.[104]

Near the end of this rejoinder, Williams passionately defends his artistic stance, reasserting the need for Brick to remain *heterosexual* in the play in much the same language he had previously used in his letter to Kazan:

> Was Brick homosexual? He probably – no, I would even say quite certainly – went no further in physical expression than clasping Skipper's hand across the space between their twin beds in hotel rooms – and yet his sexual nature was not innately 'normal.' [...] But Brick's overt sexual adjustment was, and must always remain, a heterosexual one.[105]

Kerr, like Kazan before him, had undeniably touched a nerve, yet Williams remained steadfast to both in his decision not to 'out' Brick.[106]

Worried perhaps that his message of artistic integrity would not reach posterity in such ephemeral sources, Williams added to the published version of *Cat* the now notorious extended 'bird' stage direction, which appears immediately after Big Daddy's initial intimation of Brick's latent homosexuality:

> *The bird that I hope to catch in the net of this play is not the solution of one man's psychological problem. I'm trying to catch the true quality of experience in a group of people, that cloudy, flickering, evanescent – fiercely charged! – interplay of live human beings in the thundercloud of a common crisis. Some mystery should be left in the revelation of character in a play, just as a great deal of mystery is always left in the revelation of character in life, even in one's own character to himself.*[107]

What seems now like a tempest in a teacup was fiercely played out in several media. By the 1970s, Williams was still defending himself against his representation of homosexuality on the stage, only now the accusations were coming from the gay community.

Buoyed by *Cat*'s critical and financial success, Williams sent a telegram in the spring of 1955 to Françoise Sagan, the nineteen-year-old author of the internationally best-selling novel *Bonjour tristesse* (1954). She was conducting a US book tour, and he invited her to Key West to meet him and Carson McCullers; she stayed for a 'riotous two weeks'.[108] Williams would later praise the talented novelist in his essay 'On Meeting a Young Writer', which was published in *Harper's Bazaar* in August 1956. In it, he warns her of the 'catastrophe of success' that awaits her, and Williams's predictions were borne out. Sagan's wealth fuelled her passion for sports cars, which culminated in her crashing her Aston Martin on 14 April 1957, fracturing her skull and putting her into a coma for some time. They would remain good friends despite their age difference. As Williams later recalled in his *Memoirs*: 'Françoise Sagan had adapted [*Sweet*] *Bird* for France, and she did a beautiful job on it. She was a close friend of mine; although we didn't see much of each other, whenever we did, the friendship continued as if there had been no interruption'.[109]

With the Pulitzer for *Cat* now in hand, Williams once again left for Rome, this time aboard the SS *Homeric*, coincidentally, the same name of the ship he took back in 1928 with his grandfather on his first trip to Europe. He quickly moved on to Athens, without Merlo, and then to Istanbul in June, and then finally to Valencia and Barcelona in July with an 'icy' Oliver Evans, who was cold from Williams's satiric portrait of him in the story 'Two on a Party', and a prying English theatre critic, Kenneth Tynan, who was writing a piece on Williams for *Mademoiselle*.

But Williams was not happy in any city, and with Frank returning to Rome, Williams cruised regularly, finding very little trade that appealed to him until he got to Spain.[110] All of this generally translated into the fact that his work on *Baby Doll* was not going well. Williams laconically assessed in his notebook the situation after his summer meanderings: 'Internal state: ominous'.[111] On the day before his meeting the famed bullfighter, Antonio Ordóñez, news reached him on 25 July of Margo Jones's death. Saddened as he was now by the quick parting of two central figures in his life, her and his grandfather, Williams plodded on in his work.

Williams's next trip was a flight to Stockholm in late August/early September for the Swedish premiere of *Cat*, but his unfortunate representative there, the 'dominatrix' Lilla van Saher, whom he referred to as 'the last of the crêpe-de-Chine gypsies', spoiled much of the occasion and, perhaps (as the theory goes), any chances he may have had for the Nobel Prize in Literature.[112] After another lacklustre summer in Europe, with final visits to Hamburg, Berlin, Paris, and London, Williams sailed with Merlo to New York later in the month.[113] The remaining months of 1955 were dedicated to casting *Orpheus Descending* and shooting *Baby Doll* on location in Mississippi.

Riding on the success of *Cat*, there was a revival of *Streetcar* at the Coconut Grove Playhouse in Miami that following theatre season with Tallulah Bankhead in the role of Blanche. It opened on 16 January 1956 (running till 4 February) before moving on to the City Center Theatre in New York for a two-week run in mid-February.[114] In March 1947, Audrey Wood had suggested Bankhead to Williams for the role of Blanche, but Williams was not comfortable with the choice. Two years later, when Jessica Tandy left the show, Williams wrote to Irene Selznick about the possibility of Bankhead taking over the role: 'Frankly, I am ~~very~~ frightened of her, and I don't think she should be put in the play without very earnest assurance, from her, that she would play the play and not just Tallulah as she has been recently doing. In other words, we don't yet want the "Camp" streetcar!'[115] Williams was prescient on both accounts, for when Bankhead did perform Blanche, it became a notorious revival – or a blatant disaster – depending on the party asked.

While her opening night performance was typically campy, spurred on by the gay members of the audience who came to see her, her next performance was 'legitimate and brilliant': 'She has it in her to play this part better than it has ever been played, the problem is to keep Tallulah inside the role of Blanche'.[116] *Time* magazine, however, ran a brief review of the play in its gossip column on 13 February:

> As Streetcar's wild run began, Playwright Tennessee Williams had unwarily cozied up to Tallulah in her dressing room (see cut). After catching her first performances, he began attending a nearby bar. Groaned he into his cups and to all who would listen: 'That woman is ruining my play'.[117]

Williams wrote a 'A Tribute from Tennessee Williams to "Heroic Tallulah Bankhead"' to set the record straight (or at least to bend it back to his favour), and then another 'Tribute' to her 'Tiger-Moth' character as Flora Goforth in 1963 during a revival of Williams's *The Milk Train Doesn't Stop Here Anymore*. In both pieces, he had singled out his troubled relation with Bankhead, but in the end he praised more than he damned her.[118]

From late February to April 1956, Williams began working with director George Keathley to bring an early version of *Sweet Bird of Youth* to the Studio M Playhouse in Coral Gables. He was optimistic, believing that it had 'the dynamics of a big play, which will someday emerge'.[119] In his 'Author's Note' in the playbill, Williams called the play a 'work in progress': 'At times Studio M has looked more like a printing press than a theatre, with stacks of re-writes, newly mimeographed, covering the stage and actors looking like a group of dazed proof-readers'.[120] Kazan, Crawford and William Inge all came to Miami at different times to see the play during its brief run. Kazan wanted to see if it was a vehicle that could bring to Broadway the following year, but the premiere did not take place until 1959.[121] *Sweet Bird of Youth* would prove to be Kazan's final collaboration with Williams on a play.

Williams also turned his attention – again – to *Baby Doll*, before heading off in May to Gibraltar aboard the SS *Queen Frederica*. Merlo joined him later in Rome, before Williams flew to Barcelona for the beaches and the bullfights. Very little of interest occurred that summer – 'the worst summer I have spent in Europe',[122] as Williams wrote sporadically in his notebook. And by September he was flying to the States after a brief stay in the Virgin Islands.[123] Williams and Kazan finally premiered the film *Baby Doll* on 18 December 1956. The film, with its Times Square billboard illustration of a sensuous Carroll Baker lying in a crib, sucking her phallic thumb, raised the objections of the purity league, the Legion of Decency, and the influential Francis Cardinal Spellman. Expectedly, *Time* magazine called it 'just possibly the dirtiest

American-made motion picture that has ever been legally exhibited'. In condemning it, the Roman Catholic Legion of Decency declared: 'It dwells almost without variation or relief upon carnal suggestiveness'.[124] Nonetheless, the film went on to be nominated for four Golden Globes, BAFTAs, and Academy Awards, including Best Adapted Screenplay, which Williams was again denied.

Williams had now, by the middle of the 1950s, confirmed his status as America's foremost playwright, who tackled taboos directly and without shame, and he would continue to push the moral envelope in the second half of the decade, whether with his Underwood, his Royal, his Olivetti, or later his Olympia typewriters. But with three smash hit plays, a number of successful plays and one-acts, numerous films credits, and countless published stories and poems already to his credit, Williams felt no better now than he did twenty years ago. In August 1956, after another troubled summer, he admitted in his notebook that he needed a 'little kindness, and warmth and affection' for 'just a little might have helped [him] this summer'.[125] In Rome, or Barcelona, or even Athens the summer before, there were those 'Comfortable little mercies' that he needed to get him through another day of facing the blank page. But now? Nothing. 'So? We go on from here, a little bit further, at least. [...] En Avant'.[126]

7
New York to New York
(via Miami): A Battle of Angles

In the second half of the productive 1950s, Williams's star fell, then rose sharply, then fell again, then rose once more in 1961 for the final time in his career. It all seemingly started with a dinner date at the Algonquin Hotel in 1953 with William Inge, who asked Williams if he was 'blocked as a writer'.[1] The comment troubled Williams deeply; two years later in a 20 June 1955 entry of his note, Williams wrote: 'Another possibility lies in the fact that I haven't been able to work since I got here [Rome]. An almost total impasse. (I avoid using the word 'block' – Inge scared me with it too badly)'.[2] Over the past seven years, drugs and alcohol had permanently replaced the strong coffee that once served Williams as a means to break through that block. It was now 1957, and Williams envied his former protégé's run of successes – *Come Back, Little Sheba* in 1950; *Picnic* in 1953, which ran for 477 performances and netted him the Pulitzer Prize and the New York Drama Critics' Circle Award; then *Bus Stop* in 1955, which eclipsed *Picnic*'s run on Broadway by one performance; to finally *The Dark at the Top of the Stairs* in 1957. It was clear that after the poor reviews of *Orpheus Descending* that same year, Williams needed psychological help to pull himself out of his despair. As he wrote in his notebook that February, 'Psychiatric help is imperative now'.[3]

Though Williams had spoken about undergoing psychotherapy with Cheryl Crawford as early as 1954, Williams only started analysis following the death of his father on 27 March 1957, a day after Williams celebrated his forty-sixth birthday. C.C. had been living for a while with his sister Ella in Knoxville after his legal separation from Edwina, but a quarrel with his sister sent him packing, and he eventually took up with a widow from Ohio. His father's death marked Williams in ways he never imagined it would. The older he grew, the closer Williams felt toward him. He eventually documented those thoughts about his father in his essay 'The Man in the Overstuffed Chair', which was one of the benefits of his therapy; the play *Suddenly Last Summer* was the other. Spent and nerve-wracked from the energy he put into his recent play and film productions, Williams finally realized that he needed the couch of a psychoanalyst to come to terms with his chronic hysteria, insecurity, fear, panic, selfishness, and loneliness – those 'blue devils' that had haunted him at least since his first trip to Europe with his grandfather in 1928.

On and off from June 1957 to March 1958 (sometimes daily, other times three or four times a week), Williams underwent treatment from Dr Lawrence S. Kubie, a strict Freudian analyst and President of the New York Psychoanalytic Society. On 7 June, Williams was sent to the Austen-Riggs Centre in Stockbridge, Massachusetts, for a period of psychotherapy, but he reported later to Edwina in a 28 June letter that he stayed for only five minutes.[4] To combat his 'blue devils', Kubie told Williams that he had to give up writing – to put his '[l]ife before [his] work, [...] is the message, the counsel' that Kubie gave him[5] – and to break off his relationship with Merlo. The first request was out of the question; the second had already been set in motion. Many people associated with Williams over the years have interpreted Kubie's diagnosis concerning Merlo as an attempt to 'cure' Williams of his homosexuality. Arguably, Williams had thought that himself.[6] In his interview with C. Robert Jennings in 1973, for instance, Williams noted that 'Kubie thought I should be heterosexual'.[7]

The presumption that Kubie wanted to 'cure' Williams of his homosexuality was consistent with the American Psychiatric Association's (APA) theories behind sexual orientation during the1950s when Williams underwent analysis.[8] The APA only removed homosexuality from its list of psychological disorders in 1973. However, Michael Paller has debunked the idea that Kubie, who held moderate views on homosexuality in comparison to other psychoanalysts in his day, had any plans at all to make Williams heterosexual:

According to Williams, Kubie also urged him to give up both homosexuality and writing. At this point, at least according to some of Williams's friends, Williams stopped taking the doctor seriously: after all, unlike many gay men who were urged to do so in the nineteen-fifties and sixties, Williams did not enter psychoanalysis to cure himself of homosexuality [...]. Kubie may indeed have given him such advice; if so, it was in accordance with what he described as

The Principle of Deprivation [...]. If Williams's reports are to be trusted and Kubie did suggest that he give up both writing and sex with men, these may have been the activities with which, Kubie thought, Williams was avoiding his problems.[9]

Kubie's focus was less on Williams's sexual orientation and more on his obsession with his work, which Kubie believed held all the keys to understanding, and potentially calming, his patient's 'blue devils'. When Williams could not follow Kubie's advice, he frequently fled his therapy for extended periods. His final break with Kubie in 1958, then, had to do with Kubie's pushing Williams to stop writing, and not with Williams's ending his relationship with Merlo, let alone turning straight.

Williams, of course, did not quell his desire to write and, if anything, Kubie's medical advice heightened Williams's appetite for it. Those sessions with Kubie, in fact, helped midwife his last triumph of the decade, *Suddenly Last Summer*, part of the double-bill *Garden District*, which would see its Broadway premiere in 1958, a year before the troubled flight of *Sweet Bird of Youth*. *Suddenly Last Summer* was perhaps his most violent play, and certainly his best since *Cat on a Hot Tin Roof*. Williams's theatrical response after the violence of *Suddenly Last Summer* and *Sweet Bird of Youth* was the dark comedy *Period of Adjustment*, which came to Broadway in November 1960 but closed a few months after. This chapter looks at the contexts of these four plays, from *Orpheus Descending* to *Period of Adjustment*, as well as Williams's other literary output, to explore Williams's undulating fame, which ultimately made him crash in the 1960s following the death of Frank Merlo, his partner of some fifteen years.

The year 1957 proved to be a watershed to the long-standing friendship of Tennessee Williams and William Inge, if not in Williams's career entirely. Williams was at this time writing *Suddenly Last Summer* and had *Orpheus Descending*, a rewrite of his 1940 play *Battle of Angels*, already in production. Also in 1957, Inge was presenting *The Dark at the Top of the Stairs* – again, a rewrite of an earlier Inge play, *Farther Off from Heaven* – and dedicated it, 'For Tennessee Williams'. But this marks only the beginning of the similarities they shared this year, for though Inge felt this dedication honoured his one-time mentor who was largely responsible for getting him his break on Broadway, Williams, tainted by their silent feud of the past decade, did not see any altruism in Inge's gesture. As a result, their friendship, once intimate, had by 1957 turned sour, though both maintained all friendly semblances.

In his essay 'The Past, the Present and the Perhaps', Williams notes that he revised *Battle of Angels* into *Orpheus Descending*, always having had it 'on the work bench' not because

> I have run out of ideas or material for completely new work [...] [but] because I honestly believe that it is finally finished. About 75 percent of it is new writing, but what is much more important, I believe that I have now finally managed to say in it what I wanted to say, and I feel that it now has in it a sort of emotional bridge between those early years described in this article and my present state of existence as a playwright.[10]

Orpheus Descending became for Williams not just a rewrite of his old play but a rewrite of his former career, a synthesis of all the major themes and motifs which he would recycle in his later plays. When Inge published *The Dark*, he asked Williams to write the introduction, which he begrudgingly did. The essay, 'If the Writing Is Honest', is a curious piece, never fully damning Inge but not quite praising him either:

> [...] there is no air of recent or incipient disorder on the premises. No bloodstained ax has been kicked under the sofa. If the lady of the house is absent, she has really gone to baby-sit for her sister, her corpse is not stuffed hastily back of the coal-bin. [...] In other words, they are given to believe that nothing at all disturbing or indecorous is going to happen to them in the course of their visit.[11]

The lengthy discussion of violence, or lack of it, in pre-1960 Inge is poignant for Williams, because by this time violence had become Williams's trademark. With so much personal matter going into the writing of the plays, whatever critical response it generated was sure to be interpreted as indirect commentary on the playwright himself. Thus the resulting professional success or failure of the play would say more of the *personal* success or failure of the man who wrote it than had any previous play Williams had penned.

Orpheus Descending opened on 21 March at the Martin Beck Theatre under Harold Clurman's direction, but it closed a disappointing sixty-eight performances later on 18 May. The reviews proved devastating for Williams, professionally and psychologically. Having worked on it on and off for nearly two decades, the final push to see it through production in 1956 was breaking him down: 'All that I am fit for', he wrote to Wood on 29 June 1956, 'is bits and pieces of patchwork on "Orpheus" and "Bird", if "Bird" ever flies here'.[12] William was eager to sign Marlon Brando and Anna Magnani in the principal roles and did all he could to bring their star appeal to the stage. Williams explained to Magnani in separate August and October 1956 letters the sacrifices, financial and artistic, that he was making for her.[13] Since she would only perform in the play for two months, and wanted a cut of the lucrative film deal that Wood was negotiating with Hal Wallis (who would not purchase the rights in the end), Williams explained that the shorter run would bring in less box-office receipts and diminish the play's overall worth as a Hollywood vehicle. Wood was never able to sign Brando or Magnani in the end, and Maureen Stapleton and Cliff Robertson performed the two roles. Both Brando and Magnani would eventually incarnate Val and Lady in the 1959 film version, *The Fugitive Kind* (no relation to the play *Fugitive Kind* that Williams wrote in 1937), directed by Sidney Lumet.

Despite all of Williams's efforts these past seventeen years since *Battle of Angels* to realize simultaneously his past, present, and 'perhaps', *Orpheus Descending* was 'slaughtered by the Furies of the press'.[14] Critically panned, it soon became a commercial failure, running only eight weeks (21 March to 18 May) to *The Dark*'s 468 performances. This, coupled with the sudden death of his father a week later and the ongoing fervour that Cardinal Spellman raised over *Baby Doll*'s licentiousness, pushed Williams over a psychological precipice, and he soon found himself a confused analysand on Kubie's couch. After a brief visit to London to see Peter Hall's production of *Camino Real*, based on a revised script that received a warmer welcome than it had in New York, Williams moved on to Rome that April and then to Madrid in May. By 3 June, he was back in New York, and began his initial psychotherapeutic sessions with Kubie before being transported to Stockbridge. So as not to stray far from his doctor, he stayed for most of the summer at his 323 East 58th Street apartment in upper East Manhattan, just above Johnny Nicholson's café, one of his longest stretches living in the city. It was the first summer in nine consecutive years that he did not go to Europe.

Therapy with Kubie was having mixed results. As he told his mother on 28 June 1975, he believed he needed psychotherapy 'to relieve the tensions that I have been living under, but I think it's unnecessary for me to live in a house full of characters that appeared to be more disturbed than myself'.[15] While therapy did help teach him how to release his frustrations and come to terms with his family's troubling past, his need to stay put for months on end in New York was suffocating him. He wrote Maria St Just née Britneva (Maria Britneva became the Lady

St Just in July 1956) that he needed to travel again as '[b]eing tied down in New York [was] almost unbearable'.[16] With the spectre of Rose's 'sudden deterioration' at the sanatorium no doubting haunting him, within days, Williams had fled the clinic and flew to Miami and then to Havana.[17] The Towers Hotel in Miami would be one of his preferred escapes that summer. It was still a short-flight to New York, if he needed to return to see Kubie, and it was located near to where Marion Vaccaro lived. And though it lacked the swimming pool and air-conditioning that the nearby Robert Clay Hotel had, its proprietors were discreet about Williams's choice of company. He avoided Key West as much as he could, since Merlo was there when not in New York. With Vaccaro, who was hosting him that spring and summer, they would often head further south to Havana. It is not surprising that while in Havana that June, he would begin working on the screenplay *The Loss of a Teardrop Diamond*, about Fisher Willow, a southern debutante based on Rose, and a play about his experiences under psychoanalysis, *Suddenly Last Summer*. By November 1957, he was back in his old suite at the Towers Hotel.

When he returned to New York that autumn, Williams took another apartment at 124 East 65th Street, in part because it was 'a smarter and safer neighborhood' to live in, but also because Merlo, who had taken to decorating their East 58th Street apartment, had put his mark on the place.[18] Work on *Suddenly Last Summer* was now complete – Williams makes no real mention of having worked on the play at all in his notebooks, which he always did with previous work of his – and Williams turned his attention to helping director Herbert Machiz during rehearsals. It was one of the quickest plays Williams ever wrote, going into production not long after its completion in November, barely five months after he entered therapy. Williams continued his daily, hour-long sessions with Kubie, whose office was nearby, but Williams was growing tired of it. On 7 January 1958, *Garden District* opened Off Broadway at the York Playhouse on First Avenue as a double bill, *Something Unspoken* and *Suddenly Last Summer*. *Suddenly Last Summer*, his criticism of Kubie and his psychoanalytical procedures, was praised by several of New York's theatre critics, much to Williams's earnest amazement, as he thought its violence and open treatment of homosexuality would trouble audiences and infuriate the critics.[19]

Set in a jungle-like garden of a Garden District mansion (fashioned after the Bultman's 'Green Room' that Williams visited there through his artist friend Fritz) during the heart of the Depression in 1935,

Suddenly Last Summer is ostensibly about money – not between those who have and those who do not, but rather between those who *had* and those, like the Venables, who *still* do. The play's era being that of social realism, a time when Williams began cutting his own teeth as a playwright, the true cannibal was perhaps capitalism itself. Thus, the starving of the Venus flytrap, which dramatically opens the play, is one of Williams's most poignant criticisms of the laissez-faire politics responsible for the 1929 crash and its aftermath. But Violet also refuses to keep the insectivorous plant alive because it reminds her too much of the way in which her beloved Sebastian died, consumed by everyone, including herself, for his beauty, grace, and 'illicit' desire. The multiple references to consumption or corruption, as in the 'venal' echoes of the Venable family, replicate the play's main theme of predatory social politics.

Also in 1935, a new psychosurgery procedure was being experimented with in Portugal. Invented by António Egas Moniz, who initially named it 'leucotomy' and won the Nobel Prize for it in 1949, the lobotomy, like the one performed on Rose in 1943, was seen as a new and radical option in treating mental illness when shock therapy proved ineffectual. Dr Cukrowicz is trying to secure a grant from Violet Venable to finance his experimental work in psychosurgery partly modelled on the neurologist Walter J. Freeman, who brought the procedure to America and performed the first lobotomy in the country in September 1936. In order to secure the funds, Dr Cukrowicz is being pressured into using the money to perform his first experimental lobotomy on Catherine Holly, Violet's niece, whose story of Sebastian Venable's horrific death by *quid pro quo* cannibalism on a beach in Spain threatens the mother's image of her son.

Like the religio-homoerotic undertones of another Williams tale of cannibalism, 'Desire and the Black Masseur', *Suddenly Last Summer* establishes the play's religious context with Violet's story about her and Sebastian's voyage to the Galapagos Islands, 'looking', as she says, 'for God'.[20] That cruel or indifferent God that Sebastian finds is represented in the horrific story of the 'flesh-eating birds' which ravage the baby sea turtles during their flight to freedom on the volcanic black-sand beaches of the Encatadas. The parable, of course, is repeated in Catherine's story about how the poor children from whom Sebastian has solicited sexual favours kill and eat him out of ritualized retribution for his failing to uphold his end of their economic exchange. When the starving children do devour parts of Sebastian's body, having cried out *'Pan, pan, pan!'* moments before the attack, Sebastian becomes the Holy Eucharist – the bread of life and the Bread of Life – whom these 'featherless little black sparrows' literally ingest, just as the others before had done so metaphorically.[21]

Violet relates the story to Dr Cukrowicz about how the carnivorous birds, soaring over 'the narrow black beach of the Encantadas', which earlier she had said was the 'color of caviar', had 'made the sky almost as black as the beach!'[22] As innocent as Violet's description first appears, once those hoards of black birds are translated into the hoards of those dark naked children with 'little black mouths'[23] many summers later, and the sea turtles' flesh into that of Sebastian, Williams's Holy Eucharist becomes less a tale about misappropriated consubstantiation or misrepresented homoeroticism and more one about voracious appetites for anything that can be exploited. Sebastian, too, equates desire with eating, evidenced by his rendering his trade in culinary terms: 'Fed up with dark ones, famished for light ones: that's how he talked about people, as if they were – items on a menu. – "This one's delicious-looking, that one is appetizing," or "that one is *not* appetizing" [...]'.[24] His language is purely metaphorical here (to be more accurate, they are not even *his* words but those that Catherine says he spoke), and his actions reflect Williams's own in previous summers on the San Sebastián beach outside of Barcelona, where Franz Neuner served him up local males nightly.[25] Even the language of consuming dark boys or now finding light boys more appetising came direct from a Williams letter ten years earlier to Donald Windham.[26] Williams later insisted that the play's cannibalism was not to be rendered realistically on stage or on screen, which is why he did not like the Joseph L. Mankiewicz film made from the play the following year.

Sam Spiegel, who produced the film, bought the film rights to *Suddenly Last Summer* directly from Williams after phoning him at his hotel in Miami, completely bypassing Audrey Wood as intermediary, much to her anger and frustration.[27] Williams was growing tired of his agent now, whom he suspiciously thought was trying to ruin his career in favour of Inge's. Despite a play critical of consumption and the economic manipulation of people, Spiegel saw a potential fortune to be made with the film and cast the actresses who had screen appeal: Katherine Hepburn as Violet and Elizabeth Taylor as Catherine, a casting that Williams detested.[28] In a period of four years starting in August 1958, 'Hollywood would buy seven of his plays, thus adding over four million dollars to his income'.[29] Only *Camino Real* would not be given a film treatment during the 1950s.

Williams continued his sessions with Kubie into the first few months of 1958, despite his earlier objections. After spending nearly a year now with Kubie, Williams told Maria St Just in April 1958 that he had written a letter to Kubie, breaking off their doctor-patient relationship.[30] He then wrote to Elia Kazan in June 1958 and to Audrey Wood in July, telling them both of his feelings about Kubie. To Wood, Williams wrote:

> He did give me more insight into the dark side of my nature, but it increased my depression which was already about as much as I could endure. I resented him telling me that I must 'go through hell' when I have been going through nothing but hell, with slight variations in temperature, for the past ten years of my wretched existence.[31]

If Kubie's sessions with Williams had done little to release him from his 'blue devils', they did at least give Williams one great play and allowed him to reconcile his feelings about his dead father. It also taught him free-association thinking, a technique that would figure centrally in his *Memoirs* (1975).

The year 1958 was also proving to be a watershed in Williams's life and in his memoir writing. Though Williams had spoken about undergoing psychotherapy as early as 1954, poor reviews of *Orpheus Descending* and the death of his estranged father Cornelius on 27 March prompted Williams finally to undergo psychoanalysis.[32] One of the positive benefits from his treatment was that Williams learned finally to forgive his father, a bitterness that had stayed with him for as long as his memories of C.C. reached back into his childhood. In the past decade, he saw his father only once or twice, and always coincidentally.[33] And the way Williams expressed that forgiveness was through a long essay he wrote about his relationship with the man who used to call him 'Miss Nancy' when he was a boy.

That essay, 'The Man in the Overstuffed Chair', eulogizes his father as much as it documents the past. It records the years 1932, when his father withdrew him from the University of Missouri and forced him to work in the Continental branch of the International Shoe Company, up to 1935, when Williams suffered a breakdown, quit his job, and fled to his grandparents' home in Memphis, where he wrote and produced his first play, *Cairo, Shanghai, Bombay!* In ways similar to Williams's other autobiographical essay 'Grand',[34] written a few years earlier, 'The Man in the Overstuffed Chair' is as much about Williams as it is about his subject: how he struggled with guilt after having fled the family home with all of its turmoil, abandoning those he loved in his flight (Rose in particular). The essay essentially places Williams in that same overstuffed armchair of his father, demonstrating to the playwright that he had as much in common with his father, if not more, than he did with his mother. Considered separately, the two essays, longer than most in the Williams canon, are masterpieces in their own right; read together, they demonstrate not only Williams's ability but also his flair in recalling his past and capturing it with that subtle sense of ironic nostalgia that bathes *The Glass Menagerie* in its romantic yet haunting candle light.

'The Man in the Overstuffed Chair' is important for other reasons as well. First, though not written in the 'free association' style of his *Memoirs*, it is the by-product of Williams's psychotherapy. Though Williams ultimately rejected Kubie's treatment, he drew from it the important element of confronting one's past head-on, and the result was 'free association' recollection. His discovery that 'free association' was a convenient way to access buried memories and exploit their discreet meanings to express wider personal and collective malaises both helped and hindered Williams, however. In the short term, it helped because at no other time in Williams's career did he produce as much prose writing about his life as he did in the two years leading up to *The Night of the Iguana* (1961). In the long term, it stifled his ability to produce sustained, coherent prose, and *Memoirs*, written a decade later, resembles more the stitching together of separate short pieces than it does the structuring of a master narrative of one's life and experiences, professional and personal. Harvard University holds several examples of these unpublished essay fragments written around this time that demonstrate Williams's experimentation with the form as a way to document his life. One draft titled 'Some Free Associations' was written around March 1959, when *Sweet Bird of Youth* was entering Philadelphia for its try-outs. These 'free associations' replaced his notebook entries, which he stopped writing on 22 September 1958, and eventually provided material for his *Memoirs*.[35]

Williams wrote another essay about C.C. in 1963–64, titled 'Of My Father (A Belated Appreciation)', which confirms how he felt about him and also how had not finished with the subject in 'The Man in the Overstuffed Chair'. In fact, the story of Williams's life was far from having been told.[36] If anything, writing autobiography was more than a form of psychotherapy for the playwright in 1958–59. It was a means for a man approaching fifty, who, though still at the top of his game (*The Night of the Iguana*, arguably his last great play, was just a year away from production and the New York Drama Critics' Circle Award for 1962), was anxious about confirming his place in American letters. But memoirs are written at the end of one's career, and Williams was adamant – to his critics, to his agent, and to himself – that his work was far from being finished.

In the late spring of 1958, Williams briefly retired to Key West with Merlo, and then to New Orleans, where he worked on the revisions for *Sweet Bird of Youth*, unheeding Kubie's medical advice that he 'lie fallow' and not write anything for a year.[37] He had promised Wood that he would soon have the play completed so as to send it to Cheryl Crawford, who had shown an interest in producing it. On 22 June 1958, Williams and Merlo, who was still pretty much living his own life now, flew Pan Am to Europe (Lisbon, Barcelona, Rome, Taormina, Positano, London, Paris, Cannes, and Barcelona again), bringing Marion Vaccaro along with them on the trip, in part to act as a lubricant to their frictional relationship. Jumping back and forth repeatedly between cities, Williams was extremely restless this summer, perhaps more than the previous summers he had spent in Europe. He admitted to Louise Davis in an interview earlier that year that he was becoming 'increasingly restless' as he grew older, and that was evident in his aimless sojourns this summer.[38] Williams would purposefully avoid the premiere of *Garden District* in London that August, much to producer John Wilson's dismay, and instead he would spend most of his September at the bullfights in Barcelona.

Williams was pressing on with revisions for *Sweet Bird of Youth*, but it was giving him difficulties, in particular with the second act, which he admitted to Kazan was 'too cluttered up with peripheral bits'.[39] Despite being in a state of incompletion, Wood managed an advance sale of the movie rights to MGM, which astonished and pleased and ultimately worried Williams. Williams told Crawford that he insisted on having Elia Kazan as director, and when he and Merlo returned from Europe, Williams left for the Towers Hotel in Miami to examine Jo Mielzner's set design for the play. By October, Williams was working alongside playwright Meade Roberts on the screenplay to *Orpheus Descending* that he had written the previous summer, and novelist Gore Vidal, whom Spiegel had contracted to write the screenplay for *Suddenly Last Summer*. Williams was also completing a new comedy, *Period of Adjustment*. The play underwent a try-out period that December at the Coconut Grove Playhouse in Miami, with Williams assisting during rehearsals.[40] The only other play that Williams mentions in his notebook as having worked on that autumn was the one-act *The Mutilated*, which was paired with another one-act, *The Gnädiges Fräulein*, in 1966 as *Slapstick Tragedy*.

Preparations for *Sweet Bird*'s arrival on Broadway were occupying most of Williams's time in the new year. With the cast now set by February, rehearsals would precede an early March try-out in Philadelphia, where Williams stayed at the Warwick Hotel. On the hotel letterhead, Williams typed out several versions of 'A Playwright's Prayer', in which he repeatedly pleaded for patience with his director, Kazan, and the actors, and for vision to see the play through to its success: 'Help me to receive politely and patiently all advice but to know the bad from the good and please give me the necessary faith in that which is the best I can do, after two or three yearsd [*sic*] of work on it to stand or fall by its truth as I truly see it and feel it. Give me humility, though'.[41] Perhaps because he had worked so long on the piece and had needed to finish the decade on a high note, Williams's preoccupation with the play turned into an obsession. Were it to fail, he might never recover again.

Williams had worked on the play, off and on, for over ten years. As early as December 1948, he had jotted down in his notebook his 'ghost of an idea' about a 'political play' on the life of the Kingfish Huey Long, which he would later call 'The Big Time Operators'.[42] He described it to Audrey Wood in a 18 November 1948 letter: 'The story is not at all bio-graphical but the material is drawn mostly from Huey Long, showing the main character in a mostly sympathetic light as a man very close to the people, fantastically uninhibited, essentially honest, but shackled with a corrupt machine and machine-boss'.[43] He recognized, though, that the play had a 'big and important theme' that rested outside his circle of experiences, which may be why the second act of the play never really seemed to ring true.[44] He imagined Marlon Brando in the role, no doubt given Stanley Kowalski's affinities with Huey Long. But, as he told Kazan the following July, he lost interest in the characters 'to put any fire into the writing'.[45] He would eventually leave it for a few years to work on *The Rose Tattoo, Camino Real, Cat on a Hot Tin Roof* and *Orpheus Descending*.

In 1952, Williams wrote a one-act play titled *The Enemy: Time*, which would form part of the love story for *Sweet Bird*. The story of Rose Pitts and Phil Beam is essentially that of Heavenly and Chance. Tom Finley, called Cris Pitts, plays Rose's brother, but no mention of the political father Boss Finley or his southern campaign is made in this one-act. Rose and Phil were lovers, and Phil left for New York to land a 'lead in some big musical' but 'didn't even get a job in the chorus'.[46] Phil, involved in numerous sexual encounters while away, contracts a venereal disease, which he in turn transmits to Rose upon his return. As a result, Rose had to have surgery to remove her infected uterus. All of this finds its way into *Sweet Bird*, as does the Princess (here called Pazmezoglu), who leaves

Phil at the end. Though Phil's enemy in the play is time, 'the source of corruption', Rose's antagonist is Phil himself. In combating Phil when he attempts to rape her upon his return home, Rose fights him off 'like a tiger'.[47] Now, Rose feels that she will join a convent (as Heavenly threatens Boss Finley she will do) because, as she says, 'My body doesn't exist for me anymore'.[48] Phil is not castrated like Chance for his crime, but is instead beaten up by Cris and left alone with neither Rose nor the Princess to stop the ticking of the ubiquitous clock that devours his precious youth.

On a rudimentary level, the story of *The Enemy: Time* is precisely that of *Sweet Bird*: a man returns to the town and the love of his youth in the hope of regaining lost years, while those around him try desperately to show him that they and the town have moved on. To expand the one-act play into *Sweet Bird of Youth*, Williams added the stories of Boss Finley's political machine and Princess Kosmonopolis's (i.e., Alexandra Del Largo) flight from Hollywood. While the play's dramatic conflict arises between Boss and Tom Finley and Chance Wayne over the rights to Heavenly's body, the dialectical conflict exists between Chance and the Princess alone. Chance's duality lies between two worlds: one that is locked hermetically away in the proverbial hope-chest of faded pictures of himself in *Life* magazine, the other that is irreversibly submitting to the atrophic effects of time. In coming to St Cloud, where he feels 'Time doesn't pass',[49] Chance can regain Heavenly's love and recover his lost youth. And though he tries unwittingly to stop time in this world artificially by hocking his watch and letting the Princess's wind down, Chance cannot halt the passage of his youthful triumphs into distant memories.

From 1952 to 1956, Williams attempted to graft his one-act play onto his previous work on 'The Big Time Operators', but he could not create a seamless fusion, which resulted in the structural flaw present on Broadway in 1959. In April 1956, Williams allowed George Keathley to direct *Sweet Bird of Youth* as a 'work in progress' at the Studio M Playhouse in Coral Gables. The play must have seemed convincing to Kazan, Wood, and Crawford, the three key figures responsible for the play's Broadway premiere years later, for Williams continued rewriting it the following fall, though with difficulty.[50] His greatest problem remained that rupture between the stories of Chance and the Princess and of Chance and Heavenly and Boss Finley.[51] By 11 August 1958, he wrote Kazan, '[The] discussion of the play I had with Sam Spiegel in Taormina [...] shook me up quite a bit, as it made me face up to this important problem of cohesion in the script'.[52] A year after the play's

Broadway premiere, Williams performed the theatre's equivalent of an autopsy on the play, writing to Donald Windham in April 1960 that it

> violated an essential rule: the rule of the straight line, the rule of poetic unity of singleness and wholeness, because when I first wrote it, crisis after crisis, of nervous and physical and mental nature, had castrated me nearly. Now I am cutting it down to size: keeping in on the two protagonists with, in Act Two, only one or two suitable elements beside the joined deaths of the male and female heros [*sic*] so that instead of being an over-length play it will be under length (conventionally) and the first act and third act will not be disastrously interrupted by so many non-integrated, barely even peripheral, concerns with a social background already made clearly implicit, not needing to be explicit.[53]

The cohesion that he eventually did not achieve in the play would preoccupy the rest of that autumn, when he was not working on the two film scripts or *Period of Adjustment*.

Sweet Bird of Youth eventually premiered on Broadway at the Martin Beck Theatre on 10 March 1959. Concluding the play with Chance's castration, an act of *quid pro quo* for his having infected Heavenly with VD and rendering her sterile after her hysterectomy, Williams no doubt anticipated critical condemnation of his continued obsession with violence on stage. As such, the pre-opening piece for the play, 'Williams' Wells of Violence', which first appeared in the *New York Times* two days earlier and was later reprinted as the play's foreword, announces Williams's necessity to resort to violence to access the truth. Williams wrote the piece in Philadelphia, along with another one titled 'Some Memorandae for a Sunday Times Piece that I Am Too Tired to Write', which begins as a series of personal notes to himself: 'Avoid the intimate, personal note'.[54] Both pieces were the product of his physical exhaustion and nervous prostration, but the published piece is the only coherent one of the two. In it, Williams drew on his therapeutic exercise in 'free association', describing his response to Inge's claim that Williams was 'blocked' as a writer: ' "Oh, yes, I've always been blocked as a writer but my desire to write has been so strong that it has always broken down the block and gone past it." Nothing untrue comes off the tongue that quickly. It is planned speeches that contain lies or dissimulations, not what you blurt out so spontaneously in one instant'.[55] Kubie clearly had reached Williams the previous year, and Williams was confident that his play presented the truth as he understood it with respect to Chance's and the Princess's separate crises.

Just like the play's heroine who flees Hollywood in anticipation of her latest film's critical panning, Williams ditched the Great White Way for safer havens soon after its opening. In another draft titled 'A Playwright's Prayer in Rehearsal', he had hoped to be 'booked, via jet plane, to other places and other plays'.[56] After brief stays at the Towers Hotel in Miami and his house in Key West, Williams flew to Havana where, through the help of Kenneth Tynan, he met and lunched with Ernest Hemingway at El Floridita. In his *Memoirs*, Williams recalls in detail this brief but momentous meeting with Hemingway and, later, with Castro:

> Before Castro took over Cuba, Marion [Vaccaro] and I used to have riotous weekends in Havana. Marion just as much enjoyed the frolicsome night like in Havana as I did and we would go to the same places to enjoy it. We even went back after Castro came in. The first time I went back to Havana after Castro's triumph, I was introduced to him by Ernest Hemingway, whom I met through the British theatre critic Kenneth Tynan. Tynan called me – I was staying at the Hotel Nacional in Havana – and he said, 'Would you like to meet Ernest Hemingway?' and I said, 'I don't think that's advisable, do you? I understand that he can be very unpleasant to people of my particular temperament.' And Tynan said, 'Well, I will be there to lend you what support I can. I think you ought to meet him because he is one of the great writers of your time and mine.' I said, 'Okay, I'll take a chance on it.' So we went down to the Floridita, which was Hemingway's nighttime and daytime hangout, when he wasn't at sea, and he couldn't have been more charming. He was exactly the opposite of what I'd expected. I had expected a very manly, super-macho sort of guy, very bullying and coarse spoken. On the contrary, Hemingway struck me as a gentleman who seemed to have a very touchingly shy quality about him.[57]

Williams then described his subsequent meeting with Castro. He verifies that 'Hemingway wrote [him] a letter of introduction to Castro', and that Tynan and he had visited the Palacio, the seat of the Cuban government:

> Castro was having a cabinet session at the time. His cabinet session lasted quite long. We waited it out, sitting on the steps outside the room in which the session was being held. After about a three-hour wait, the door was thrown open and we were ushered in. Castro greeted us both very warmly. When Kenneth Tynan introduced me,

the Generalissimo said, 'Oh, that cat,' meaning *Cat on a Hot Tin Roof*, which surprised me – delighted me, of course. I couldn't imagine the generalissimo knowing anything about a play of mine. Then he proceeded to introduce us to all of his cabinet ministers. We were given coffee and liqueurs and it was a lovely occasion, well worth the three-hour wait.[58]

Both encounters would have a profound effect on Williams.[59]

During this time, *Sweet Bird of Youth* was enjoying a successful run on Broadway despite its lukewarm to hostile reviews. Among those critics who panned the play was Tynan himself, who felt 'dismayed and alarmed' by it.[60] Another critic who attacked Williams was a relative new comer, Robert Brustein, whose scathing review of the play as 'cornball' and its pre-opening piece as 'embarrassingly explicit' haunted Williams for more than a decade. In his June 1959 review for *Encounter* titled 'Sweet Bird of Success', Brustein charged Williams with writing dishonestly by hiding his clear interest in incest:

> the play is interesting primarily if you are interested in its author. As dramatic art, it is disturbingly bad – aimless, dishonest, and crudely melodramatic – in a way that Williams's writing has not been bad since his early play, *Battle of Angels*. But if the latter failed because its author did not sufficiently understand his characters, *Sweet Bird of Youth* suffers both from his ignorance of, and obsession with, himself.[61]

The charge resembles the one that George Jean Nathan had levelled against *The Glass Menagerie* nearly fifteen years earlier, which elicited a similar retort from Williams: 'Truth is something that I have set up as my single standard, both as a writer and as an individual'.[62] In a 1957 interview with Don Ross, Williams repeated the claim: 'The moral contribution of my plays is that they expose what I consider to be untrue'.[63]

Here, Brustein's charge of dishonest writing sparked a flurry of attempted rejoinders that Williams had planned to send to the press. Some are called, appropriately enough, ['Reply to Professor Brustein']; others are titled 'Some Philosophical Shop-Talk' or 'These Scattered Idioms', two titles that he would use for the memoirs he was currently drafting. In one, Williams writes, 'Dear Professor Burstein [*sic*]: I read your piece in "Encounter" with understanding and appreciation of some valid points made, but I would like to discuss with you the charge of "dishonesty" that you make against me'.[64] In another draft, he expounds upon his idea that all creative writing is a form of psychotherapy (Kubie again) that should produce a catharsis, both in the playwright and in his audience: 'I cannot be cured of explicitness in my plays or my efforts at prose. You see, I feel with all my heart that writing must not be separated from the total truth of the writer's self, and I am by nature explicit'.[65] This, and the more polished responses that came later, were not the angry and frazzled attempts at a reply of a beleaguered playwright to one of his critics, but rather an open and detailed letter intended for the *Times*'s readers about the nature of contemporary American thea- tre and the relationship between its 'intellectual' playwrights and its 'pedantic' critics.

Though Williams had frequently responded to his critics (e.g., George Jean Nathan, Walter Kerr, Eric Bentley) and thanked others for their support (e.g., Brooks Atkinson), there was something new about these academic critics like Brustein. They were not 'old school' enough for Williams. The theatre criticism emerging from these 'Groves of the Academy', as Williams would often refer to Brustein, came out of books and not out of years of exposure to Broadway. Witnessing post-war thea- tre criticism quickly migrating from newspapers like the *New York Times* to magazines like *Time*, *Harper's*, or *The New Yorker*, to finally erudite and academic books like Bentley's *The Dramatic Event* (1954) or Brustein's *The Theatre of Revolt: An Approach to Modern Drama* (1964), Williams saw the need more and more to defend his brand of theatre against its rising hostility and misinterpretation, and he took up arms against them with his manual Olivetti typewriter.

In May 1959, Williams flew out to London to see the English premiere of *Orpheus Descending* at the Royal Court Theatre. By early June he was back in New York, where Williams attended rehearsals of the film *The Fugitive Kind* (certain exterior shots were filmed in Milton, New York, just north of the city). In July, Williams then drove south to Pennsylvania to see Diane Barrymore as Blanche in *A Streetcar Named Desire*, whose iden- tification with the role of a neurotic spinster compounded the alcohol abuse that led to her death the following January. Later that summer, Williams and Merlo began their three-month trip around the world. On 22 August, they flew to the Orient, where Williams's exposure to Kabuki and Noh theatre greatly influenced the direction his theatre would take in the following decade. Williams worked on several projects this sum- mer, including revisions of *Period of Adjustment* and 'Man Bring This Up Road', a story he had started in Positano and finished in Rome in August/September 1953 that he was now preparing for publication in

Mademoiselle for July. He returned to this story in a couple of years when he began drafting the play *The Milk Train Doesn't Stop Here Anymore* (1963). The fact that Williams wrote fewer short stories in the 1950s than he had in the previous decade owes to the exhaustion he felt working consistently on his full-length plays. While a story often gave birth to a play later, just as 'Three Players of a Summer Game' inspired *Cat on a Hot Tin Roof*, for the most part, the 1950s was a decade devoted to the theatre and non-fiction prose.

This non-fiction prose, most of which rests in an unpublishable state, evinces the notion that Williams saw the urgency to record his life and document his theory of the theatre. Though some of it was written before Brustein's attacks against Williams, much of it dates from just after *Sweet Bird*. Williams had repeatedly claimed since 1959, and more adamantly in 1971, that he was never going to write his memoirs. He would betray himself, of course, when he completed the first full draft of his *Memoirs* in the fall of 1972, an autobiography that he had actually begun in 1959. Audrey Wood once asked him a year later if he would ever change his mind, and Williams responded with the fragmented essay 'Twenty Years of It': 'I thought my agent should know that my biggest and last indiscretion would be to come out with the sort of autobiography that I would write if I wrote one. I would have to write it in the psycho-analytical style of free-association, and if I did write it, which I am not about to do, now or ever'.[66] Williams had always felt that autobiography would never explain his life and his art to his public better than his plays. 'Why do I resist writing about my plays?' Williams later asked himself in the *Memoirs*. 'The truth is', he responded,

> [...] I feel that the plays speak for themselves. And that my life hasn't and that it has been remarkable enough, in its continual contest with madness, to be worth setting upon paper. And my habits of work are so much more private than my daily and nightly existence.[67]

But that did not stop him from writing about both, then or now.

From 1959 to 1961, Williams produced well over four hundred pages of manuscripts for what he once called 'The Tennesee [*sic*] Williams Story', which he half-jokingly imagined being picked up by 'an independent producer who operates on a low-budget without stars and whose product is exhibited in the small houses'.[68] Many of these essay fragments, at times called 'These Scattered Idioms' or 'Sequitors and

Non-Sequitors', were first intended as pieces for the *Times* but bear the mark of Williams's extended foray into autobiographical writing. They range in topics from discussions of his plays *Period of Adjustment* and *Orpheus Descending* to his past experiences in becoming a writer; the disillusioned middle-aged men and playwrights like John Osborne of the 'New Wave' theatre; the role of women in his play; the memories of his grandfather, Walter Edwin Dakin; and the creative process. Several other drafts discuss his life during the 1930s and 1940s, the role of alcohol in his work, and his genealogy: 'Incomplete... (some fragments of my life)' (c. 1953), 'Lean Years' (c. post-1958), 'The Middle Years of a Writer' (March 1959), 'Life before Work' (c. 1959), and 'The Mornings, Afternoons, and Evenings of Writers' (c. 1960).

In the piece 'Incomplete... (some fragments of my life)' (c. 1953), Williams writes, 'This morning, like most mornings since last Spring, almost as soon as I had had one weak cup of coffee and started toward my work-table, the anxiety started, the incipient stir of tension that sometimes builds into a wave of panic, that freezes my fingers and makes me gasp for breath'.[69] The 'Lean Years', a 'compilation of accurate data from the horse's mouth, meaning mine, on the subject of my lean years', hopes to 'inspire be of moral value to writers who are young now as I was then, and very likely as hard-pressed for a subsistence living, which is to keep them alive and remaining at work'.[70] Just before his forty-eighth birthday and the opening of *Sweet Bird of Youth,* Williams typed out 'The Middle Years of a Writer', a 'free association' exercise in which he expresses his surprise to have ever made it to middle age:

> I have gone much further, in the sense of surviving much longer, as a playwright or than any kind of writer than I expected when I could still be classified as a young writer. I harbored, you almost might say cherished, the idea of a premature extinction in the romantic style of Thomas Chatterton, Arthur Rimbaud, Hart Crane or John Keats. I could not imagine myself as a middle-aged writer or even as a middle-aged man.[71]

In 'Life before Work', he discusses how his therapy with Kubie has forced him to reconsider the relationship between his work and his life. And in 'The Mornings, Afternoons, and Evenings of Writers', he outlines the 'three lives' of a writer's career, noting that he has recently entered the third life where 'all that has been learned or discovered along the way' of life 'may not be enough to compensate for the reduction of raw, youthful energy in the writer, and that is when the writer has to put up or shut up'.[72] As Flora Goforth would do a few years later in *Milk Train*, Williams was composing his life story for posterity's sake.

Other Sunday pieces that he began writing at the time, and would rework over the next year, were also intended to establish his dramatic theory. 'Prelude to a Comedy' (1960), which was a pre-opening piece for *Period of Adjustment*, discusses the nature of the American theatre. The fragments linked to this essay, as well as to 'The Man in the Overstuffed Chair', are many, and they demonstrate a playwright in full defence of his art. 'These Scattered Idioms', 'Some Philosophical Shop Talk, or An Inventory of a Remarkable Market', 'Some Philosophical Shop-Talk', 'Sam, You Made the Interview too Long', 'Personal as Ever', 'Bits and pieces of shop-talk', 'Shop Talk', and 'Deepest Instinct, or Fate... .' (all c. 1959/60) – in each, Williams presents his ability to weave pedestrian details about his life with loftier sentiments about the state of the American theatre and of the country in general. They not only show that Williams was working towards *both* essays simultaneously, but that Kubie's 'free association' exercise and Brustein's gauntlet-throwing criticism led Williams to devote a good portion of his writing day to non-fiction prose. Is there any wonder why he stopped writing in his notebooks and penned fewer letters at the end of the 1950s?

Recollections about his life and work were inextricable in Williams's mind at this time. He thought about his life, as he had about his characters' lives, in terms of scenes and acts, of entrances and exits, of climaxes and denouements, and each of these fragments demonstrates how he wrote and rewrote each scene until he found its proper spine. And just as with his plays, Williams could not leave a polished piece of writing alone, fiddling with dialogue or scenes long after the play ended its Broadway run or appeared in print. In the many fragments he wrote during 1959–60, it is difficult to tell which he had envisioned as familial anecdotes for his Sunday pieces and which as philosophical 'shop talk' on the nature of violence (such as he had known in his father) for 'The Man in the Overstuffed Chair'. In other words, we find throughout most of these late 1950s and early 1960s fragments a Williams recalling his youth either to recuperate new material for a play or to express what ills mankind on the whole had to face as the Cold War began heating up. If the open letter to Brustein was never finally sent, the response itself preoccupied Williams for more than a decade. Brustein's comment had cut Williams so deeply that if forced him into a mode of self-reflection deeper than even what Kubie had managed with him. Thus, if Kubie indirectly gave the world *Sudden Last Summer*, Brustein paved the way to Williams's best non-fiction writing.

Williams and Merlo were back again in New York on Thanksgiving to attend the preview of *The Fugitive Kind*. Their relationship was amiable for the most part but lacking in emotional commitment from either of them. Williams was not happy with himself throughout the decade, in particular his treatment of Frank Merlo. But Merlo's suddenly illness did not give Williams much time to make amends, if that was what he really wanted to do anyway.

On the professional side, following the letdown of *Sweet Bird of Youth*, Williams returned to an earlier story and began writing a dramatic treatment of his time in Acapulco in 1940, what would become his last successful play on Broadway, *The Night of the Iguana*. Williams was also completing the final revisions on his dark domestic comedy, *Period of Adjustment*, which he described to Maria St Just as 'an unimportant and charming little play'.[73] Its premiere at the Coconut Grove Playhouse in Miami in December 1958 was strong enough to see it transferred to New York in November 1960.

The end of the 1950s was an important period in Williams's recollection about his past life and where his future was taking him, personally and professionally. While many critics have often divided Williams's career between the pre- and post-*Iguana* plays, it would be more accurate to divide it between the pre- and post-*Sweet Bird* plays. Williams cracked seriously in 1959, but he had already cracked in 1957; yet that madness was safely hidden behind the mask of genius that gave the world *Suddenly Last Summer*. *The Night of the Iguana*, if anything, is more the anomaly of the second half of his career, one noted by the palpable shift in his voice and style from melodrama to black comedy. The real cusp of Williams's second life, then, is found in *Period of Adjustment*, Williams's self-claimed 'Serious Comedy'. The title was vastly appropriate at this time in Williams's life, since he was undergoing his own period of adjustment that would see him into the 1960s.

That adjustment, however, held more problems for Williams than it did triumphs. By the start of 1960, Williams was still very much an eminent figure on Broadway and in Hollywood. Yet, the depression, the drugs, the insomnia, the restlessness, the alcohol, the infidelities, and the artistic exhaustion were all contributing to his sense of having reached bottom. He could not predict that, after one more rise to the top, he would fall even farther. When he stopped this past year or so to examine his life from its various angles, what he came to realize was that the battles he confronted daily – over drugs, alcohol, love, and work – were more often than not the ones of his own making.

The last decade would indeed prove to be a battle of angles, those peaks and troughs that represent the triumphant reception of some plays and the vituperative rejection of others. Monitored as such, his career these past ten years resembled a chart that tracked the stock market or the beat-by-beat palpitations of a heart on an electrocardiogram. There was still one systolic push ahead of him, *The Night of the Iguana*, but then Williams's career would flatline, briefly, before entering freefall, resembling something like the New York Stock Exchange on the months following the Black Tuesday he had predicted back in November 1928.

8
Tokyo to St Louis (via Spoleto): The Stoned(wall) Age

The 1960s are commonly referred to as Williams's 'stoned age', a term he himself used to explain the years of drug and alcohol dependency and depression that forced his brother Dakin to place him unwillingly in a mental ward for several months in 1969. In many ways, the various diversions that Williams's playwriting was experiencing at this time mirror the numerous directions his personal life was leading him. What remained unclear for many of his audiences and critics, though, was whether Williams's art during the decade was imitating life or his life was imitating art.

The plays of this decade are unlike those that established and confirmed his reputation in the 1940s and 1950s. Despite these new directions for Williams, few critics were unable, or unwilling, to discern his plays' experimental natures and thus deemed them all, one after the other, as being largely inferior to *A Streetcar Named Desire* or *Cat on a Hot Tin Roof*. Williams once said that he was through composing 'symphonies' and wanted instead to devote his time to 'chamber music'.[1] More recent critics, like Annette Saddik and Linda Dorff, have begun reclaiming these forgotten or rejected 'chamber' pieces for the Williams canon. The tenor of Williams criticism today is that Williams's career did not end with *The Night of the Iguana* in 1961 but that a second career began just after it with the Noh-inspired play, *The Milk Train Doesn't Stop Here Anymore*. Perhaps that second career had already begun with *Period of Adjustment*.

Not all of the 1960s was amiss, however. Williams did open the decade with one last critical and commercial success, *The Night of the Iguana*. That the play evoked the poetic naturalism of the theatre that Williams produced in previous years was no doubt one of the reasons behind its success. Williams had again become retrospective, and the play's mix of personal philosophy and national nostalgia struck the right balance of sex-laced melodrama and catharsis-producing tragedy for Broadway audiences. Moving from its Chicago try-out on 23 December to the Royale Theatre on Broadway on 28 December 1961, *Iguana* ran for 316 performances, and the following April Williams was awarded another New York Drama Critics' Circle Award. He had erased the failures of *Sweet Bird of Youth* and momentarily felt alive again. But it would be the last time that he would sit atop Broadway's summit. When personal crisis hit in the death of Frank Merlo, theatrical crisis soon followed. The rest of this decade would prove a rocky one for Williams, who seemed to fall a little bit farther down that northern stone mountain called the Great White Way with each subsequent play he produced.

Hannah's Eastern philosophy in *Iguana* was conspicuously Williams's at the time. Forming part of the itinerary of his three-month trip with Merlo around the world in the late summer and fall of 1959, Williams stopped over in Tokyo to see the novelist and playwright Yukio Mishima, whom he had previously met in New York through Jay Laughlin at New Directions. Mishima introduced Williams to the Kabuki and the Noh theatre traditions of his country, which profoundly altered his thinking and his writing. The result of those reflections led to Williams's next play, *The Milk Train Doesn't Stop Here Anymore*. Following try-outs at the Spoleto Festival in July 1962, the play opened at the Morosco Theatre on 16 January 1963, but closed soon after. At this time, Merlo was in a hospital dying of lung cancer, and much of Williams's anxieties over Merlo's suffering can be felt in the play's 'Angel of Death', Christopher Flanders, the young gigolo who helps Flora come to terms with her mortality.

Williams's response to Merlo's death was to pursue comedy, but his brand of black humour barely cracked a smile in the stone faces of his critics. They erringly dismissed the next play, *Slapstick Tragedy* (a double bill joining *The Mutilated* with *The Gnädiges Fräulein*) as a pale copy of the classics of 'Theatre of the Absurd', a term coined by Martin Esslin in his book on the experimental plays of Samuel Beckett, Arthur Adamov, Eugene Ionesco, and Jean Genet. Instead, his plays were written in a style 'kin to vaudeville, burlesque and slapstick, with a dash of pop art thrown in' – not unlike 'news' stories published in the tabloid *The National Inquirer*.[2]

Williams saw *Slapstick Tragedy* as fitting more into the tradition of the carnivalesque Grand Guignol, a theatre of violent excess in the Pigalle district of Paris that Williams knew well for its notorious prostitution and *Moulin Rouge*.[3] The Grand Guignol's tradition of mounting short naturalistic horror shows, whose gratuitous use of blood and gore were set against light comedies to heighten their dramatic effect, seemed to capture well Williams's artistic vision at the time. An early title for *Suddenly Last Summer* was, in fact, 'A Play for the Grand Guignol', and Williams even imagined a theatre evening as late as the summer of 1982 titled 'Williams's Guignol'.[4] He did offer a night of the Grand Guignol in the mid-1960s, and it cost him his career. When the double bill finally opened on 22 February 1966 at the Longacre Theatre in New York, it closed after only seven performances. No one was laughing, least of all Williams. It seemed as if his career had reached its nadir.

Unfortunately, Williams would explore depths even lower than Maxim Gorky's with his next three plays, *Kingdom of Earth*, *In the Bar of a Tokyo Hotel*, and *The Two-Character Play*. *Kingdom of Earth*, or *The Seven Descents of Myrtle*, opened on 27 March 1968 at the Ethel Barrymore Theatre, but ran for only twenty-nine performances until 20 April. Williams had predicted (or even announced) the play's failure in his pre-opening piece, 'Happiness Is Relevant', which was published in the *New York Times* just three days before the premiere. In the essay, Williams recalls how his mother wanted to attend the play's opening 'if it isn't closed out of New York', a self-damning phrase that is only slightly attenuated when Williams ensures his readers that 'we trust' the New York opening 'will occur'.[5]

In the Bar of a Tokyo Hotel did not fare much better, opening Off Broadway at the Eastside Playhouse on 11 May 1969 and closing on 1 June, twenty-two previews and twenty-five performances later. In his pre-opening piece for this long one-act, '"Tennessee, Never Talk to an Actress"', also published in the *New York Times* a week prior to the premiere, Williams once again acted as 'the spokesman for the party of doom'.[6] As was typical in Williams's short pieces for the *Times*, he never discussed the play directly but often commented upon it through parables of personal anecdotes that many of his readers probably did not understand. Here, the essay enumerates Williams's several run-ins with celebrity actresses who bristled at his honest evaluation of their performances. Always self-damning before being publically vilified for the production that lay ahead, Williams is unmistakably substituting one actress's line for his own: '"At this point in an out-of-town tour," she told us, "I can always tell if a play is going to be well or poorly received in New York"'.[7] Yet faithful to his signature line that he must always go forth in spite of the setbacks, Williams added, 'Must silence always follow the loss of a star? In my opinion, no'.[8] The star here is not an actress who leaves a show midway through its successful run, as Bette Davis had left *Iguana*, but a playwright who needed to justify his literary output when one failure followed on the heels of another.

Not only would Williams *not* remain silent in the face of the growing hostile criticism levelled against him, but he would cry out in retaliation with yet another play more outrageous than the one before. Williams's next play, which in fact had its first production in 1967, was *The Two-Character Play*. The play's ill reception by confused or outraged critics and audiences obsessed Williams for years, who rightly recognized it as his best work of the decade, if not of his later career in its entirety. The play, which would undergo several rewrites and productions, serves as a bridge between his stoned 1960s and his paranoid 1970s. There was, of course, more at stake with the play than simply its critical and commercial acceptance, but *that* issue only really became relevant after he spent time as a mental patient. This chapter will explore the decade's radical changes with respect to Williams's plays, which many critics once believed were simply lagging behind his earlier work but which are now accepted as having been clearly ahead of their day.

In spite of the fact that it would all end rather tragically for Williams by the end of the decade, the 1960s began on several high notes. In April 1960, Williams was working with Louise de Rochemont and screenwriter Gavin Lambert on the film adaption of his novel *The Roman Spring of Mrs. Stone*, which was to begin filming that fall in Rome and open the following autumn of 1961. It would be the only film made of his work that he really liked. He improved relations with his family, one positive by-product of his father's death and his psychotherapy with Dr Lawrence Kubie. Instead of going off to Europe as he had planned that June 1960, Williams took Edwina, Dakin, and his wife Joyce with him to the West Coast, where they hobnobbed with celebrities like Mae West and Elvis Presley.

Later that month, Williams returned to Key West to continue work on a new major play that he had begun the previous fall. His Key West studio was a distraction as much as it was a benefit to his writing, however, for its was always filled with the various characters he surrounded himself with, like Marion Vaccaro and Lilla van Saher. In one letter to Donald Windham, Williams even described the trouble he was having with a local 'Conch', who was disturbing the peace by threatening everyone who came near him with a kitchen knife.[9] As was typical, Williams never managed to rid these distractions from his life, and if anything he even encouraged them. As for this undesirable 'Conch' guest, Williams noted later in a daily prose piece that he went on to sort his life out and became one of the best electrical mechanics on the keys.[10] Score one point for Williams's fugitive kind. But if Williams could frequently forgive a certain nobody for his social digression, he would never deprive those close to him of the sting of his deception.

Williams stayed in sultry Key West that summer to see an early production of *The Night of the Iguana*, which had been prepared at the Actors Studio under the direction of Frank Corsaro. This one-act version of the play, which was first performed at the Spoleto Festival in Italy on 2 July 1959, was brought to the Coconut Grove in Miami that August and drew the attention of several key figures in the play's future success. Williams completed the story 'The Night of the Iguana' in Rome back in 1948, though he had begun writing it in New Orleans two years earlier, about the same time that he was drafting *Ten Blocks on the Camino Real*, *Summer and Smoke*, and *A Streetcar Named Desire*. Unlike Hannah in *The Night of the Iguana*, a would-be Brahmin from New England, Edith Jelkes in the story is a southerner, a former school teacher of art at an 'Episcopalian girls' school in Mississippi' who, like many of the early avatars of Blanche DuBois, 'had suffered a sort of nervous breakdown and had given up her teaching position for a life of refined vagrancy'.[11] Also like Blanche, this 'spinster of thirty with a wistful blond prettiness and a somewhat archaic quality of refinement' is a lady from an historical southern family of great but now moribund vitality whose later generations had tended to split into two antithetical types, one in which the libido was pathologically distended and another in which it would seem to be all but dried up.[12] Aside from the title, the setting, the roped iguana, and Miss Jelkes's surname, the story and this one-act and the 1961 full-length play have little in common. Most of this material, well worn in the Williams canon by this time, was rightly rejected for a different take on people's 'blue devils'.

The fall of 1960 was an important time in Williams's literary life. With echoes of Robert Brustein's 1959 charge against him still ringing in his head, Williams frequently continued his auto-writing about his life, his family, his career, and his vision of American theatre. He felt the mounting need to attend to the image of himself as an American playwright and so, along with his work on *Iguana*, Williams spent hours documenting his theory of the American theatre. In a later version of an essay that he began the previous year, titled 'Some Philosophical Shop Talk, or An Inventory of a Remarkable Market' (c. autumn 1960),Williams speaks extensively about actors, playwrights, directors, and the theatre of the day.[13] He goes into detail about an actress's tantrum against a producer for a shoddy set designer; about an actor who arrived at rehearsal without knowing his lines; about American versus French theatre; and about the vampiric egos of vain playwrights, 'those unattractively

awkward, embarrassed, ~~graceless~~, blushing, fidgeting, shuffling, stam-
mering, wretches who hang over the production of a play like ~~a stench~~
~~of xxxxx~~ the ~~stench~~ smell of ~~a rotting~~ an over-ripe ego'.[14]

Midway through the draft, Williams begins discussing the relationship between a playwright and his director in words that echo a previous essay of his, 'Author and Director: A Delicate Situation' (1957). His
definition here is as good as anything he said about the theatre:

> [...] the thing that distinguishes the theatre from the world, of which
> it is ~~our~~ a mirror, is a beautiful thing: it is a xxxxxxxxxxx choice, in
> crisis, of both finding and losing one's self, or, to put it somewhat
> better, the finding of xxxxxxxxxxxx one's best self through the
> abnegation of the more selfish self, in the creation of something
> <u>collaboratively</u>, and if this means 'togetherness', that over-worn word,
> then let's bear in mind that most cliches become cliches because they
> mean the most to the most: in other words contain truth.[15]

Williams concludes his thoughts about the 'Broadway society', those
who make up his audiences. They are not 'cultural cannibals' but 'ter-
rifically knowing' creatures fully aware when a scene is being overacted
to counter its lack of poetry, or when a set is 'lovely to look at but awful
to play on', and able to distinguish 'a gag line from one that is honestly
amusing', or 'color-blind to purple patches in a sometimes pretentious
script'.[16] If they could not understand his brand of theatre, it was not
because they were ignorant; rather, it was because the nation was wean-
ing them on a syrupy pap that soured their tastes to anything that was
not sugar-coated.

All of this material was originally intended for his essay 'Tennessee
Williams Presents his POV' (1960), which he wrote as a direct response
to Marya Mannes's May 1960 essay 'Plea for Fairer Ladies', wherein she
describes recent Broadway plays as 'snake pits' and how only a 'psychiatrist or a nurse in a mental institution would have spent several hours
of so many nights in the company of addicts, perverts, sadists, hysterics,
bums, delinquents, and others afflicted in mind and body'.[17] Given the
obvious allusion to violence in Williams's plays (such as rape, castration, immolation, and cannibalism), Williams felt the need to defend
himself and the American theatre in general. In one essay fragment
titled 'The Good Men & the Bad Men' (c. 1960), previously titled 'Get
the Corpse Out of the 'Copter', Williams complains that, while violence
is allowed to permeate American television screens, he is not allowed to
bring it onto the American stage.

Williams's view was that popular culture, fuelled by post-war jingoism, was generating a binary violent impulse in American mores in the 1950s that pit the good 'white hat' guys against the bad 'black hat' guys, and that this epistemological banality was keeping audiences from recognizing that violence in his plays was not diametrically opposed. In short, TV Nation was killing Theatre Nation by proscribing certain modes of acceptable social interaction and by anaesthetizing the public to real forms of human tragedy. As the nation thickened its skin to violent projections, Williams felt forced to up the stakes in his plays. But where could Williams logically go, having already dramatized rape, castration, and murder? Williams had only two viable directions: the absurd, such as the Grand Guignol violence of *The Gnädiges Fräulein*, or the surreal, such as the tragedy-within-the-tragedy of *Out Cry*.

Williams wrote a few years back in 'The World I Live In' (1957) that he did not 'believe in villains or heroes – only right and wrong ways that individuals have taken, not by choice but by necessity'.[18] Here, in 1960, he still believed

> that evil ~~is not~~ is not identifiable with places or beings in them, but a <u>thing</u>, a <u>disease</u>, afflicting these beings and places, with nothing to show that xxxxxxxx is was ever ~~consciously~~ deliberately and consciously chosen. And finally, this: I don't buy the cynical comment, made by someone somewhere, that God, in whom I believe, is on the side of the heaviest artillery. I believe as much as I am able that He prefers a butterfly to a cannon.[19]

Williams felt that it was 'risky' for him to show the nation that American pop culture was persuading it 'to believe that the human race is really and truly divided between cops and robbers, ranchers and cattle-rustlers: the good and the bad':

> My message is that I don't believe there is any such sharp definition, certainly none sharp enough to excuse the bang-bang and the rat-a-tat-tat, and the upliftingly, musical, and luminous finale of a movie or TV drama in which there has been great carnage with the good men walking off, smiling, ~~or kissing~~ to kiss their sweethearts.[20]

Williams voiced a similar opinion to Edward R. Murrow in May 1960 on his 'Small World' broadcast for CBS, arguing his case for 'the light and the shadow' sides to human nature and how emotional violence is the necessary obstacle to love.[21]

In another, one-page essay fragment from this time, Williams again tried setting down his theory of dramatic art, one that also makes reference to Brustein's attack against his overly personal writing:

> My theory about creative art is that it must, or should be, as close to your intensely personal experience as possible and even if you should betray that dreadful and somewhat disgusting thing, an excessive concern with yourself, you must go for broke with the hope that there are people enough, with the same inclination or disease, for your work to be understood and partly excused by a majority of them.[22]

He continues in this draft about how art in general cannot be anything but personal and about how a writer's confrontation with life's frightening experiences is an expression of that art. In another passage, he illustrates this idea by explaining how prehistoric cave drawings told personal tales of the animals the caveman encountered in battle.

This last image would eventually make it into his pre-opening piece for *Period of Adjustment*, 'Prelude to a Comedy', which is really more a coda to his earlier 'POV' essay. Here, Williams's discussion of violence in American culture and how he saw all couples, gay and straight alike, working through their relational problems was no doubt inspired by his own troubled life with Merlo. Merlo, like Brustein and Mannes, precipitated in Williams the need to re-examine his life, his love and his art, and Williams's period of adjustment was, for the moment, working well.

In a fragment to 'Prelude to a Comedy' that begins 'and in this way we fight the bang-bang' (c. 1960), Williams writes:

> In my new play about human adjustments, and the enormous difficulties of them, the misunderstandings xxxxxxxx, the pride and the wounds of pride, the aggressions and counter aggressions, it may be that I was all the time trying, without knowing I was, to state my total disbelief in and rejection of the black-and-white differences among individuals, nations, and hemispheres on this planet, my conviction that the world is passing through a period of adjustment like the two young married couples in my play, and that the only hope lies in our finding patience, insight and tolerance, (those things that are the trinity of wisdom,) to stop thinking in terms of 'My daddy can beat your daddy', the yells of little boys, the bang-bang and the rat-a-tat-tat or last big boom of the 'good men' destroying

the 'bad men', but in the infinitely difficult but infinitely necessary [texts breaks off here].[23]

We can only wonder what that 'infinitely necessary' actually was for Williams; to some extent, the break in the text is itself like a Hollywood film, where the hero, who is about to reveal the name of the murderer, is suddenly killed himself before the declaration is finally made. Life *can* imitate art, and that will perhaps remain one of Williams's greatest gifts to American culture.

By November 1960, Williams was planning to head to Rome to take part in the filming of *The Roman Spring of Mrs. Stone*, but he was stuck stateside due to pneumonia. The difficulties that he had experienced with *Sweet Bird of Youth* were still taxing his nerves and taking their toll on his general well-being, despite a relative uplift from good reviews and audience approval of his new 'serious comedy', *Period of Adjustment: or, High Point Is Built on a Cavern*. The play, which opened on Broadway at the Helen Hayes Theatre on 10 November and closed on 4 March 1961 after a reasonable run of 132 performances, was written concurrently with *Suddenly Last Summer*, and though it announced a new direction for Williams's theatre, it could certainly be read as a black comic companion piece to the darker one-act play on the nature of psychological trauma formed in couples.

Period of Adjustment juxtaposes the marital problems of two couples on Christmas Eve, one newly wed and the other married for five years. George Haverstick, a Korean War veteran who suffers from posttraumatic stress, gets drunk on his honeymoon and forces himself on his wife Isabel. His friend Ralph Bates feels emasculated working for his wife Dorothy's father. The story in many ways prepared audiences for Edward Albee's tragicomic play, *Who's Afraid of Virginia Woolf?* which was produced the following year. As with Albee's two couples, Williams's pair finds stasis to their relational plight, with the Bates and the Haversticks accepting in the end that what they have with their spouses is better than the void they would have to face alone – a decision, no doubt, inspired by Williams's failing relationship with Merlo. *Period of Adjustment* might have been a greater success, Cheryl Crawford mused, had younger actors been cast, which would have made their marital problems more pronounced for the audience.[24] Film rights were sold quickly, with the movie, like the play, being directed by George Roy Hill for MGM (1962). Complete now was the Williams–Kazan rift that began when Kazan refused to direct the play, citing other professional engagements that included the filming of Inge's script *Splendor in the Grass*.[25]

Williams knew that *Period of Adjustment* was not going to be a Broadway smash, but he had hoped that it would be one step up from the abyss that *Sweet Bird* had thrown him into the previous year. By December, Williams was worn out, convinced that *Iguana* was going to be his last play for Broadway, a line that he would repeatedly use throughout his professional life since *A Streetcar Named Desire*. As he confided to Maria St Just in a letter that month,

> Anyhow I had planned to stop work in the sixties. I am so far out of fashion, now, that I am almost back in. Withering attacks from all critical directions, they even hold me responsible for the corruption of other playwrights. I think I should enjoy resting now for ten years on my withered laurels, I am sick of my work myself.[26]

Williams did not rest on his laurels, however; he was physically and psychologically incapable of walking away from his typewriter, which was something he had learned from psychoanalysis in spite of his therapist's advice. Williams not only continued writing but also pursued artistic avenues that he had not ventured down before in his theatre, at least not since *Camino Real*.

In early 1961, Williams was busy in Key West working on *Iguana*, but then decided he needed to head off again to Europe. As his and Merlo's relationship was souring beyond the point of reconciliation, Williams took Marion Vaccaro alone with him this time. After a brief stay in London, they went to Rome, where in April they met up with Windham and his partner Sandy Campbell, and then on to Taormina and Rhodes, staying at the 'model prison-farm, Hotel Miramare'.[27] By the summer, he was back in New York, and in Key West by autumn, where he returned to Merlo. His life with Merlo was all but over, but Williams was nonetheless concerned about his partner's health. Merlo's four-packs-a-day cigarette habit was bringing about the lung cancer that would soon kill him. Williams's own alcohol and drug habit increased during this time, and the combination of drugs, professional paranoia, and personal resentment toward those who had previously cared for him, put Williams on the one-way track of his own 'Cemeteries' streetcar.

The collapse of his relationship with Merlo would be echoed in the destruction of other close relationships Williams had had over the past decade or more. His first break came with Cheryl Crawford, who had produced four of his last plays. Williams was under the wrong impression that she did not want to produce another of his plays for fear of losing money, which is why he sought out Charles Bowden to produce

Iguana. Next up was Audrey Wood. Though he would maintain a part-nership with Wood over the next decade, the strain that finally ended their working relationship in July 1971 was already palpable. Wood had recently obtained the manuscripts of two books about Williams earlier that year, Benjamin Nelson's *Tennessee Williams: The Man and his Work*, and Nancy Tischler's *Tennessee Williams: Rebellious Puritan*, both pub-lished in the fall of 1961 and reviewed by Brooks Atkinson in the *New York Times* on 26 November.[28] Wood felt that it was time for Williams to capture his life on paper, a request he openly refused and quietly honoured through the various essays that he had already begun drafting about his life and his work.

Williams was irritated with Wood in the same way that he would become irate with Jay Laughlin a decade later for his wanting Williams to publish his *Collected Plays* with New Directions.[29] Williams inter-preted both suggestions as indications of their feelings that his career was now over and that his memoirs and collected works represented his final legacy. Williams, though, was adamant that his legacy was only half over, which indeed it was by 1961, given that he would write and produce plays for another twenty-two years. Williams quickly took revenge on Wood in his essay 'The Agent as Catalyst', which was pub-lished in *Esquire* in December 1962. In it, Williams describes Wood, with whom he had worked for twenty-two years up to this point in time, as a 'mother-image' – with all the ambiguity that that epithet carried for Williams with regards to his rocky relationship with Edwina – and a woman who is 'nothing if not impressive' in her 'domination' of him.[30] As he had done with Inge in a similar type of piece, Williams damns Wood through his praise for her, and the highly perceptive Wood no doubt felt the shot fired across her desk.

Williams returned to New York in October 1961 to prepare for rehears-als of *Iguana*, and, by the end of November, he was in Chicago for the try-outs before its Broadway premiere just after Christmas. As he later described in his pre-opening piece for the play, 'A Summer of Discovery' (1961), *The Night of the Iguana* was based on his first trip down to Mexico – his North via south, as it were, given his moral compass and his need to return to a time just prior to success. Back in August 1940, Williams wrote in his notebook, 'I have just read an article about travel in Mexico. Perhaps this proposed trip will revive me'. The next day, he added, 'Thursday I may leave for Mexico. [...] (I think I will start a new Journal with the Mexican period and make it more complete)'. Then, on 21 August, he noted: 'Met the car-owners and they seem to be a comfortable sort of couple. It may be bearable after all'.[31] In his

Memoirs, Williams described the couple who drove with him to Mexico in detail:

> I determined upon a course of action, flight to Mexico. In those days there was an advertised service by which someone desiring trans-portation by car to some other city – in this case, another country – could contact a driver going that way and arrange to share the expenses of the journey. I applied to that service, when I'd returned to Manhattan in my state of shock [over the break-up with Kip], and was quite speedily introduced to a young Mexican who had come to New York by car to see the 1940 World's Fair and who had married a prostitute in Manhattan and now was taking her home to meet his wealthy family in Mexico City.[32]

While in Acapulco that summer, Williams stayed at Todd's Place, 'a resort run by a drunken "Georgia cracker" and his "fat Mexican" wife' and 'occupied mainly by lizards – and Tennessee Williams'.[33] Williams left this hotel after the proprietors 'vamoosed' and moved to the Hotel Costa Verde, where he 'sw[am] before breakfast and again after supper' and spent his 'evenings in a hammock talking to the other Americans and drinking iced coconut milk right out of the shell – sometimes with a little rum in it'.[34] All of this, save the actual drive down to Mexico, which is reworked into the bus tour company, becomes the locale and the plot of *Iguana*.

Williams added an entirely new dramatis persona and storyline to his story 'The Night of the Iguana' when he adapted it to the play, keeping only the symbols of the raging storm and the tethered iguana. Edith in the story is now the defrocked Episcopal clergyman, Reverend T. Lawrence Shannon, who is torn between his affections for the God he once served and the sexual appetite he now gratifies with an under-aged girl. Shannon retreats to the Costa Verde Hotel to find solace and to hide – from God, from the authorities, and from himself. Yet his 'spook in the rain forest' – those 'blue devils' borne out of the guilt he carries with him for having rescinded his holy vows – follows him there, taunt-ing him with its equal propositions of the spirit (rejoining his religious order) and of the flesh (seducing young Charlotte Goodall, one of the many young girls he has taken advantage of on the Mexican tours he guides). In order to dramatize what is occurring internally in Shannon, Williams added two other characters – Maxine Faulk and Hannah Jelkes. Maxine supplies the argument for the flesh and tries desperately to sway Shannon's attention away from Hannah, who conversely provides spirit. If Williams's prior allegories about the human struggle between the flesh and the spirit – from *Spring Storm* to *Battle of Angels* and from *Summer and Smoke* to *A Streetcar Named Desire* – all ended with the flesh ultimately winning out (in Williams's earlier equation, the flesh simply *was* the spirit), his final message in *Iguana* is endurance.

In Williams's dramatic and fictional worlds, people need each other. Those who are fugitives often think they are running from society when, in fact, they have only been running from themselves. Such is the case in *Iguana*. Only Shannon, though, undergoes any such epiphany here, as Charlotte, Maxine, and Hannah remain by the end essentially what they were at the beginning of the play. *Iguana* thus becomes another of Williams's medieval morality plays with Shannon cast as Everyman and those around him as allegorical renderings of humours. Charlotte, a girl of almost seventeen, represents Shannon's impotent quest for innocence in himself; and when he makes love to her, he recognizes that he has not regained his lost innocence but instead has corrupted her, a theme diametrically opposed to Williams's Beauty and the Beast pantomime in his earlier play, *Stairs to the Roof*. Maxine, on the other hand, is for Shannon, an '*affable and rapaciously lusty*'[35] woman who instructs Shannon to give up his heavenly aspirations for those of the physical world. Lastly, Hannah represents spirit, a '*remarkable-looking – ethereal, almost ghostly* [woman]. *She suggests a Gothic cathedral image of a medieval saint, but animated* [....] [and] *totally feminine and yet androgynous-looking – almost timeless*'.[36] Williams even describes her later as a '*medieval sculpture of a saint*'.[37]

Iguana managed to draw upon many of the themes and characters of Williams's previous plays but, unlike them, it offered audiences a new character in Hannah, one based in part of Williams's experiences in the Orient. Shannon, like most of Williams's protagonists, exists on 'two levels [...] the realistic level and the fantastic level, and which is the real one, really.... [...] But when you live on the fantastic level as I have lately but have got to operate on the realistic level, that's when you're spooked, that's the spook ...'.[38] The spook is the manifestation of guilt resulting from indulging in illicit pleasure. To Hannah, this is Shannon's Passion Play: 'Who wouldn't like to suffer and atone for the sins of himself and the world if it could be done in a hammock with ropes instead of nails, on a hill that's so much more lovelier than Golgotha ...'.[39] Hannah, too, was haunted once by her blue devils and 'had quite a battle, quite a contest' with them.[40] But now she is at peace, one of the few Williams characters ever to achieve such a state of grace. Her answer to Shannon's question on how one can dispel one's spook is the same answer she had learned from her grandfather Nonno, and one Williams had discovered in the East – endurance: 'Endurance is something that spooks and blue devils respect'.[41]

Hannah's message to Shannon that one's spook or blue devil was what made that person unique was perhaps not entirely lost on audiences or critics who witnessed Williams's battle of angles throughout the previous decade. Nor was it lost on Williams himself. Endurance was surely not as new a message to Williams as it was to Shannon, but it was the first time Williams ever allowed one of his major characters up to now to embrace it fully. 'You have always traveled alone except for your spook, as you call it', Hannah says. 'He's your traveling companion. Nothing, nobody else has traveled with you'.[42] When Shannon finally expiates his guilt and cuts the iguana loose and Nonno reaches the end of his long endurance and completes his valedictory poem, Williams achieves a poetic moment on stage to rival Blanche's exiting on the arm of her kind stranger or Laura's blowing out of her candles. Audience and critics alike were mesmerized, and Williams won back the accolades that had escaped him the last few years. In *The Night of the Iguana*, Shannon learns the lesson Williams had to learn himself: the only response to the suffering was not to end it, or resolve it, but endure it. This was the lesson that Williams put repeatedly to the test throughout the rest of the decade after plunging into a quagmire of death, drugs, and alcohol, from which he would only momentarily emerge.

When *Time* magazine put Williams on its 9 March 1962 cover, and titled its piece on him rather appropriately 'The Angel of the Odd' (given his tense history with the Luce mouthpiece of American conservatism), it would seem that Williams was once again on top. He was, momentarily, for *Iguana* would be his final curtain call. He would never again in his lifetime achieve the Broadway success that *Iguana* had given him. There would be flickers of greatness witnessed in a few plays of his over the next twenty years, but mostly his Broadway presence was blacked out. Some critics would agree with Williams that it was a conspiracy against him involving New York's homophobic critics and Broadway's moneymen (and women) who grew tired of his formula or wary of his bankability. Williams's productions were never really given the time or the money needed for a production that would win awards or the hearts of dwindling audiences.

The rest of the decade would be littered with a series of ones: one mishap too often, one failed relationship after another, one pinky and scotch too many, one dramatic line too few, and one character named One in his one-act play *I Can't Imagine Tomorrow* (1966) who wants Two to leave her alone. The title seemed to capture perfectly all that Williams wanted to say about his depression. Though he knew that his relationship with Merlo was as mundane and routine as that between One and Two in this play, Williams could not escape the fact that Merlo's death had affected him. But for the moment, Merlo was still alive, barely, and Williams could not deal with the thought of facing death and the inescapable blood that would recall Grand's violent haemorrhaging. If *Iguana* was Williams's encomium to his past, his next play, *The Milk Train Doesn't Stop Here Anymore*, was obviously an analgesic to his, and Merlo's, present.

In January 1962, he admitted to Lewis Funke that his 'pseudo-literary style of writing for the theatre' was 'on its way out' and that he wanted to explore new directions, and *The Milk Train Doesn't Stop Here Anymore* was one of them.[43] Based on the promise of its try-outs at the Festival of Two Worlds in Spoleto, Italy, on 11 July 1962, Williams brought *Milk Train* to the Morosco Theatre the following January, but the play closed sixty-nine performances later on 16 March a critical and a commercial failure. Ten months and several rewrites later, a third production was mounted in September at the Barter Theatre in Abingdon, Virginia. Again, its promising reviews convinced Williams to bring the play once again to New York, now with Tallulah Bankhead replacing Hermione Baddeley as Flora Goforth. In his 1963 essay 'T. Williams's View of T. Bankhead', Williams admitted (no doubt retroactively) that he wrote the play for Bankhead, but at the time 'it wasn't ready' for her:

> so I tried it out in Spoleto with an English actress, Hermione Baddeley, and she was so terrific that I staggered into her dressing room, after the Spoleto opening, and said, 'Hermione, this play will be yours if you want it next season on Broadway.' What did Tallulah say? She said: 'Well, darling, you did the right thing and that's that. But if it doesn't work because it isn't ready, well, you know me. And I know you wrote it for me and sometime I'm going to play it'.[44]

Although the try-outs 'limped through several cities',[45] the revival opened at the Brooks Atkinson Theatre on 1 January 1964 and closed disastrously three days later.

One of *Milk Train*'s obvious inspirations, besides Merlo's impending death, was the Japanese Kabuki theatre. At their request, Williams had provided promoters with a statement on Kabuki's introduction to the American theatre in June 1960, drawn from his exposure to the form after meeting novelist Yukio Mishima in 1957 and visiting him two years later in Tokyo:

> The great traditional Theatre of Japan, the Noh-plays and the Kabuki theatre which grew out of them, deserve to be ranked in importance and influence with such historical flowering of drama, verbal and plastic, as the ancient Greek and Elizabethan theatres, and the theatre of Chekhov and Stanislavsky.[46]

Williams dresses Flora in a Kabuki dancer's robe and has her recount her time as a Kabuki artist to the Witch of Capri, the Marchesa Constance Ridgeway-Condotti.[47] He even adds in the 'Author's Notes' to the play that he included 'a pair of stage assistants that function in a way that's between the Kabuki Theatre of Japan and the chorus of Greek Theatre' in order to make the play less 'conventional' and more 'allegorical' like a '"sophisticated fairy tale"'.[48] Williams had already been experimenting with the Kabuki tradition in a play he worked on for several years, *The Day on Which a Man Dies: An Occidental Noh Play* (1960), which he dedicated to Mishima. The play, which is about the death of Jackson Pollock as told to him by his artist friend, Tony Smith, would inspire his last play of the decade, *In the Bar of the Tokyo Hotel* (1969).

But there were clearly other influences besides Kabuki working on Williams at the time. The late Gilbert Debusscher scrutinizes Williams's *Milk Train* against Jean Cocteau's *L'aigle à deux têtes* in terms of their similar stage designs, characters, plots, and symbols, concluding that 'there is a strong probability that Williams took a great deal of his inspiration' from Cocteau's play.[49] Granted, there are enough differences between the two plays to make a strong case for 'inspiration' rather than 'imitation' – or worse – but Debusscher's convincing argument that '*Milk Train* turns into a faithful copy of *L'aigle* [...]' nonetheless raises questions about Williams's intentions.[50] In a later Williams play, however, one might push that notion of 'inspiration' even further, for the one-act *The Pronoun 'I'* (c. 1975) again closely resembles Cocteau's play.

L'aigle à deux têtes is set in Krantz Castle in Tyrol on the tenth anniversary of King Frederick's wedding day *and* assassination. His reclusive widow, whom many in her court and government deem mad, arrives to spend the night in the bed chamber that was to be their nuptial suite. Stanislas, a '*haggard, disheveled*' young anarchist poet whom the Queen greatly admires and who '*closely resembl*[es] *the portrait of the King*',[51] climbs over a balcony, looking to assassinate her for her lack of interest in international affairs affecting the nation: 'I despise the people, I ruin them. That's the kind of malicious tale which is circulated about me'. The Queen, who has hidden her face behind a veil now for ten years, shelters Stanislas because she sees him as her angel of death, a point Williams makes in the unpublished essay 'A Woman Owns an Island' about his own Chris Flanders in *Milk Train*.[52] In return for not having handed him over to the minister of internal affairs, Count von Foehn, the Queen demands Stanislas to kill her after three days: 'And I repeat: if you don't kill me, I shall kill you'.[53] Both inevitably keep their contracts, though in a rather melodramatic end: Stanislas poisons himself to save the Queen's life, and she pretends to have tricked him so that in his vengeful anger he will stab her to death, which he does.

In addition to the similarities that Debusscher details between the Queen and Flora Goforth or Stanislas and Christopher, what becomes evident is how Williams's *The Pronoun 'I'*, brief as it is, replicates many of the same stage designs, characters, plots, and even symbols of Cocteau's *L'aigle*. *The Pronoun 'I'* is also about a revolution being led against a mad queen, May, for her own lack of interest in international affairs affecting the nation. While her young lover, Dominique – a narcissistic poet who cannot *'begin a poem without the pronoun "I"'* – lays about at her feet half naked in her throne room, a *'ragged young revolutionary steals into the room'* and sets about to assassinate the Queen.[54] The Queen becomes aware of his presence but does not expose him. Like Stanislas, he, too, struggles to carry out his task when he becomes transfixed by the Queen, who also hides her beauty behind an *'artfully designed mask over which is usually drawn a veil'*.[55] Just as Stanislas had told his Queen, 'Lift your veil. Show your face to them. Display yourself',[56] Williams's revolutionary convinces his Queen to remove her disguise. When he sees her unmasked, the assassin says: 'I came to assassinate a demented old hag – not you ... .'.[57] Once unveiled, Cocteau's Queen tells Stanislas and Duke Willenstein, 'I'm showing myself naked before two men. I'm giving up the veil, Felix, and I'm ten years older'.[58] While Cocteau's Queen is left figuratively naked after the unveiling, Williams's Queen literally stands naked at the end, allowing her and her assassin-lover to escape the mob.

Williams shares Stanislas's role as Cocteau's poet–assassin between two characters, the revolutionary and the solipsistic poet Dominique, an androgynous French *prénom*. Why he does so is worth exploring. Though Williams's Queen counters the poet's infatuation with the 'great gilded assertion of the first person singular' by employing the royal 'we', she is not altogether ignorant of the fact that she, too, is obsessed by the '[e]normity of personal concern, disregard of all others on earth'.[59] As the city burns around her and her guards have all fled, she faces with stoicism her imminent death. As Dominique flees, the Queen exposes his escape to the approaching mob. The revolutionary stays, however, but instead of leading the mob to the Queen, he protects her (as Stanislas does in *L'aigle*) by stripping the Queen of her royal garb just as the mob breaks into 'the *thrown* [*sic*] room'.[60] The Queen tells the mob that the Queen has fled, and the revolutionary chooses not to disclose her lie. With the poetic 'I' now destroyed, both utter an ambiguous second person 'You' as curtain-lines, ostensibly to demonstrate the Queen's shedding of her egoism.

Both *Milk Train* and *The Pronoun 'I'* resemble Cocteau's *L'aigle*, but Williams was not interested in plagiarism. Rather, he was moving closer toward a European aesthetic in his drama, which proved to be detrimental to the reception of his work at home. He had written admirably about French playwrights just a few years previously, and saw Beckett's work as manna for the post-war theatre. Cocteau's play certainly intrigued Williams, perhaps because of its ability to play with European history in ways no American playwright could do. Perhaps it was also that European theatre was more catholic in its tastes and welcoming to experimental plays like Williams's plastic theatre more than conventional Broadway or West End audiences were. Having spent so many summers in Europe, Williams was beginning now to turn to the old continent for inspiration and resources. In another of Williams's unpublished one-act plays, titled 'Dame Picque' (c. 1955?), Cocteau's Queen even turns out to be a man in royal drag, which may surely have been a wink and a nod to the openly gay French poet-playwright, who would die a couple weeks after Merlo.[61] Annette Saddik is surely correct when she describes *The Pronoun 'I'* as 'a campy frolic with touches of absurdity', believing the play to be 'a parody of classical forms and contemporary mores'.[62] Perhaps it was more than camp; perhaps the evolution of the three plays demonstrates how Williams's own dramaturgy was moving away from dramatic Modernism toward Postmodern pastiche, paying homage to (and taking the cheek of) a fellow playwright along the way.

The simultaneous build up to and sharp demise of *Milk Train* paralleled the final descent of Merlo, and for the next seven years Williams would himself fall into a drug-hazed depression that could not find a way to separate the two tragic events. Despite his claim in his self-interview 'The World I Live In' (1957) not to 'believe in "guilt"', to a great extent Williams's depression was based on guilt over having neglected Merlo at his time of need, though the relationship was so confrontational that there was little Williams could do.[63] So he wrote, and he materialized his partner's suffering in the form of a play, just as he had done before with Rose's fateful day under a lobotomizer's scalpel (a procedure he frequently blamed himself for not having stopped). It was cannibalism to Williams, plain and simple, a literary equivalent to Sebastian Venable's, a *quid pro quo* exchange of bodies. But Williams was not dying of cancer (though he always thought he was), nor was he lobotimized (though he clearly saw the potential for madness in him), so he suffered instead for his loved ones.

One of Williams's guilty associations at the time was his installation of a young poet from Columbus (OH), Frederick Nicklaus (golfer Jack Nicklaus's cousin), in his Key West home along with Merlo, who was sick without yet knowing the gravity of his illness. Nicklaus, with whom Williams said he 'could barely communicate with except in bed',[64] was his latest in a long line of past and future secretaries/lovers/travelling companions that he put on the pay roll before and after Merlo's death. Poignantly, Williams took Nicklaus, and not Merlo, to Tangier in the summer of 1962. Merlo underwent a battery of exams in the spring of 1962 to discover the reasons for his recent weight loss. By the fall, he grew weaker and then came north in January 1963 to New York to see Williams, who was preparing *Milk Train* for its Broadway debut. In New York, a doctor diagnosed Merlo's illness as inoperable lung cancer. Though briefly returning to the warmth of Key West, Merlo flew back to New York in April with Williams and Nicklaus.

After a brief stay with Williams and his 'Angel' poet in Nantucket the following July (Williams and Nicklaus again went to Europe in the summer of 1963), Merlo returned to New York one final time that August for treatment at the Memorial Hospital, but he would not recover, having already outlasted the cancer by several months. Williams did not plan on staying long in the 'States when the present situation has run its inevitable course' and asked Anna Magnani to find him a small villa with a pool in Rome.[65] Merlo died later that September, a death that would shatter Williams's world: 'My first reaction was a hard thing to analyze now. I think it must have been relief that his and my torture was finished. His, yes. Mine, no. I was on the threshold of an awful part of my life. It developed slowly'.[66] In his revisions for *Milk Train*, Williams would insert in the mouth of his 'Angel of Death', Christopher Flanders, many of the words he never said to Merlo while he was still alive.

It is not entirely clear if Merlo's death and *Milk Train*'s failure together precipitated Williams's demise, as Williams often recalls in his writing and in his interviews, or if the path had already been laid since 1959 following his traumatic experience with *Sweet Bird of Youth*. Whatever the cause – Merlo's death, Williams's increased drug and alcohol abuse, his mounting paranoia against those who loved him or worked with him, or his rabid fear of writer's block – Williams's physical life took a downward spiral for seven years. His career quickly followed suit, though the post-Merlo/*Milk Train* plays are today enjoying more favourable critical assessment than they did in the 1960s, thanks to the work of Linda Dorff, Annette Saddik, Philip Kolin, Thomas Keith, David Kaplan, and others. Following Merlo's funeral, Williams flew with Nicklaus down to Mexico for the filming of *The Night of the Iguana* with director John Huston. Then he was back in New York that October preparing for *Milk Train*'s ill-fated 1964 revival. Bankhead was in poor health, exacerbated by her alcohol and drug abuse, and reportedly could not be heard onstage. Like his actress, Williams was now on a road to self-destruction from a lethal cocktail of alcohol and drugs: Seconal, Nembutol, Luminal, the hallucinogen Doriden, the tranquillizer Miltown, and phenobarbital.[67]

Depression had set up shop – or a pharmacy – wherever Williams travelled, which was less frequently now. When Nicklaus could no longer stand Williams's mood changes, he left him and the Key West compound in March 1964.[68] It did not take long to replace him with a new paid companion, William Glavin, who moved in with Williams the summer of 1965 into his penthouse at 145 West 55th Street, before moving again to 15 West 72nd Street that July.[69] After changing New York addresses from his East 65th Street apartment that held too many memories of Merlo to the penthouse, Williams sought ways to escape his pain. He returned to psychotherapy that summer after Nicklaus left him, but it was a new doctor who drew much of his attention while living in New York: Dr Max Jacobson, drug supplier to the stars, which included John F. Kennedy. Though Williams would defend the good doctor later in a December 1972 letter to the editor of the *New York Times*, Jacobson, whom Williams calls 'Dr. Feel Good' in his *Memoirs*, would later lose his licence to practise based in part of what he did to Williams and other celebrities like him in prescribing vitamin shots laced with amphetamines, painkillers, and human placenta. As Williams confessed to John Gruen in their 1965 interview (then to Walter Wager a year later),

I begin [the writing day] with two cups of coffee, rather strong coffee. And then I go to my bedroom and I give myself an injection to pick me up. At first, I was terrified of taking the injections – giving them to myself. But I've gradually learned to do it. And I give myself one c.c. of whatever the thing is, the formula – I don't know what it is. I just know that immediately after it I feel like a living being! Then I can go to my table and work.[70]

Even with the injections, Williams's writing did not come any easier, and when it did come at all, what he produced was exceedingly different from what he had previously written. The news was not all bad, however. Brandeis University gave Williams their Creative Arts Award in March 1965, and in May Maureen Stapleton brought *The Glass Menagerie* to life again for its twentieth anniversary. But the revival would do more damage than good since it reminded the audience what they had expected from Williams, and that was hardly the type of play that he was giving them now. Two one-act plays, *The Mutilated* (begun in July 1958[71]) and the *Gnädiges Fräulein*, were grouped together under the title *Slapstick Tragedy*, but the whore Celeste and the cacaloony-fighting the Gnädiges Fräulein are no Amanda Wingfield. It was not entirely a new direction for Williams, since he had already experimented with the absurd or black humour elsewhere in his canon, most notably in *Camino Real*. But for Broadway audiences who were used to the Williams of *The Glass Menagerie* revival or the more recent *Night of the Iguana*, these plays were not only irreverent (and even irrelevant) but downright distasteful.

In his 'Preface' to *Slapstick Tragedy*, published along with the plays in the August 1965 issue of *Esquire*, Williams was a little more than apprehensive, if not entirely self-effacing, in his explication of the two one-acts. Having repeatedly said that he would never 'explain' a play in the press before its premiere, Williams attempts here to do just that, fully aware that his plays no longer did simply speak for themselves:

> [...] since I can't just stop working, I divert myself with some shorter project, a story, a poem, or a less ponderous play. These diversions are undertaken simply as that, as diversions, and they nearly always have a quality in common, which is experimentation in content and in style, particularly in style.[72]

Referring to them as 'diversions' was readily translated as 'inferior' by the public, which is what Williams predicted but did not mean; he had called *The Glass Menagerie* a diversion as well. Instead, these plays were two of his 'chamber' pieces, standing alongside the great symphony of *The Glass Menagerie*, which would run for 175 performances during its revival and close triumphantly at the Brooks Atkinson Theatre on

2 October. But a symphony can cast a great shadow, just as the silver anniversary of *Streetcar* or the *Cat* revival would do in the mid-1970s, eclipsing any new play that Williams was offering to his public. And what is more, like many of his late plays, these two one-acts speak more in performance than on paper: 'I think, *in production*, they may seem to be a pair of fantastic allegories on the tragicomic subject of human existence on this risky planet'.[73] Williams knew that good productions meant everything to the life of his work, but he also recognized that a printed play had more shelf life than a performed one.

The production/print dilemma would not affect *Slapstick Tragedy* in the end, as it did not matter which the public saw first: both were dismissed as nonsensical. Williams normally decided to publish his later plays during or just after production, which he frequently did in *Esquire*, so as to give audiences the time to digest them. In the case of *Slapstick Tragedy*, delays in the production caused the plays to be printed first. A loyal Williams collaborator in his later career, for whom Williams had snubbed Cheryl Crawford to produce *The Night of the Iguana*, Charles Bowden was chosen to produce *Slapstick Tragedy*. In late January 1965, Williams considered that the premiere was imminent, and he was preparing for rehearsals in early February, as he wrote St Just: 'I am going into rehearsal in a couple of weeks with a couple of very odd plays. I don't suppose the critics or public will know what to make of them, and I can't say that I do either'.[74] Production was postponed, however, as Williams explained in a 5 February letter to Donald Windham:

I am caught right now in a very strange and nerve-wracking professional situation. I have two short plays that are supposed to go into rehearsal on Monday next. Everything is ready, director, cast, designer, costumer, composer, but the producer, [Charles] Bowden, has not yet raised the money.[75]

Rehearsals were cancelled in May 1965 because Bowden could not raise the $150,000 still needed to see the play through production. By May, Williams confided to Gruen in their interview: 'I don't think they'll work'.[76] Whether he truly felt this or used it, as he had often done, as a means to derail criticism by pronouncing the play's death beforehand remains uncertain.

Following the successive failures of *Milk Train*, financial angels were hesitant to back any new Williams play, especially since Broadway had seemingly moved on from staging plays of poetic naturalism or personal lyricism. Production of *Slapstick Tragedy* would thus be delayed a year until February 1966. As he had nearly always done before one of his play's premieres, Williams sent the *New York Times* a pre-opening piece, 'The Wolf and I', which it published on 20 February two days before the plays opened at the Longacre Theatre in New York. The essay begins in the fall of 1960 in Rome, where Williams, on the advice of Anna Magnani, bought a black Belgian shepherd *lupo*, which he called Satan. Given his rather poor track record with a string of bull dogs, Williams thought the more robust dog would survive the endless travels that he and Merlo would subject it to. On Christmas Day, 1960, Williams wrote to Maria St Just, 'I'll probably have to travel [to London] alone, since we now have two dogs, one a big black wolf, the other a bitch bull-dog [...]'.[77] A few months later, Williams told her that the 'big black wolf-dog we bought in Rome stands off looking at [a big rat] respectfully although he, the dog, has inflicted bites on some pretty tough friends here which required five or six stitches, when they came near him when he was having his horse meat'.[78] That bite would eventually become Williams's during the two-week try-out for *The Night of the Iguana* at the Fisher Theatre in Detroit in November 1961. The attack made such an impression on Williams that it later inspired the story about the death of the Champagne Girl in *I Never Get Dressed Till after Dark on Sundays* (1973), a one-act that Williams merged with his story 'The Angel in the Alcove' to become *Vieux Carré* (1976).[79]

The dog-bite anecdote in the *Times* essay was hardly gratuitous. Williams knew that the proper function of a pre-opening piece was not to provide fanfare for a play, which was why he chose parable over interpretation, using allusion to negotiate his way through the paradox of explaining his work while appearing to have said nothing at all. Williams had long perfected this style of deferral, innuendo, connota-tion, and parable in his essays, and he was recounting the *lupo* story in such detail now either to persuade the drama critics not to bite too hard in their press notices or, more probably, to show them that no matter how hard they did bite, he would survive and continue writing. In one unpublished fragment draft to his piece for *Cat*, 'Person–To–Person', titled 'A Thing Called Personal Lyricism' (c. 1955), Williams shows his recognition of a piece's potential to 'soften-up the New York critics at just the proper moment', though a history of having received mixed press notices had also taught him that 'an author's disarmingly modest "pitch" in front of the tent will have little if any effect upon the show's reception in the press'.[80] Consequently, Williams was simultaneously eager and hesitant to write these invited pieces of what he called his 'Apologia':[81] eager because he understood the author's role in promoting himself within the economy of Broadway, and hesitant because he knew that perceived personal self-promotions could readily backfire.

Williams concluded the essay on the sombre note that *Slapstick Tragedy* forewent any 'pre-Broadway tour' (probably to save the producers' money), which is 'very hard on a wolf and is torture to a playwright'; as such, the play's producers 'decided not to go out of town with *Slapstick Tragedy*. Two weeks of previews in New York at reduced prices has a peaceful sound to it'.[82] When *Slapstick Tragedy* finally did open on 22 February, it closed after only seven performances. By April, Williams was again off to Rome and Taormina with Glavin and Merlo's Boston terrier Gigi.[83] One of his latest projects was to write the film script of *Milk Train*, for which Audrey Wood had managed to procure a very lucrative deal with Universal Studios. He drew inspiration from his seaside hotel at Positano to write about 'Sissy' Goforth's villa on the Divina Costiera. The 1968 film, titled *Boom!*, would bring to the screen Richard Burton and Elizabeth Taylor in one of Williams's favourite film adaptations of his plays. When he was not working on the film script, he devoted his time to revising the adaption of his 1942 story 'Kingdom of Earth', which he had begun dramatizing in 1953 and planned to run opposite the early short version of *Cat on a Hot Tin Roof* in 1954. He also worked on another full-length play, *The Two-Character Play*, hoping for a London premiere. Wary now of the prejudices against him at home, Williams began looking to produce his plays abroad.

The year 1967 was a haze for William, whose drug addiction grew stronger the more he built up resistance to those drugs that he was taking daily. Early in the year, he travelled with Glavin to the Virgin Islands to continue work on *Boom!* and *Kingdom of Earth*, which he published that February in *Esquire* as a one-act play. The story about 'Chicken [being] King!'[84] is essentially the same story as the full-length play expanded a year later; the major differences are that Lot is not yet a transvestite and Chicken's mother is mulatto and not Cherokee. By July, he and Glavin were in Spain, and then in Rome and Sardinia, where *Boom!* was to be filmed.[85] Glavin underwent gastrointestinal surgery, for which he needed post-op medication, and Williams, whose paranoia was rabidly increasing, was convinced that Glavin was stealing his drugs.

In the fall of 1967, Williams completed work on the first version of a play he would revisit frequently in the 1970s, *The Two-Character Play*. It was an ambitious play about the warped relationship between a brother and sister, Felice and Clare, and one that Audrey Wood genuinely liked. It was offered to the Edinburgh International Festival, which spawned its more celebrated Fringe Festival there, but the play was rejected. It was first produced instead in Williams's 'drunken or stoned' presence in London at the Hampstead Theatre Club on 11 December 1967.[86] Williams pursued writing the play the following summer, and in the years after that, but it would be a long time before he brought the play to New York, under its new title, *Out Cry*. Also in December, he continued working on his 'period piece', *Will Mr. Merriwether Return from Memphis?*, which he references in his pre-opening essay for *Kingdom of Earth*, 'Happiness Is Relevant',[87] as well as on the film adaptation of his one-armed boxer story, 'One Arm'. Williams envisioned Joe Dellasandro, an actor associated with Andy Warhol with whom Williams was fascinated at the time, in the role of Oliver Winemiller.[88]

Back in the summer of 1967, Wood had informed Williams that David Merrick wanted to produce *Kingdom of Earth*, which panicked Williams because he felt the play was not yet ready and that he lacked the energy to complete its full-length version.[89] By February 1968, *Kingdom of Earth* was finally ready for production and, after a try-out in Philadelphia, it opened on 27 March at the Ethel Barrymore Theatre in New York under a new title at Merrick's request, *The Seven Descents of Myrtle*; it closed on 20 April. A gothic tragicomedy, *Kingdom of Earth/The Seven Descents of Myrtle* mixes some of Williams's earlier themes with his more recent characters: Myrtle, a disillusioned prostitute who finds the security of a home through her hasty marriage to Lot; Lot a consumptive transvestite who returns with his bride to his Mississippi homestead to reclaim it from his half-brother Chicken; and Chicken, a mulatto whose mother 'wasn't black but she wasn't white neither',[90] who runs the house and who seduces his brother's young wife to annul an earlier agreement that the house would pass onto Lot and his kin if he ever married. As a result of having 'some black blood in him', Chicken is ostracized by everyone in the county, 'talked about in whispers' and denied ownership of the land because of Lot's birthright.[91] A film version of the play, *The Last of the Mobile Hot Shots*, would be made in 1970, starring Lynn Redgrave and James Colburn.

Williams's drug and alcohol-induced paranoia continued to grow out of control. Following a fight at a New York restaurant with Glavin, Williams wrote to his brother Dakin in June 1968 that he thought he was about to be assassinated. The news eventually appeared in the *New York Times*, which reported on 30 June that the playwright 'surfaced in New York long enough yesterday to telephone his brother in Collinsville, Ill., and assure him he was alive and well' and just depressed over the failure of *Kingdom of Earth* and *Boom!*[92] By the end of the year, Dakin felt it was time to intervene, as Williams was incoherent and repeatedly falling down. Glavin had taken Williams back down to Key West after the events of the previous summer, and Dakin flew down to see what could be done.

Dakin arrived in Key West in the beginning of 1969 to accompany his brother back to St Louis, where he would check him into a hospital. Dakin's first and only step this trip was to get Williams accepted into the Catholic Church (Merlo was Catholic, and they often discussed religion when he was alive, and Dakin had converted during his military service in Burma in 1945[93]). Dakin also wanted him committed into the psychiatric ward of the Barnes Hospital in St Louis, but that would not happen for another few months. After meeting for several days with Father Joseph LeRoy at the start of the new year, Williams was baptized into the Catholic Church, St Mary Star of the Sea, in Key West on 10 January 1969.[94] By the end of the month, he flew to Rome to visit LeRoy's superior general of the Jesuits, the Reverend Pedro Arrupe, known as the 'black pope'. During the meeting, which was supervised by John Navone, Williams asked Arrupe to bless the manuscript of his new play, having forgotten to bring his wooden rosary for just that purpose.

Following a week in a Miami hospital recovering from the Hong Kong flu, Williams was back in New York in February to prepare the rehearsals for the play *In the Bar of a Tokyo Hotel*, which was to be directed by Herbert Machiz.[95] At this time, he attended a birthday party for Robert Whitehead hosted by Maureen Stapleton, where he apparently took an overdose of sleeping pills, which she quickly forced him to vomit up. Williams recounts the story with such insouciance in his pre-opening piece for the play, '"Tennessee, Never Talk to an Actress"', that he either failed to see the seriousness of his drug addiction or, more probably, he was aware of it but dealt with it through the same black humour that saw him through most of his 'stoned age'.

Later that spring, Dan Isaac interviewed Williams, who had postponed the premiere of *In the Bar of a Tokyo Hotel* because he felt it was not finished, and saw in him evidence of this contradictory manner in which he conducted himself daily. Williams was heavily under the influence of both the Eastern poetry he was reading at the time to find serenity and the drugs he was obviously taking to achieve that serenity artificially. Williams was to Isaac 'depressed and uncommunicative': 'There were moments when nothing was said and a thick silence hung between us. [...] Tennessee looked tired and moved slowly', and, like the characters in his recent play, did not always finish his sentences.[96]

But those incomplete sentences were not evidence of a playwright who had lost his ability to think and write clearly. Rather, they demonstrate, in both *In the Bar of a Tokyo Hotel* and *The Two-Character Play*, ways of representing the cognitive dissonance in geniuses and madmen, of which Mark, Felice, and Williams were both. In his open 'letter' to the cast of *Tokyo Hotel*, which the *New York Times* published on 14 May, Williams tried to explain this philosophy of human incompletion. An artist needs to cannibalize those around him for the sake of the art, but he regrets that behaviour when he grows older, thinking now that his art has failed. It is only after the artist's death that the rejected loved one can again love the artist, but principally through his or her appreciation of the art that had usurped their place in the artist's life.[97]

In the Bar of a Tokyo Hotel was thus Williams's apology to Merlo (or justification to himself) for what he had done to him, for Mark was as much an avatar of Williams as he was meant to be Jackson Pollock vis-à-vis his wife, the artist Lee Krasner. The play ended up being about 'the particular humiliating doom of the artist'[98] – both Pollock's and Williams's – but the drama critics were not thrilled by either testament. By early May, it was obvious that the play was in trouble. Herbert Machiz was fired, and Williams took over as director, and, in spite of his habit of falling down, Anne Meacham, who played Miriam, said that he directed her and Donald Madden, who played Mark, well enough. The play opened 11 May at the Eastside Playhouse after twenty-two previews; its failure to receive good notices forced it to close twenty-five performances later.

Williams soon left for Tokyo with Meacham that June (Glavin was too ill for the trip due to his recurrent intestinal problems), for a Japanese production of *Streetcar*, but returned to New York the following month, before restlessly heading on to Key West then San Francisco then New Orleans. After a scalding incident that involved the spilling of hot coffee on himself in his Key West home (he was having a new, modern kitchen installed, and the stove was placed temporarily out back), Williams suffered second degree burns on his shoulder. Dakin flew in from his Collinsville, and, after several previously aborted attempts, finally convinced Williams to return to St Louis with him and enter Barnes Hospital, where he stayed for three months and claimed to have suffered two heart attacks. As Dakin recalled, the Renard psychiatric division of the hospital was the only block where a patient did not have the possibility to sign himself out before ten days, and given Williams's fears about his sister's fate and his own dislike of being denied his pills and alcohol, there was no way Williams was going to stay on his own will; Dakin never informed him about his legal rights to check himself out after ten days.

Though his intervention would cost Dakin his brother's love (they had a partial reconciliation in Key West years later[99]), Dakin repeatedly said that he felt that he saved his brother's life, and thus gave the world several more of Williams's plays, poems, stories, and memoirs, which is not entirely an exaggeration. As a form of punishment, he cut Dakin mostly out of his will, which he had updated at this time, 'for my said brother [...] is well provided for',[100] leaving him only $25,000 to be paid out only after the death of his sister Rose. As for the rest of his Estate, Williams would endow the Walter E. Dakin Memorial Fund to be created for 'the purpose of encouraging creative writing and creative writers in need of financial assistance' and which was to be administered by the University of the South in Sewanee, his grandfather's alma mater.[101] His entire Estate was to be put into a trust and used to care for Rose until her death, at which time the trust would terminate, and all his income would be 'paid over and distributed'[102] to the University of the South. On her death in 1996, the university received $7 million. Williams later added a few codicils that would guarantee a lifetime annual salary of $7500 to Robert Carroll and full royalties of *The Two-Character Play* to Maria St Just, a gesture, John Lahr blithely points out, that was as 'impudent a joke as Shakespeare's leaving his wife his "second best bed"'.[103]

Williams also took out his revenge on Dakin and his political aspirations – he was running for Illinois's US Senate seat at the time[104] – and on the 'Friggins Division of Barnacle Hospital in the city of Saint Pollution' in a long prose-poem titled 'What's Next on the Agenda, Mr. Williams?', which was later published in the *Mediterranean Review* in the winter of 1971.[105] He read the poem at the Waterfront Playhouse in Key West in the spring of 1970, then at the London Poetry Festival that summer, and then once again for Tom Buckley and others during an extended interview at his house in Key West later that same fall.[106] Rambling and poisoned with acid, the prose poem set the tone for much of the next decade to come for Williams.

In the autumn of 1969, when Williams was just entering his 'cell'[107] number 9126 at the psychiatric ward of the Barnes Hospital, several members of the gay community were breaking out of theirs. Many had clashed with homophobic New York City police forces at the Stonewall Inn on Christopher Street in the late and early morning hours of 27/28 June, marking the birth of gay power. What could have been a turning point in Williams's career, however, turned into another apparent war front against his critics. In the opening years of the 1970s, Williams was battling certain members of the gay community as much as he was the homophobic theatre critics in New York. With nowhere to turn but inward, Williams rejected nearly everyone that was close to him – family members, lovers, friends, and agents – and began surrounding himself with the sycophants who would fill his New York apartment or his homes in New Orleans and Key West. The 1970s is as much their story, as it is Williams's.

9
Key West to New York (via Bangkok): In Search of Androgyny

The 1970s found Williams awakening from his self-proclaimed 'stoned age' to the social angst of the Cold War and to his personal struggle to conclude his life's work, and reconfirm his rightful place in America's literary pantheon. Consequently, the repeated attacks against his work of the 1960s would not deter Williams from continuing to write stories and plays, many of which were growing more sexually and homosexually explicit in the nation's libertine years of the early 1970s. He saw these plays as his 'chamber' pieces, those works on a scale much smaller than his opus plays of the 1940s and 1950s. It was also the decade that he wrote his pot-boiler *Memoirs*, a *cause célèbre* that seriously impeded any chance he had for a Broadway comeback. As was the case in the 1960s, Williams fought the critics, the producers, his agents, and his audiences in these early years of the 1970s over issues pertaining to his waning artistic abilities, but now that he was fully out of the closet, his sexuality became more important an issue to his audiences than his art, something Williams did not exactly try to counter.

In 1970, Williams produced *I Can't Imagine Tomorrow* (1966), a Pinter-esque sketch about a lonely man and an equally lonely woman, aptly called One and Two, and their mutual search for meaning to life. In June 1971, Williams published *Demolition Downtown*, a fantastic portrayal of two suburban couples during a military coup in the nearby capital city. After the androgynous *Out Cry* (1971/1973) came the queer *Small Craft Warnings*, which premiered on Easter Sunday at the Truck and Warehouse Theatre on 2 April 1972 and limped through several months of production largely due to Williams's celebrity. It was Williams's first openly gay play, in politics more than aesthetics, though many in the gay community found it a bit too little too late. Williams then wrote *Creve Coeur* (1975), producing it in 1978, then again in 1979 under the title *A Lovely Sunday for Creve Coeur*. In Bodey, Williams returned to the strong female characters of his earlier works; and in Dotty, he had exhumed his archetypal southern woman who lets fantasy supplant reality. Critics felt Williams was returning to the poetic naturalism of his early work in order to appease mounting criticism and hostility toward his newer dramatic trends.

The same would be said of his next play, *Vieux Carré*, which Williams wrote while touring the Orient during his 1973 summer voyage on the 'Cherry Blossom' cruise. *Vieux Carré was* an attempt to return to the 'poetic naturalism' that characterized Williams's earlier dramatic triumphs but through the prism of a postmodern aesthetic or a cataract eye. Williams had, in fact, begun *Vieux Carré* as early as the winter of 1939 during his first stay in New Orleans, which may account for its similarities in style to these earlier plays. Neither play was a success, owing perhaps more to their lacklustre productions and promotions than to the quality of Williams's playwriting in either.

Again in 1975, Williams completed *The Red Devil Battery Sign*, a surrealistic impression of Dallas set sometime after the Vietnam War, where the wasteland between the city and its environs, called the Hollow, is ruled by anarchic rival gangs. Because of its disastrous try-out in Boston that June, Williams turned to overseas productions, and *The Red Devil Battery Sign* was again performed in the winter of 1975–76 at Vienna's English-speaking theatre to mixed reviews, and another production followed at the Phoenix Theatre in London from 7–23 July 1977. *Red Devil* was later revived at the Vancouver Playhouse, opening on 18 October 1980. That fall, Williams accepted the offer of a Distinguished Writer-in-Residence post at the University of British Columbia, and part of the deal was that they produce *Red Devil*. On 17 October, Williams wrote to Maria St Just that he was in Vancouver for 'the definitive production of *Red Devil Battery Sign* being staged by a brilliant director'.[1] In the many essay fragments Williams left behind, he repeatedly describes the play as his best work after *The Two-Character Play/Out Cry*. The university also asked for the rights to a Williams premiere, and he gave them *The Notebooks of Trigorin*, his free adaptation of Chekhov's play *The Sea Gull*. The play's Canadian premiere was at the Vancouver Playhouse in 1981, and its American premiere took place at the Cincinnati Playhouse in 1996, starring Lynn Redgrave as Madame Arkadina.

The second half of this decade witnessed the continued decline of his reputation and his vigorous pursuit of androgyny. Another surreal play, a comedy for Maria St Just called *This Is (An Entertainment)* (1976) about a countess who cuckolds her munition-making husband during a revolution, also failed to resurrect Williams's name. He would continue working on the play until at least April 1978, and as of today it remains the only full-length play that Williams wrote which has not been published. Nor did the lengthened and dramatized version of the 1943 story 'The Angel in the Alcove' or the play *Tiger Tail* (1978), the stage adaptation of his 1956 movie *Baby Doll*, help his cause, though both received promising reviews. Also in the late 1970s came two short plays, *Lifeboat Drill* (written around early 1970) and *This Is the Peaceable Kingdom; Or, Good Luck God* (1979). The first depicts the absurd struggle an aged couple engages in over life preservers, literal and metaphoric; the second describes the breakdown of the societal microcosm in a nursing home during the 1978 New York strike. Lastly, the subtitled 'ghost play' about F. Scott Fitzgerald's selfish destruction of wife Zelda's literary career, *Clothes for a Summer Hotel*, which was begun in 1975 but not produced until 1980, proved to be Williams's final curtain call on Broadway.

The 1970s was difficult decade for Williams, perhaps more so than the 1960s because he was more lucid, no longer protected by an impermeable drug-induced bubble. The decade began well enough, with his being awarded the 'Gold Medal for Drama' from Lillian Hellman by the American Academy of Arts and Letters, a medal that seemingly carried little significance for him, as he makes clear in his acceptance speech: 'I think I'm essentially a humorist you know, so I'm going to try and tell you something that will make you laugh. I hope it does. If it doesn't, then I'm no good'.[2] The audience did not laugh, just as they had not laughed at any of his black humour plays of the preceding decade. The tone was set for a difficult decade ahead. This chapter balances his literary productions against his non-fiction, in particular the mountains of draft fragments that he left of his work, to show how conscious Williams was of his struggle not to write a better play but to convince his public that he indeed already had.

Williams entered the 1970s reeling from anger and paranoia brought on by his alcohol and drug abuse of the previous decade, by his internment in the psychiatric ward at Barnes, and by his growing distrust of people closest to him. The first to feel his wrath was his brother Dakin. Then came Bill Glavin, whom Williams fired at the start of the new decade, out of suspicion that he was stealing from him or only befriended him for his wealth. Later, Williams would turn his sights on Audrey Wood.

In April 1970, Williams travelled to Durham, North Carolina, with John Young, Glavin's replacement as secretary/companion. In spite of the drugs, Williams gave a coherent reading at Duke University of a play he had been working on, *I Never Get Dressed Till after Dark on Sundays*, which was generally well received by the student audience. In early summer 1970, he attended a poetry reading at the Institute of Contemporary Arts in London, joined by W. H. Auden, Stephan Spender, Allen Tate, and Wole Soyinka. He read his embittered prose poem 'What's Next on the Agenda, Mr. Williams?' that he had written following his treatment at Barnes the year before.[3] He had lost his best friend Marion Vaccaro to illness in Miami earlier that April, preparing her funeral arrangements with Audrey Wood. By September, the day after an interview he had given with Don Lee Keith in New Orleans, he headed for the Orient aboard the SS *President Cleveland* with long-time friend Oliver Evans. The trip was paid for from the $10,000 that Evans raised by selling several of Williams's manuscripts to UCLA, which are now housed in its library's Department of Special Collections. The fact that Williams believed he needed to sell his manuscripts to pay for the trip lends some credence to his comment a few years later that he wrote *Memoirs* because he was broke and that he needed Doubleday's generous advance, which he did not. Though rich until his death in 1983 (bequeathing Rose and her trust some $11 million dollars), Williams always feared poverty awaited him. He was a product of the Depression after all.

In that extended and, at times, bitchy interview with Don Lee Keith, Williams spoke about his interment in Barnes, his imaginary 'breast cancer', as well as the advances he made in a 'revised version of a new play called *The Two-Character Play* [...]'.[4] He and Evans flew on to Yokahama, where he met up with Mishima, who not long after committed suicide, and then on to Hong Kong and Bangkok for surgery to remove a benign tumour that had formed in Williams's left breast. Evans assured Williams that the doctor who would perform the surgery was the surgeon to the Thai king. A military doctor did operate, but he was not the King's physician, nor did he find any cancer in his breast. During the visit, Williams almost overdosed on opium that Evans had purchased among his coterie of young boys in Thailand. Though he was no longer taking the injections that had made him an addict in the 1960s, Williams was anything but on the wagon. Staying in the Orient until 10 December 1970, they sailed back to the US, disembarking at Honolulu on Christmas Eve. Williams then returned to Key West alone.

Williams escaped the national and personal trauma of the 1960s, but not entirely unscathed. Famous now is Gore Vidal's replay to Williams's claim to have slept through the previous decade: 'Don't worry, you didn't miss a thing'.[5] Williams had missed much, of course, most singularly a theatrical hit on a par with those of the 1940s and 1950s, the reasons for which are as varied as Williams's plays are themselves. No doubt the most important reason was that Williams's style had changed rather abruptly, veering toward the gothic, the absurd (a theatrical term that he did not like in reference to his later plays), the minimalist, or at least the Postmodern. But Broadway was changing as well, and so was its theatre criticism, and none for the better as far as Williams was concerned. More than ever, Broadway meant money, and producers were no longer willing to take chances on 'art' plays that would not guarantee a high end return on their investments. Williams saw that his future in the theatre was Off Broadway or even Off-off Broadway, though secretly he coveted that Cinderella comeback that would put his name once again on a Broadway marquee next to the title of a runaway smash hit.

Williams concentrated on two plays in the opening years of the decade, a revision of the 1967 play *The Two-Character Play*, and the one-act *Confessional* (1967) that was now showing promise in a limited run at the Maine Theatre Arts Festival in Bar Harbor in July 1971. He felt that *The Two-Character Play*, which he now called *Out Cry*, was his great late play, on par with the best of Beckett, Pinter, and Albee. He said as much in many of his unpublished essay fragments written at the time, such as 'Final Materiel' [*sic*] (1972) and 'Stylistic Experiments in the Sixties ~~While Working Under the Influence of Speed~~' (c. 1973). His critics, however, felt that the play was over-indulgent, and that what Williams was presenting was not a story of social or philosophical importance but one that put the worst of Williams's substance abuse and increasing paranoia and personal bitterness on stage for all to see.

Out Cry first premiered in the summer of 1971 under the direction of George Keathley at the Ivanhoe in Chicago. It was revised again and reopened in New York in March 1973, but closed after only twelve performances, only to be revised once more in 1976, with the original titled, *The Two-Character Play*, restored. After the notices for the 1973 performance were dismal, Williams fled to Key West, then to New Orleans, before heading out to Los Angeles to begin his second Pacific crossing. As Williams noted later in his essays 'Let Me Hang It All Out' (1972) and 'Where My Head Is Now and Other Questions' (1973), one of the reasons for the play's failure were the successful revivals of Williams's *Streetcar* in 1973 and *Cat* in 1974, just as *The Glass Menagerie*'s revival in 1965 had overshadowed *Slapstick Tragedy*. The public was still relishing the older Tennessee Williams, or so Williams figured, and the new Tennessee Williams was consequently jettisoned along with yesterday's trash. While Williams was partly correct in his assessment of the play's failure (though it does not explain why the play was rejected back in 1967), what was also true was that the American public, which had been force-fed on Broadway the in-yer-face politics of the 1960s, no longer desired personal lyrical theatre, particularly one that seemed to lack much social resonance. The play was viewed simply as a realistic portrayal of the playwright's own mental crack-up.

Comparisons in *Out Cry* to Williams's lifelong battle with psychosis are inevitable. When Felice and Clare perform their play-within-the-play, titled 'The Two-Character Play', in *Out Cry* – for their audience as well as for Williams's – both publics left midway through the show. Felice and Clare continue performing their play to an empty house, just as Williams saw himself writing plays for an imaginary audience who long since abandoned him, because for them (and for him) it was a form of psychotherapy. To stop the performance all together was to invite senility and ultimately death – as much for Williams as for the brother and sister in the play. Similarly, the two *characters* in the play-within-the-play, who are also called Felice and Clare, battle their own demons of sanity and insanity, reality and illusion, flesh and spirit, just like the two *actors* Felice and Clare who portray them. So lost in their ability to distinguish between reality and performance, the actors Felice and Clare border on the same schizophrenia to which the characters Felice and Clare have already fallen victim. When the acting company of which they were members leaves Felice and Clare because, as they write in their cablegram to the two, ' "Your sister and you are – *insane! – "* ', it is surely not difficult to substitute the names 'Tennessee' and 'Rose' here.[6] This insanity stems in part, many reviewers suggested, from their incestuous relationship, depicted by Felice's '*sort of lovemaking*' gesture with Clare's opal ring.[7]

Though incest had been a leitmotif throughout most of Williams's writings, as Robert Brustein claimed back in 1959, evidenced in the countless references in name or in person to his lobotomized sister Rose, it had never before become central to the plot of one of Williams's major plays. For that reason, most of Williams's critics at the play's two distinct eras (1967 and 1973) dismissed it either as a *cri du coeur*, of the type they had witnessed in Williams throughout the 1960s, or as a 'confessional', which would find its non-dramatic equivalent in the one-act play of the same name and in the *Memoirs*. Either interpretation took the play literally, or as literally as any psychodramatic parable such as this one could be taken, and as a result attacked it for its incestuous theme or its solipsistic nature. After having repeatedly treated antisocial topics on a supra-realistic level, Williams was dumbfounded that his critics once again failed to discern the play's non-realistic impetus. Sex, if it were there at all, was just another means for Williams to access the truth about this brother and sister, and, in the days of celebrating sexual difference and transgression, Williams simply had a different truth in mind from the one his liberal (or liberated) audiences had considered. Williams called it instead a *'Liebestod'*.[8]

The characters of *Out Cry*, Felice and Clare – 'vulnerably deviant persons confronted by these implacable forces of the familiar world'[9] – have grown inseparable in their prison/house, just as the two actors Felice and Clare who perform the roles of 'The Two-Character Play' have become trapped, literally in the locked theatre doors at the end of Williams's play and figuratively in the unending play they perform as they search for its conclusion. But for both the actors and the characters that they perform, entrapment is not entirely undesirable for Felice and Clare, since it allows them to explore the limits of their attraction. That attraction is not based on any physical desire, however latent or manifest. Rather, their uncleavable bond is metonymic of an unlobotomized brain, with each character representing half of the healthy human psyche. The play they perform for themselves and for us is thus representational of the conscious and unconscious struggle of daily existence. The character Felice can no more leave the character Clare than the frontal lobe can function independently from the cortex. To divide Felice from Clare would result in a figurative lobotomy.

Incest here is thus no more realistic than cannibalism is in *Suddenly Last Summer*. It is a theatrical means to an epistemological end, 'a parable'.[10] For Williams, as he explained in his 'Notes for *The Two Character Play*' (1970), an essay he wrote to shed light on the play's 'emotional obscurity',[11] that end was androgyny. Like schizophrenia, androgyny was one of Williams's literary obsessions, which, after Stonewall, also became one of his political ones as well. Williams frequently voiced in his interviews during the 1970s that what he had been experimenting with in his drama (*Out Cry*), in his fiction ('Miss Coynte of Greene' [1972] and *Moise and the World of Reason* [1975]), and in his poetry (*Androgyne, Mon Amour* [1977]) was a poetics of androgyny, 'a duality not reconciled'.[12] As Kari Weil has argued in *Androgyny and the Denial of Difference*, the androgynous differs from the hermaphrodite in a political sense in that while the latter describes more a physiological phenomenon, the former recalls the transcendental signified that 'asserts original difference (the male and the female "halves" it unites), and claims to transcend that "most virulent" of binary oppositions by defining our origin as one'.[13]

This 'oneness of the origin posited by the androgyne' and the 'differ-ences it engenders through opposition' are best defined 'by the exclusion of an origin that is not determined by the phallus, in other words, by the exclusion of a "differ*a*nt" sexual and textual body'.[14] Williams was not only attracted to the androgynous physically, but ideologically as well, since it was for Williams 'the truest human being'.[15]

In her 1971 interview with Williams, Jeanne Fayard asked him if his work was 'a quest of the androgynous', and Williams wholly agreed, but he replied that it could never be achieved because individuals prefer recognizing sexuality as distinct social categories rather than as degrees of psychological completeness.[16] Much of this he would repeat for *Playboy* a couple of years later: 'If you understand schizophrenics, I'm not really a *dual* creature; but I can understand the tenderness of women and the lust and libido of the male, which are, unfortunately, too seldom combined in women. That's why I seek out the androgynous so I can get both'.[17] Lee Quinby has argued that Williams believed in the power of the sexual life force in his early plays and thus employed hermaphroditic symbols like the rose, which reinforces the 'union of opposites' since it represents both spiritual and physical love.[18] Williams viewed these symbols, Quinby maintains, as manifestations of the androgynous because they exhibit 'a unity involving the fusion and balance of the masculine and the feminine, the spiritual and the physi-cal within the individual's psyche'.[19] This pursuit of the androgynous would thus lend unity to Williams's most heterogeneous decade in the literary arts.

The years 1970 and 1971 were proving to set the tone for the rest of the decade, and the message Williams was sending, or was being sent through his name by others writing biographical essays on him, was not flattering. His campy, drunken, interview on *The David Frost Show* in January 1970, when he finally admitted that he had 'covered the waterfront', as well as his candid (Williams called them fictive) interviews with Donald Newlove for *Esquire* ('A Dream of Tennessee Williams', November 1969), Tom Buckley for *The Atlantic* ('Tennessee Williams Survives', 1970), and Rex Reed for *Esquire* ('Tennessee Williams Turns Sixty', 1971), all made public the open secret of his homosexual-ity. But it came across at the time as a homosexuality of excess, one that he would celebrate in his *Playboy* interview with C. Robert Jennings in 1973 and his *Memoirs* two years later. Williams, of course, felt betrayed by his interviewers, who favoured the camp side of his lifestyle to a discussion of his theatre. As Donald Spoto suggests, 'Perhaps he wanted to be controversial – the hard-drinking, openly homosexual writer with nothing to hide – and at the same time, a man of *his own* time, a Southern gentleman from a politer era who would never abandon propriety and privacy'.[20]

So bothered was he by Buckley's 'exposé-type' essay, which he discovered while in Bangkok with Oliver Evans that November 1970, that Williams wanted to sue him and the *Atlantic Monthly* for libel and even asked his brother Dakin to begin the proceedings. Dakin told him that the suit would cost too much money and that he was not likely to win anyway.[21] Williams told Maria St Just that Buckley made him out to be 'an ass and an absolute vulgarian'.[22] In the January 1971 edition of *The Atlantic*, Williams published his rebuttal, 'Letter to the editor: An Open Response to Tom Buckley', charging him with libel over a series of inaccuracies, falsifications, and misquotations (Buckley claimed to have recorded the interview over several days on a tape recorder). Gore Vidal had warned Williams around this time that his 'dreadful personal publicity' was killing his theatre reviews,[23] which was mostly true, and Williams understood that with such bad press 'it would be practically impossible for [him] to have another play produced in the States and possibly not even in England'.[24] But instead of tempering the publicity, Williams exacerbated it with more unflattering interviews, candid memoirs, and gratuitous self-promotion as the drunken Doc Delaney in *Small Craft Warnings*: 'I guess I have to admit that I am a ham and that I loved it: appearing again tonight'.[25]

In the summer of 1971, several important stars were aligning, and he began to group his entourage between those who still thought he could succeed in American theatre and those who did not. The 'did' camp was diminishing rapidly. While Maria St Just continued to support Williams (as much out of love as out of self-promotion), others, like Marion Vaccaro, who died in April 1970, were fewer and farther between. Williams had always needed companionship, but now the bevy of retainers was disrupting his work habits. The first to be grouped in the 'did not' camp was his long-time agent, Audrey Wood. His break with Wood, to whom he had grown increasingly hostile over the last decade, was founded on his belief that she was partly responsible for derailing his career.

Williams was paranoid of Wood's attitude toward him, exacerbated by comments she was reported to have given Buckley about her love-hate relationship with Williams. During that summer, Williams was staying at the Ambassador Hotel in Chicago, trying out the first revised version of *The-Character Play*, now called, *Out Cry*, at the Ivanhoe Theatre, when the break-up took place. Wood apparently seconded director

Keathley's suggestions that Williams rewrite some of the play's lines, and Williams exploded. She overhead his final comment to Marie St Just just before parting: 'That bitch! I'm glad I'm through with her!'[26] It was a break long in the making, and Wood arranged for a younger agent from International Creative Management (ICM), Bill Barnes, to represent Williams. Barnes would retain his role for most of the decade before leaving ICM in 1979, replaced by Mitch Douglas.

Also that summer, Williams turned his attention more seriously to writing his memoirs. Though he had begun drafting his memoirs as far back as 1959, he dropped it for a while, and then picked it up again sometime in the early 1970s. He was still calling his autobiography 'These Scattered Idioms' at the time, but would change the title for *Esquire* to 'Waiting for that Sea Gull' or 'Which Sea-Gull on What Corner?', which the magazine eventually published dully as 'Survival Notes: A Journal' (1972). Kate Medina soon took interest in the memoirs for Doubleday after hearing Williams read from his private notebooks at a 'Conversations with Playwrights' talk in New York in the winter of 1971–72. In the summer of 1971, while rummaging through his unit at the Morgan-Manhattan Storage in New York for furniture from two of his apartments in the city that he now needed for an apartment in New Orleans,[27] Williams stumbled across his lost notebooks:

> But what I found that was most important to me was (were) a number of old journals which I kept in the innocent days when I thought my daily and nightly existence should be recorded. I had no idea at all – this I promise you – that I thought that [they] were worth recording for anyone but myself. But for myself it was useful to read back over old entries and be comforted by the discovery that I was going through much the same turmoil that I was now, meaning then. It gave me a reassurance of my [breaks off].[28]

Medina tried persuading Barnes to let Doubleday publish these note-books, but instead he turned her on to the *Esquire* piece already in progress, which 'became the basis of the contract for the memoir' that he signed in the summer of 1972.[29] By early July 1971, Williams had written a good number of polished pages of the memoirs, now titled 'Some Memoirs of a Con-Man', which he gave separate copies of to Marie St Just and Dotson Rader.[30] This version was similar in language and detail to the final piece that he eventually published in *Esquire*.[31] In a 30 December 1971 letter, he told St Just that he 'got up at four a.m. to continue work on my memoirs', which suggests that he wanted to continue writing his autobiography where he had left it the previous July, long before Doubleday showed any interest in publishing it.[32]

That autumn 1971, Williams also began reworking *Confessional*, buoyed by the reviews it was receiving in Bar Harbor. In November, he attended a revival of *Camino Real* in Houston, and then lent his voice to an anti-Vietnam demonstration for The Peoples' Coalition for the Peace and Justice benefit that took place in New York City on 6 December at the Cathedral of St John the Divine. Norman Mailer's antiwar play, *D.J.* or *A Fragment from Vietnam: A One-Act Play*, based on his 1967 novel, *Why Are We in Vietnam?*, was given a stage reading, which Williams did not appreciate (he was bothered by Mailer's liberal use of expletives within a holy place[33]) and left the church in a huff. About his speech, Williams admitted that he 'had only recent and limited contact with The Movement' and was 'not yet a reliable reporter upon its program': 'I am not the right person to write this. Not yet, not at this time: but they said they needed me to say something and I've said what I could…'.[34] A couple of years later, Williams would even mock the Movement in his one-act play *I Never Get Dressed Till after Dark on Sundays* (1973), when Jane tells the Playwright, 'You see, in New York, I was into the Movement a little, on the fringes of it till the Cathedral thing that opened my eyes to it'.[35] A lot of his spleen against the nation and its 'bastions of pig-dom' was vented in his most political (if not entirely incoherent) essay, 'We Are Dissenters Now', published in *Harper's Bazaar* a month later,[36] which was inspired by his benefit talk. Williams would confess the following year, when he began preparing the manuscript for his memoirs, that despite his political attachments to protecting Bohemia in America, he was never politically active outside of his plays: 'But you know and I know thatt regardless of how intensely I may feel about politics, that that is still not where my head is at this moment'.[37] If someone asked Williams what his politics were then, he said that he was 'a (an) humanitarian'.[38]

Also in December, Williams began drafting his pre-opening announcement for his expanded, two-act version of *Confessional* for the *New York Times*, though he still had not yet settled on the present title for the play. He called his piece 'Sunday Peace' and used the space to talk less about the play and complain more about his critics. He singled out 'something ominous' in Lewis Funke's misspelling of his name in his 19 December essay, 'One from Tennessee, One from Tom, Two on Way':

'The Times' has forgotten holw to spell myh first name, they omitted the final 'e'e and I think just about several one is aware that the state of Tennessee has two 'e's at the end of it. [...] I suppose I must be a very immodest as well as immoderate playwright to expect The Sunday Times drama section to spell my name correctly after all their experiences with me in the Sixties. [...] I have turned [in]to the bad-man, the bogeyman, of the American theatre and you would prob-ably much prefer to see my name in the obituary column than the announcement of a new play of mine on a dramam page.[39]

Neither this, nor his essay 'Too Personal?' (written 26 March 1972), whose defensive stance against the 'devastatingly bad write-up[s]' he was receiving was meant to be the pre-opening piece for *Small Craft Warnings*, was published prior to the premiere. Instead, the *New York Times* ran on 31 March Mel Gussow's interview, 'Williams Looking to Play's Opening'.

Now called *Small Craft Warnings*, the expanded play opened at the Truck and Warehouse Theatre on 2 April 1972. Though it was not the first play that Williams wrote which dealt frankly with homosexuality, it was the first that had been given a New York production. It is an hon-est, at times brutal play, about the devastation of various souls seeking comfort in the company of other battered 'crafts' adrift in Monk's bar. Though its use of the confessional, a spot-lighted stage area where each main character exposes his or her bruised heart in a monologue, was not new to the theatre, it was highly effective – for those who bothered to listen. *Small Craft Warnings* received mixed, though not damning, reviews, and it opened the following year in London at the Hampstead Theatre Club. On 6 June, it was transferred uptown from the Truck and Warehouse to the New Theatre, where Williams held nightly symposia after the performances; it was then rushed out of the New Theatre by mid-September to make room for *Noël and Gertie*, a revue about Coward and Lawrence that Williams made adlib assaults against when he was again taking up the role of Doc Delaney. All told, his play ran for a respectable six months.

During the summer and fall of 1972, Williams completed the major-ity of the first draft of his manuscript for *Memoirs*, which he would spend much of 1973 revising.[40] In July 1972, just before dedicating his next two months to the project, he wrote to Maria St Just:

I am also writing my 'memoirs' for Doubleday – so you'd better stay on my good side if there is one. I have already made some *guarded* references to you....

I enjoy writing the stuff, I am knocking it out at an average of about 16 pages a day and – although I may have to emigrate permanently from the States when it is published – I feel there's a cool million in it!

It's about time I struck it rich with something....[41]

St Just rightly notes that 'Tennessee later complained that the publisher had wanted too many cuts' but wrongly asserts that Doubleday 'had wanted him to concentrate too much on his sensational sex life'.[42] The opposite, in fact, was true: Medina had repeatedly voiced her concern that Williams was speaking too much about his nightly quests and not enough about his theatre. In one draft dated 'Materiel: January 14, 1973', Williams wrote: 'An obvious change has occurred in her [Medina's] attitude toward me since I wrote her that there was a fundamental difference in her concept and mine of these memoirs'.[43]

By late September, Williams was hard at work with Michael York and Cara Duff-MacCormick on the second attempt at *Out Cry*: 'I guess tomorrow is "D" day [for the play]. Either we pull it off – or I return to the writing of my memoirs....'.[44] The play was scheduled for rehearsals in Canada (for reasons related to York's tax problems in the US), and Williams was growing confident that the play would make it to New York by the start of the new year. He had wanted at the end of the month to return to Rome, then Taormina, taking with him the three-year Vietnam veteran Robert Carroll (age twenty-five), whom Williams wrongly considered to be one of the best, up-and-coming writers in America. But problems with his eyes forced Williams to return to Key West, where he continued work on the *Memoirs*, finishing the first draft, 650 pages of it, on 10 November 1972 with the final line, 'What a very strange year, between beginning and ending!'[45]

After having stayed in rooming houses and then hotels for the past thirty or so years, Williams finally purchased a small house in the French Quarter in 1972. Located at 1014 Dumaine Street, it was divided into two apartments; he occupied the top floor, apartment B, with its wrought iron balcony, and rented out the lower apartment. Slave quarters and a small, unused swimming pool were in the back. When Williams was not in Key West or in New York, he often stayed here, which was looked after by his then-secretary/lover Victor Campbell, whom he calls 'Miss Mary' or 'Poppins' in his letters to St Just. Campbell, a former Bell Telephone employee who eventually fell in love with long distances and left Williams in 1976, took care of Williams's Boston terrier Gigi and his house in New Orleans. Campbell, like Carroll in Key West, was now on Williams's payroll.

The year 1973 would again not prove kind to Williams personally. Several of his close friends and distant acquaintances tragically died: Jane Bowles (for whom he dedicated his recent gazebo at his Key West home), William Inge (for whom he wrote 'An Homage'), Anna Magnani (for whom he delivered a speech at her requiem mass in New York), and W. H. Auden (for whom he wrote 'An Appreciation' for the Harvard *Advocate*). Professionally, however, he was not dead, though he often felt like he was. He started working on a screenplay called 'A Second Epiphany for my Friend Maureen [Stapleton]' that would eventually become *Stopped Rocking* (1979–81).[46] He wrote stories like 'The Inventory at Fontana Bella' and 'Miss Coynte of Greene' (both 1972, July and November), and completed 'Sabbatha and Solitude' while crossing the Atlantic back to Europe that May. And he was all the time working on *Vieux Carré* and *The Red Devil Battery Sign*, not to mention his corrections for *Memoirs*. All in all, the year was very fruitful in terms of Williams's literary production.

In terms of his theatrical production, however, the news was not as sterling. On 1 March 1973, *Out Cry* opened at the Lyceum Theatre – and closed on 10 March after only twelve performances; there would be another revival the following year in June in Greenwich Village, and one more in October 1976, again called *The Two-Character Play*, at the Showcase, Lyle Leverich's theatre in San Francisco. Williams was deeply affected by the failure; he had put everything into the play over these past six years, and once again the critics and the public refused to like or even try to understand it. He responded to this 'latest flop' in two essays, 'Let Me Hang It All Out', which appeared on 4 March in the *New York Times* as a post-production response to the harsh notices, and 'Where My Head Is Now and Other Questions', which was published in *Performing Arts* a few weeks later in April. Both essays address the upcoming revivals of *A Streetcar Named Desire* and *Cat on a Hot Tin Roof* and how he was glad to have major productions in the works. But he intimates in both essays how these revivals of his classic plays were fuelling the antagonism toward his more recent, experimental plays.

'At the moment', he wrote in the latter essay, 'I am more interested in writing than in publishing or having further productions, but that is probably only the consequence of having gone through a Broadway production of *Out Cry*, which I honestly didn't think I would survive and am still not quite sure that I did'.[47] Devastated by *The Two-Character Play/Out Cry*'s third rejection, Williams flew to California, where he gave

an introduction to the projection of *A Streetcar Named Desire* at the Los
Angeles County Museum and then, on 18 March, spoke at a luncheon
at the University of Southern California. In a 12 April letter to St Just
from Bangkok, Williams mentioned, somewhat ironically, that the West
Coast silver anniversary revival of *Streetcar*, starring Faye Dunaway and
Jon Voight, 'out-grossed any show in the country the second week'
thanks in part to his '"spectacular appearance"'.[48]

After leaving Los Angeles near the end of March, Williams boarded
the cruise ship *Oronsay* in Honolulu en route to Sydney. Williams was
heading to Australia for a 'kangaroo' gig, where he had a theatre appoint-
ment planned and where he wanted to make a new career for himself
in the Aussie theatre. He wrote to St Just that he was working on a new
play 'and writing [my]self into the first one as an "aged playwright"
attending a reading with an "aged director"'.[49] That play was *I Never
Get Dressed Till after Dark on Sundays*, which would become, after some
unfortunate changes from the innovative play, the more traditional
play *Vieux Carré*.

To his quick dismay, Williams learned that the 'Cherry Blossom' cruise
he was booked on with Robert Carroll was generally for geriatrics, several
of whom died in passage, and once they reached their first port of call in
Yokohama, he and Carroll jumped ship:[50]

> The customs-officials, with big Japanese grins, enquired:
> 'How many not make it this far?', meaning how many demises had
> already occured [*sic*] at this point on 'The Cherry Blossom Cruise'.
> 'Only three that we know of'.
> They exchanged looks of surprise.
> 'Usually twice that many before they see cherry blossoms!'[51]

From Yokohama, they flew to Hong Kong to meet Norman Wingrove,
a radio newscaster there who later produced and presented a nightly
programme on technology. Next, they flew on to Bangkok and headed
to the beach resort at Pattaya, where Williams often ate at Ed Headley's
restaurant. In a cottage beside a pool at Pattaya, Williams envisioned
finishing his memoirs, which he did not succeed in doing.[52] Instead of
heading to Australia, they made their way to Istanbul, then to Rome,
a city he no longer liked with its 'suffocating traffic' and the 'up-tightness
of the Romans'.[53] He and Carroll finally returned to New York to catch
the East Coast silver anniversary production of *Streetcar* with Rosemary
Harris, and by the end of April, a little over a month after they left for
the East, he was back in Key West.

He did not stay there long, though. On 31 May, he wrote St Just again, this time from Positano, telling her that he has 'not yet opened [his] great box of memoirs which has been around the world with [him]': 'I will open it tomorrow when I am settled. I have an interesting new title for it: *Flee, Flee This Sad Hotel* – it is a quote from Rimbaud [it actually comes from Anne Sexton's poem, "Flee On Your Donkey"]. Hotel is a metaphor for life'.[54] In Rome that June, he learned of Jane Bowles's death, and then a few days later of Inge's suicide. He could now count his closest living friends, including Jane and Tony Smith, Oliver Evans, Paul Bowles, and Maria St Just, on just one hand. The 'Enfant Terrible', Carroll, was no longer included in his inner circle, since he and Williams were constantly fighting. He wrote his agent Barnes in June to send him 'a large section of [his] memoirs', but it was missing 'in the box when [he] opened it and he promised to send it at once along with an earlier draft of a short long play', *The Latter Days of a Celebrated Soubrette*, a rewrite of *The Gnädiges Fräulein* that Anne Meacham raised money to produce in May 1974, but which ran for only one performance in a New York church. 'Nevertheless, I have completed editing all the memoirs that were in the box [...]'.[55]

After Carroll returned to the States a second time that spring, Williams continued travelling with a new companion, Tom Field (who was often sick), for two weeks in July to visit Bowles in Tangier with the intent to head to Madrid to visit the Goyas and Velazquez at the Prado. He was growing anxious now to complete both the *Memoirs* and *Red Devil*. By October, he headed to Austin, Texas, where he was welcomed by 5000 students and toured the archives at the Harry Ransom Center, which had purchased or acquired many of his early papers and correspondences from 1962 to 1969.

During the fall of 1973, Williams saw several of his works published, from the poem 'Miss Puma, Miss Who?' to the stories 'Sabbatha and Solitude' and 'Miss Coynte of Greene', one in *Playgirl* and the other in *Playboy*, where he had previously published his strange story, 'A Recluse and His Guest', in 1970. Williams collected five of the early 1970s stories and published them the following year in a collection titled *Eight Mortal Ladies Possessed* (1974); 'The Red Part of a Flag or Oriflamme', the sixth story in this collection, was actually written in 1944. As Williams's short stories (and one-act plays) became more sexually explicit, he found that he could no longer place them in mainstream literary magazines; he later published in the gay New York magazine, *Christopher Street*.

One of these stories, 'The Inventory at Fontana Bella', which was also published in *Playboy* in March 1973, describes how Principessa Lisabetta,

102 years old, cannot find androgynous harmony to her antinomic desires for the flesh and obeisance to her spirit. Clutching her groin, she cries out for her fifth and last husband Sebastiano, dead fifty years, because 'in her dream she had felt the ecstasy of his penetration'.[56] While at Fontana Bella, her treasure-laden hideaway, where she has gone to put the material side of her life in order, Lisabetta disturbs a 'great white female stork'. The stork, 'alarmed for the safety of her young ones', repeatedly dives at Lisabetta (like the bird in the story 'The Night of the Iguana'), 'inflicting wounds' on her breast and stomach 'with its beak and blows with its wings'. To satisfy her sexual urges in this spiritual battle, the old woman grabs the bird and forces its beak 'to penetrate her vagina'.[57] The bird dies, suffocating inside her uterine passage; Lisabetta dies later, too, still clutching her insatiable groin. Such stories were hardly material for *The New Yorker* or *The Saturday Evening Post*.

If Williams was recently experimenting at length with the sexually androgynous, he was also interested in exploring racial intercourse. In 'Miss Coynte of Greene', Williams describes Miss Coynte as 'not a lady of the new South' but as having a mission in life to begin the 'great new race in America', one which will inevitably come from 'the total mixing together of black and white blood [...]'.[58] Williams had already dabbled with interracial sex in *Kingdom of Earth* between Chicken and Myrtle, as well as between a young bride and a sailor on leave in the one-act *Green Eyes* (1970), whom the groom suggests was black or mulatto. But in the novel he was writing alongside his *Memoirs*, *Moise and the World of Reason* (1975), whose revised first draft Williams completed in May 1974,[59] Williams explores interracial homosexual sex between the narrator and Lance, the only black ice skater on the circuit, who admits to being 'a product of miscegenation'.[60] Williams's gradual progression from portraying mixed blood as a societal ill to a genetic panacea mirrors to a certain extent his generation's own gradually shifting attitudes toward racial segregation. But in terms of representing interracial homosexual sex in his writing, Williams was clearly ahead of his times.

Moise and the World of Reason is as much about racial integration as it is about hypersexuality. And it is also about madness and the pursuit of androgyny, with each character containing fragments of a self-portrait of the playwright trying to pick up the 'scattered idioms' of his life. The narrator Lance and the artist Moise are both facets of Williams's own personality. A 'distinguished failed writer at thirty'[61] from Thelma, Alabama, the narrator is looking for his third lover, as his second one has just left him and his first one had overdosed. Lost for most of his life in the uncertainty about his homosexuality and the frustration of a failing career, this southern writer reaches an epiphany one night that his life exists in absolutes. He has seen this in both Lance and Moise but is now struggling to discover it in himself. Lance, the writer's lover, is 'an oversexed cat', a 'hellcat' with 'green eyes', who exists more for the 'flesh' than for 'the skin and its color'.[62] Moise, a burnt-out artist based in part on the 'mad' artist Olive Leonhardt whom Williams had met back in 1942 and whose work both Tony and Jane Smith admired,[63] is throwing her own creative wake as she departs from the 'world of reason'; she has a 'certain vanity' about her 'vaginal entrance' and wishes to remain a virgin. The narrator finds himself in the midst of this dialectical predicament, being both 'a very sensual person' with 'a chronically inflamed libido' and a '"child of God"' who sees that it is 'time for purification of my forsaken and ailing body by thoughts upon the absolutes of existence, and on the non of it before it occurs and after'.[64]

Written roughly at the same time as *Memoirs*, *Moise and the World of Reason* can be read as Williams's shadow memoirs. Both share many passages, including the story of Marion Vaccaro peeing on herself in Rhodes; of the Irish truck-driver who knocked out the 'middle-aged queen's' front teeth; of his trip to Bangkok and his staying in Somerset Maugham and Neil Coward's bedroom; of the March 1968 atrocities at My Lai and the cover-up which followed; of Rimbaud's *Bateau ivre*, and also the story of his finding his name in the *International Who's Who* in Maria St Just's library in 1952.[65] *Moise and the World of Reason* unlocks some of the mysteries of Williams's *Memoirs*, just as the *Memoirs* help unravel the novel's at times incoherent narrative structure.

The narrator of *Moise and the World of Reason* comments once about the looseness of the novel's structure in words that echo what Williams had said himself about the rather unorthodox organization of his thoughts and recollections in *Memoirs*:

> It's seldom my practice to observe sequence. When I try to, my thoughts blur and my fingers shake [...]. Now I have got to discontinue this *thing* for a while, even though I never ignore the possibility that some inadvertence, a sudden subway of sorts, may stop it permanently in its tracks [...].[66]

'Truth is the bird we hope to catch in "this thing"', he writes midway through *Memoirs*, and 'truth' for him was something 'better approached through my life story than an account of my career'.[67] Accessing the 'truth' about his life was not bound by rules of chronology or even coherency but rather by the 'free association' exercises he had learned years before in psychotherapy:

> This whole book is written by something like the process of 'free association,' which I learned to practice during my several periods of psychoanalysis. It concerns the reportage of present occurrences, both trivial and important; and of memories, mostly much more important. At least to me.
>
> I will frequently interrupt recollections of the past with an account of what concerns me in the present because of many of the things which concerned me in the past continue to preoccupy me today.
>
> Whether or not it will be acceptable to you will depend in part on your tolerance for an aging man's almost continual scuttling back and forth between his recollections and his present state.[68]

When Williams finally published his *Memoirs* in November 1975, it was an immediate best-seller and a *cause célèbre*. In December of that year, Williams broke all records at Doubleday by signing more than eight hundred copies in what has been termed 'the Great Fifth Avenue Bookstore Riot'.[69] In spite of its success, or rather because of it, *Memoirs* also became a lightning rod for the continued harsh, and ostensibly homophobic, attacks levelled against him by many of the nation's leading theatre critics. *Time*'s typically acerbic T. E. Kalem called *Memoirs* a 'gamy, scarcely edifying spectacle' of Williams's '"cruising" tours', while the *New York Times* triumvirate – Christopher Lehmann-Haupt, Jack Richardson, and Mel Gussow – found it 'unorthordox', out of control, and 'graphic'.[70] *Memoirs* offers readers little in the way of insight into Williams's dramatic theory or his creative process, teetering between a string of disjointed anecdotes, several of which detail his sexual escapades, and his daily struggles over the production of *Small Craft Warnings*.

'Of course, I could devote this whole book to a discussion of the art of drama', he writes in *Memoirs*, 'but wouldn't that be a bore?'[71] Instead, Williams offers in its place an endless list of his sexual conquests that are for him and his poetic namesake, Tom Wingfield, 'truth in the pleasant disguise of illusion': 'Why do I resist writing about my plays? [...] The truth is, I feel that the plays speak for themselves. And that my life hasn't and that it has been remarkable enough, in its continual contest with madness, to be worth setting upon paper. And my habits of work are so much more private than my daily and nightly existence'.[72]

Williams himself never felt that his *Memoirs* was artistic, certainly not after the editors at Doubleday had censored it, and he repeatedly inserted jibes at Doubleday editor Kate Medina in the manuscript version, which were edited out, just to see what would get in and what would not. Williams admitted as much to the *Atlanta Constitution* when he blamed Doubleday 'for deleting material and distorting the book's balance'.[73] In another fragment of his titled 'These Scattered Idioms' (c. 1977), written after the book's critical pasting, Williams acknowledged its literary shortcomings:

> About my recent book of Memoirs, there have been some complaints that they were not well-organized ~~or~~ nor in a very good literary style. Now I will let you in on <u>one</u> disgraceful secret about the <u>Memoirs</u> which <u>they</u> did not ~~contain confess~~ let you in on.
>
>   I did all my writing on them while I was working on a play, and I only worked on the <u>Memoirs</u> when I was too exhausted to continue work on the play. No excuses: just an explanation....[74]

For many of Williams's theatre critics, *Memoirs* justified the venom they had been spewing against him over the past ten years. Williams to them was not only past his literary prime but was now just a spectacle or a pastiche of his former self. Further crushed by the review about his novel (published in May) and now his *Memoirs*, Williams summed up his life in a 1975 interview with Patrick O'Haire: 'Very scattered. Psychoanalysis didn't put me together at all. I am about as together as Humpty Dumpty after the fall'.[75]

When *Memoirs* was harshly reviewed in the press, Williams never really expected anything less from the 'macho' critics like Stanley Kauffman, Robert Brustein, Frank Rich, or Clive Barnes, who had set out to destroy his reputation since *Slapstick Tragedy* or even as early as *Sweet Bird of Youth*. What caught him off guard was that even the gay community took its vindictive shots at him now. In a long statement that he published in *Gay Sunshine* in 1977, Williams castigates the magazine's reviewer, Andrew Dvosin, for his short-sightedness concerning the autobiography:

> At the end of your review of my *Memoirs* (mostly dedicated to an attempt to annihilate my work for the theatre), you make these extravagant charges. You call my plays 'lies' and 'lies not like truth' but 'complicated misrepresentations of reality' and you really blast off about this in a very militant vehemently self-righteous way. [...] But please believe me, there are no lies in the creation of these characters. Nothing repels me more than untruth and nothing attracts me more strongly than honesty – I mean on a spiritual level.[76]

This review stung Williams more sharply than those that had appeared elsewhere in print because this was, in his own words, 'the only completely literate and serious Gay journal' published in America.[77] Williams knew he was not going to get positive reviews in, say, *Time* magazine or the *New York Times*, whose 'chauvinistic put-downs [...] delivered by "macho" critics' was infamous as far as Williams was treated over the years; he had thought, however, or at least had hoped, that he would have found sympathetic reviewers in a magazine devoted to the gay community. As Williams concluded his rebuttal, 'I could say what I needed to say as easily through love-scenes between a man and a woman as I could have between two Gays, that I swear. So, where's the lie?'[78]

Similar charges from gay artists began to accumulate after the publication of *Memoirs*. Gay playwright 'Lee Barton' in his article 'Why Do Homosexual Playwrights Hide their Homosexuality?' also castigated Williams for having sensationalized heterosexuality for pecuniary reasons, while slighting homosexuality throughout his career because he knew it would not sell:

> One work of art dealing truthfully with homosexual life is worth a hundred breast-beating personal confessions. Who really gives a damn that Tennessee Williams has finally admitted his sexual preferences in print? He has yet to contribute any work of understanding to gay theater, and with his enormous talent one of his works would indeed be worth any amount of personal data.[79]

But Williams insisted here, and elsewhere, that he never wrote a gay play because sex itself was not the play's main concern. Rather, sex was more the manifestation of truth between two people, regardless of their orientation; if they had sex at all in a Williams play, it was because that was the only way the two characters could ever communicate on a human level. As Stella tells her sister Blanche in *A Streetcar Named Desire*, 'there are things that happen between a man and a woman in the dark – that sort of make everything else seem – unimportant'.[80] Williams documents his sex life in *Memoirs* and in *Moise and the World of Reason* simply because it was essential to his artistic life, and to leave sex out of the books' pages would have been akin to denying the process toward artistic creation itself. If anyone knows the importance sex plays in reaching the type of sublime that Stella speaks about, it is surely Blanche, in spite of her puritanical posturing – and Williams.

Williams dismissed his gay critics by arguing in 'Let Me Hang It All Out' that his plays were never about homosexuality from the outset since his themes were much larger than the sexual identification of one character:

> Frankly, and at the risk of alienating some of my friends in Gay Lib, I have never found the subject of homosexuality a satisfactory theme for a full length play, despite the fact that is appears as frequently as it does in my short fiction. Yet never even in my short fiction does the sexual activity of a person provide the story with its true inner substance.[81]

Significantly, Williams would repeat this sentiment often, even directly to the gay community itself, where, in his taped 1976 interview with George Whitmore at the Hotel Elysée for *Gay Sunshine*, Williams reiterated that he did not want to 'write a gay play' simply because he did not 'find it necessary'.[82] Williams knew that such a comment would 'bring down on my cracked head the wrath of all the Gay Libs to whom my heart is committed, categorically, in a bruised-ass way', as his self-identified narrator says in *Moise and the World of Reason*.[83] Yet he also knew that his Broadway audience and theatre critics were not yet warm to the idea of an honest 'gay' play, despite the financial and critical success that plays like *The Boys in the Band* had enjoyed years earlier.

Even sexuality was not the 'truth' that Williams sought in *Memoirs* or in anything he had written up till then. Instead, he was championing the idea that we all have a certain amount of heterosexual and homosexual nature in us, an idea Freud and other psychosexual theorists had been claiming for half a century. As Williams wrote,

> Now, surely, Mr. Dvosin, you don't believe that the precise sexual orientation of a character in a play is what gives validity to the play. Is there such a thing as precise sexual identity in life? I've never encountered it in my sixty-five years of living and getting about widely. Nearly every person I've known has either two or three sexual natures, that of the male, the female and that of the androgyne which is far from being a derogatory classification to my way of feeling and thinking. Now a confession. I contain all three.
>
> But I have always had something to say in my plays which was more important to the play, to me, to the audiences, than the non-existent thing, a precise sexual identity of a character.[84]

This belief of his in androgyny, which Williams repeated later in many interviews, was essential to the expression of his indiscrete truth, which was politically more dangerous at the time than declaring one's homo-sexuality. Outing oneself was a political act, but it still served social ends by creating social categories in which a person could situate him- or herself. Proclaiming in interviews or dramatizing on the stage that the hetero-/homo-divide was not unique to any one individual, and that the sexual categories themselves were as false as the people placed in them, allowed Williams to parry attacks against him from the gay and straight communities alike and to uphold his lifelong pursuit of disclosing the indiscrete truth of human existence. *Out Cry*, like *Small Craft Warnings*, was not about sexual impropriety; it was instead about how sexual taboos keep society from exploring the depths of its own psychosexual identity out of fear of what it might find there.

In spite of the fact that 1974–75 was a critical year in the public's solidification of Williams's homosexuality, his drug and alcohol addic-tion, and his apparent incoherence in print and on stage, Williams pursued writing plays. He was fully conscious of his unwinnable war with the theatre critics and knew that his final reputation would lay with his theatre. Producing long non-fiction that required attention to assure structural unity would keep him from writing his plays. As such, he concentrated all of his efforts on two plays these past few years that he had hoped would restore his reputation: one was *Out Cry*, which was now playing in Paris, and a London production with Paul Scofield as Felice was in the negotiation stage; the other was *The Red Devil Battery Sign*. Throughout 1974, while Medina and Doubleday were trying to sort through Williams's *Memoirs*, Williams worked feverishly on *Red Devil* and other plays.

One of those new plays was the dreamlike fantasy *This Is (An Entertain-ment)*, which Williams initially completed in January 1974 but which was again extensively revised for the 1976 production. Williams had begun work on the play in 1971, around the time that he saw Françoise Sagan's adaption of *Sweet Bird of Youth* at the Théâtre de L'Atelier in Paris, but the majority of writing was done during the winter of 1973–74, when negotiations with *Red Devil* stalled its production. David Merrick, Williams's on-again/off-again producer for *Red Devil*, was trying to get Elia Kazan to direct, but Williams soon grew impatient with the stand-off between the two egos (Kazan was concentrating on his own literary work now) and just wanted his play produced and suggested they hire the director Milton Katselas, who had directed revivals of *The Rose Tattoo* and *Camino Real* in 1966 and 1970, respectively. St Just was trying to help Williams get *This Is* performed at the Greenwich Theatre in London in the summer 1974, but it eventually premiered at the American Conservatory Theater (ACT) in San Francisco in January 1976. It ran at the ACT in rep until May, with Williams adding changes to the script during his three month stay on the West Coast between San Francisco and Palm Springs. The play, directed by Frank Dunlop, received mixed reviews. During rehearsals for the play at the end of December 1975, Williams fled to Vienna to see the European premiere of *Red Devil* at the city's English Theatre.

Back in August 1975, Williams had completed a second draft of *The Red Devil Battery Sign*, which he had begun in Tangier with Bowles during the summer of 1973. Williams felt that it was his most important play of the decade after *Out Cry*. Merrick was back on board the project, and, by September, the play finally had a director, Edwin Sherin, who had just successfully directed Claire Bloom as Blanche in the London revival of *Streetcar* in March 1974. In September, and then again in January 1975, Williams and Sherin met in Guadalajara to audition various mariachis.[85] Rehearsals for *Red Devil* were to start in late spring, but Anthony Quinn kept pushing the dates back, delaying the play's production indefinitely. Preparing for its June premiere, Williams started writing in its pre-opening piece for the *New York Times*; though untitled, and eventually unpublished, it begins 'in my present and future plans'.[86] *Red Devil* eventually opened on 18 June at Boston's Shubert Theatre but ran for only two weeks. It was 'slated' for a five-week run at Washington's National Theatre before moving on to Broadway's Broadhurst Theatre.[87] Despite good reviews in Boston, Williams bemoaned in his 'White Paper' (August 1975) the fact that 'big-time producer, Mr. David Merrick, for some reason of a sort that I don't want to and cannot explore at this point, decided to post the closing notice four days after we opened'.[88] Quinn wanted to bring the play to New York, or even make it in to a film, and Williams was making changes in the script based on what he saw in Boston. Many of Williams's fragmented essays written around this time, including an 'Afterword' that he had hoped to insert into *Memoirs* before its release later that November, discuss the play's opening and its brief 'coup-de-desgrace' closing and his frustration with Merrick.[89]

All told, *The Red Devil Battery Sign*'s try-out in Boston was cut short to ten performances. Following several revisions, it reopened the following winter in Vienna, where it was a minor success.[90] Williams felt that its sharp social criticism and reference to the various cover-ups in the 1963 assassination of President John F. Kennedy that were coming to light in 1972, made it inappropriate and even 'dangerous' for an American production. In his 1975 interview with Charles Ruas, Williams boldly stated, 'It's the moral decay of America, which really began with the

Korean War, way before the Kennedy assassination. The main reason we were involved in Vietnam was so two hundred billion dollars worth of equipment could be destroyed and would have to be bought again. We're the death merchants of the world [...]'.[91] It was this blend of moral disgust and political outrage that fuelled the incoherent essay 'The Misunderstanding and Fears of an Artist's Revolt', which he would only publish in his collection of essay, *Where I Live: Selected Essays* (1978).[92] The essay, which echoes the 1948 piece 'On the Art of Being a True Non-conformist', which appeared in *Where I Live* under the 1953 title 'Something Wild ...', equates the 'Artist' with the 'Revolutionary'.[93] This 'political' Williams was becoming more pronounced now, evident in several one-act plays he had been writing ever since the late 1960s, from the dark vision of a suffocating totalitarian world of *The Municipal Abattoir* (1966), where an older man succumbs to the pressures of a Fascist regime and turns himself in for extermination, to the post-atomic world of *The Chalky White Substance* (1980). In his 'Playwright's Preface' programme note for *The Red Devil Battery Sign*, which was first printed in the *Vancouver Playhouse Program Magazine* in October 1980, Williams offered a reflection on the play's half-decade long excursion, describing it as a representation of the nation's 'raw, bloody wound' that it has self-inflicted and left to fester since the start of the Cold War.[94]

In January 1976, Williams was interviewed by a German television company, and Carroll, whom Rose was mistaking as Williams's son, was causing more and more problems. Williams could never find it in himself to finally cut ties with him, despite the fact that Carroll was looking for a hundred thousand dollars to leave him. Later that spring, Williams was invited to Cannes to serve as President of the film festival's jury, just as he had done for the Venice Film Festival four years earlier in August 1972 with Bill Barnes, Michael York and his wife, and the film director Paul Morrissey, whose film *Heat* Williams greatly admired. Williams arrived, with his new bulldog Madam Sophia under one arm (Gigi, his thirteen-year-old terrier, died the previous year), and Maria St Just on the other (Sophia, whom Williams adored, died a year later when she was put into the hold of an airplane that Williams thought was air-conditioned and suffocated). Just prior to his visit in April, he provided a short piece for *Le Figaro*, which the French paper titled 'Le cinéma et moi'. In the English version, the message he wanted to send to 'you in Europe' was essentially the same that he had been saying to everyone in America: 'This may sound to some of you like that paranoiac plaint of a bitter, defeated old man. But I am not bitter, I am not yet defeated'.[95] Also that spring, he moved Rose out to Key West, hoping the change from Ossining would do her good, but the stay was not long in the end. In the summer of 1979, he finally purchased a house for her near his own in Key West.[96] Spending time at Stoney Lodge and in Key West was hard on Rose, who needed the structure of the institute, and Williams finally accepted by 1979 that her 'transfer to Key West [was] fizzling out'.[97]

The rest of 1976 was devoted to bringing *Vieux Carré* and *The Eccentricities of a Nightingale* to Broadway. While more time and energy was devoted to revising *Vieux Carré*, the second play was given priority in production, owing to the fact that Williams had already completed most of it back in 1951 when he had wanted to substitute it for the *Summer and Smoke* production in London and a version of it had already been produced at Chicago's Goodman Theatre in January 1967. After a quarter of a century, *The Eccentricities of a Nightingale* finally made it to Broadway via the Arena Theatre in Buffalo, opening at the Morosco Theatre on 23 November 1976, again under the direction of Ed Sherin. In his pre-opening piece, 'I Have Rewritten a Play for Artistic Purity', published in the *New York Times* on 21 November 1976, Williams describes the reasons for this new version of the play, denoting a 'semantic variance between the more popular concept of the word "purity"' and 'the meaning that purity has for those who practice the literary or plastic arts'.

For Williams, 'purity' in the first sense denotes 'morality', and in the second, artistic 'truth':

> purity means the disciplined excision from the work of those elements that are inessential or extraneous, and so by one agile leap I bring myself, and possibly you, directly to the stripping away of much inessential, distracting and often incredible material that somehow formed an accretion about the bare and true being of a play [...].[98]

In a draft version of this essay written back in 1961, Williams recalled being 'elated to find, last June, that I had removed the corn and the melodrama that had spoiled the play for me in its original form':

> I have always wanted to make more drafts of a play than the exigencies of Broadway have allowed, but from time to time, I have profited from the faults observed in their original exposure to write a full draft of them afterwards, for publication or just as a typed revision.[99]

From 1951, when he wrote the new play, to 1961 when he recovered it from Maria St Just, to 1976 when it was finally produced, Williams remained loyal to its androgynous message. Unfortunately, his public did not, as the play closed after twenty-four performances on 12 December. Following its premiere, Williams booked his escape to St Thomas on the Virgin Islands but returned in early December for his lifetime induction ceremony into the American Academy of Arts and Letters.

As if his professional battles were not enough, Williams faced several personal crises as well. In Key West, with Carroll now more out of his life than in (though he would be back the following year), Williams could find the peace and tranquillity to paint next to his pool, opening up the horizons of a potential new career opportunity. Several of his paintings would be exhibited in Charleston in 1978. But loneliness traumatized him, and he quickly ran through a number of secretaries/ travelling companions. In New York, trouble was equally brewing with Truman Capote and Donald Windham. Though Williams had already distanced himself from both of them for over a decade, his long-time friendship with the two writers would now come back to haunt him. In the 'Unspoiled Monsters' chapter of his novel-in-progress, *Answered Prayers*, published in *Esquire* in May 1976, Capote captured Williams cruelly (if not inaccurately) in his unflattering and thinly veiled portrait of Mr Wallace, a 'paunchy, booze-filled runt' who was America's greatest playwright.

Also compiled in 1976, Windham's *Tennessee Williams' Letters to Donald Windham, 1940–1965* painted Williams, particularly later in his life, as a self-centred paranoid depressive – again, not an entirely inaccurate portrait of his later years. Though Williams had signed over to Windham the copyrights to his letters that he had written to him since the 1940s, Williams felt that the way Windham went about acquiring the copyrights was devious. Williams wrote to the editors of the *New York Times* that Windham had provided him with paperwork that would transfer ownership of the letters over to Windham, but that he did not have his proper reading glasses and thus could not read what the letter actually said. Williams admits that he was inebriated at dinner when he signed the contract in front of Windham and Sandy Campbell – 'Les Soeurs Bitches'[100] – which he thought limited publication of the letters to a small press in Verona, Italy. No doubt Williams was angered when the 'far from private firm' of Holt, Rinehart and Winston published the letters in the US in 1977. Williams was 'certainly not' ashamed of the letters' content (how could he be after revealing much the same sexual content in his *Memoirs*?) and did regard them as 'a valuable documentation of a young writer's way to survive the difficult climb to achievement'. He was angered more by Windham's bitter commentary 'peppered' in between the letters that portrayed Williams in a less than favourable light.[101]

Williams looked past these many professional hurdles and personal crises and ahead toward his next production. He returned to the story of the 'Cherry Blossom Cruise' (c. 1976–77) in preparing a pre-opening piece for *Vieux Carré* and wrote a significant number of versions of the essay that described the genesis of *Vieux Carré* from its initial one-page draft in January 1939 to the two one-act plays of 1975 that he eventually fused together aboard the *Oronsay* to create the full-length play. One of those essay drafts is titled 'What Is "Success" in the Theatre?' (c. 1977), written in Key West during and after the play's try-out period.[102] It not only describes the geriatric cruise he and Carroll had taken, but it also ruminates on the failure of *Out Cry* in March 1973, one of the reasons why he had fled the country for the Orient in the first place. In another draft of this essay, Williams wrote, 'I can't honestly deny that I haven't derived a great deal of satisfaction from all these revivals of old hits of mine, here and there about the country as it approached and passed through its bicentennial year'. Yet he also knew that the revivals were affecting the reception of his newer work and, as a 'glutinous creature', he wanted more plays produced.[103] 'Success' for Williams in the 1970s often translated as 'the past', and he was determined to revise that definition to include, as one essay fragment was titled, 'Finally Something New'.

In *Vieux Carré*, however, Williams returned to the characters and themes of his earlier work and updated them for his contemporary audiences. Jane Sparks – an avatar, or pastiche, of Mrs Hardwicke-Moore in *The Lady of Larkspur Lotion* (c. 1941) – suffers from an unnamed disease (probably leukaemia) that has been in remission ever since her first meeting with Tye McCool. She often wonders why an educated, well-bred woman from the North stays with Tye, a Bourbon Street strip-joint barker. Williams suggests that the answer lies in her dual nature: like the game of chess she plays with herself, Jane is trapped in fighting a battle where victory would simultaneously announce her defeat. As such, she purposely avoids the endgame in the chess match and accepts the gradual loss of chess pieces as the necessary prolongation of the inevitable. Her daily clashes with Tye push Jane to leave him, but her sensual desires to remain alive forbid it: 'I've been betrayed by a – sensual streak in my nature'.[104] That 'sensual streak' of hers is more than pure lust, however: to keep her disease in remission, Jane needs Tye's life-supporting sexuality, as much as Blanche needed Stanley's to release her from the 'epic fornications' that have ruined her southern family.

Unlike Mrs Hardwicke-Moore and Blanche, Jane is able to fight and preserve her flesh at the expense of her spirit – not because it is a violation of her person, but because it has terminated the life force to which she so desperately clings. She sought no androgynous harmony between her disparate natures, as most of Williams's heroes and heroines do, but instead struggles like Flora Goforth to stave off the impending departure of the spirit. Her journey is the exact opposite of the play's Writer, who enters the boarding house ill-prepared for his homosexual encounter with Nightingale. The tubercular painter initiates the younger Writer into accepting his sexual nature, and the Writer seeks spiritual comfort for his sexual 'transgressions' in the angel of his dead grandmother.

The *Vieux Carré* that premiered at the St James Theatre in New York on 11 May 1977 shares little in common with the play that Williams conceptualized back in 1973 and reworked over the next two years. In September 1975, Williams mentioned to St Just that he was working on 'a pair of one acts called *Vieux Carré*' and asked William Prosser in March 1976 to direct them for the Greene Street Theatre in Key West. The play still 'consisted of two parts': 'Part 1 was titled "The Angel in the Alcove" after the short story of the same name and relating the same basic incidents. Part 2 was called "I Never Get Dressed till after Dark on Sundays" and was set in a different New Orleans apartment with totally different characters'.[105] This earlier version of Jane and Tye's story was more experimental, a play about the rehearsal of the play, where actors address the director and the playwright provides running commentary from the wings. It was a style not far from the metatheatre of *Out Cry* but less esoteric. Arguably, Williams significantly altered *Vieux Carré* from this experimental conception to something resembling the poetic naturalism that had established his reputation because he wanted to please the critics and audiences. The last three failed attempts to ensure his critics of the genius of *Out Cry* and the recent public demand for revivals of his older plays may have convinced him that he had to return to the style of the 1940s if he were ever to conquer Broadway again.

When the play was nearing production in the winter of 1977 (the initial opening was set for his sixty-sixth birthday), Williams returned for promotional purposes to New Orleans with director Arthur Alan Seidelman and a reporter and photographer from *People* magazine. Describing what Christopher Harris captured with his camera lens, Williams writes, 'Our little "People" party dispersed in Jackson Square amidst a great fluttering of pigeons beneath the equestrian statue of Andrew Jackson'.[106] The nostalgic trip to his French Quarter haunts had a noticeable impact on Williams, for not only did he change the essential structure of the play, but now he would completely rewrite his essay destined for the *New York Times*. In preparing his pre-opening piece for *Vieux Carré*, Williams suddenly abandoned all that he had already written about the 'Cherry Blossom' cruise. In its place, Williams offered an essay that talks about his last string of failures dating back to *The Night of the Iguana* and 'how certain radically and dreadfully altered circumstances of [his] life compelled [him] to work in correspondingly different styles'.[107]

The essay 'I Am Widely Regarded as a Ghost of a Writer', which was published in the *New York Times* on 8 May, was actually an earlier essay that Williams wrote for an awards ceremony in the spring of 1973, just before the ill-fated third run of *Out Cry*. That essay, titled 'Stylistic Experiments in the Sixties ~~While Working Under the Influence of Speed~~', describes precisely how he has moved away from his poetic naturalism and toward newer styles.[108] Williams simply updated that essay with events involving the recent production of *The Eccentricities of a Nightingale*. Gone now was the history to *Vieux Carré*'s composition aboard the 'Cherry Blossom' cruise, though he mentioned it a few days later in his interview with the *Village Voice*, 'Orpheus Holds his Own: William Burroughs Talks with Tennessee Williams',[109] and he may have even spoken about the ocean crossing during his February 1977 appearance at the Sophomore Literary Festival at the University of Notre Dame, again in the company of Burroughs.

The substitution of this essay for his 'Cherry Blossom' piece was surely a calculated manoeuvre on Williams's part. In his 'Ghost' essay, Williams tried both to remind his audiences that *Vieux Carré* was really not the nostalgic play that it actually was, and to convince his critics not to judge his new material by the old standards, as they had done with *Out Cry*, though by now the play was already denatured of its potentially troubling experimental style. Williams had simply wanted it both ways: to ride the momentum established by the recent successful revivals and to remain loyal to the experimental directions that his theatre was taking. Neither effort paid off in the end, however. Though Bill Barnes had booked try-outs for *Vieux Carré* in New Haven and Boston in early February 1977 to ensure its smooth ride into Broadway, when *Vieux Carré* finally did premiere on 11 May, it closed after only five performances. Williams was now indeed the 'ghost' of a writer that he had feared becoming back in 1973.

With the current frenzy in America over the conspiracy theory surrounding Kennedy's death sparking interests abroad, Vanessa Redgrave wanted to bring *Red Devil* back to the stage. Burt Shevelove, who saw the

Vienna production, offered to direct the play at the Roundhouse Theatre in London, which was for Williams a 'totally unsuitable mock-up of a theatre with no acoustics fit only except for rock bands [...]'.[110] Eventually directed by Keith Baxter, who played King Del Rey in the Vienna production, *Red Devil* was quickly transferred to the city's Phoenix Theatre and ran throughout the month of July 1977. A year later, Williams praised Baxter's 'stunning abilities, both as actor and director' in the Vienna production and sympathized with his efforts at the Phoenix, for Barnes had put on the play 'without even sufficient funds to pay the Round House [*sic*] for tenancy, nor any promotion, nor, at the end, after we'd transferred to the Phoenix, salaries for a number of actors'.[111]

'En avant' was always Williams's direction in his professional life, and so forward ahead he marched on. His aborted attempt in 1973 to fulfil his theatre commitments in Sydney, Australia, revisited him in the summer of 1977, when he was offered another 'Project Kangaroo'.[112] He worked the remaining months of the year on the teleplay *Stopped Rocking*, ostensibly about him and his sister Rose, which he wrote for Maureen Stapleton, and on *Tiger Tail*, a theatrical adaptation of the film *Baby Doll*. Canadian filmmaker Harry Rasky, whose documentary about Williams in 1973, *Tennessee Williams' South*, had secured a friendship between the two men, was asked to direct the try-out of *Tiger Tail* in Atlanta at the Alliance Theatre in 1978, which enjoyed such success that there was a buzz about bringing it to Broadway. But the play never made it out of Atlanta. Williams had asked Rasky to direct *Stopped Rocking* back in 1975 but that production, too, never materialized.[113]

By June 1978, Williams had a new play, *Creve Coeur*, in production, directed by Keith Hack at the Dock Street Theatre in Charleston, South Carolina, for the American version of the Italian Spoleto Festival. Williams wrote the one-act *Creve Coeur* while in San Francisco back in 1976, after having discovered a lost screenplay of his in New Orleans, *All Gaul Is Divided*, that he had written in the late 1950s around the same time that he wrote his other southern film script, *The Loss of a Teardrop Diamond*. *Creve Coeur*'s unanimous praise, including from New York critic Mel Gussow, was the first for a Williams play in decades. Williams scored a double victory in Charleston that summer as his paintings were also exhibited for the first time. The potential now of bringing his last two out-of-town successes, *Tiger Tail* and *Creve Coeur*, together to New York excited Williams immensely, but only *Creve Coeur* would eventually make it there a year later, lengthened slightly and retitled *A Lovely Sunday for Creve Coeur*.

Similarly nostalgic, though more conventional, than *Vieux Carré*, *A Lovely Sunday for Creve Coeur* is about several women and the men who affect their lives, though the men never appear on stage. The women, among them Dorothea (Dotty) Gallaway, are '[c]apable of flight' but perch themselves like pigeons waiting 'for a moment in this absolute desolation' for life to begin.[114] Suffering from her 'Southern belle complex', Dotty must confront her delusions that T. Ralph Ellis, a society gentleman who took advantage of her in his REO sedan, has any intentions of marrying her. She sits lifeless between Bodey, the boisterous German who tries to set Dotty up with her twin brother Buddy, and Helena, the superficial socialite who has '*the eyes of a predatory bird*'.[115] Metaphorically speaking, Bodey and Helena are at metaphysical odds over Dotty's being and, in fact, represent the life and death forces that control her, just as Maxine and Hannah battle for Shannon's spirit in *The Night of the Iguana*. Bodey struggles to preserve Dotty from heartbreak, literally in the heart pills she must distribute to Dotty and figuratively in the inevitable rejection Dotty will receive from Ralph. As Bodey says to Helena, 'I don't want heartbreak for Dotty. For Dotty I want a – life'.[116] Helena, the 'hawk' and the 'buzzard' represents the death force in Dotty, wanting to break the news to Dotty about Ralph's recent engagement.[117]

Dotty survives her eventual *crève coeur*, and so did Williams, temporarily. When Craig Anderson, director of the Hudson Guild Theatre, read the play in March 1978, he agreed to produce it for the Festival.[118] Keith Hack, who had just directed the London premier of *Vieux Carré* in August 1978, brought most of the Charleston cast with him to New York, including Shirley Knight in her role as Dotty. The revised version focused on creating more of a climax in act two, but Williams preferred the long one-act version of the play to its rewrite. During rehearsals at the Hudson Guild, Williams was his usual nervous self, and apparently for cause. When the play opened Off Broadway on 10 January 1979, its reviews, far more mixed than in Charleston, forced its closing after a disappointing thirty-six performances. Ironically, the play would find wide approval when it served as the basic scenario for the highly successful TV series *The Golden Girls* in the 1980s.[119]

Following the New York production, Williams returned to Key West to various forms of tragedy. His home had been burglarized twice, his gardener Frank Fontis was murdered (probably for his connection to the drug underworld), and he was assaulted on Duval Street. Williams's persistent paranoia that people close to him were stealing from him all the time was not really that unfounded when it was discovered that Fontis had taken some of Williams's manuscripts, no doubt to sell or to keep as insurance policies against his mounting debts. Since his homes were near half-way houses for a variety of fugitive characters – some close to him, others not – it is certainly possible that several unknown manuscripts of his might one day make an unannounced appearance.

The fact was that Williams was writing all the time, and perhaps even more feverishly since his release from the Barnes Hospital in 1969. He had wanted that Cinderella comeback that would silence his naysayers from critics to audiences to even sceptical friends. Any potential production was thus welcomed. In one, Sylvia Miles was planning on bringing *Goforth*, a rewrite of *The Milk Train Doesn't Stop Here Anymore* that he began for her and Michael York back in 1973, to the English theatre in Vienna, which Williams hoped would be transferred to London the following fall; neither production ever materialized.[120] He began work on a screen treatment of his story 'Hard Candy'. He even wrote and published some of his poems and stories from 1975 to 1979, which he read on various college campuses like New York University and Williams College in that spring 1979. Poems included 'Wolf's Hour' (1975), 'Turning Out the Bedside Lamp' (1976), 'The Rented Room' (1979), and 'Arctic Light' (1978), which Prosser recalls Williams having read at a dinner party at his house.[121] Another poem, written on a draft page of *Clothes for a Summer Hotel*, begins 'The wayward flesh has made me wise'.[122] As for his stories, Williams wrote 'Mother Yaws' (1977), a gothic tale about Barle McCorkle's rejection from her family after acquiring a rare, African disease, and 'The Killer Chicken and the Closet Queen' (1978), a story he wrote in November 1977 about the predatory wolves and closeted homosexuals who struggle daily at work among colleagues and at home among family members for love and acceptance for who they are.

Also in the spring of 1979, Williams started writing 'Mes Cahiers Noirs', a cross between his notebook entries and his fragmentary essays of the past nine years or so. In it, he mentioned his daily activities, such as swimming at the New Orleans Athletic Club, and his personal impressions about the people with whom he was in contact regularly, such as Mitch Douglas, his new agent at ICM, with whom he planned on having a 'cards on the table' confrontation: 'I have hung on ten years to have one more success in the American theatre, if only to defy my detractors'.[123] Williams was very much alone during these final years, and he speaks frequently about inviting strangers back home with him or onto trips to Europe. As it had been in his *Memoirs*, loneliness is a leitmotif in these entries. Williams soon recognized that he did not want his final autobiography to be uniformly bitter, writing: 'Perhaps the title (<u>Black Pages</u> in English) should be changed to <u>Mes Cahiers Noirs et Blancs</u>, since I hope I do not intend to restrict myself to comments of a dark nature'.[124]

He did focus mostly on the dark side of these 'cahiers', however, including this final self-assessment, which is perhaps as lucid a comment as Williams made in any piece of prose of the last decade:

> Did I die by my own hand or was I destroyed slowly and brutally by a conspiratorial group? There is probably no clear cut answer. When was there ever such an answer to any question related to the individual human fate?
>
> [...] But I am observing my life and approaching conclusion of my life and I see a long, long stretch of desolation about me, now at the end.
>
> [...] The best I can say for myself is that I worked like hell.[125]

From here, the 'Cahiers' degrade considerably into a *règlement de comptes* against those people who had discredited or crossed him over the years – Robert Carroll, Donald Windham, Audrey Wood, and John Simon, whose most recent pan of *Creve Coeur* in June 1978 was still stinging. 'At random', he writes, 'I offer you a list, and the charges against them'.[126] The 'Cahiers' also becomes an encomium to those people whom he held dear: his sister Rose, his grandmother Grand, his grandfather, and his childhood sweetheart Hazel Kramer (as well as Marion Vaccaro and Maria St Just).

By extending his commentary over the duration of his lifetime, as opposed to focusing solely on his most recent years, Williams perhaps envisioned 'Mes Cahiers Noirs' as being the autobiography that would supplement, if not replace entirely, *Memoirs*. In it, he attempts to become philosophical, as he had tried to be back in 1959–60, writing (albeit sophomorically): 'What are artists? Desperate searchers after whatever can be found of truth and beauty, even when the two may be poles apart. I am in no condition to arrange this material in any kind of sequence: but does it matter now?'[127] He speaks forthcoming about his critics: 'Critics: I recognize them as potential assassins, before, now, and after'.[128] He even returns to the daily bitter ruminations found throughout the fragments that never quite made it into *Memoirs*, about which he adds that 'I am in transit, my work prematurely finished': 'Now I must suspend these cahiers to see what I can do with the final bit of my last important dramatic work, "Red Devil Battery Sign". (Remember to have it copyrighted as soon as typed)'.[129] Even when he was pining, or whining, Williams always returned to his work.

Williams closed out the decade preparing his play *Clothes for a Summer Hotel*, which he began negotiating with Elliot Martin in 1979 at the request of José Quintero. Williams had been working on the play for the better part of two years, conducting extensive research into the lives of F. Scott and Zelda Fitzgerald. As he told Paul Bowles in a 31 August letter, the play had received 'auspicious reactions in manuscript and is booked into the Royale': '[It] required enormous documentation, but I think it's worth it, as I feel in it a surging undercurrent of power that I've not felt in a long time'.[130] Rehearsals for *Clothes for a Summer Hotel* began the following January, the same month that the Tennessee Williams Theatre (still the only theatre in America to bear his name) was inaugurated at the Fine Arts Center of the Florida Keys Community College with the first performance of his 1969 play, *Will Mr. Merriwether Return from Memphis?*

While his place on Broadway was growing more and more tenuous by the end of the decade, his reputation elsewhere in the country was solidifying. In 1979, there was a panel of the Modern Language Association on 'Tennessee Williams: The Plays of the Seventies', Stephen S. Stanton was founding the *Tennessee Williams Newsletter* (later *Review*), and Jac Tharpe was at work editing the enormous volume, *Tennessee Williams: A Tribute*, published the following year. On 2 December, Williams received perhaps the most important accolade: along with Ella Fitzgerald, Henry Fonda, Martha Graham and Aaron Copeland, he was honoured by President Carter at the Kennedy Center for his lifetime contribution to the arts.

On his sixty-ninth birthday in March 1980, Mayor Ed Koch declared Tennessee Williams Day in New York City, and *Clothes for a Summer Hotel* opened at the Cort Theatre on Broadway for a short, fourteen-run performance. In early June, President Carter pinned onto him the Presidential Medal of Freedom at the White House in the presence of Rose, Maria St Just, and Tony and Jane Smith, who remained his closest friends during these turbulent years. Carter congratulated Williams for having shown all of America that 'the truly heroic in life or art is human compassion'.[131] The new decade held promise for the playwright, whose last ten years were filled with seemingly endless personal and professional struggles. As Rexford Stamper wrote in 1977,

Everyone concerned with modern American drama recognizes [...] that Williams' recent plays have been failures; and although many

244 Tennessee Williams: A Literary Life

reasons have been offered, perhaps not enough attention has been paid to the most apparent reason for this failure: he is no longer writing the type of drama which won him his reputation.[132]

Though more critics would begin seeing these changes in the following decade, when Williams enjoyed more popular and critical success on stage in three years than he had in the previous fifteen, it would all be a little too late. Critics would take another twenty years or more to catch up with what Williams was now attempting on the American stage.

10
Chicago to St Louis (via Vancouver): '<u>Right (Write) On</u>!'

Williams had used his motto '*En avant*' ever since 1937 to close his note-book entries, conclude his letters, or terminate his fiction, just as he did the short story 'Miss Coynte of Greene': 'It's time to let go, now, with this green burning inscription: *En Avant!* or 'Right on!'[1] The expression, as Felicia Hardison Londré has recently pointed out,

> [...] does not seem to have meant exactly 'Forward!' to Williams. When we look at his use of the motto in his letters and notebooks, it almost always connotes something more like 'Keep going!' or '*Bon courage!*' or perhaps even something not too different from Sarah Bernhardt's motto '*Quand même!*' – 'Never mind!' 'So what!' 'No matter!' 'In spite of everything!' Indeed, in his plays and fiction as well as in his letters and notebooks, Williams seems to have associated the phrase '*En avant!*' with the concept of endurance.[2]

Williams did not mean 'Forward, March' in the sense that French General 'Papa' Joffre meant it in September 1914, when he ordered his troops to advance during the battle of the Marne. It was just his way of ensuring himself that he would wake up tomorrow morning and write.

Williams did write, and he produced several works in the 1980s whose quality belied the general attitude in the 1970s that he was finished as a writer and as a playwright. Be it short fiction, one-acts or full-length plays, he never stopped writing (or painting), nor did he allow his gothic and camp style explored in the previous decade to alter his vision of his art. Though the decade proved short for Williams, who, given his family's longevity, could have potentially lived to see the 1990s, it was thus very productive. Three major plays (and many more are being uncovered each year as scholars scour the archives) were given productions and met with varied degrees of success. *Clothes for a Summer Hotel*, his pastiche of the Fitzgeralds, was his final play for Broadway. *Something Cloudy, Something Clear*, his other 'ghost' play about his first summer in Provincetown, premiered at The Bouwerie Lane Theatre in New York on 24 August 1981 by the Jean Cocteau Repertory. Like *Clothes* before it, the play was a critical disappointment, though today it is finding newer audiences more open to its poetry and its theatricality. Hopes of a success were brewing once again in Chicago, where Williams had first found fame with *The Glass Menagerie*. The respected Goodman Theatre had produced *Tennessee Laughs* for its 1980 season, a triple-bill including, *A Perfect Analysis Given by a Parrot*, *The Frosted Glass Coffin*, and *Some Problems for the Moose Lodge*, and now it was working with Williams to expand *Moose Lodge* into the full-length play, *A House Not Meant to Stand*, for the following season. Williams was reportedly at work on several other plays at the time of his tragic death in February 1983.

'Right on' he shouts at the start of his rather unorthodox essay 'We Are Dissenters Now', but, throughout the 1970s, he would turn that phrase to mean 'Write on!', concluding many of his 'Which Sea-Gull on What Corner?' drafts with the pun. Williams entered the 1980s with exactly that new meaning in mind. He would not let the last decade's critical assault on his reputation deter him from the one thing that kept him alive: his writing. This chapter will study these last three plays, and several one-acts and unpublished plays that Williams was writing at the time, in an attempt to defend Williams's defiant cry of *'En avant!'* in the face of two decades of criticism that had goaded him to stop writing plays.

Returning occasionally to writing in his notebooks these remaining years of his life, Williams opened the decade on a sombre note. 'I think soon we will fly away from the whole gig here in the States. [...] Leave all behind. Travel under Tom Williams. Forget the world a while'.[3] Williams was no more capable of leaving his world at Key West or New Orleans or New York as Felice and Clare were able to venture from their home in *Out Cry*. Nor could he have abandoned his writing or his troublesome partner, Robert Carroll. There was plenty, of course, to keep him in America, or at least in North America. That January, there was 'conspirator[ial]' talk of a Writer-in-Residence position in Vancouver in exchange for a production of *The Red Devil Battery Sign*; *Will Mr. Merriwether Return from Memphis?* was premiering at the Fine Arts Center of the Florida Keys Community College; and *Clothes for a Summer Hotel* was donning its winter coat for a frigid Broadway reception.

Williams had been working on *Clothes for a Summer Hotel* for at least half a decade, reading all that there was to read on the Fitzgeralds and the Hemingways. He later told Dotson Rader in their 1981 *Paris Review* interview that it was the play on which he had done the most research. The story's subtext of Williams's guilt over his own appropriation of Rose's pre- and post-lobotomized life is thinly veiled in this period piece. Disappointing try-outs in Washington, DC, and in Chicago followed the play to Broadway, where, on Williams's sixty-ninth birthday, it opened at the Cort Theatre, with Geraldine Page playing the role of Zelda, the delusional southern belle who blames her life's failures on the fact the she sacrificed all to become her husband's literary material. *Clothes for a Summer Hotel* was soon headed for disaster, beginning with the fact that the *New York Times* refused to publish his embittered pre-opening piece for the play.[4] Williams admitted to Elia Kazan in a 5 July letter that the play was 'victim of a bad first act'.[5]

Williams subtitled *Clothes* a 'ghost play' since he took 'extraordinary license with time and place'[6] to dramatize Scott and Zelda Fitzgerald's failed marriage and mutual artistic sabotage. Since Scott is already dead when he visits his wife at the Highland Hospital in Asheville, and Zelda has premonitions of her death by immolation at the asylum in the spring of 1948 (and not in the autumn of 1947, as Williams suggests), *Clothes for a Summer Hotel* was not meant to be a historically faithful account of the Fitzgeralds' break-up. Time knows no bounds for the artist, or for his work, and Zelda's death in the play occurs in the autumn because the red, yellow, and orange leaves of the October foliage visually reproduce the flames that would eventual consume her, locked away in a room awaiting electroshock therapy.

The point of the play during its self-proclaimed duration of an hour and forty-five minutes is to exhibit the gossamer thread that writers like Williams must cling to emotionally and psychologically during the excruciating and exhausting process of artistic creation. As Zelda says near the end of the play, 'Between the first wail of an infant and the last gasp of the dying – it's all an arranged pattern of – submission to what's been prescribed for us unless we escape into madness or into acts of creation....'.[7] The 'ghosts' drift in and out of time – their time, Williams's time, our time – speaking in the past and in the future, conscious, if not self-conscious, all the time that they are now on stage as Williams's puppets, just as Zelda feels her life had been in her husband's novels. The play's intertextual references with Nancy Milford's feminist biography *Zelda* and Hemingway's *A Moveable Feast* did not cannibalize art any more than both writers had cannibalized their own subjects,

Hemingway in particular in his curious chapters on Scott's beauty and emasculation. Instead, they demonstrate Williams's evolving knowledge of and experience with the metatheatre since writing *Camino Real*, a view his critics could not have seen at the time but which is becoming a more commonplace theory in Williams scholarship as the years press on.

Like most of Williams's late plays, *Clothes for a Summer Hotel* was considered at the time as another embarrassing blemish on a rather illustrious career. It is not coincidental, then, that such a work of minor standing should have met with so little critical attention from the theatre public whose ennui could not keep the play's Broadway production alive for even a month, nor sustain its 1995 York Theatre revival. The theatre critics were typically scathing. Walter Kerr called it 'wasteful', the result of 'Tennessee Williams holding his tongue', and Clive Barnes wrote that it 'needs some tailoring' since it 'seems more smoke than summer'.[8] Most critics dismissed the play as another psycho-dramatization of Williams's guilt-ridden relationship with his sister Rose,[9] a mimetic representation of his *auto-da-fé* at the hands of belligerent critics,[10] or a personal exegesis on the tortured psyche's struggle to produce art with impunity.[11]

A recent spate of academic criticism on the play, however, is changing the way the play is being appreciated today, a welcomed trend in Williams scholarship that is revisiting many of his anti-mimetic late plays with new critical tools to analyse his Postmodern literary aesthetics. Michael Paller even suggests that gay theatre in general could be considered Postmodern given that it 'bumped comedy against tragedy, quoted works from literature, comic books and film, could be heavily ironic, was aware of itself as theatre and made its theatricality part of its subject-matter'.[12] Linda Dorff shows how the play 'rejects the earlier plays' redemptive paradigms' of Modernist resurrection mythologies from which he frequently drew in the 1940s and 1950s by using fire and ash metaphors within a Postmodern discourse of doubt and distrust to foreground 'the artificiality/artifice of the denaturalized ghost form as an ultimate simulacrum [...] a reproduction of a reproduction', what Jean Baudrillard defined as hyperrealism.[13]

Similarly, George Crandell looks at the Postmodern representation of time in *Clothes* which 'substitutes for historical time an *aesthetic space*, a representation of time that permits the exploration of an alternative temporality and a virtual reality that bears no mimetic relationship to the world outside of the play's dramatic boundaries and yet, paradoxically, illuminates that *real* world'.[14] Finally, Norma Jenckes examines the play's Postmodern flippancy toward serious modern issues, here love, to demonstrate how 'an historically constructed emotion and state of being [...] can be and is affected by the material conditions of society in which it rises and falls' – in other words, how love has become a commodity, a Postmodern spin on Romanticism.[15] Their enlightened readings of *Clothes for a Summer Hotel* are influencing the way the later Williams plays are now being re-read, and much to their advantage.

By June 1980, Williams was finalizing proofs for publisher William Targ of his surreal duologue between Hart Crane and his mother Grace, *Steps Must Be Gentle*, which was released that August. Then a week following the death of his mother Edwina (an event he did not deem relevant enough to put down in his notebook), he attended the White House to receive the Medal of Freedom, along with Eudora Welty, the late John Wayne, Rachel Carson, Ansel Adams, and Robert Penn Warren (to name but a few). Not long after, Williams was back again in Europe, travelling this time with artist Henry Faulkner, and their destination was the San Domenico Palace Hotel in Taormina, Sicily. While on his terrace, Williams painted and wrote a new one-act play, 'The Everlasting Ticket, or As I Lay Going Mad in Santo Domingo', which he dedicated to Joe Orton.[16] His patience with Faulkner's antics with the local boys grew thin,[17] and Williams quickly returned to Chicago via London to work with Greg Mosher, then artistic director of the Goodman Theatre.

Gary Tucker introduced Mosher to Williams at a restaurant in Chicago, where Mosher was offered to produce *Some Problems for the Moose Lodge*. Mosher accepted, and not long after he put together an evening of three of Williams's shorter plays collectively titled 'Tennessee Laughs', which ran for three weeks from 8–23 November 1980. Two other one-acts accompanied *Some Problems for the Moose Lodge – A Perfect Analysis Given by a Parrot* and *The Frosted Glass Coffin*, a black comedy about ageing first written in 1970. *Some Problems for the Moose Lodge*, though funny, relies on a grotesque, gothic sense of humour: Cornelius and Bella McCorkle have just buried their son Chips in Memphis, and Bella soon begins to mistake her other son Charlie for the dead Chips. Based on the positive public reception to *Moose Lodge*, Mosher invited Williams to expand the one-act play, which he was to work on over the next few months before the longer version was tried out once again in the Goodman's Studio Theatre later that spring.[18]

At the start of that autumn 1980, Williams accepted the Distinguished Writer-in-Residence position at the University of British Columbia in Vancouver, where part of the agreement, in addition to his paid lectures (to the sum of $2000 per week), was a renewed production of *The Red*

Devil Battery Sign, which was now cut down to eighty pages, 'about twenty less than it was in England [...]'.[19] Williams did not like being tied down by the teaching post and quickly escaped to San Francisco, but he was coaxed back to Vancouver when it was made clear to him that he would be well entertained. He regretfully brought one of his companions back with him to Key West several months later. Williams complained to St Just that he was 'highly efficient' as a secretary but generally 'cold as a fish'[20] to his advances.

After the play opened on 18 October, Williams returned to Chicago where the triple bill 'Tennessee Laughs' was scheduled to open the following month. Williams informed St Just in a 14 October letter that Gucci was inviting him to Rome via a Concord jet to celebrate the thirtieth anniversary reissuing of his 1950 novel *The Roman Spring of Mrs. Stone*. He was already talking about spending a luxurious time in Russia, living high off the royalties his plays had earned him there, which would include the purchasing of several mink coats.[21] He had considered going there as late as December 1971 with Oliver Evans and would consider going there again in 1982 with Jane Smith. By Christmas, though, he was in Key West preparing Rose's transfer back to Stony Lodge in Ossining.

During the winter holidays, Williams devoted most of his writing energy to expanding the one-act play *Some Problems for the Moose Lodge*, which he first called 'The Dancie Money' but now titled it *A House Not Meant to Stand*. Mosher was worried about Williams's depression and thought it best to bring him to Chicago for the rewrites. Mosher and others in Chicago threw Williams a big seventieth birthday celebration that March, attended by Jane Smith, whose husband Tony died the previous December, and Vassilis Voglis, a Greek painter and partner of the actor/playwright John Cromwell, for whom Williams had written an obituary in the *New York Times* in the fall of 1979. Death was following Williams everywhere at this time: Audrey Wood would suffer a stroke in April that left her in a coma for several years, and Oliver Evans would die in December. Logically, death would become one of the central themes to his new play.

A House Not Meant to Stand received its premiere on 1 April 1981 in the Goodman's Studio Theatre, and then on the main stage the following year, running for forty-one performances and garnering Williams positive reviews. Subtitled 'A Gothic Comedy' though called 'A Spook Sonata' in various drafts, the Strindbergian play freed some of the ghosts of Williams's past, including his coming to terms with his father's belligerence and his feud with Dakin over his placing him in the Renard

Psychiatric Division of Barnes Hospital in 1969. Williams would never entirely forgive his brother, however. When Dakin asked Williams to write the foreword to his 1980 book, *The Bar Bizarre*, Williams wrote what Dakin later recalled 'a generous foreword'.[22] But his dashed-off tribute was devoted more to Lucy Freeman's editorial hand in Edwina's memoirs, *Remember Me to Tom* (1963), than to Dakin's legal memoirs. The fact that Williams did not type the foreword, as was his chosen method of writing, but instead handwrote it suggests how little time and effort he had wanted to spend promoting his brother's book.

If Williams's recent full-length plays were generally consistent in style and structure to those of the second half of the 1970s, his one-act plays were of a different beast all together. He wanted to push American theatre to its limits, so much that many of these plays were barely performable in their day and have only recently seen the light of production at the annual Provincetown Tennessee Williams Theater Festival, founded by David Kaplan. Williams admitted in the introduction to 'Williams' Guignol', an evening of theatre that he planned in August 1982, that each of these plays has a particular attention paid to style and that 'their intention [was] to shock'.[23] As Annette Saddik has pointed out, these, and other late plays that Williams was writing at the time, 'were clearly influenced by cultural and artistic developments such as pop art, vaudeville, camp, and a sense of the outrageous in the style of Charles Ludlum's Ridiculous Theatrical Company, for example, which Ludlum founded in 1969'.[24]

Perhaps the most bizarre or notorious of these one-acts is *The Remarkable Rooming-House of Mme. Le Monde*, which Williams began drafting back in 1975 under the title 'A Rectangle with Hooks' (a phrase we find used in *Moise and the World of Reason* published that year) as part of an evening of theatre, 'Tragedies of the Drawing-Room', which was set in the 1920s and included a very early version of *Clothes for a Summer Hotel*, whose principal characters were Valerie and Mallory.[25] Set in a boarding house in London run by Mme Le Monde, the campy play contains the outlandish antics of Williams's 'most salacious outcasts, worthy of meritorious inclusion for bad behavior in his *Memoirs*'.[26] Paralysed from the waist-down, Mint moves around his attic by swinging from hooks attached to the ceiling. Mme Le Monde's son, Boy, repeatedly rapes Mint, but at no point does Mint ever perceive of it as illicit, given his own bent for sado-masochism: 'Oh, no, no, no! Well, maybe, since you've come with – lubricant, is it?'[27] The play ends when Mme Le Monde kills her son, Mint, and Hall, Mint's school friend from Scrotum-on-Swansea. According to Philip Kolin, the play 'reveals a Tennessee Williams wickedly exaggerating and punishing his own personna, egregiously magnifying the grostequeries for which he was (in)famous in the public consciousness'.[28]

Williams considered several other one-act plays as part of his 'Three Plays for the Lyric Theater', which he submitted to New Directions in August 1980. The trilogy, which evoked the common theme of youthful death, included *A Cavalier for Milady*, written from the mid-1970s to 1980 and alternatively titled 'Magic Is the Habit of Our Existence'; *The Youthfully Departed*, also written during the mid-1970s; and *Now the Cats with Jewelled Claws*, a play Williams told Frederick Martin that he had written when he was 'quite ill in the Sixties', but that may have been his way of 'sabotag[ing]' the play before his critics could.[29] In the final entry of his notebooks, spring 1981,Williams feared that his agent Mitch Douglas lost the play altogether: 'Under circumstances, I cannot submit any more original copies of work to I.C.M. – All new work was securely bound or fastened by secure clips! Where do I from here [*sic*]?'[30]

A Cavalier for Milady portrays two ageing Park Avenue widows, Mother and Mrs Aid, who are waiting for the babysitter to arrive so that they can leave. They have planned to go to the Plaza for the evening to meet male companions who have promised them a good time. The 'child' who is to be looked after, however, is a mentally disturbed young woman, Nance, whose masturbating tendencies (like those attributed to Rose Williams with alter candles) trouble the sitter. Nance soon summons the apparition of Nijinsky, who dances for her and narrates the story of his rise to fame and his decline into madness. *The Youthfully Departed* is about two young lovers, drowned while making love when their car rolls into a lake, who now appear as ghosts seated on separate benches. Kept apart by two Laments, or figures of mourning, the youths break free and perform their ecstasy in an erotic dance.

In *Now the Cats with Jewelled Claws*, two women, Madge and Bea, meet for lunch during the Christmas shopping rush and discuss the trivialities of their daily lives with two doomed homosexual men, who prepare for their destinies. The young men, dressed in 'pink leather jackets' that carry the inscription, 'The Mystic Rose', on their backs, are ill-fated when the First Young Man, called 'Green Eyes' (recalling the title of another one-act play of his), sees a man outside the restaurant carrying a placard paging a Mr Black. His fear that Mr Black is Death is proven correct when the Second Young Man is killed moments later in a motorcycle accident. The two men believe their destinies are to be united with the first Mystic Rose – Christ – who 'ended up high, too, on crossed beams between two thieves'.[31] Such religious sentiment comes true when the manager, 'an aging queen with dyed hair', says immediately after the Second Young Man's death, 'And now the cats with jewelled claws/glide down the wall of night'.[32] Life, like the cat, makes its escape, at least with the First Young Man, who discovers that his destiny was not to die but instead to become, or at least to become like, the manager, who tells him, 'Your future. I'll introduce you to it'.[33]

Williams wrote two other one-act plays around this time, *The Chalky White Substance* and *The Traveling Companion*. The chalky white substance that lends the first play its title is the dust of the obliterated bones of God destroyed years ago in a nuclear war that permeates the air and chokes Mark and Luke, two Beckett-like survivors of the holocaust. *The Traveling Companion*, published later in *Christopher Street* in November 1981, describes the symbiotic relationship between a young hustler from San Francisco named Beau and an ageing playwright named Vieux, undoubtedly reflective of Williams's personal anxieties about being an ageing gay man.

In July 1981, Williams wrote that he wanted Eve Adamson to direct *Now the Cats with Jewelled Claws* since she had done such a masterful job with *Kirche, Küche, Kinder* (1979). As Williams recalled, Adamson took 'a play that was a work-in-progress and despite the limitations of a company not all of whom could be properly cast in their roles (characters that would horrify the Moral Majority)', and she staged it 'with such inventiveness, both lyrical and comical, that it played to good houses although it had been stipulated that the press could not be admitted'.[34] In Adamson's 1979 production of *Kirche, Küche, Kinder* at the Jean Cocteau Repertory Company, 'no press was admitted', allowing Williams 'to work with the director and actors with complete freedom'.[35] The privacy felt needed, given the rather delicate nature of the play, which included a hypersexed and pregnant ninety-nine-year-old woman, 'Hotsy', being played by a man in drag. For Linda Dorff, *Kirche, Küche, Kinder* was one of Williams's 'theatricalist cartoons', calling for those '*invisible canaries*' in cartoon strips that sing as the Wife '*turns slowly and dizzily about*' after getting hit over the head with the Minister's umbrella.[36] If Williams was still concerned about writing plays that he hoped would appeal to Broadway and appease his many doubting critics, this certainly was not one of them. He was simultaneously following his own dramatic voice, while thumbing his nose at them, too. 'It may very well be', Williams concluded,

that I no longer have critical following in New York, with the exception of two or three exceptional members of the press, uptown and downtown. But let them all come who care to. Neither Eve nor I see any reason to evade them.[37]

Now the Cats with Jewelled Claws, which, despite its exotic nature, was pretty tame next to plays like *The Remarkable Rooming-House of Mme. Le Monde* and *Kirche, Küche, Kinder*, eventually premiered on 2 October 2003 at the Hartford Stage in Connecticut as part of the 'Rose' programme of '8 by Tenn' that performed four of eight Williams one-acts in two separate productions.

Williams would return to Eve Adamson and the Jean Cocteau Repertory Company for one of his last original plays staged in his lifetime. *Something Cloudy, Something Clear* (1981) is a dramatization of Williams's first visit to Provincetown and his love affair there with Kip Kiernan, which drew upon a play he had begun drafting notes for back in 1940 and completed in 1962, titled *The Parade*. Like *Clothes for a Summer Hotel*, the play takes liberties with chronology, as Williams is describing in 1979 his memories of Kip back in 1940. As Saddik has noted,

> *The Parade* was begun in Provincetown in the summer of 1940, where Williams fell in love, completely and unguardedly, with a dancer named Kip Kiernan, who ultimately disappointed him. The play, based on the events of that summer, was revised and finished in 1962, and submitted to his publisher in 1979 in a collection of 'various odds and ends titled *Pieces of My Youth*'.[38]

Something Cloudy, Something Clear, subtitled 'The Silver Victrola', is thus another 'ghost' play that divides its author into two people at two different stages of his life. Figuratively and literally recalling his way of seeing the world, *Something Cloudy, Something Clear* represents some of the best writing that Williams was doing in his late career. Dotson Rader recalls what Williams told him in 1981 about the play:

> I prefer the title *Something Cloudy, Something Clear* because it refers to my eyes. My left eye was cloudy then because it was developing a cataract. But my right eye was clear. It was like two sides of my nature. The side that was obsessively homosexual, compulsively interested in sexuality. And the side that in those days was gentle and understanding and contemplative. So it's a pertinent title.[39]

The play opened Off-off Broadway at the Bouwerie Lane Theatre on 24 August 1981, but it received little praise from the New York critics, who saw in it the familiar Williams ghosts who have haunted his pages and plays since *Memoirs*.

Later that year, Williams chased an uncontrollable Carroll out of his Key West and welcomed a new secretary, Scott Kenan.[40] Williams also published privately the long short story *It Happened the Day the Sun Rose* (1981) about his days in Tangier in the late 1940s and 1950s with Paul and Jane Bowles. Half camp, half magical realism, the story is about a witch who has the power to turn men she does not like, or grows sexually tired of, into birds. Madame La Sorcière, 'seductive enough to satisfy her sexual appetite for every attractive young employee of the Grand Hôtel Des Souhks',[41] fails to seduce the one boy whom she desires most – Ahmed, the evening barman. Angered by his insolence in rejecting her amours, she transforms Ahmed into a crow. When he finally returns to his job three days later in human form, Ahmed still 'make[s] sudden wing-like motions with his arms',[42] until Madame La Sorcière frees him from his trance. In the second part of the story, Ahmed, disgusted with Mme La Sorcière, informs the local authorities that she is harbouring five jewel thieves in her room. When they search her room, she changes the five men into crows and places them, marsupial-like, in a pouch near her stomach. When Ahmed refuses to reacquaint himself with her later at a dinner party, she turns him into the sixth crow. Ahmed is collected by his rich lover, Lord Buggersmythe, who places him in a cage as his devoted pet. Some time later, while still in his cage, Ahmed transforms back again into a human; as he metamorphoses, the cage is broken about him, just as the spirit breaks out of its *ban-hus*: 'it is not good, it is God'.[43] Whether in his plays or in his fiction, Williams's recent experiments with 'the strange, the crazed, the queer', the famous opening from a 1941 poem he composed for Paul Bigelow, seemed now to know no limits.[44]

In March, he gave a public reading of a story that he began the previous May, titled 'The Donsinger Women and their Handyman Jack', which was based on a recent visit to Texas with his Key West friend and neighbour, 'Texas' Kate Moldawer. As he described the reading to Maria St Just, 'There was too big a crowd for the amplification system and the rude ones kept shouting "Louder". Finally I got up and said I would leave if they did not shut up'.[45]

In April 1982, Vanessa Redgrave invited Williams to Boston to do a reading with her. She was now interested in appearing in his teleplay, *Stopped Rocking*. *A House Not Meant to Stand* also opened later that month on the Goodman's main stage, and Williams was preparing another play for the 'Miami Festival', perhaps 'The Lingering Hour'. While in

Chicago, he met a new companion, a young Sicilian who reminded him a lot of Merlo, and Kenan left quietly.

That May, Williams travelled to Charleston to visit Robert Carroll, who had taken up residence there, living off Williams's weekly stipend. Williams wrote St Just that he was working on a new play, 'The Lingering Hour'.[46] It was another 'fantasy' play, one that he had begun the previous November. It appears that most of Williams's directive to '<u>Right (write) on!</u>'[47] in this brief decade entailed writing fantasy; like Blanche or T. S. Eliot, Williams could not 'bear very much reality' anymore.

On 10 June, Williams received an honorary doctorate degree from Harvard University, partly in exchange for his having promised to bequeath his manuscripts to the Houghton Library upon his death.[48]

He then boarded the Concord in July 1982, heading to Taormina, this time with long-time friend Jane Smith. While there, Williams continued to write every morning, despite the arthritic pains in his right shoulder that he had had for several months and which he treated with powerful pain killers that kept his writing sessions shorter than usual. The pain also kept the two of them from heading on to Russia, where they had planned on spending some of his millions of rubles 'which had accumulated in the royalties that he had to spend inside the country'.[49]

They returned to New York via Rome in August, where Jane Smith and John Uecker accompanied Williams to a production of *Gideon's Point* (1979–82) on 'The Other Stage' of the Williamstown Theater Festival that ran throughout the month. He had worked off and on for the past few years on the play, which was based on his 1945 short story 'Tent Worms' and would later be titled *In Masks Outrageous and Austere*.

By early September, he was back in Key West, but not for long. Later in the month, he went to New York to visit Voglis on Long Island, and then returned to Key West.

In October, like a southern bird heading north for the winter, he would repeat the roundtrip voyage, twice, in the space of a month. Such restless trips taken in apparent haste make it seem as if Williams was trying to outrun the Reaper, or at least to hide from him long enough to write that comeback play he had so desired since *The Night of the Iguana*. His life was speeding headlong to its terminus.

On 31 May of that year, Williams had written to Kate Moldawer that he no longer understood 'life itself': 'Death seems more comprehensible to me'.[50] Though he was always an alarmist about his mental health and impending death, there seemed more of a ring of authenticity in his words this time. He was growing increasingly weak and depressed, and he felt that his work was slowly coming to an end. That did not stop him, however, from trying to put together the following August a selection of his short, dark 'way out' comedies collectively titled 'Williams' Guignol' at his 'old try-out theatre, The Coconut Grove Playhouse'.[51] On the programme, Williams envisioned producing *Sunburst*, *The Chalky White Substance*, 'Night Waking: Strange Room', *The Remarkable Rooming-House of Mme. Le Monde*, and 'A Monument for Ercole', a 'savage play in one act' that has Ercole, a revolutionary partly based on Raul Castro and named after Anna Magnani's agent, capture Tre and Jan Hunter, 'a young ruling-class couple', during a coup d'état.[52] The production never came to fruition.

Back in Key West, just after noon on Christmas Eve, 1982, Williams apparently tried to kill himself through a drug overdose, typing out a suicide note on which he handwrote 'Valediction' at the top, though it reads like much of his rambling thoughts of the previous decade. In it, he wrote, 'What are you writing? This. And you're not sure what it is. [...] Now let you and I go without knowing where to turn next. Turn the motor onto automatic and it may decide upon something'. He signed it 'T.W.' and added post-mortum financial arrangements for Leoncia McGee (his black housekeeper), Tatiana Schvetzoff (Rose's guardian), and Robert (Carroll). His final words read: 'Love, TW. God is here. I salute Him!'[53] He had not been eating anything and had locked himself in his bedroom for three days. Kate Moldawer and Gary Tucker found him comatose and rushed him to the Depoo Psychiatric Hospital, where he was admitted under the name 'George Clemmons'. Donald Spoto suggests that the short-term hospital stay was more for extreme dehydration from alcohol and drugs, which it certainly was, but he makes no mention of the possible suicide attempt. And there may not have been one in the end. Williams loved life too much to have ended it, as friends Mishima and Inge had done, by his own hand.

Williams told Jane Smith and his current secretary/companion, John Uecker, that he was heading back to Taormina, this time alone.

Williams returned north to New York via New Orleans, where he concluded the sale of his house on Dumaine Street, and travelled to London alone, where he attended Pinter's triple bill at the National Theatre, *Other Places*, with St Just. He left alone to head to Rome, then to Taormina, where he stayed at the San Domenico Palace Hotel.

After only five days, he returned to New York, where Williams took up residence once again at the Hotel Elysée, refusing to eat or entertain visitors. On the night of 24/25 February 1983, Tennessee Williams died as he had chosen to travel these past months – alone, in his bed, the victim of an accidental barbiturate overdose. Uecker was in the other bedroom of their two-room suite when he heard a noise around 11 pm that Thursday evening, but had been given strict instructions not to disturb him. At around 10:45 Friday morning, Uecker went to Williams's room and found his body lying next to his bed.[54]

The feet, finally, had stopped moving.

New York medical examiner Elliot Gross listed the cause of death as 'asphyxia due to obstruction of the glottis' when he found a 'thin rubber medicine bottle stopper' in Williams's mouth (but not lodged in his throat).[55] Gross sent tissue samples from Williams to a toxicology lab 'under another name', and six months later, 'after the press had lost interest, Gross quietly issued another cause of death [...]'.[56]

His body was publically waked in a closed casket at the Frank E. Campbell Funeral Home in Manhattan, a sort of funeral home to the stars.

Against his stated, though never legalized, wishes to be buried at sea in the Gulf of Mexico to lie near his idol Hart Crane, Williams made his one last voyage from New York to the Calvary Cemetery in St Louis, where he was buried next to his mother, proving that irony can touch anyone, even beyond the grave.

11
Epilogue

In Williams's one-act play that was originally to be part of *Vieux Carré*, *I Never Get Dressed Till after Dark on Sundays*, the playwright offers these final words:

> A play's not stopped by a curtain, I mean if it's a true thing it continues after the curtain the way life does after sleep. It comes out of the night stop and goes into the next day. And maybe it goes on in the minds and hearts of the audience after [...].[1]

Williams's curtain never descended that tragic night in February 1983. While it did come down for a long while, when Maria St Just was still alive and ruled the Williams Estate with an iron fist, that pause proved only to be an *entr'acte*, or, as Williams would have preferred, an *intermezzo*. He left behind him a rich theatre legacy, whose centennial was recently celebrated by academics throughout the world in cities as far as New Orleans and Narni (Italy), Clarksdale and Cáceres (Spain), and St Louis and Nancy (France); but he also bequeathed the world numerous unpublished or recently published plays, stories, poems, film scripts, and paintings that are now enjoying the life denied them in Williams's final years alive.

New Directions, his publisher, has worked with the Williams Estate for a decade and a half in bringing these 'new' Williams works to print, and Peggy Fox and Thomas Keith have been the driving force behind much of these publications: *Something Cloudy, Something Clear* (1995), *Not about Nightingales* (1938; Hale, 1998), *Spring Storm* (1937; Isaac, 1999), *Stairs to the Roof* (1942; Hale, 2000), *The Selected Letters of Tennessee Williams. Vol. I: 1920–1945* (Devlin and Tischler, 2000), *The Fugitive Kind* (1937; Hale, 2001), *Collected Poems* (1925–81; Moschovakis and

Roessel, 2002), 'In Spain There Was Revolution' (1936; Moschovakis and Roessel, 2003), *Candles to the Sun* (1937; Isaac, 2004), *The Selected Letters of Tennessee Williams. Vol. II: 1945–1957* (Devlin and Tischler, 2004), *Mister Paradise and Other One-Act Plays* (1935–62; Moschovakis and Roessel, 2005), *Notebooks* (Bradham Thornton with Yale University Press, 2006), *A House Not Meant to Stand* (1982; Keith, 2008), *The Traveling Companion and Other Plays* (1960–82; Saddik, 2008), *New Selected Essays: Where I Live* (Bak, 2009), and *The Magic Tower and Other One-Act Plays* (1936–73; Keith, 2011).

Now that several of these plays have been unearthed from the archives and others made available in print for the first time, countless directors and producers throughout the world have finally been devoting to them the attention, the time, and the money necessary to see them brought to the stage, either for the first time or in highly respectable revivals that Williams would have been proud of. David Kaplan and the annual Provincetown Tennessee Williams Theater Festival has provided the venue for the productions of many of these 'strange' or 'crazed' or 'queer' plays, and audiences are finally understanding what Williams had been telling them since the 1960s: his later plays were written in an entirely different style and needed to be judged by standards that differed from those used to propel his early works into the American canon. While many of these later plays will not enter the nation's literary canon as such – nor did Williams intend for them to – they do attest to the genius of a writer who was not 'dead' at the age of fifty but in full artistic chrysalis.

In sum, with over *half* of his oeuvre having been published posthumously, and many of his one-acts or full-length plays receiving lavish productions that they never would have been given during his lifetime, it is safe to say that Tennessee Williams is enjoying a fertile literary afterlife.[2]

Not all of the plays that Williams left behind for posterity, however, should be brought to the stage, and the recent fiasco with the production of *In Masks Outrageous and Austere* is a lesson worth noting. A dark play at times called *Gideon's Point* (which was produced at the Williamstown Theater Festival in August 1982), and *Tent Worms* (as the 1945 short story it was based on), *In Masks Outrageous and Austere* is about the hypersexual Clarissa 'Babe' Foxworth, the richest woman on earth, and her bisexual third husband, Billy, who are being held by Gideon security guards. Williams told Bruce Smith that Babe was based on an 'immensely wealthy' Hungarian woman he never met who 'corresponded with me occasionally'.[3] William Prosser, who discusses the play at length in the penultimate chapter of *The Late Plays of Tennessee Williams*, admits that, given the play's 'nightmarish' atmosphere, 'going from a basically realistic play with some fantastic overtones to becoming one of Williams' most outlandish creations', it is 'doubtful that *Masks Outrageous* would [have been] well received by the critical establishment'.[4] But given the recent productions of several of Williams's other 'wild' plays, surely audiences today would not be shocked by the play's content or style. Given this theory, the play received its world premiere on 16 April 2012 at the Culture Project in New York, with Williams veteran Shirley Knight incarnating the role of 'Babe'.

It was not the play's content or style this time, however, that made it problematic. Instead, it was the nature in which the play's script, which Williams never completed before his death, was prepared for production, despite his will's stipulation that 'no poem or literary work of [his] be changed in any manner, whether such change shall be by way of completing any such work or adding to it or depleting from it [...]'.[5] In 2007, Gore Vidal and Peter Bogdanovich undertook the task of completing *In Masks Outrageous and Austere*, which Williams had worked on, on and off, for the better part of a decade, though most seriously since 1978 until his death. Gavin Lambert, who had at one time helped Williams edit the manuscript, released the play from his control before his death in 2005, when it seemed as if it would finally be produced. Production was delayed for various reasons, and Vidal and Bogdanovich each submitted their versions of the play separately to the US Copyright Office under slightly varying titles. Both were granted copyrights in January 2008, roughly a week apart. Legal wrangling ensued over who owned the rights to the play, which blocked its production for years. Eventually, director David Schweizer laid his hands on the various versions of the play and fed them into a forensic computer called Juxta to try and reproduce what Williams might have actually written were he still alive and able to finish it – that is, *if* he had wanted to finish it. In his *New Yorker* review of the play, John Lahr cleverly quips that the play's unfortunate reconstruction through a 'compilation of six different versions by six well-meaning collaborators' is 'the theatrical equivalent of trying to clone Christ from shreds of the Shroud of Turin'.[6]

In spite of this one isolated miscue in Williams's posthumous career, he has enjoyed great success over the past years, in the US and abroad. While it is true that his classic plays, like *A Streetcar Named Desire* and *The Glass Menagerie*, are receiving most of the productions and attention of the critics, his other plays are also being given a second chance on stage and in academic articles.[7]

Posthumous premieres of his work include: *Steps Must Be Gentle* at the Trueblood Arena Theatre in 1983; *The Chalky White Substance* and *The Traveling Companion* at the Running Sun Theater Company in 1996; *Not about Nightingales* at the Royal National Theatre in London in 1998; *Spring Storm* at the Actors Repertory of Texas in 1999; *The One Exception, Now the Cats With Jewelled Claws,* and *The Palooka* at the Hartford Stage Company in 2003; *The Municipal Abattoir, And Tell Sad Stories of the Death of Queens...,* *Summer at the Lake,* and *These Are the Stairs You Got to Watch* at the Kennedy Center, Washington DC, in 2004; *Adam and Eve on a Ferry* and *The Fat Man's Wife* at the Manhattan Theater Club in 2004; *Mister Paradise, Escape, Interior: Panic,* and *Thank You, Kind Spirit* at the Tennessee Williams/New Orleans Literary Festival in 2005; *The Parade* at the Provincetown Tennessee Williams Theater Festival in 2006; *The Pink Bedroom* and *Why Do You Smoke so Much, Lily?* at the Dream Engine Theatre Company in 2007; *The Pronoun 'I'* and *Sunburst* at the Provincetown Tennessee Williams Theater Festival in 2007; *The Day on Which a Man Dies* at SummerNITEs, in 2008; *The Dog Enchanted by the Divine View* and *Green Eyes* at the Boston Center for the Performing Arts in 2008; *The Enemy: Time* at the Gremlin Theater in 2009; *The Remarkable Rooming-House of Mme. Le Monde* at the Beau Geste Moving Theatre in 2009; *I Never Get Dressed Till after Dark on Sundays* and *A Cavalier for Milady* at the Cock Tavern Theater in London in 2011; *Every Twenty Minutes, The Magic Tower,* and *The Pretty Trap* at the Southern Rep Theater/New Orleans in 2011; and *The Big Game* at the Tennessee Williams Project in Toronto in 2012.[8]

Abroad in France, a country that has never really warmed to Williams (or American drama in general) as have the theatre cultures of Italy and Spain, several solid productions of his plays have made a lasting impression: *Baby Doll* at the Théâtre de l'Atelier in 2009 (dir. Benoît Lavigne); *La nuit de l'iguane* at the Théâtre MC 93 Bobigny in 2009 (dir. Georges Lavaudant); *La ménagerie de verre* at Théâtre de la Commune in 2009 and in 2011 (dir. Jacques Nichet); *Soudain l'été dernier* at the Théâtre de la Tempête in 2009 (dir. René Loyon); *Un Tramway d'après A Streetcar Named Desire,* at the Théâtre de l'Odéon in 2010 (dir. Krzysztof Warlikowski); *Parle-moi comme la pluie et laisse-moi écouter* and *La propriété condamnée* at the Théâtre Ça Respire Encore in 2011 (dir. Daniel Pierson); *Le paradis sur terre* at the Théâtre d'Edouard VII in 2011 (dir. Bernard Murat); and, of course, *Un tramway nommé Désir* at the Comédie-Française in 2011 (dir. Lee Breuer), the first American play ever to have been performed as part of the Comédie's repertoire in its august Salle Richelieu.

And that is only listing what has taken place in France recently. In the countries were Williams is most respected, the lists would extend beyond the space allotted for this book. What both lists are meant to demonstrate is that – at home or abroad – Williams is not only alive again, and thriving; he is also 'in', he is hip, he is cool, he is now, and he is here to stay.

Thomas Lanier Williams III must be cackling in his grave.

Notes

Preface

1. Qtd. in *T*, 202.
2. *N*, 457.

1 Columbus to Columbia (via St Louis): Separating Fact from Fiction

1. *T*, 37.
2. Ibid., 42–44.
3. Allean Hale, an eminent Williams scholar, has made this point repeatedly, the latest effort coming from her article, 'Tennessee Williams' St Louis Blues', in David Kaplan's *Tenn at One Hundred: The Reputation of Tennessee Williams*.
4. *T*, 39.
5. Ibid., 79. The Williamses were to live in the flat for nearly ten years.
6. *NSE*, 27.
7. *RMT*, 19.
8. *T*, 44–45.
9. Ibid., 44. Leverich notes that Cornelius would escape the War due to his near blindness in one eye, the result of a childhood injury (39, 46). Prophetically, eye problems would be the reason for his son having been declared IV-F years later and thus ineligible for the draft during World War II.
10. *L I*, 5. The widow Rose Williams in the comic is 'so strict' that her previous nine husbands have all 'commided suicid' (6, *sic*). Violence in Williams's writing was already well established from an early age.
11. Kolin, '"Isolated"', 33–39.
12. Williams, 'Isolated', 2.
13. Ibid.
14. Qtd. in Kolin, '"Isolated"', 35.
15. *T*, 77, 65.
16. *KS*, 48. As Esther Jackson notes, 'In his concept of form, then, Williams recapitulates certain ideas drawn from the romantic tradition' (31; see also 34–36).
17. *T*, 140.
18. Written when he was a ninth grader, Williams's ecological tract, 'Demon Smoke', about the smog problem that St Louis faced daily, appeared in *Blewett Junior Life Yearbook* in June 1925.
19. Qtd. in *T*, 73.
20. Qtd. in *RMT*, 43, 76.
21. Hale, 'Early Williams – The Making of a Playwright', 13.
22. *M*, 4.
23. *NSE*, 223.
24. Williams, 'Can a Good Wife Be a Good Sport?', 13.

25. Ibid., 9.
26. *T*, 81.
27. Editorial head note to 'Can a Good Wife Be a Good Sport?', 4.
28. *RMT*, 45.
29. *L I*, 9–10.
30. *RMT*, 46, 50.
31. *CS*, 11.
32. *L I*, 26.
33. *T*, 98.
34. *N*, 469.
35. See *L I*, 11–21 (especially letters of 5 and 10 August 1928, where he talks about Montreux, Sorrento, Milan, and especially Cologne, since they do not appear among his travel pieces). See also *M*, 19–23 and *T*, 89–96.
36. Williams, 'A Day at the Olympics', 5.
37. Ibid.
38. Ibid.
39. Ibid.
40. *L I*, 20.
41. *M*, 21.
42. *CTW*, 271.
43. Williams, 'A Flight over London', 3.
44. Ibid.
45. Anon., 'Airports'.
46. Williams, 'A Flight over London', 3.
47. Ibid.
48. *L I*, 17.
49. Williams, 'A Tour of the Battle-fields of France', 2.
50. Ibid.
51. *TTW*, 4.261.
52. Williams, 'A Trip to Monte Carlo', 2; *TTW*, 3.415.
53. Ibid.
54. *M*, 20, 21.
55. Ibid., 23.
56. *N*, 19.
57. *T*, 113–14.
58. Williams, *Beauty Is the Word*, 187, 188, 187, and 189.
59. *L I*, 23.
60. *CS*, 19.
61. *T*, 119.
62. HRC, 'The Wounds of Vanity', [1].
63. Ibid., [2].
64. Smith, *My Friend Tom*, 60.
65. Williams, *American Blues*, 13, 9, 11, and 13.
66. *L I*, 62.
67. *CS*, 33.
68. *M*, 35.
69. *L I*, 60.
70. HRC, ['Yesterday morning the city of Midland ...'], [1].
71. Ibid., [2].

72. *T*, 126.
73. HRC, 'Somewhere a Voice. ...', [1, 4].
74. *T*, 125.
75. Smith, *My Friend Tom*, 7.
76. *L I*, 65.

2   University City to Clayton (via Memphis): Looking for a Publisher in Spring

1. *RMT*, 62.
2. Tischler, *Rebellious Puritan*, 38.
3. *SR*, xi, xviii.
4. HRC, ['To Psyche']. An untitled draft in holography on recto-verso of Friedman-Shelby Branch, International Shoe Company, 'Red Goose Shoes' letterhead, [1-2]. See another page of this poem in *T*, 196 ff.
5. *N*, 7.
6. Ibid.
7. *T*, 117, 146.
8. Qtd. in *T*, 131.
9. *L I*, 69.
10. Ibid., 71.
11. Ibid., 73.
12. Ibid., 70–71.
13. Ibid., 72.
14. *N*, 47.
15. Qtd. in *IB*, 49.
16. *T*, 137.
17. *CP*, 177.
18. HRC, 'Return to Dust', [1]. William Jay Smith writes in the foreword to *Candles to the Sun* that Williams attended the weekly meetings of The League 'at the old courthouse near the St Louis riverfront' (*CTS*, xxii).
19. *IB*, 41.
20. *CTW*, 5.
21. HRC, 'The Darkling Plain (For Bruno Hauptmann who Dies Tonight)', [1].
22. Ibid.; cf. *N*, 28.
23. *N*, 29.
24. HRC, 'The Literary Mind by Max Eastman', [4].
25. *N*, 7.
26. Qtd. in *RMT*, 80.
27. *N*, 13.
28. Founded in 1890 by artistic- and civic-minded women of St Louis, the Wednesday Club was located at 4506 Westminster Place.
29. *CP*, 180; *RMT*, 76.
30. *L I*, 69.
31. Ibid., 83. As Devlin and Tischler note, Williams published 'forty-odd lyrics from 1933 to 1938, nearly all in collegiate or little magazines, but he did not appear in *Poetry* until 1937' (*L I*, 69).
32. *CP*, 201.
33. Ibid., 200.

34. HRC, 'Cut Out', [1].
35. HRC, 'This Spring', [1].
36. *N*, 11.
37. Ibid., 15. Margaret Bradham Thornton suggests in her note to this entry that Williams's stream of consciousness style was influenced by William Saroyan's story 'The Daring Young Man on the Flying Trapeze', which appeared in *Story* in 1934. I suggest later that Williams's discovery of James Joyce's *Ulysses* continued his interests in the stream of consciousness, which included finding a dramatic equivalent to it for his plastic theatre.
38. *N*, 13.
39. Ibid., 12.
40. Qtd. in Ibid., 20.
41. Ibid.
42. Ibid., 21.
43. Ibid., 25.
44. *MT*, 38.
45. HRC, 'Nirvana', [1].
46. Originally from a typescript housed at the HRC (box 35, folder 14), this essay was written to mark the recent successes of a local poet, Clark Mills. Suggesting that he had planned to submit it to a St Louis newspaper (or was asked to write it), Williams typed at the top of the six-page manuscript: 'Feature Story about Clark Mills (McBurney), Clayton, Mo.'.
47. *T*, 125, 159. Williams referred to a similar party in his notebook in the entry dated Sunday, 3 Jan. 1937: 'Helen Longmire's delightful dinner and theatre party [...]' (*N*, 71; cf. 70).
48. HRC, 'Return to Dust', [4].
49. Ibid.
50. Ibid., [5].
51. Ibid., [6].
52. *N*, 51.

3 University City to New Orleans (via Iowa City): Academic Blues versus 'American Blues'

1. *N*, 35.
2. Ibid., 82.
3. For a fuller treatment of Williams's activist plays, in particular their relationship to Conroy's Depression-era work, see Hale, 'Tom Williams – Proletarian Playwright', 13–22.
4. *Spring Storm* was originally titled 'April Is the Cruelest Month', after T. S. Eliot's *The Waste Land*.
5. Hale, 'Tom Williams – Proletarian Playwright', 20.
6. The notebook's insert reads, 'Dead Planet, The Moon I salute you! (a writer's journal)' (*N*, 3). In January 1939, following his introduction to life in the French Quarter, Williams began writing a play titled 'Vieux Carré', over which he pencilled a new title, 'Dead Planet, the Moon' (*N*, 138).
7. Devlin, 45.
8. *N*, 155.
9. *T*, 170.

10. *L I*, 90.
11. The HRC (box 11, folders 1–2) contains the following college essays written by Williams around the same time as this essay (all are undated but written during the academic years 1930–32, 1936–37, and 1937–38): 'Tristam by Edward Arlington Robinson', 'DAISY MILLER by Henry James', 'The "Nigger" of the Narcissus by Joseph Conrad', 'Art, Clive Bell', 'The Literary Mind by Max Eastman', 'Antigone', 'An Ancient Greek Poet's Address to a Convention of Modern Artist', 'Thinking Our Own Thoughts', 'Rain from Heaven', 'You Never Can Tell The Depth Of A Well', '"Holiday" by Philip Barry', 'The Wind and the Rain (Merton Hodge)', '"The Late Christopher Bean" by Sidney Howard', 'Candida', 'Review of Two Plays by John M. Synge', 'Some Representative Plays of O'Neill And a Discussion of his Art', 'Candide ou L'Optimisme', 'Tucaret', and 'Merope'.
12. *L I*, 90–91.
13. HRC, [College spiral notebook], n.pag., all *sic*.
14. *N*, 59. Brown was Williams's professor for 'French 16,' 'Origins of the Philosophic Movement'.
15. Ibid., 61; cf. *T*, 183.
16. HRC, 'Some Representative Plays of O'Neill And a Discussion of his Art', [6].
17. Ibid., [16].
18. HRC, 'Birth of an Art (Anton Chekhov and the New Theatre)', [1].
19. *T*, 217.
20. HRC, 'Candide, ou L'Optimisme', [1].
21. HRC, [College spiral notebook], n.pag.
22. HRC, 'Merope', [1].
23. *N*, 71.
24. Ibid., 73.
25. HRC, 'The Literary Mind by Max Eastman', [1].
26. Ibid., [2].
27. HRC, [College spiral notebook], n.pag. Also in the spiral notebook is an interesting comment which suggests that, even now, Williams was not entirely sure which sex attracted him the most: 'It is so exciting this time of year to sit in a room full of women. [signed] A scholarly mind'.
28. *NSE*, 244.
29. Ibid.
30. Ibid., 245.
31. Williams was planning on writing a 35,000-word novella 'about a year in the lives of a number of young people – terminating in the apocalyptic experience of Spring – the scene a University campus' (*N*, 47), but he feared that his novel was becoming 'cheap' and he did not 'want to write that kind of stuff' (*N*, 51).
32. *CTW*, 220–21.
33. TWPHL, MS Thr 397 (764a), 'Some Random Additions to my Memoirs', 1, all *sic*.
34. HRC, 'A Report on Four Writers of the Modern Psychological School', [1]-2, 3. It is not certain if the handwritten page numbers at the top right corner of each page are Williams's or Heller's, since Williams rarely paginated his homework assignments. I have faithfully reproduced the portions of this essay about Joyce as they appear on the typed manuscript page. All errors in fact, formatting, punctuation, or language, including spelling, are Williams's own.

35. HRC, ['I: Mr. Krutch is probably correct'], [1–2].
36. Ibid., [7].
37. Moscato and Le Blanc, 311. For excellent essays on Joyce's legal battles in the US over the censorship of *Ulysses*, see Carmelo Medina Casado, 'Legal Prudery: The Case of *Ulysses*', and Robert Spoo, 'Copyright Protectionism and Its Discontents: The Case of James Joyce's *Ulysses* in America'.
38. *N*, 59, 61.
39. *RMT*, 33.
40. HRC, 'A Report on Four Writers of the Modern Psychological School', 5.
41. *N*, 55.
42. Ibid., 56–57.
43. *TTW*, 1.161.
44. *RMT*, 33. For more on Lawrence's influence on Williams during these years, see Linda Dorff, 'Collapsing Resurrection Mythologies'.
45. *TTW*, 7.56.
46. HRC, 'A Report on Four Writers of the Modern Psychological School', 5.
47. HRC, 'Comments on the Nature of Artists with a few Specific References to the Case of Edgar Allan Poe', [1]. Concerning this essay, Williams mentioned it in his notebook (and then struck it out) as a 'silly paper on Poe' (*N*, 111). See also *NSE*, 254.
48. This is something Alma Winemiller, paraphrasing Oscar Wilde, would later say in *Summer and Smoke*:

    How everything reaches up, how everything seems to be straining for something out of the reach of stone – or human – fingers? [....] To me – well, that is the secret, the principle back of existence – the everlasting struggle and aspiration for more than our human limits have placed in our reach... Who was [it] that said that – oh, so beautiful thing! – 'All of us are in the gutter, but some of us are looking at the stars!' (*TTW*, 2.197)

49. *KS*, 48; cf. Jackson, 31.
50. Qtd. in *T*, 155.
51. Williams also greatly admired Rainer Maria Rilke's *Duineser Elegien* (*Duino Elegies*) and was probably also familiar with his 1906 poem 'Blaue Hortensie' ('Blue Hydrangea'). In it, Rilke associates the same 'fleetingness!' of life with the Blue Flower that Novalis had described in 1801 with his 'Die blaue Blume' ('The Blue Flower') and the novel *Heinrich von Ofterdingen* (1799–1801). The blue flower was the one symbol most embraced by the *Romantiker* to describe wanderlust, an endless search for the unattainable ideal. For Williams's admiration for Rilke, see *N*, 488, 647, 661, and his letters to Maria Britneva (later the Lady St Just), *FOA*, 60–61. For two essays on Williams's relationship to the *Romantiker* tradition, see Cora Robey, 'Chloroses – Pâles Roses and Pleurosis – Blue Roses', and Bert Cardullo, 'The Blue Rose of St Louis: Laura, Romanticism, and *The Glass Menagerie*'.
52. Burnett's story is a fantasy set in the mythical Far East. In it, the boy-king Amor, the son of the last reigning King Mordreth, grows up in the mountains under the tutelage of a sagacious philosopher called the Ancient One, who teaches the boy an ontology that unifies man with beast and flora. Baring's story repeats this same motif of the search for the unattainable

in yet another myth about a Princess in the Far East. In it, the emperor's beautiful daughter is about to wed, and many suitors present themselves to her through her father. To assure that his daughter would marry well, the emperor orders that only 'the man who found and brought back the blue rose' (139) could marry his daughter. Kipling's poem is a rather sardonic take on Novalis's quest for the blue flower, where the young lover returns only to find that his beloved has long since died.

53. Williams, 'In Spain There Was Revolution', 53–54. As the late Gilbert Debusscher notes in his essay ' "Where Memory Begins": New Texas Light on *The Glass Menagerie*', 'The story is on a typed manuscript of eight pages by Thomas Lanier Williams with a penciled note on the title page that reads "Not a bad story and rather prophetic. T. W. (written about '36)." A small slip in the same file indicates that the text was originally "rejected by Story – sept. 21, 1936" ' (53).

54. Though written in 1935, 'Twenty-seven Wagons Full of Cotton' was published in August 1936 by *Manuscript*. A previous story by Williams was accepted in 1934 for *The Anvil*, *The Magazine of Proletarian Fiction*, an 'important radical magazine' published by Jack Conroy in Missouri (*L I*, 72–73), but it was later rejected by his successor, Philip Rahv, when it was taken over by *The Partisan Review*. For more on Williams's experiences with *The Anvil* and its editorial staff, see Hale, 'Tom Williams – Proletarian Playwright', 14–15, 16–17.

55. *CS*, 44.

56. Ibid., 46. For more on the rape in the story, see my article '*A Streetcar Named Dies Irae*: Tennessee Williams and the Semiotics of Rape'.

57. William dedicated *Battle of Angels* (1940) to Lawrence, and on one manuscript for the play he wrote, 'For D. H. Lawrence / Who was while he lived the brilliant adversary of so many dark angels and who never fell, except in the treacherous flesh, the rest being flame that fought and prevailed over darkness' (*N*, 56).

58. *N*, 65.

59. Ibid.

60. Ibid.

61. Qtd. in *N*, 80.

62. Ibid., 27.

63. *CTW*, 5.

64. Pawley, 67.

65. Bigsby, *Critical Introduction to Twentieth-Century American Drama*, 31.

66. *MT*, 59.

67. Williams called this play Sartre's 'finest piece of theatre' whose 'intellectual freshness and purity is really quite wonderful' (*L II*, 204).

68. *N*, 89.

69. *FK*, xiii. When writing this in 2001, Hale was working directly from Williams's unpublished notebooks at Texas, which explains the many discrepancies in her transcription from them and the published version in *Notebooks* that appeared five years later.

70. *N*, 93, 99.

71. Ibid., 103.

72. Ibid., 21. As Thornton notes, ' "Gift of an Apple" was not accepted, but in a letter dated 6 May 1936 (HRC), the editor, Wilbur Schramm, wrote: "Some of these days you are going to burst out and write some fine stuff" ' (*N*, 20).

73. Ibid., 51; cf. *L I*, 88, 90.

74. Ibid., 61; cf. 79. Throughout the year 1937, Williams made repeated references to sending his work to *American Prefaces*. For example, in October 1937, Williams wrote a letter to his mother Edwina, informing her that 'AMERICAN PREFACES have definitely accepted a short-story and I think will publish it in two or three months. It was read and highly approved by the whole staff which includes some very well-known literary figures. Schramm, the editor, thinks it has a good chance of being chosen for the annual O'Brien short-story anthology, which would do a great deal for my literary reputation' (*L I*, 113).
75. Ibid., 105. In a 22 August 1937 letter to Wilbur Schramm, Williams wrote, 'I know it will surprise you to learn that I am intending, if possible, to enter the University of Iowa this Fall' (*L I*, 100).
76. HRC, 'American Gothic', 11.
77. Ibid., 11, 13.
78. *T*, 245.
79. *FK*, 25.
80. O'Connor, 'Moving into the Rooming House: Interiority and Stage Space in Tennessee Williams's *Fugitive Kind* and *Vieux Carré*', 27.
81. *N*, 105.
82. *L I*, 101.
83. *N*, 93, 119.
84. Qtd. in *T*, 263.
85. *SS*, 31; cf. 116.
86. Ibid., 121–22; *FK*, 104, 106.
87. *SS*, 122.
88. *N*, 121–23.
89. *T*, 235. Mabie helped her obtain a Rockefeller fellowship to work on her master's thesis, the same one that Audrey Wood would later acquire for Williams (cf. *T*, 263; *L I*, 128).
90. *L I*, 147.
91. *NN*, 37.
92. *MT*, 272.
93. *MP*, 61.
94. Ibid., 47.
95. Ibid., 121.
96. Ibid., 141.
97. *N*, 127.
98. Ibid.
99. Ibid., 129.
100. Ibid., 131.
101. Ibid., 131.
102. *T*, 274; cf. *L I*, 160–61, 176. Williams sent a third play, *Not about Nightingales*, but it arrived too late to be considered.

4 New Orleans to Hollywood (via Acapulco): *Mañana Es Otro Día*

1. *CTW*, 4.
2. Ibid., 25, 257.

3. *RMT*, 97.
4. *L I*, 162–63.
5. *CTW*, xii, viii.
6. *N*, 325; cf. *N*, 253.
7. *L I*, 503. Dakin shipped out for northern Burma via North Africa on the day Rosina Otte Dakin ('Grand') died.
8. *N*, 335.
9. Qtd. in *T*, 335.
10. *N*, 131.
11. Ibid., 133.
12. *L I*, 145.
13. Ibid., 146.
14. *NSE*, 5.
15. *L I*, 220.
16. HRC, 'A Letter to Irene' (box 23, folder 8), [2]. The manuscript of the same title at the TWPHL, MS Thr 397 (732) is a longer version.
17. *L I*, 158.
18. *N*, 141; *L I*, 143, 148–49.
19. *L I*, 157–59, 161. Cornelius told Williams to contact Sam J. Webb, a salesman in Los Angeles, who worked for the International Shoe Company.
20. *N*, 161.
21. FTTW, MSS 562 (610) 'Final Materiel' [*sic*], [4].
22. *N*, 145.
23. *L I*, 164.
24. Ibid., 678–69.
25. *TTW*, 7.56.
26. Though *Steps Must Be Gentle* was published quite late in Williams's career, various arguments have been made for dating the play much earlier than 1980. Echoing Stephen S. Stanton in his essay 'Some Thoughts about *Steps Must Be Gentle*', Gilbert Debusscher argues in '"Minting their Separate Wills": Tennessee Williams and Hart Crane' (a point he reiterates in his 1989 essay on *The Gnädiges Fräulein*) that the play was actually written in 1947, just after Grace Hart Crane's death, and was the precursor to *Suddenly Last Summer* (468). While neither critic offers conclusive evidence to date the play as 1947, there is a twenty-five page typescript of a play titled 'Suitable Entrances to Springfield or Heaven' about Vachel Lindsay's suicide by drinking Lysol that may shed some light on the date of composition of *Steps Must Be Gentle*.
   The typescript of 'Suitable Entrances to Springfield or Heaven', held in the Special Collections at the University of Delaware, bears a note on its cover page that curator Timothy D. Murray cites in *Evolving Texts: The Writing of Tennessee Williams*, a catalogue to the Collection's exposition of its Williams holdings back in 1988:

> *Suitable Entrances to Springfield* has not yet been published or produced, although Williams's note on the title page suggests that it could go with *Steps Must Be Gentle* under the title 'Two American Poets' (n.pag.). Nancy Tischler, who has written about Williams's fascination with Lindsay in her essay 'Tennessee Williams: Vagabond Poet', adds that the 'cover page indicates – in his handwriting – that it was never produced. It is "an old

ms. revised for Art Center," which "could go with *Steps Must Be Gentle* 7); [*sic*] under combo title 'Two American Poets'"' (77).

Tischler suggests that 'Suitable Entrances' was the play evolved from a scenario that Williams first described to Audrey Wood in a series of letters dating from June to July 1939, which is likely the one-page scenario 'Springfield, Illinois' now held at the HRC (box 42, folder 6). Williams began writing 'Suitable Entrances' around this time period, for he had informed the Rockefeller fellowship board in his application that June that the play was a 'work in prospect' (*L I*, 178). A month later, he had 'shelved the Lindsay idea for a much more compelling impulse to dramatize D.H. Lawrence's life in New Mexico' (*L I*, 179), which eventually became *I Rise in Flames, Cried the Phoenix*. None of this validates a 1947 composition date for *Steps Must Be Gentle*, whose style does resemble Williams's later plays, and Williams may have simply returned to his older Lindsay manuscript around the time he first started working on the Crane play before it was published privately in 1980. Yet it is at least possible that the play was first drafted long before its 1980 publication date since Williams's other play was as well, and he revisited it in the late 1970s, as he had frequently done with other older manuscripts, to revise and update it for a potential production.

27. *MT*, 7.
28. *N*, 173.
29. *NSE*, 12.
30. *L II*, 14.
31. Ibid., 267.
32. *N*, 619, 621.
33. Ibid., 179.
34. *L I*, 259.
35. FTTW, MSS 562 (648), [Medical prescription], [1].
36. *L I*, 244.
37. Ibid., 228–29.
38. *N*, 187, 189.
39. *NSE*, 216.
40. *N*, 193.
41. Ibid., 137.
42. Ibid., 182–83.
43. Qtd. in *T*, 354.
44. *L I*, 239. By 1 May, Williams expressed to Langner and Helburn that he was 'completely confident' that the play would be 'a critical and a commercial success' (*L I*, 252). He even thought it would win that year's Pulitzer Prize (*L I*, 268).
45. *T*, 358.
46. Ibid., 328; *L I*, 261.
47. *NSE*, 135.
48. *LDW*, 134; Steen, 195.
49. *NSE*, 197.
50. For more on Williams's first encounter with Kip Kiernan in Provincetown, see the first five chapters of David Kaplan's biography, *Tennessee Williams in Provincetown*.

51. *LDW*, 11–12.
52. *T*, 352.
53. Ibid., 369; *L I*, 263, 272.
54. Moschovakis and Roessel claim that such an early date is suspect, however: 'Its first sentence suggests that the narration takes place in late October, 1940, "about a month" after the author's departure from Acapulco, yet before his play's calamitous Boston premiere. However, it would be rash to affirm that the narrator's opening statement, or indeed anything in this essay, is reliable as autobiographical testimony. [...] The most that can be said with some confidence, then, is that "Amor Perdido" was written between the end of September 1940 and the summer of 1945, when Williams made his second trip to Mexico' (537–38).
55. *L I*, 250.
56. Ibid., 277.
57. Andrew Gunn, 'a spoiled creature [...] who has never learned honesty and is now too old to learn it' (*L I*, 277), was one of Williams's lovers during his summer visit to Acapulco in 1940. He would become the older writer in Williams's story 'The Night of the Iguana'. In an 11 October letter to Donald Windham, Williams wrote:

> Had one brief, exciting affair with a native – Carlos from Vera Cruz! – and a long, dull, complicated one with a neurotic American writer from Tahiti who wants me to share an apt. with him in New Orleans this winter, or in Key West, Florida, but that appears to be out of the question now, if I wanted to, even. He was a football star at Michigan some yrs. ago and son of General Mgr. of [Pullman] Co. – extremely wealthy – but always talking about suicide. (*LDW*, 16)

58. *SR*, xxi.
59. Ibid, xxi–xxii, Williams's ellipses.
60. *CTW*, 5.
61. *L I*, 18.
62. *NSE*, 43.
63. *CS*, 33.
64. *SR*, 72–73.
65. *SR*, 73.
66. *SR*, xiv.
67. Williams, 'A Movie by Cocteau', 3.
68. *NSE*, 18, 19; Smith, *My Friend Tom*, 53.
69. Ibid, 24.
70. *CTW*, 5.
71. *T*, 394; cf. *L I*, 281–82 and *N*, 299. Audrey Wood sent him a Photostat copy of the card and kept the original, knowing he would probably lose it (*T*, 436). He would also spend a night in a New York jail in the spring of 1944 after FBI agents arrested him for what amounted to vagrancy when he could not produce his card (*L I*, 522).
72. *M*, 58.
73. *LDW*, 21; cf. *L I*, 302.
74. *L I*, 302; cf. *N*, 219.

75. *NSE*, 168.
76. *M*, 64–65.
77. *L I*, 308.
78. *T*, 405; *N*, 225.
79. *N*, 225.
80. HRC, 'Te Moraturi Salutamus', [1].
81. *T*, 418.
82. *L I*, 330.
83. On 12 January 1942, he wrote in his notebook: 'I write a great deal of drivel which I think is good – till afterwards. I refer to "A Woman Not Large but Tremendous" – and the preceding filth in this journal. I do not want to keep that kind of journal' (*N*, 277).
84. Ibid., 251.
85. *L I*, 342. In an earlier 1941 letter to Bigelow, Williams wrote, 'It was really a frightful sad sort of thing. Queens! Oh, God, what a mess it all is!' (*L I*, 334).
86. *L I*, 353.
87. *M*, 50.
88. *NN*, xx.
89. Qtd. in *FOA*, 236.
90. *M*, 72; qtd. in *FOA*, 236.
91. *T*, 446; *N*, 282. In 1945, Williams described to Jay Laughlin a request he was given to write a critique for *View* magazine on 'The Plastic Theatre' and how he planned on writing about Federico García Lorca and Ramon Naya (*L I*, 538). Williams was no doubt moved by Lorca's surrealist play, *If Five Years Pass*. Written in 1931, the play was not produced until after Lorca's assassination in 1936 at the hands of Francisco Franco's Nationalists' militia in Grenada. While the play's first Spanish production had to wait until 1954, there was an English performance of *If First Years Pass* in April 1945 by the Jane Street Cooperative at the Provincetown Playhouse. The first artist cooperative in New York, Jane Street consisted of a group of artists, including Hyde Solomon, Nell Blaine, Judith Rothschild, Leland Bell, Louisa Matthiasdottir, Ida Fischer, Larry Rivers, and Albert Kresch, who were all heavily influenced by Hans Hofmann's Abstract Expressionist paintings. The group designed the sets for *If Five Years Pass*.
92. *N*, 281.
93. Qtd. in *T*, 446. Leverich takes this passage, as he writes, from Williams's 'notebook' but, unlike with his other passages, Leverich fails to cite the date of the entry. Curiously, in the published *Notebooks*, this passage – one extremely important to Williams's dramaturgical theory – does not appear. The *Notebooks* do mention that, after the 'post-war artist' reference for 25 February 1942, there is a '[*page missing*]' (*N*, 283). Furthermore, Devlin and Tischler note that Williams's term 'sculptural drama' came from his '*Journal* c. Apr. 1942' (*L 1*, 441). Williams had only two entries in April 1942 in his notebook, neither of which carries this passage. Moreover, Richard E. Kramer makes reference to this passage in his essay ' "The Sculptural Drama": Tennessee Williams's Plastic Theatre', but relies on Leverich's source and not on the original: 'Aside from the passage quoted by Leverich and the lines Bray cites [in his introduction to New Directions's 1999 reprinting, which he drew from Leverich], the remainder of this entry is currently available

only in manuscript at the Harry Ransom Center' (8). Nowhere are these
very important words available for verification outside of Leverich's book.
94. HRC, 'The Sculptural Play (a method)', [1], all *sic*. An earlier version of this
essay is housed at TWPHL, MS THR 397 (759), 'The Sculptural Play'.
95. Cocteau, Préface, 45.
96. *LDW*, 24.
97. *L I*, 387.
98. *L I*, 374.
99. *N*, 327.
100. Qtd. in *T*, 445.
101. *T*, 446.
102. *N*, 195.
103. Qtd. in ibid., 197.
104. Ibid., 249.
105. Ibid., 265.
106. Ibid., 269.
107. Qtd. in ibid., 274.
108. Ibid., 275–76.
109. Ibid., 279. See also his 17 December 1941 letter to his mother and his
6 January 1942 letter to Audrey Wood (*T*, 439), and his 21 June 1942 notebook entry.
110. *L I*, 536.
111. *T*, 471.
112. *N*, 301–303.
113. Ibid., 321.
114. Qtd. in *T*, 483.
115. *N*, 299. See also *T*, 538 and *L I*, 522 for a similar occurrence in New York in
1944, when Williams had to spend a night in jail until his papers arrived
from his parents' home in St Louis.
116. *N*, 299.
117. Ibid., 327.
118. Ibid.
119. Ibid., 339, 343.
120. Qtd. in *T*, 480.
121. *L I*, 429.
122. *N*, 253.
123. Ibid., 345.
124. Ibid., 343.
125. *L I*, 439; *N*, 361, 360.
126. Hayman, 84.
127. *N*, 285.
128. *N*, 301.

5   Hollywood to Rome (via Chicago): The 'Catastrophe' of his Success

1. Qtd. in *N*, 365.
2. Ibid.

3. *T*, 499.
4. *L I*, 455.
5. Ibid., 451.
6. *T*, 495.
7. Palmer and Bray, 20.
8. *L I*, 486.
9. FTTW, MSS 562 (574), 'Provisional Film Story Treatment of "The Gentleman Caller"', 1.
10. *L1*, 476; *N*, 380.
11. *MT*, 165.
12. *LDW*, 91.
13. *N*, 421.
14. *L I*, 440.
15. *N*, 447.
16. *L I*, 457.
17. *N*, 401, 407.
18. For more on the prefaces and on the reviews, see *LDW*, 68, 147–48; *CP*, xv–xvi; and *N*, 371 and 391.
19. *L I*, 455.
20. Ibid., 540.
21. Ibid., 540–41.
22. Ibid., 494.
23. *N*, 393.
24. *M*, 77; *T*, 502.
25. *N*, 357.
26. *L I*, 493.
27. *LDW*, 176.
28. *N*, 386.
29. Ibid., 409.
30. *RMT*, 143.
31. *L I*, 500–501.
32. Ibid., 502.
33. *T*, 533–34.
34. *L I*, 511. Williams would later betray Hunter by offering *You Touched Me!*, which was not a hot commodity due to the success of *The Glass Menagerie*, to Guthrie McClintic (*L I*, 550).
35. *T*, 538.
36. *LDW*, 143. See also *L I*, 517; *T*, 540. Laughlin had a hard time getting the first issue of *Pharos* printed. The magazine was printed in Utah (its editorial address was at Murray, 'near Laughlin's ski lodge at Alta' [*L I*, 529]), and the Mormon printers found the play objectionable. In a July 1944 letter to Laughlin, Williams asked if *Pharos* was 'still at the mercy of the Mormons' (*L I*, 529).
37. Qtd. in *L I*, 527.
38. Ibid., 532; *N*, 413.
39. Schvey, 58. As Schvey writes,

> They had already seen evidence of the young man's extraordinary talent in a series of short sketches based on his home life that he had produced for the class. Classmate A. E. Hotchner described them as 'the most

wonderful, little fragile vignettes about a mother and daughter and a son in St Louis,' leading him to conclude they were precursors to Williams's first great Broadway success, *The Glass Menagerie* (1944). 'They were quite lyrical,' he continued, 'and we took it for granted that he would turn in a play based on these people'. (qtd. in Givens, 30)

40. Williams wrote in his *Memoirs* that Dowling and Nathan conspired to write the drunk scene for Tom, which Williams detested and rewrote himself (*M*, 82). See also *N*, 429; *T*, 552–53; and *CTW*, 14–15.
41. Though the line does not appear in the Random House edition of 1945, it is retained in the Drama Play Service's edition of 1948, much to Williams's chagrin: 'I was surprised to find that the acting edition of Menagerie contained practically all of the little vulgarisms which Babs and I spent practically a whole day weeding out. How did they get back in? I particularly detest that closing line * * "And this is where the play ends and your imagination begins"' (*L II*, 186; cf. *L I*, 555).
42. Their literary war began when Nathan castigated the Theatre Guild in an April 1943 issue of *Esquire* for having turned down productions of Sean O'Casey's plays and instead produced 'Tennessee Williams' cheap sex-shocker, *Battle of Angels*, which shut down after a few days' engagement out of town [...]' (*N*, 360).
43. *DLB*, 65; cf. *CTW*, 14–15.
44. *T*, 563.
45. *TTW*, 1.131.
46. HRC, 'A Report on Four Writers of the Modern Psychological School', [1].
47. *L I*, 25–26.
48. *TTW*, 1.131.
49. HRC, 'A Report on Four Writers of the Modern Psychological School', 4.
50. Durham, 63. Allean Hale argues that the lantern slides, which were influenced by Erwin Piscator of the Dramatic Workshop at the New School for Social Research, who was known for his use of cinematic techniques on the stage. Williams briefly studied with Piscator in the spring of 1940 and worked for him in 1942. Williams had used placards in earlier plays like *Candles to the Sun* and *Fugitive Kind* to introduce scenes: 'It reminds one of the vaudeville shows which accompanied most films in those days in St Louis, where each act was announced by a printed placard' (Hale, 'Early Williams', 19). For more on Williams and Piscator, and on Piscator's use of the screen device, see Richard E. Kramer, '"The Sculptural Drama": Tennessee Williams's Plastic Theatre', and John Willett, *The Theatre of Erwin Piscator: Half a Century of Politics in the Theatre*, 113.
51. *TTW*, 1.132, emphasis added.
52. Qtd. in Parker, 'The Composition', 422.
53. For fuller treatment of the screen device in the play, see Lori Leathers Single, 'Flying the Jolly Rogers: Images of Escape and Selfhood in Tennessee Williams's *The Glass Menagerie*', 69–85.
54. *L II*, 203.
55. In several plays decades later, Williams continued his quest for a theatrical 'interior monologue' (*HNMS*, 77). In *Confessional* (1970), he set characters off by spot lights on a darkened stage where they then address the audience in

confessional-like speeches that reflect their inner thoughts: '[...] *there should be an area in the downstage center that can be lighted in a way that sets it apart from the bar at those points in the play when a character disengages himself from the group to speak as if to himself. This area is the* "confessional"' (*TTW*, 7.153). Not simply theatrical 'asides' to the audience, these are interior monologues meant to capture the complex thought processes of various characters experiencing significant psychological or emotional epiphanies.

56. *L I*, 545.
57. William wrote in a letter to his parents postmarked 12 February 1941 that he had had 'quite a bad ordeal':

> I suffered very severely for the first few days after the operation and they had to give me typhoid fever injections to combat the inflammation in the eye – it seems an artificial fever will accelerate the absorption. The injections gave me a high fever and chills that nearly shook me to pieces: I got wonderful attention at that hospital, though. (qtd. in *T*, 400; cf. 441, 534 and 588)

58. *T*, 441; *M*, 71–72. As Leverich adds, 'In her wildest imaginings, [Edwina] could never have conceived of her Tom wearing a black eyepatch, on which Fritz [Bultman, a painter friend from New Orleans] had painted a glaring white orb [...]' (*T*, 441).
59. *NSE*, 33–34; cf. *M*, 74–75.
60. *L I*, 557–58.
61. *L II*, 14. When Williams passed back through Dallas en route to New York later in summer 1945, Jones apparently asked him for a $1,500 contribution to 'the Project', which Williams declined, though he blamed Audrey Wood (*L II*, 21–22).
62. *NSE*, 29.
63. *L I*, 561.
64. Ibid.
65. Ibid., 565; *L II*, 7; and *LDW*, 174.
66. *L II*, 3.
67. Ibid.
68. *L I*, 549–51.
69. *N*, 435.
70. Ibid., 437.
71. *L II*, 40.
72. Ibid., 45.
73. *M*, 99.
74. *L II*, 36, 45.
75. Ibid., 39.
76. Ibid., 48–49, 67–68, 139, and 211.
77. Ibid., 53–54; *N*, 441.
78. Ibid., 50. Most of this trip is described in a letter Williams wrote to Kenneth Tynan that was reproduced in *LDW*, 303–305.
79. *L II*, 55.
80. McCullers's *The Member of the Wedding*, outlined in 1939, was published in 1946, following the success of *The Ballad of the Sad Café* (1943). In a March

1948 letter to Audrey Wood, Williams wrote, 'Please tell Carson that I am utterly and truly entranced by her story "The Ballad of the Sad Café" which she recently sent me' (*L II*, 173).

81. *NSE*, 122.
82. *L II*, 61.
83. *NSE*, 48, 50–51.
84. Bak, Homo americanus, 137.
85. *NSE*, 49.
86. *L II*, 62, 64, 77, 83.
87. Williams, 'The History of *Summer and Smoke*', [3]. Williams began reworking *Streetcar* in late December 1946, after he sent a draft of *Summer and Smoke* to Audrey Wood by 19 December (*N*, 453).
88. Qtd. in *N*, 446.
89. *N*, 455.
90. *L II*, 85, 86–87.
91. *N*, 457.
92. *L II*, 91.
93. Ibid., 105.
94. Ibid., 107–108.
95. *M*, 132.
96. *L II*, 89.
97. Porter, 127–28.
98. Qtd. in Porter, 128–29.
99. *L II*, 116.
100. *L II*, 118; *M*, 131. See also *L II*, 96.
101. It is possible that Williams, who was working on *Streetcar* and *Summer and Smoke* simultaneously that autumn 1946, eventually saw his Blanche and Ralph (who was not yet called Stanley in this version of 'The Poker Night'; perhaps Cocteau's Stanislas helped Williams decide to restore the name of his St Louis friend that he had used in an earlier draft of *Streetcar*) in terms of Brando's Stanislas and Bankhead's Queen. There are plenty of lines from Cocteau's *Eagle* that later appeared in *Streetcar*. There is a scene in the first act when Brando's Stanislas becomes angry and '*snatches off the tablecloth and sends the cutlery and crockery, etc. flying*' (252), becoming for the Queen a 'storm': 'Upset things, break them, send them flying!' (252). Stanley's comment about Blanche and Stella being 'a pair of Queens' (*TTW*, 1.371) is also appropriate given the Queen–Tallulah–Blanche connection. Von Foehn, during his interrogation of Stanislas, says, 'Let us put all our cards on the table', just as Blanche tells Stanley during his interrogation of her about the loss of Belle Reve (*TTW*, 1.281). Also the Queen's contract that forces Stanislas to kill her after three days resembles Blanche's line about Stanley being her potential executioner, a role Stanley is attributed only in the late stages of the play's composition, probably March 1947. Stanislas also tells von Foehn about his transformation vis-à-vis the Queen and her government: 'The real tragedy is the distance which separates human beings, and the fact that they do not know each other. If they did, many a sad spectacle and crime would be avoided' (288). These are nearly the same words Williams used to describe *Streetcar* as a 'tragedy of incomprehension' in his 1948 essay 'Questions without Answers' (*NSE*, 42).

102. Atkinson, 42.
103. Nathan, 14; McCarthy, 358.
104. Adler, *The Moth and the Lantern*, 11.
105. Krutch, 129.
106. Ibid., 129–30, emphasis added.
107. *N*, 343.
108. HRC, 'What Is "Success" in the Theatre?' (box 51, folder 13), 2.
109. *L II*, 150.
110. *M*, 139–40; cf. *L II*, 147 and *N*, 469.
111. *N*, 615–17.
112. *N*, 469. Williams added: 'the country is full of flowers and the sea is turquoise. Snow-covered Alps are visible way off. (I probably wrote the same things when I passed through here at 16 [*sic*]!)'.
113. These were books he listed as 'My Current Reading' in a 6 March 1948 insert of the *Saturday Review of Literature*.
114. *N*, 477.
115. *TTW*, 3.375.
116. *M*, 142; cf. *FOA*, 25–26. Donald Downes, in addition to having worked for American and British intelligence and foreign correspondent, was Zeffirelli's lover *(N*, 472). For more on the film and his time in Sicily, see *L II*, 162–65; on Visconti, see *L II*, 483–84. See also *FOA*, 23, for a photo, which Maria St Just incorrectly places in the summer of 1949.
117. The essay is a faithful reproduction (with some minor editorial changes) of the typescript 'A Film in Sicily' (FTTW, MSS 562 [602]). Williams explained to Margo Jones, in a 3 February letter, that he had seen photographs taken during the production of the film which he said were 'the best most moving photography and lighting I've seen ever!' (*L II*, 157). Some of these photos, taken by Paul Ronald, still photographer for the film (as he would be for Visconti's 1951 film, *Bellissima*), are reproduced along with the article in *'48*.
118. Years later, Williams, along with his Roman muse, Anna Magnani, wanted Visconti to direct the film version of *The Rose Tattoo*, which Daniel Mann eventually did. Williams helped write some English dialogue for Visconti's 1953 film *Senso*, a film he did not like when he learned that his script was rewritten (*CTW*, 203; cf. *FOA*, 78–80, 82–86). Visconti also directed *The Glass Menagerie* in 1946 and would later direct (with Zeffirelli's set design) a 'Communist' version of *A Streetcar Named Desire* with the 'focus to make Stanley the hero' (*CTW*, 159; cf. *LDW*, 229–30).
119. *N*, 473.
120. *L II*, 162; cf. *L II*, 435.
121. *N*, 472.
122. Hayman, 123.
123. *N*, 479; *M*, 146–47.
124. *N*, 483.
125. Ibid.
126. *L II*, 198–99.
127. *N*, 485.
128. *L II*, 198.
129. See his note to his family about Congress's plan to revise the tax brackets (*L II*, 20, 84).

130. Back then, he told Margo Jones that he could not contribute the requested $1,500 to her 'Project' because 'Until I know where I stand financially it would be foolish to make any large disbursals, even to anything so important' (*L II*, 21). See also Williams's uncertainty about his 'economic security' (*L II*, 45).
131. *L II*, 199.
132. Williams even gave Donald Windham a signed affidavit to authenticate the sale of his manuscripts (*LDW*, 311–12).
133. Ibid., 199; *LDW*, 222.
134. *L II*, 205.
135. *M*, 149.
136. *L II*, 487.
137. *CTW*, 121.
138. *M*, 150–51.
139. *N*, 489.
140. The expression, which Stanley uses metaphorically to describe sexual inter-course with Stella in *Streetcar*, was often erroneously taken literally as if they made love under a string of Christmas lights strung across the room. Like Williams's term for homosexual intercourse – e.g., 'the nightingales sang sweetly once last week' or 'The nightingales busted their larynx! And Miss [John] Keats swooned in her grave' (*N*, 225 and 468; cf. 227, 241, 271, 301, 387, and 435) – the 'colored lights' are what Williams's 'saw' during sexual or creative climax.
141. *L II*, 102.

6   Rome to Rome (via Nearly Everywhere Else): 'Comfortable Little Mercies'

1. *N*, 495.
2. Ibid., 561.
3. Qtd. in ibid., 560.
4. Ibid., 493.
5. Qtd. in *N*, 506.
6. *NSE*, 63, 60–61.
7. The introduction evolved out of numerous typescripts at: HRC, 'Some Words of Introduction' (box 42, folder 1) or 'This Book' (box 37, folder 5); TWCD, 'Praise to Assenting Angels' (box 3, folder F107); and FTTW, 'Praise to Assenting Angels' (MSS 562 [616], a revision of the Delaware manuscript). All of the manuscripts begin with several pages of commentary on McCullers's relation to writers of the previous generation, as well as her inauspicious beginnings at the Julliard School of Music, that are cut from the final version (apparently by Williams himself). Some material in the larger folder called 'This Book' do not appear in the essays 'Praise to Assenting Angels' but find their way into the final essay, suggesting that it is the first preface (along with 'Some Words of Introduction') that Williams describes in his 17 August 1949 letter to Jay Laughlin, and that the essay 'Praise to Assenting Angels' (a phrase Williams uses in the first version) is the second preface. The published introduction, as Williams noted in his letter, combines the two versions, grafting the Southern Gothic discussion and the references to E. E. Cummings and Picasso's *Guernica*

of 'This Book', on to the second half of 'Praise of Assenting Angels', which finishes with the comment on Herman Melville's writing (which is subsequently used in the various book blurbs from Williams on McCullers).

8. *L II*, 240. On 8 April, Williams informed Donald Windham that he had 'completed an introduction to the reprint of Carson's "Reflections in a Golden Eye"' – the first version he would later completely revise (*LDW*, 239). From April 1949 to August 1949, Williams made several attempts to write the introduction. In an entry of his notebook, dated 14 July 1949, Williams wrote, 'Meant not to work but did – a little on Carson's preface', and on 18 July, he added that he 'rewrote Carson's preface with some progress' (*N*, 509). He finally submitted the two versions of the preface to Laughlin:

> Whatever decision you and Carson reach about the two prefaces is O.K. with me. My feeling was, when I read over the first version, that I appeared in that version to be talking too much about myself. If you revert to that original version I hope that you will preserve the cuts that I have made in it, particularly the long portion about 'imitators'. I believe that I scratched out (in the returned proofs) all but about two sentences of the material which was provoked mainly by the personal antagonism for Truman [Capote] which I think should not be indulged in this place. I also wish you would compare the two versions very carefully, again, and perhaps something from the second, which I still believe had a great deal more dignity in keeping with the novel, could be appended or worked into the other. (*L II*, 265)

9. *NSE*, 50, 51.
10. *TTW*, 3.114–15; *M*, 173.
11. HRC, 'Some Words of Introduction', [1]; FTTW, MSS 562 (616), 'Praise for an Assenting Angel', [6].
12. *L II*, 174; cf. 267.
13. See ibid., 440.
14. In 1951, Williams transferred Rose to Stoney Lodge in Ossining, New York, where she lived out the majority of her final years. Williams tried moving her down to Key West in 1976 then again in 1979, but she was more disoriented there. Williams moved her back up to Ossining in 1980 and into the Bethel Methodist Home, where she died in September 1996.
15. *LDW*, 249.
16. *KS*, 182.
17. *L II*, 329, 339, and 342.
18. *N*, 551; *L II*, 439; *M*, 204–208.
19. *L II*, 447–51.
20. *N*, 513.
21. Ibid., 515.
22. *NSE*, 54.
23. *N*, 519.
24. *NSE*, 64.
25. *L II*, 369.
26. *M*, 165.
27. *L II*, 390.

28. *N*, 551.
29. *N*, 531.
30. *L II*, 396; cf. 397.
31. *N*, 533, 537.
32. In his 1976 essay 'I Have Rewritten a Play for Artistic Purity', which accompanied the play's premiere, Williams tried convincing his critics and the public of *Eccentricities'* superiority for reasons of its 'disciplined excision' of 'inessential or extraneous' words found in the original play (*NSE*, 181–82).
33. *L II*, 402; *N*, 535. In his letter, Williams mentions having attended Ingmar Bergman's Swedish premiere of *The Rose Tattoo* in Göteborg with Merlo, which Spoto places in August 1951, with Williams and Merlo driving there in a rented car (*KS*, 194). The problem is that the Swedish premiere was not until 15 November 1951, and Williams was in London at the time and departed for New York on the 12th of the month.
34. *N*, 537.
35. Ibid.
36. *FOA*, 46; *N*, 537.
37. *N*, 543; cf. 537 and *L II*, 403–404.
38. *L II*, 419–20; *FOA*, 53–54.
39. Williams wrote Oliver Evans that his new chameleon, called Fairy May, was catching 'almost as many gnats and mosquitos [*sic*] as Bigelow does sailors' (*L II*, 421).
40. *N*, 548.
41. Ibid., 553.
42. Ibid., 559.
43. *NSE*, 46. Though begun in 1938, the House on UnAmerican Activities investigation committee was currently terrorizing left-leaning artists in the film industry, with the 'Hollywood Ten' being convicted in early 1948. Williams's boldness to write so blatantly 'leftist' here at this time should not be considered lightly.
44. An earlier production for *Camino Real* in 1951 was put on hold because of casting and financial problems. As Williams wrote to his mother in December 1951: 'Nobody came forth with much money for it!' (*L II*, 410). By June 1952, Williams was still looking for producers for the play (*L II*, 434; cf. 436–37).
45. *N*, 559.
46. Qtd. in ibid., 538.
47. *L II*, 463.
48. *DLB*, 139.
49. Williams, 'The Theatre', 3. See also *LDW*, 273–80 and 283–90.
50. Before departing, Merlo's female friend, Ellen, had become 'hysterical over his departure and had to be supported off the boat' (*N*, 566). Given this event, and the naked photo of herself that Williams and Merlo's landlady at 45 via Aurora in Rome, Mariella, had given to Merlo, it is altogether possible that some of Merlo's sexual encounters while living with Williams were also heterosexual. Even if this were true, and there is no irrefutable proof, there is no evidence that Williams knew of Merlo's potential bisexuality.
51. *N*, 569.
52. *L II*, 483–84.

53. Steen, 149.
54. Though Williams had already written a poem with the same title, it is possible that his encounters in Barcelona in mid-July 1953 with Jean Cocteau and his 'fils adoptif', Jean Marais, might have influenced his change of title. Cocteau had adapted his 1926 play into the film in 1950.
55. *L II*, 490; *N*, 575. In a 29 June 1953 letter to Wood, Williams wrote that he and Britneva had just seen the final performances of *The Rose Tattoo* in Paris. Britneva, whose mother knew the actress playing Serafina, 'hit it off like a house afire, to the tune of thousands of francs at Russian night-clubs at my expense' (*L II*, 489). As Williams wrote in his notebook a year later in August 1954, 'It's hard for my friends to realize that my economic resources are less than infinite' (*N*, 651). Once Britneva married Lord Peter St Just in July 1956, Williams asked Wood to take her off 'my pay-roll': 'I think we might drop her, now, and the funds can be diverted to my old maid Aunt in Knoxville if that venerable spinster survives [...]' (*L II*, 626). By October 1956, she was back on his pay roll (*L II*, 636).
56. *LDW*, 281.
57. Bowles described this voyage in detail to Mike Steen in *A Look at Tennessee Williams* (148–49).
58. Visconti was not happy with Bowles's work, so out of a sense of obligation to the Italian master who had hired Bowles on his recommendation, Williams completed the work and shared the film credits.
59. *L II*, 497, 499; *LDW*, 284.
60. *N*, 595.
61. Ibid.
62. Ibid., 583.
63. *L II*, 502.
64. *L II*, 593, 625; *M*, 126–27; *KS*, 206.
65. *N*, 607; cf. 677.
66. Ibid.
67. In June 1954, he wrote in his notebook about planning a trip to the Orient: 'A lot depends on what sort of money comes through from the films. Next year, unless the films pay, I'll be in a much lower income bracket' (*N*, 641).
68. *N*, 609, 611.
69. *M*, 109.
70. *N*, 633.
71. *L II*, 545.
72. Ibid., 535.
73. Ibid., 532, 537. His notebook entry about this event contrasts sharply with Britneva's version in *Five O'Clock Angel* (*FOA*, 91, 93): 'Maria is with us. I am getting adjusted to the situation but at first it seemed a rather trying complication, fond as I am of her. A girl in the house is a strain! And Maria does need attention, and I am selfish ... mostly the last item is relevant' (*N*, 643).
74. Ibid., 540.
75. On 5 August 1954, he wrote in his notebook:

Thurs. A.M. – A bright day without the weight of Roman summer. I woke too early, about 6:30, and applied medication and sat in hot water (bidet) to relieve rectal trouble, which is not serious, so far, except as an apprehension. Read 'Death In the Afternoon' by Hemingway with ever increasing respect for it as a great piece of prose, and honest acknowledgment of a lust which is nearly always concealed. H's great quality, aside from his prose style, which is matchless, is this fearless expression of brute nature, his almost naively candid braggadocia. If he drew pictures of pricks, he could not more totally confess his innate sexual inversion, despite the probability that his relations have been exclusively (almost?) with women. He has no real interest in women and shows no true heterosexual eroticism in any of his work.

(I don't think this is just the usual desire to implicate others in one's own 'vice'.)

Hemingway calls El Greco, whom he greatly admires, 'El Rey de Maricones' – perhaps in literature H. deserves the same crown. (*N*, 649)

76. Ibid., 657; cf. *FOA*, 105–106. For a detailed account of Britneva's complex friendship with Williams, see John Lahr's excellent essay, 'The Lady and Tennessee', and most of Bruce Smith's *Costly Performances*, especially chapter eight (96–106). See also Paul Bowles's comment about her to Mike Steen (*A Look at Tennessee Williams*, 149).
77. Steen, 60.
78. *L II*, 369.
79. Ibid., 374.
80. Ibid., 517–18.
81. The essay has nothing in common with the piece he published in *Harper's Bazaar* in February 1955, 'The Rose Tattoo in Key West'.
82. FTTW, MSS 562 (615), 'Notes on the Filming of "Rose Tattoo"', 2–3.
83. See Palmer and Bray, 99–121.
84. Cf. *N*, 511: 'Wrote a pretty good poem this A.M.'. Williams often thought his poetry was 'Piddling' or 'dull, most of them' (*N*, 549, 547). Yet he did spend a lot of time as well on certain poems: 'This evening, to get something <u>done</u>, I sent off a bunch of poems to Laughlin after working more on "The Dangerous Painters". It <u>could</u> be a fine poem with more work on it' (*N*, 341).
85. *KS*, 306.
86. *FOA*, 58. In July 1952, en route from Paris to Rome, Williams wrote the story, then penned the amended sentence in his letter to her: 'Will send you a story to sell for me (with commission) in London, wrote on the train'. That he gave it Britneva and not to Audrey Wood to place in a publication is a good indication of what he thought the story was worth, artistically and financially speaking. It is not by chance that the stories Williams rated among his best, such as 'Three Players of a Summer Game', took him over a year to finish.
87. *N*, 525.
88. Parker, 'A Preliminary Stemma', 81.
89. *L II*, 521.
90. *KS*, 220.
91. *N*, 633.
92. Ibid.; *L II*, 524.
93. *N*, 631.
94. *L II*, 536.
95. Ibid., 549.

96. *N*, 663.
97. *L II*, 554.
98. *FOA*, 103.
99. Ibid., 555–58. If Kazan was never convinced of Brick's paralysis, or of Williams's explanation for it, it may have been due to the fact that Kazan was battling his own identity politics before HUAC and needed clarity and resolution in Brick, as he did in himself.
100. *N*, 667.
101. *NSE*, 73.
102. *L II*, 570; cf. 555–56 and *N*, 663.
103. Kerr, 'A Secret Is Half-Told', 4: 1.
104. *NSE*, 76.
105. *NSE*, 77–78.
106. A few months later, in an interview for *Theatre Arts*, Williams would reiterate his theory to Arthur Waters:

> Brick is definitely not a homosexual [...]. Brick's self-pity and recourse to the bottle are not the result of a guilty conscience in that regard. When he speaks of 'self-disgust,' he is talking in the same vein as that which finds him complaining bitterly about having had to live so long with 'mendacity.' He feels that the collapse and premature death of his great friend Skipper, who never appears in the play, have been caused by unjust attacks against his moral character made by outsiders, including Margaret (Maggie), the wife. It is his bitterness at Skipper's tragedy that has caused Brick to turn against his wife and find solace in drink, rather than any personal involvement, although I do suggest that, at least at some time in his life, there have been unrealized abnormal tendencies. (73)

Ironically, Williams wrote the editors of *Theatre Arts* in the fall of 1955, complaining to them that he never said what Water's quoted him as having said:

> It is true that the interview took place; it took place very dimly, almost unconsciously, during the dreadful last week before the New York opening of my play *Cat*. But even considering the conditions under which I had this interview, I am not able to believe that I actually said the things that I am directly quoted as having said... [...] My article in the [New York] *Herald Tribune* deals accurately with my attitude toward Brick's sexual nature, not the one given in quotes in this interview. (*L II*, 589–90)

107. *TTW*, 3.114–15.
108. *L II*, 572; *FOA*, 112–13.
109. *M*, 176. Sagan translated Williams's *Sweet Bird of Youth* in 1971 at the request of André Barsacq, director at the Théâtre de l'atelier in Paris, though it remains unpublished (*FOA*, 245–46; cf. 276, 278, and 321).
110. Williams and Merlo did not hide their cruising from each other, often bringing trade back home when the other one was there. Williams even told Merlo that he was 'being careful, as careful as I can be' while in Spain, and hoped that Merlo was being careful, too (*L II*, 582).

111. *N*, 671.
112. *CTW*, 357. See Gindt, 'Tennessee Williams and the Swedish Academy: Why He Never Won the Nobel Prize', for more on the Swedish reception of *Cat on a Hot Tin Roof* and on Williams's nomination for the Nobel Prize.
113. *FOA*, 126–27; *N*, 687.
114. *L II*, 599–605.
115. Ibid., 236.
116. Ibid., 599; cf. *M*, 98 and *CTW*, 122. Another version has it that Bankhead camped up her performance in her final dress rehearsal, which is the night Williams attended, but played the role straight after that.
117. 'People'. *Time* 13 February 1956. See also *Time* 12 March 1956 for the follow-up story and Williams's 'tremulous letter' to the *New York Times*.
118. See also *L II*, 601–603.
119. Ibid., 604.
120. Playbill, n.pag.; rpt. in *N*, 686.
121. Hayman, 164; *FOA*, 138.
122. *L II*, 625.
123. It was around this time that *Time* magazine published a review by Robert Elliot Fitch, who cited Williams and Hemingway as being 'high priests' of the '*mystique de la merde*'. Williams's rebuttal, 'Mal de Merde', defended *Cat*'s moral message.
124. 'New Picture', 61.
125. *N*, 689.
126. Ibid. Nearly all of his notebook entries over the next couple of months end with his signature salutation, evidence of the nadir he had reached.

7   New York to New York (via Miami): A Battle of Angles

1. *M*, 146; *L II*, 502.
2. *N*, 671.
3. Ibid., 701.
4. Ibid., 706; cf. 705, 707. Williams told Windham that he was to enter the Centre on 18 June (*LDW*, 294).
5. TWPHL, MS Thr 397 (733), 'Life before Work', [3].
6. *M*, 173. Tom Buckley, for instance, writes that 'Dr. Kubie tried unsuccessfully to change his sexual orientation' (*CTW*, 169), and Ronald Hayman writes that 'Dr. Kubie was hoping to turn his patient into a heterosexual […]' (170).
7. *CTW*, 245.
8. See Paller, 'The Couch and Tennessee'.
9. Ibid., 46–47.
10. *NSE*, 82.
11. Ibid., 90.
12. *L II*, 615.
13. Ibid., 628–29 and 636–37.
14. *N*, 701.
15. Qtd. in *N*, 706.

16. *FOA*, 150.
17. Ibid., 141. Williams explained to his mother and brother that the doctor looking after Rose at Stoney Lodge, where Williams had recently placed her, suggested mild shock treatments as a treatment for her 'present phase of disturbance' (*L II*, 643).
18. Ibid., 145. Merlo requested the help of café owner and proprietor Johnny Nicholson in decorating the apartment. Williams makes reference to Nicholson's '*Victorian chic*' style in the stage setting to his one-act play *A Cavalier for Milady* (c. mid-1970s–1980) (*TC*, 49).
19. *M*, 173, 174–76; *NSE*, 94–95.
20. *TTW*, 3.357.
21. Ibid., 3.415, 3.422.
22. Ibid., 3.355, 3.356.
23. Ibid., 3.415.
24. Ibid., 3.375.
25. *N*, 649.
26. *LDW*, 215.
27. Palmer and Bray, 153.
28. *CTW*, 154.
29. *KS*, 251.
30. *FOA*, 151.
31. Qtd. in *N*, 716.
32. In the fragment titled 'Bits and pieces of shop-talk' (TWPC, box 25, folder 2), Williams attempted to psychoanalyse himself by trying to figure out why he told Rip Torn that he was glad Geraldine Page was through and why he did not like her during the run of *Sweet Bird of Youth*:

    > But why did I say 'Oh, good!' when informed that she thought I didn't like her? Was it because I thought that she was demonstrating more taste and intelligence than I had credited her with, despite the fact that I credited her with such an exceptional amount of those qualities? No, that's probably not the reason, the true explanation. The closest I can come to figuring out the impulse back of my odd response is that I feet a betterr relation can exist between two persons who assume, rightly or wrongly, that they function better together, ~~collaboratively~~ as artists, without any kind of sentimental involvement. [1]

33. *KS*, 238.
34. Though written in March 1953 after the death of his adored maternal grandmother, Rosina Maria Francesca Otte Dakin, 'Grand' was published much later in a limited edition of 326 copies by House of Books, 15 December 1964. See TWPHL, MS Thr 397 (727 and 728).
35. TWPHL, MS Thr 397 (764), 'Some Free Associations'.
36. That his mother's biography was just published in 1963 probably added to his taking up the subject of his father once again. Williams no doubt wanted to proffer his version of his family, particularly of his father, whom he had by now come to respect.
37. *N*, 711.

38. *CTW*, 48.
39. Qtd. in *N*, 718.
40. *KS*, 254.
41. TWPHL, MS Thr 397 (753), 'A Playwright's Prayer in Rehearsal', [1]. This was crossed out in pencil. Multiple versions of this prayer exist in the Houghton collection.
42. *N*, 493.
43. Qtd. in *N*, 492.
44. Ibid.
45. Qtd. in *N*, 506.
46. Williams, *The Enemy: Time*, 16.
47. Ibid., 15.
48. Ibid., 16.
49. *TTW*, 4.85.
50. *N*, 695–97.
51. Ibid., 717, 723.
52. Qtd. in *N*, 716.
53. *LDW*, 299–300.
54. TWPHL, MS Thr 397 (765), 'Some Memorandae for a Sunday Times Piece that I Am Too Tired to Write', [1].
55. *NSE*, 93.
56. TWPHL, MS Thr 397 (753), 'A Playwright's Prayer in Rehearsal', [3].
57. *M*, 67; cf. 65, 111, and 112.
58. *M*, 68. Tynan's version recalls that 'Castro strode over to meet us' and in 'clumsy but clearhearted English' he had told 'Tennessee how much he had admired his plays, above all the one about the cat that was upon a burning roof' (*Right and Left*, 336).
59. For more on Williams's meeting with Hemingway, see my book, Homo americanus.
60. Tynan, [Review of *Sweet Bird of Youth*], 98. In *Right and Left*, Tynan adds that was he nervous when seeing Williams at the Hotel Nacional in Havana the following month: 'I flinched; because a few days earlier I had given his latest play, *Sweet Bird of Youth*, an extremely damaging review that included references to dust bowls and sterility' (*Right and Left*, 332).
61. Brustein, 59.
62. *NSE*, 193.
63. *CTW*, 40.
64. TWPHL, MS Thr 397 (756), ['Reply to Professor Brustein'], [14].
65. Ibid., [1].
66. TWPHL, MS Thr 397 (780), 'Twenty Years of It', [1].
67. *M*, 153–54.
68. TWPHL, MS Thr 397 (780), 'Twenty Years of It', [1].
69. TWPHL, MS Thr 397 (729), 'Incomplete ... (some fragments of my life)', [1].
70. TWPHL, MS Thr 397 (730), 'Lean Years', [1].
71. TWPHL, MS Thr 397 (740), 'The Middle Years of a Writer', [3], [1].
72. TWPHL, MS Thr 397 (742), 'The Mornings, Afternoons, and Evenings of Writers', [1].
73. *FOA*, 169.

8   Tokyo to St Louis (via Spoleto): The Stoned(wall) Age

1. Rader, 257.
2. *NSE*, 149.
3. As Thomas Keith writes of Williams's sense of comedy, 'On the page the drama dominates, but performance can reveal wit, earthiness and comic rhythms found in most of Williams's plays. In much of his later work, from the 1960s and 1970s, the humor is often recognizable or broad – slapstick, grotesque, even the Grand Guignol – and sometimes even reads like comedy' (*HNMS*, xv).
4. TWPHL, MS Thr 397 (370 and 470) and (804), 'Williams's Guignol', [1].
5. *NSE*, 154.
6. Ibid., 156.
7. Ibid.
8. Ibid., 157.
9. *LDW*, 309.
10. TWPHL, MS Thr 397 (818) and (822), 'Unidentified essays'. [2] and [20], respectively.
11. *CS*, 240.
12. Ibid.
13. TWPC, 'Some Philosophical Shop Talk, or An Inventory of a Remarkable Market' (box 25, folder 2). It constitutes ten pages of free-association writing that was written in the fall of 1960 after Hurricane Donna struck the Florida Keys that September.
14. Ibid., [3].
15. Ibid., [4–5].
16. Ibid., [5].
17. Mannes, 16. Mannes's title refers to the success of Alan J. Lerner and Frederick Lowes's 1956 Broadway musical, *My Fair Lady*, which ran for a then-record 2,717 performances.
18. *NSE*, 85.
19. TWPHL, MS Thr 397 (725), 'The Good Men & the Bad Men', [5].
20. TWPHL, MS Thr 397 (726), 'The Good Men & the Bad Men', [1].
21. *CTW*, 77.
22. TWPC, ['The last time I wrote …'] (box 25, folder 2), [1].
23. TWPC, ['and in this way we fight the bang-bang'] (box 25, folder 2), [3].
24. *KS*, 271.
25. *CTW*, 64–65.
26. *FOA*, 158.
27. Ibid., 175. Of the trip with Vaccaro, Williams called it not a 'vacation-trip but the seven stations of the cross' (*FOA*, 175).
28. *CTW*, 79.
29. Williams referred to the incident with Laughlin as the 'Pigeon Drop'. See *FOA*, 242. In one page of an 'Unidentified essay' [c. 1971] (TWPHL, MS Thr 397 [818]), Williams writes:

> Recently a friend and business-associate said to me over the phone, 'Tennessee, why don't you write your autobiography now?'
> I disliked and resented this suggestion because I felt there was an implication in it that my career as a playwright was now completed, and,

      although I am now in my fifties, I am no more interested in retirement
      honorable or dishonorable, than I was when I first started to write plays,
      about thirty years ago. [18]

30. *NSE*, 130, 131. Wood, who founded the Liebling-Wood Agency in 1937, worked for the Music Corporation of America (MCA) when it was purchased 1954. MCA was the giant in the talent industry, representing so many of the biggest stars in Hollywood that the Justice Department, under directions from Robert Kennedy, ordered its break-up in July 1962 as part of an anti-trust suit. She then worked for Ashley-Steiner-Famous in 1962, which became the International Famous Agency and was later acquired by the International Creative Management in 1974.
31. *N*, 205, 207, and 209.
32. *M*, 56. See also *LDW*, 12 and *L I*, 268, 270.
33. *L I*, 279; *L I*, 277.
34. Ibid., 278; *L I*, 281.
35. *TTW*, 4.255.
36. Ibid., 4.266.
37. Ibid., 4.339.
38. Ibid., 4.317.
39. Ibid., 4.344.
40. Ibid., 4.352–53.
41. Ibid., 4.353.
42. Ibid., 4.359.
43. *CTW*, 99.
44. *NSE*, 138–39.
45. *M*, 191.
46. Playbill, 'Grand Kabuki', May 1960, n.pag.
47. *TTW*, 5.43.
48. Ibid., 5.3.
49. Debusscher, 'French Stowaways on an American Milk Train: William, Cocteau and Peyrefitte', 405. He argues that Williams was probably working from the original French text (1946) instead of Ronald Duncan's 1947 translation. While it is true that Williams read French (though how well remains uncertain), there was another English edition of *L'aigle à deux têtes* available to him: the Carl Wildman translation for Hill and Wang in 1961. Given this version's later date, which coincides more closely with the drafting of *Milk Train*, it is more probable that Williams used this translation, which is a much more accurate one than the Duncan version.
50. Ibid., 403.
51. Cocteau, *The Eagle with Two Heads*, 243.
52. TWCD, 'A Woman Owns an Island', [1].
53. Ibid., 271, 260 and 253.
54. *TC*, 79.
55. Ibid., emphasis added.
56. Cocteau, *The Eagle with Two Heads*, 281.
57. *TC*, 83.
58. Cocteau, *The Eagle with Two Heads*, 282.

59. *TC*, 84.
60. Ibid., 87.
61. 'Dame Picque' (TWPC, box 8, folder 8) is undated but it might have been written in the autumn of 1955, or at least that autumn inspired its writing. Williams called Carson McCullers 'Dame Picque' in a 17 July 1955 letter to Maria Britneva, and in September 1955 he was staying in a plush hotel in Hamburg that 'looks like the throne-room of a very pretentious nineteenth-century Balkan monarch!' (*FOA*, 128).
62. *TC*, front matter.
63. *NSE*, 85.
64. *M*, 187.
65. *FOA*, 185; *CTW*, 110.
66. *M*, 194.
67. Hayman, 200.
68. Ibid.
69. *KS*, 294.
70. *CTW*, 114; cf. 'wonderful doctors like Doctor Max', 120. See also *CTW*, 130, 148.
71. *N*, 715.
72. *NSE*, 147.
73. Ibid., 149, emphasis added.
74. *FOA*, 190.
75. *LDW*, 316.
76. *CTW*, 120; cf. 109.
77. *FOA*, 169.
78. Ibid., 174.
79. *MT*, 224–25. Williams recalls in his essay (*NSE*, 152) and in *Memoirs* that Merlo had the dog put to sleep, which added another degree of separation to their life together (*M*, 180–82).
80. HRC, 'A Thing Called Personal Lyricism', [5, 6].
81. In one fragment to 'Prelude to a Comedy' (c. 1960) that begins ['The last time I did a piece for the Sunday Times …'] (TWPC, box 25, folder 2), Williams wrote, 'You see I'm still doing it! Justifying, explaining, the facts of my life. I guess this is a dodge. I do it to avoid doing another kind of piece, an "Apologia" for the work about to be exposed on the Broadway stage' [1].
82. *NSE*, 153.
83. *KS*, 296–97. Maria St Just claims that this trip was made not with Glavin but with a new travelling companion, Harry O'Lowe: 'I know nothing about him' (*FOA*, 194).
84. *MT*, 207.
85. *KS*, 300.
86. *FOA*, 194.
87. *NSE*, 153. T. E. Kalem of *Time* reviewed the play's 24 January 1980 premiere at the Tennessee Williams Fine Arts Center of Florida Keys Community College: 'Pensive and muted, a violin to *Camino Real*'s trumpet, *Mr. Merriwether* laces together reality and fantasy, the romantic spirit and the appearance of actual cultural heroes of the past, such as Van Gogh and Rimbaud'.

88. Rader, 137.
89. *KS*, 300.
90. *TTW*, 5.205.
91. Ibid., 5.201, 5.207.
92. Hofmann, 54.
93. *L I*, 538.
94. Hayman, 207; *KS*, 307.
95. *KS*, 309.
96. *CTW*, 139, 134–35.
97. *NSE*, 211.
98. *CTW*, 208.
99. Ibid., 173–74.
100. Williams, 'Last Will and Testament', 84.
101. Ibid., 85. In his interview with Buckley in 1970, Williams describes the essential articles to his 11 September 1980 will and testament, though he calls the Fund here the 'Rose Isabelle Williams Foundation for creative writers' (*CTW*, 176–77).
102. Ibid., 84.
103. Lahr, 'The Lady and Tennessee', 242.
104. Dakin took to driving around the state on a motorcycle with an American flag painted on the helmet. Williams believed he was 'running for [...] the title or office of America's biggest eccentric. – Possibly that could be a successful campaign, in view of Tricky Dick's triumph this week' in the November 1972 elections. By 1977, Dakin was running for Governor of Illinois. By 1984, he was hoping to run for President (*FOA*, 277).
105. *CP*, 151.
106. *FOA*, 203; *CTW*, 179–80.
107. *CP*, 153.

9   Key West to New York (via Bangkok): In Search of Androgyny

1. *FOA*, 381.
2. Williams, 'Proceedings', 28. In one fragment of his essay 'Which Sea-Gull on What Corner?' (TWPHL, MS Thr 397 [801]), Williams had this to say about the event:

> And, gosh but this is one hell of a deviation from the straight story-line, but I recall that a journalist present at this occasion said, later, that I wobbled up to the dais to receive the gold medal as if I were walking on post-toasties and that I received and acknowledged this award with a very vulgar anecdote, which is the only accuracy of which this particular journalist can be accused, since on that same occasion he asked me if he could interview me for Esquire, and I had just sufficient awareness of situation to tell him that I was not in condition to be interviewed, as so he wrote for Esquire a piece called "A Dream of Tennessee Williams" [...]. [2]

This refers to Donald Newlove's essay on him in November 1969.

3. *FOA*, 203.
4. *CTW*, 158; cf. 186.
5. Ibid., 233.
6. *TTW*, 5.321.
7. Ibid., 5.328.
8. *NSE*, 211.
9. Ibid., 212.
10. Ibid.
11. Ibid., 213. He offered these notes to Thomas P. Adler at Purdue University in April 1972, when the play was given a stage reading by Olive Deering and her brother Alfred Ryder. He came to West Lafayette, Indiana, to speak at the university's Literary Awards Ceremony. Later that year, he travelled to the University of Hartford in Connecticut to receive an honorary doctorate.
12. *CTW*, 209.
13. Weil, 11.
14. Ibid.
15. *CTW*, 212.
16. Ibid., 209.
17. Ibid., 229.
18. Quinby, 12.
19. Ibid.
20. *KS*, 325.
21. *FOA*, 217–21. There is a folder containing drafts of Williams's rebuttal, ['An open letter to Mr. Tom Buckley'] (TWPHL, MS Thr 397 [774]). Even as late as 1974, he complains about Buckley in his 'White Paper' (TWPHL, MS Thr 397 [802]), where he notes Dakin's response to his request for a law suit.
22. *FOA*, 217.
23. TWPHL, MS Thr 397 (808), 'Unidentified Essay for the Sunday *New York Times*', [2].
24. *FOA*, 219.
25. Ibid., 263.
26. Qtd. in *KS*, 330; cf. *FOA*, 231–32.
27. See *FOA*, 269.
28. TWPHL, MS Thr 397 (822), 'Unidentified essays', [37].
29. *DLB*, 313.
30. In his handwritten note to Williams that was attached to a Photostat of the memoirs, Rader wrote that he 'ought to tell <u>more</u> about the early years' [1]. See TWPHL, MS Thr 397 (787), 'Waiting for That Sea Gull, or Some Memoirs of a Con-Man'.
31. *FOA*, 233.
32. Ibid., 253.
33. Rader, who accompanied Williams to the rally, recounts the events more fully in *Tennessee: Cry of the Heart*, 85, 107, and 111–15.
34. FTTW, MSS 562 (637), ['... are its social aims ...'], [1].
35. *MT*, 229.
36. *NSE*, 164.
37. FTTW, MSS 562 (610), 'Final Materiel' [*sic*], [2].
38. *NSE*, 160; cf. *NSE*, 66.

39. TWPHL, MS Thr 397 (769), 'Sunday Peace', [1–2]. This piece is connected to one at the FTTW, MSS 562 (646; cf. 645), that opens ['We are now into the seventies …'] and that is dated 20 December 1971.
40. *FOA*, 287.
41. Ibid., 270.
42. Ibid.
43. TWPHL, MS Thr 397 (764a), 'Some Random Additions to my Memoirs', n.pag. Williams was now using the French spelling *materiels* of the word 'materials' for the title of his memoirs because of its military connotations.
44. *FOA*, 271.
45. Ibid., 276. By early December 1972, Doubleday contacted Williams to work with him on editing the book. Writing to St Just on 4 December, Williams noted: 'Also the Doubleday editor [Medina] wants to start working with me immediately on my memoirs which look like telephone books of a big city, the boroughs Manhattan and Brooklyn' (*FOA*, 279; cf. Rader, 247). Then, on 18 April 1973, he sent St Just two more pages of what he called '*Material*' (she corrected Williams's French spelling of the word) for memoirs that he hoped still to insert into the manuscript (*FOA*, 288–89).
46. Palmer and Bray, 288.
47. *NSE*, 176.
48. *FOA*, 287; cf. 302.
49. Ibid.
50. *CTW*, 302; *FOA*, 286.
51. TWPHL, MS Thr 397 (782), '"Vieux Carré" and the "Cherry Blossom Cruise"', [1]. See also HRC, ['Vieux Carré was started on a steamship …'], [1].
52. *FOA*, 287.
53. Ibid., 288.
54. Ibid., 295. Williams was no doubt drawn to the lines 'They are my two thin ladies/named Blanche and Rose'.
55. Ibid., 296.
56. *CS*, 506.
57. Ibid., 510.
58. *CS*, 529. Miss Coynte takes it upon herself to resolve the Southern struggle for black/white hegemony by having a child with one of the identical black twins, Mike and Moon. She believes herself, after what she interprets as a sign from God, to be the new Madonna, and Mike or Moon will be the Joseph to the new Messiah. Twenty years later, the child, a 'duskily handsome' (*CS*, 530) girl named Michele Moon, engages 'the young colored gatekeeper in shameless sexual play', and Miss Coynte feels she has left her 'mission in good hands' (*CS*, 531–32).
59. *FOA*, 311.
60. *MWR*, 99. Several times in his later interviews, Williams said, apparently in jest, that he was an octoroon (*CTW*, 90; *NSE*, 154).
61. Ibid., 18.
62. Ibid., 81, 115, and 137.
63. *KS*, 101, 346.
64. Ibid., 174, 11, 106, and 135.
65. *M*, 261–62, *MRW*, 50–51; *M*, 280–81, *MWR*, 79–80; *M*, 299, *MWR*, 128; *M*, 313, *MWR*, 139; *M*, 155, *MWR*, 150–51; and *M*, 1–2, *MWR*, 162–63.
66. *MWR*, 38–39, emphasis added.

67. *M*, 173.
68. Ibid., xviii.
69. *DLB*, 301.
70. Kalem, 'Of Sin and Grace', 84; Lehmann-Haupt, 35; Richardson, 42; and Gussow, 49.
71. *M*, 144.
72. Ibid., 153–54. He repeated this in an interview with William Burroughs in 1973, saying, 'There's something very private about writing [...]. Somehow it's better, talking about one's most intimate sexual practices – you know – than talking about writing' (*CTW*, 304–305).
73. *Atlanta Constitution*, B8.
74. HRC, 'These Scattered Idioms', [1].
75. Qtd. in *KS*, 338.
76. Williams, 'Tennessee Williams Writes', 26.
77. Ibid.
78. Ibid.
79. 'Barton', 2: 1.
80. *TTW*, 1.321.
81. *NSE*, 172.
82. Whitmore, 315, 320.
83. *MWR*, 139.
84. Williams, 'Tennessee Williams Writes', 26.
85. *FOA*, 317, 323.
86. FTTW, MSS 562 (639), ['in my present and future plans'], [1].
87. Kolin, *Tennessee Williams: A Guide to Research and Performance*, 199.
88. TWPHL, MS Thr 397 (803), 'White Paper', [1].
89. FTTW, MSS 562 (640), 'Afterword', [2]. See also MSS 562 (641, 643 and 644).
90. Kolin, *Guide to Research and Performance*, 200. See Lothar Schmidt-Mühlisch's 1975 interview with Williams, 'Life Is a Black Joke', just prior to the opening (*CTW*, 296–98).
91. *CTW*, 292.
92. The near-final version of the essay is at TWPHL, MS Thr 397 (741), 'The Misunderstanding and Fears of an Artist's Revolt'.
93. *NSE*, 189.
94. Ibid., 218. In the fall of 1980, Williams accepted the offer of a Distinguished Writer-in-Residence post at the University of British Columbia. Part of the deal was that they produce *Red Devil*. On 17 October, Williams wrote to St Just that the 'play is now tight as a fist, cut to 80 pages, about twenty less than it was in England, every superfluous bit eliminated' (*FOA*, 381–82).
95. TWPHL, MS Thr 397 (809), 'Unidentified Essay on Artists' Reputations', [1]. Parts of this fragment version were translated into French for the newspaper.
96. *N*, 739.
97. *FOA*, 372.
98. *NSE*, 181–82.
99. TWPHL, MS Thr 397 (810), 'Unidentified Essay on the Genesis of *Eccentricities of a Nightingale*', [2].
100. *FOA*, 360.
101. Williams, 'Tennessee Williams – Donald Windham', 14, 18. See also *N*, 749.

102. There are variations of this essay fragment at the HRC (box 51, folder 12) and the TWPHL, MS Thr 397 (782, 783, and 91), '"Vieux Carré" and the "Cherry Blossom Cruise".
103. See both TWPHL, MS Thr 397 (782), '"Vieux Carré" and the "Cherry Blossom Cruise"', [3] and HRC, 'Finally Something New', [1].
104. *TTW*, 8.82.
105. *FOA*, 331; Prosser, 101.
106. TWPHL, MS Thr 397 (782), '"Vieux Carré" and the "Cherry Blossom Cruise"', [9].
107. *NSE*, 185.
108. This fragment at the HRC uses the expression 'ghost of a writer' who was 'still ambulatory' – terms that come straight from his *New York Times* essay on *Vieux Carré* – and is similar in title and general theme to two other essays that he wrote in 1973, 'Experiments of the Sixties' (HRC, box 51, folder 12) and 'Experiments of the Sixties and Further Plans' (TWPHL, MS Thr 397 [717]). The second essay is the same as the one at HRC but edited in Williams's hand. He had crossed out the reference to his receiving an award that evening, which prompted the initial writing of the essay, and on top of the first page he typed in the existing titled, 'and Further Plans'.
109. *CTW*, 302.
110. FTTW, MSS 562 (643), ['Keith Baxter has been ...'], [1].
111. Ibid.
112. *FOA*, 360.
113. Hayman, 231; *FOA*, 323.
114. *TTW*, 8.167.
115. Ibid., 8.136.
116. Ibid., 8.173.
117. Ibid., 8.172, 8.173.
118. *CTW*, 309. The history of the play from genesis to production is recounted in Ira Bilowit's 1979 interview, 'Roundtable: Tennessee Williams, Craig Anderson and T. E. Kalem Talk about *Creve Coeur*'.
119. Harris, 183.
120. *N*, 753; *FOA*, 372.
121. Prosser, xviii. 'Arctic Light' is currently miscataloged at TWPHL under 'D: Essays', MS Thr 397 (707).
122. TWPHL, MS Thr 397 (32).
123. Ibid., 737.
124. Ibid., 739.
125. Ibid.
126. Ibid., 741.
127. Ibid.
128. Ibid., 747.
129. Ibid., 753.
130. Qtd. in ibid., 755.
131. Carter, 'Presidential Medal of Freedom Remarks at the Presentation Ceremony', 9 June 1980. Online by Gerhard Peters and John T. Woolley, *The American Presidency Project*. Available at http://www.presidency.ucsb.edu/ws/?pid=45389 (3 April 2012).
132. Stamper, 355.

10 Chicago to St Louis (via Vancouver): '<u>Right (Write) On</u>!'

1. *CS*, 533.
2. Londré, n.pag. I thank her for having pointed out the reference to Joffre to everyone in Nancy, France, during the centennial conference there on Williams in June 2011.
3. *N*, 757.
4. *KS*, 383.
5. Qtd. in *N*, 759.
6. *TTW*, 8.202.
7. Ibid., Williams's ellipses.
8. Kerr, 'The Stage', 15; Barnes, 1.
9. Thomas P. Adler sees the play less as biographical drama and more, like *Vieux Carré* before it in 1978, as autobiographical drama, with it emerging, just as *The Glass Menagerie* had, as a 'play of guilt, spawned by the author's betrayal of the person closest to him' ('When Ghosts Supplant Memories', 6).
10. Elliott Martin, the play's Broadway producer, suggested this from the beginning when he told Donald Spoto, '[...] it's a play with a certain transferred paranoia – from the situation of Rose to that of Williams himself who [...] was blaming the critics and media for his own failures' (qtd. in *KS*, 384).
11. Kroll, 95; Sandomir, 5, 12.
12. Paller, *Gentlemen Callers*, 16.
13. Dorff, 'Collapsing Resurrection Mythologies', 157, 158.
14. Crandell, '"I Can't Imagine Tomorrow"', 170. Crandell reads the play as Williams's Postmodern 'critique of realism's and modernism's great faith in the future to remedy or cure the present (Kolin, *The Undiscovered Country*, 171).
15. Jenckes, 189.
16. *FOA*, 380. Another version of the play existed with the title 'The Everlasting Ticket, or The Fruit-Bat's Droppings' (TWPHL, MS Thr 397 [65-69]). Zelda makes reference to 'The Everlasting ticket that does not exist' (8.273) in act two of *Clothes for a Summer Hotel*.
17. Faulkner died in a tragic car accident a year later, bequeathing to Williams his Kentucky farm in Falling Timber.
18. *HNMS*, ix–x.
19. *FOA*, 381.
20. Ibid., 382–83.
21. *FOA*, 382.
22. *IB*, 330.
23. TWPHL, MS Thr 397 (804), 'Williams' Guignol', [1].
24. *TC*, xxvi.
25. Though published posthumously in a limited edition, *The Remarkable Rooming-house of Mme. Le Monde* 'was written two or three years before *Clothes for a Summer Hotel*', as Williams noted in June 1981 (TWPHL, MS Thr 397 (403), [verso 1]).
26. Kolin, 'Little Shop of Comic Horrors', 40.
27. *TC*, 102.
28. Kolin, '*The Remarkable Rooming-House of Mme. Le Monde*: Tennessee Williams's Little Shop of Comic Horrors', 40, all *sic*.

29. Hale, 'Three Plays for the Lyric Theatre', 93.
30. *N*, 763.
31. *TTW*, 7.324.
32. Ibid., 7.302, 7.329.
33. Ibid., 7.330.
34. Williams, 'Something Tennessee', 7.
35. Dorff, 'Theatricalist Cartoons', 19.
36. *TC*, 112.
37. Williams, 'Something Tennessee', 7.
38. *TC*, 308.
39. Rader, 154–55.
40. Kenan describes how Carroll, so wigged out on drugs, went over the edge and threatened Williams's cook, Roy, with a gun. Williams knew that his manuscripts were in danger as long as Carroll, whom he still loved but no longer considered a lover, was around (chapter two).
41. *IHDSR*, 1.
42. Ibid., 3.
43. Ibid., 34.
44. *CP*, 150.
45. *FOA*, 386. See TWPHL, MS Thr 397 [1246–1250].
46. Ibid., 390.
47. TWPHL, MS Thr 397 [730], 'Lean Years', [1].
48. Article VI of Williams's last will and testament, which was enacted on 11 September 1980, has all of his 'personal journals, diaries and other literary properties' destined to be given to the University of the South upon his death. However, a codicil was added in December 1982, just a couple months before his death, deleting the phrase 'University of the South' and replacing it with 'Harvard University' (90). The 'Chairman of the Creative Writing Department of Harvard University' was also made sole administrator of the Walter E. Dakin Memorial Fund, to which Williams bequeathed his entire Estate upon Rose's death.
49. Hayman, 237.
50. Qtd. in *N*, 765.
51. TWPHL, MS Thr 397 [804], 'Williams' Guignol', [1].
52. TWPHL, MS Thr 397 [219], 'A Monument for Ercole'.
53. TWPC, 'Valediction' (box 25, folder 1), [1–2].
54. Daley, 1: 1. Conspiracy stories around Williams's death began almost immediately after his body was cold. Dakin, Williams's brother, was certain that he was murdered and wrote a book about it, *His Brother's Keeper: The Life and Murder of Tennessee Williams*. More recently, fellow playwright Larry Myers announced his version of the cause of death to *The New York Post*: 'Williams did not choke on a nasal spray cap lodged in his windpipe as reported then ... No booze, no AIDS, no suicide, no murder – what media hungered for! "Acute Seconal intolerance" is what the autopsy report reveals. This has never been reported.' Scott Kenan, one of Williams's last secretaries, has charged *The New York Post* with adding unfounded details to Myers's story. See http://scottkenan.blogspot.fr/2010/02/fox-news-changes-tennessee-williams.html (5 April 2012).
55. Baden, 73.
56. Ibid.

11 Epilogue

1. *MT*, 235.
2. Other significant unpublished or unproduced Williams works worth exploring include 'Edible, Very' (1972, subtitled 'A Whore Sings at Daybreak: A Charade with Music'), 'The Wild Horses of the Camargue' (1976, also called 'Chien dans la Chambre'), 'The Everlasting Ticket' (1980), 'The Intruder, or Finally, at Dusk' (1980), 'Virgo' (1981?), 'A Monument for Ercole' (1982), 'The Lingering Hour: A Fantasy' (1982), 'Ivan's Widow' (1982), and 'Lady's Choice' (1982), to name only nine.
3. Smith, *Costly Performances*, 173.
4. Prosser, 235.
5. Williams, Article VIII of his 'Last Will and Testament', 86.
6. Lahr, 'Past Imperfect', 76.
7. Since 1996, monographs, articles and notes on Williams have largely surpassed those written on any other American playwright, Eugene O'Neill and Arthur Miller included.
8. I would like to thank Thomas Keith for having shared with me his compiled list of Williams's posthumous premieres.

Bibliography

Primary Sources

Williams, Tennessee [as Thomas Lanier Williams]. 'American Gothic'. Unpublished play [30 August 1937]. HRC, University of Texas at Austin, n.d.
—— '"Beauty Is the Word" and "Hot Milk at Three in the Morning"'. *Missouri Review* 7 (1984): 186–200.
—— 'Birth of an Art (Anton Chekhov and the New Theatre)'. Unpublished college essay [c. Spring 1937]. HRC, University of Texas at Austin, n.d.
—— 'Can a Good Wife Be a Good Sport?' *Smart Set*, May 1927: 9, 13.
—— [College spiral notebook] [c. 1936–37]. HRC, University of Texas at Austin, n.d.
—— 'Comments on the Nature of Artists with a few Specific References to the Case of Edgar Allan Poe'. Unpublished college essay [c. 1937]. HRC, University of Texas at Austin, n.d.
—— 'Cut Out'. Unpublished short story [8 March 1936]. HRC, University of Texas at Austin, n.d.
—— 'The Darkling Plain (For Bruno Hauptmann who Dies Tonight)'. Unpublished essay [c. 1936]. HRC, University of Texas at Austin, n.d.
—— 'A Day at the Olympics'. *U. City Pep* 9.2 (30 October 1928): 5.
—— 'A Festival Night in Paris'. *U. City Pep* 9.9 (5 March 1929): 2.
—— 'A Flight over London'. *U. City Pep* 9.4 (27 November 1928): 3.
—— ['I: Mr. Krutch is probably correct']. Unpublished college exam [c. 1936]. HRC, University of Texas at Austin, n.d.
—— 'In Spain There Was Revolution'. Eds. Nicholas Moshchovakis and David Roessel. *The Hudson Review* 56.1 (Spring 2003): 50–56.
—— 'Isolated'. *The Junior Life* 14.4 (7 November 1924): 2.
—— 'The Literary Mind by Max Eastman'. Unpublished college essay [c. 1936]. HRC, University of Texas at Austin, n.d.
—— 'Nirvana'. Unpublished short story [29 April 1936]. HRC, University of Texas at Austin, n.d.
—— 'A Night in Venice'. *U. City Pep* 9.5 (20 December 1928): 2, 4.
—— ['To Psyche']. Untitled poem on 'Red Goose Shoes' letterhead [c. 1933]. HRC, University of Texas at Austin, n.d.
—— 'A Report on Four Writers of the Modern Psychological School'. Unpublished college essay [c. 1936]. HRC, University of Texas at Austin, n.d.
—— 'Return to Dust (Via the Sorbonne and Cornell Universities)'. Unpublished essay. HRC, University of Texas at Austin, 1938.
—— 'Some Representative Plays of O'Neill and a Discussion of his Art'. Unpublished college essay [c. 1936]. HRC, University of Texas at Austin, n.d.
—— 'Somewhere a Voice....'. Unpublished college essay [c. 1932]. HRC, University of Texas at Austin, n.d.
—— 'Thinking Our Own Thoughts'. Unpublished essay [c. 1932]. HRC, University of Texas at Austin, n.d.

────── 'This Spring'. Unpublished short story [c. 8/9 March 1936]. HRC, University of Texas at Austin, n.d.

────── 'The Tomb of the Capuchins'. *U. City Pep* 9.3 (12 November 1928): 2, 5.

────── 'A Tour of the Battle-fields of France'. *U. City Pep* 9.8 (19 February 1928): 2.

────── 'A Trip to Monte Carlo'. *U. City Pep* 9.6 (16 January 1928): 2.

────── 'The Wounds of Vanity'. Unpublished college essay [c. 1930]. HRC, University of Texas at Austin, n.d.

────── ['Yesterday morning the city of Midland ...']. Unpublished college exercise [c. 1931]. HRC, University of Texas at Austin, n.d.

Williams, Tennessee. 'Afterword'. Fragment of essay [c. 1975]. MSS 562 (640). FTTW, Williams Research Center, Historic New Orleans Collection, n.d.

────── *American Blues*. 1948. New York: Dramatists Play Service, 1968.

────── ['and in this way we fight the bang-bang']. Fragment of the essay 'Prelude to a Comedy' [c. 1960]. TWPC, Rare Book and Manuscript Library, Columbia University, n.d.

────── *Androgyne, Mon Amour*. New York: New Directions, 1977.

────── ['... are its social aims...']. Fragment of a speech [c. December 1971]. MSS 562 (637). FTTW, Williams Research Center, Historic New Orleans Collection, n.d.

────── 'Bits and pieces of shop-talk'. Fragment for the essay 'Prelude to a Comedy' [c. 1960]. TWPC, Rare Book and Manuscript Library, Columbia University, n.d.

────── *Candles to the Sun*. Ed. Dan Isaac. New York: New Directions, 2004.

────── *Collected Poems*. Eds. Nicholas Moshchovakis and David Roessel. New York: New Directions, 2007.

────── *Collected Stories*. New York: New Directions, 1989.

────── *Conversations with Tennessee Williams*. Ed. Albert J. Devlin. Jackson: University of Mississippi Press, 1986.

────── 'Dame Picque'. Fragment of a play [c. 1955]. TWPC, Rare Book and Manuscript Library, Columbia University, n.d.

────── *Eight Mortal Ladies Possessed*. New York: New Directions, 1974.

────── *The Enemy: Time*. *Theatre* (March 1959): 14–17.

────── 'Experiments of the Sixties'. Fragment of an essay [c. 1973]. HRC, University of Texas at Austin, n.d.

────── 'Experiments of the Sixties and Further Plans'. Fragment of an essay [c. 1973]. MS Thr 397 (717). TWPHL, Houghton Library, Harvard University, n.d.

────── 'A Film in Sicily'. Finished essay. [c. 1948]. MSS 562 (602). FTTW, Williams Research Center, Historic New Orleans Collection, n.d.

────── 'Finally Something New'. Fragment of an essay [c. 1977]. HRC, University of Texas at Austin, n.d.

────── 'Final Materiel'. Fragment of *Memoirs* [c. September 1972]. MSS 562 (610). FTTW, Williams Research Center, Historic New Orleans Collection, n.d.

────── *Five O'Clock Angel: Letters of Tennessee Williams to Maria St Just, 1948–1982*. Ed. Maria St Just. New York: Knopf, 1990.

────── *Fugitive Kind*. Ed. Allean Hale. New York: New Directions, 2001.

────── 'The Good Men & the Bad Men'. Fragment of an essay [c. 1960]. MS Thr 397 (725 & 726). TWPHL, Houghton Library, Harvard University, n.d.

────── *Grand Kabuki*. Playbill, May 1960, n.pag.

────── 'The History of *Summer and Smoke*'. Playbill, 7 November 1949, n.pag.

—— *A House Not Meant to Stand*. Ed. Thomas Keith. New York: New Directions, 2008.

—— 'Incomplete... (some fragments of my life)'. Fragment of an essay [c. Fall 1953]. MS Thr 397 (729). TWPHL, Houghton Library, Harvard University, n.d.

—— ['in my present and future plans']. Fragment of an essay [c. June 1975]. MSS 562 (639). FTTW, Williams Research Center, Historic New Orleans Collection, n.d.

—— *It Happened the Day the Sun Rose*. Los Angeles: Sylvester & Orphanos, 1981.

—— ['Keith Baxter has been ...']. Fragment of an essay [c. September 1978]. MSS 562 (643). FTTW, Williams Research Center, Historic New Orleans Collection, n.d.

—— ['The last time I did a piece for the Sunday Times ...']. Fragment of the essay 'Prelude to a Comedy' [c. 1960]. TWPC, Rare Book and Manuscript Library, Columbia University, n.d.

—— ['The last time I wrote ...']. Fragment of an essay [c. 1960].TWPC, Rare Book and Manuscript Library, Columbia University, n.d.

—— 'Last Will and Testament of Tennessee Williams' (including the 1982 codicil). *Tennessee Williams Review* (Spring 1983): 83–90.

—— 'Lean Years'. Fragment of an essay [c. mid-1960s]. MS Thr 397 (730). TWPHL, Houghton Library, Harvard University, n.d.

—— 'A Letter to Irene'. Fragment of an essay [c. December 1940]. HRC, University of Texas at Austin, n.d.

—— 'A Letter to Irene'. Fragment of an essay [c. December 1940]. MS Thr 397 (732). TWPHL, Houghton Library, Harvard University, n.d.

—— 'Life before Work'. Fragment of an essay [c. 1959]. MS Thr 397 (733). TWPHL Houghton Library, Harvard University, n.d.

—— *The Magic Tower and Other One-Act Plays*. Ed. Thomas Keith. New York: New Directions, 2011.

—— 'Mal de Merde'. *Time*, 22 October 1956: 11–12.

—— [Medical prescription] [c. 1974]. MSS 562 (648). FTTW, Williams Research Center, Historic New Orleans Collection, n.d.

—— *Memoirs*. 1975. New York: New Directions, 2006.

—— 'The Middle Years of a Writer'. Fragment of an essay. MS Thr 397 (740). TWPHL, Houghton Library, Harvard University, 26 March 1959.

—— *Moise and the World of Reason*. New York: Simon and Shuster, 1975.

—— 'The Mornings, Afternoons, and Evenings of Writers'. Fragment of an essay [c. 1960]. MS Thr 397 (742). TWPHL, Houghton Library, Harvard University, n.d.

—— *Mister Paradise and Other One-act Plays*. Eds. Nicholas Moshchovakis and David Roessel. New York: New Directions, 2005.

—— 'The Misunderstanding and Fears of an Artist's Revolt'. MS Thr 397 (741). TWPHL, Houghton Library, Harvard University, March 1978.

—— 'A Movie by Cocteau'. *The New York Times*, 5 November 1950: 3, 41.

—— *New Selected Essays: Where I Live*. Ed. John S. Bak. New York: New Directions, 2009.

—— *Not about Nightingales*. Ed. Allean Hale. New York: New Directions, 1998.

—— *Notebooks*. Ed. Margaret Bradham Thornton. New Haven and London: Yale University Press, 2006.

—— 'Notes on the Filming of "Rose Tattoo"'. Unpublished essay. MSS 562 (615). FTTW, Williams Research Center, Historic New Orleans Collection, 21 April 1952.

—— ['An open letter to Mr. Tom Buckley']. Fragment of an essay [c. 1970]. MS Thr 397 (774). TWPHL, Houghton Library, Harvard University, n.d.
—— 'A Playwright's Prayer in Rehearsal'. Fragment of an essay [c. 1959]. MS Thr 397 (753). TWPHL, Houghton Library, Harvard University, n.d.
—— 'Praise for an Assenting Angel'. Draft of 'Introduction' to *Reflections in a Golden Eye* [c. May–July 1949]. MSS. 562 (616). FTTW, Williams Research Center, Historic New Orleans Collection, n.d.
—— 'Praise for an Assenting Angel'. Draft of 'Introduction' to *Reflections in a Golden Eye* [c. May 1949]. TWCD, (Ms 112). Special Collections Department, University of Delaware Library, n.d.
—— 'Proceedings of the American Academy of Arts and Letters and the National Institute of Arts and Letters'. New York, 1970: 28.
—— 'Provisional Film Story Treatment of "The Gentleman Caller"' [c. 1943]. MSS 562 (574). FTTW, Williams Research Center, Historic New Orleans Collection, n.d.
—— ['Reply to Professor Brustein']. Fragment of an essay [c. July 1959]. MS Thr 397 (756). TWPHL, Houghton Library, Harvard University, n.d.
—— 'The Sculptural Play'. Fragment of an essay [c. 1941–42]. MS THR 397 (759). TWPHL, Houghton Library, Harvard University, n.d.
—— 'The Sculptural Play (a method)'. Fragment of an essay [c. 1942]. HRC, University of Texas at Austin, n.d.
—— *The Selected Letters of Tennessee Williams.* Vol. I: *1920–1945.* Eds. Albert J. Devlin and Nancy M. Tischler. New York: New Directions, 2000.
—— *The Selected Letters of Tennessee Williams.* Vol. II: *1945–1957.* Eds. Albert J. Devlin and Nancy M. Tischler. New York: New Directions, 2004.
—— 'Some Free Associations'. Fragment of an essay [c. March 1959]. MS THR 397 (764). TWPHL, Houghton Library, Harvard University, n.d.
—— 'Some Philosophical Shop Talk, or An Inventory of a Remarkable Market'. Fragments of an essay [c. 1960]. TWPC, Rare Book and Manuscript Library, Columbia University, n.d.
—— 'Some Memorandae for a Sunday Times Piece that I Am Too Tired to Write'. Fragment of an essay [c. March 1961]. MS Thr 397 (765). TWPHL, Houghton Library, Harvard University, n.d.
—— 'Some Random Additions to my Memoirs'. Fragments of *Memoirs* [c. 1972–73]. MS Thr 397 (764a), TWPHL, Houghton Library, Harvard University, n.d.
—— 'Something Tennessee'. *Other Stages* 3.23 (30 July 1981): 7.
—— 'Some Words of Introduction'. Draft of 'Introduction' to *Reflections in a Golden Eye* [c. April 1949]. HRC, University of Texas at Austin, n.d.
—— *Something Cloudy, Something Clear.* New York: New Directions, 1995.
—— *Spring Storm.* Ed. Dan Issac. New York: New Directions, 1999.
—— *Stairs to the Roof.* Ed. Allean Hale. New York: New Directions, 2000.
—— 'Stylistic Experiments in the Sixties ~~While Working Under the Influence of Speed~~'. Fragment of an essay [c. 1973]. HRC, University of Texas at Austin, n.d.
—— 'Sunday Peace'. Fragment of an essay [c. December 1971]. MS Thr 397 (769). TWPHL, Houghton Library, Harvard University, n.d.
—— 'Survival Notes: A Journal'. *Esquire* 78.3 (September 1973): 130–34, 166, 168.
—— 'Te Moraturi Salutamus'. Unpublished essay [c. April 1941]. HRC, University of Texas at Austin, n.d.

—— 'Tennessee Williams – Donald Windham'. *New York Times*, 15 January 1978: 14, 18.

—— *Tennessee Williams' Letters to Donald Windham, 1940–1965*. Ed. Donald Windham. New York: Holt, Rinehart and Winston, 1977.

—— 'Tennessee Williams Writes'. *Gay Sunshine* 31 (Winter 1977): 26.

—— ['That Greek Island in times so ancient ...']. Fragment of an essay [c. post-April 1961]. TWPC, Rare Book and Manuscript Library, Columbia University, n.d.

—— 'The Theatre'. *The Playhouse*, program note, 13 May 1953, n.pag.

—— *The Theatre of Tennessee Williams*. 8 vols. New York: New Directions, 1971–92.

—— 'These Scattered Idioms'. Fragment of an essay [c. 1960/61]. MSS 562 (625). FTTW, Williams Research Center, Historic New Orleans Collection, n.d.

—— 'These Scattered Idioms'. Fragment of an essay [c. 1960/61]. TWPC, Rare Book and Manuscript Library, Columbia University, n.d.

—— 'These Scattered Idioms'. Fragments of an essay [c. 1960–Summer 1971]. MS Thr 397 (773 to 777), TWPHL, Houghton Library, Harvard University, n.d.

—— 'These Scattered Idioms'. Fragment of an essay [c. January 1977]. HRC, University of Texas at Austin, n.d.

—— 'A Thing Called Personal Lyricism'. Fragment of an essay [c. 1955]. HRC, University of Texas at Austin, n.d.

—— 'This Book'. Draft of 'Introduction' to *Reflections in a Golden Eye* [c. April 1949]. HRC, University of Texas at Austin, n.d.

—— *The Traveling Companion & Other Plays*. Ed. Annette Saddik. New York: New Directions, 2008.

—— 'Twenty Years of It'. Fragment of an essay [c. 1960]. MS Thr 397 (780). TWPHL, Houghton Library, Harvard University, n.d.

—— 'Unidentified Essay for the Sunday *New York Times*' [c. 1974]. MS Thr 397 (808). TWPHL, Houghton Library, Harvard University, n.d.

—— 'Unidentified Essay on Artists' Reputations'. MS Thr 397 (809). TWPHL, Houghton Library, Harvard University, Apr. 1976.

—— 'Unidentified Essay on the Genesis of *Eccentricities of a Nightingale*' [c. 1961]. MS Thr 397 (810). TWPHL, Houghton Library, Harvard University, n.d.

—— 'Unidentified Essays' [c. 1960–75]. MS Thr 397 (822). TWPHL, Houghton Library, Harvard University, n.d.

—— 'Unidentified essays' [c. 1949–71]. MS Thr 397 (818). TWPHL, Houghton Library, Harvard University, n.d.

—— 'Valediction'. TWPC, Rare Book and Manuscript Library, Columbia University, 24 December 1982.

—— '"Vieux Carré" and the "Cherry Blossom Cruise"'. Fragment of an essay [c. 1977]. MS Thr 397 (782 and 783). TWPHL, Houghton Library, Harvard University, n.d.

—— ['Vieux Carré was started on a steamship ...']. Fragment of an essay [c. 1976–77]. HRC, University of Texas at Austin, n.d.

—— 'Waiting for That Sea Gull, or Some Memoirs of a Con-Man'. Fragment of *Memoirs*. MS Thr 397 (787). TWPHL, Houghton Library, Harvard University, 1971.

—— ['We are now into the seventies ...']. Fragment of an essay. MSS 562 (646). FTTW, Williams Research Center, Historic New Orleans Collection, 20 December 1971.

—— 'What is "Success" in the Theatre?'. Unpublished essay [c. 1977]. HRC, University of Texas at Austin, n.d.

—— 'Which Sea-Gull on What Corner?' Fragment of *Memoirs* [c. 1971]. MS Thr 397 (801). TWPHL, Houghton Library, Harvard University, n.d.

—— 'White Paper'. Fragment of essay [c. 1974]. MS Thr 397 (802). TWPHL, Houghton Library, Harvard University, n.d.

—— 'White Paper'. Fragment of essay. MS Thr 397 (803). TWPHL, Houghton Library, Harvard University, August 1975.

—— 'Williams' Guignol'. Fragment of a list of plays. MS Thr 397 (804). TWPHL, Houghton Library, Harvard University, August 1982.

—— 'A Woman Owns an Island'. Unpublished essay. TWCD, (Ms 112). Special Collections Department, University of Delaware Library, 8 March 1967.

Williams, Tennessee, and Donald Windham. *You Touched Me!* New York: French, 1947.

Secondary Sources

Adler, Thomas P. *American Drama, 1940–1960: A Critical History*. New York: Twayne, 1994.

—— *A Streetcar Named Desire: The Moth and the Lantern*. Boston: Twayne, 1990.

—— 'Tennessee Williams's "Personal Lyricism": Toward an Androgynous Form'. *Realism and the American Dramatic Tradition*. Ed. William W. Demastes. Tuscaloosa: University of Alabama Press, 1996: 172–78.

—— 'When Ghosts Supplant Memories: Tennessee Williams' *Clothes for a Summer Hotel*'. *Southern Literary Journal* 19.2 (Spring 1987): 5–19.

Anderson, Hilton. 'Tennessee Williams' *Clothes for a Summer Hotel*: Feminine Sensibilities and the Artist'. *Publications of the Mississippi Philological Association* (1988): 1–9.

Anon. 'Airports'. *Time*, 29 April 1929.

Atkinson, Brooks. 'First Night at the Theatre'. *New York Times*, 4 December 1947: 42.

Atlanta Constitution, 11 February 1976: B8.

Baden, Michael M., MD. *Unnatural Death: Confessions of a Medical Examiner*. New York: Ballantine, 1989.

Bak, John S. '"Celebrate her with Strings": Leitmotifs and the Multifaceted "Strings" in Williams's *The Glass Menagerie*'. *Notes on Mississippi Writers* 24.2 (July 1992): 81–85.

—— *Homo americanus: Ernest Hemingway, Tennessee Williams, and Queer Masculinity*. Madison: Fairleigh Dickinson University Press, 2010.

—— '*A Streetcar Named* Dies Irae: Tennessee Williams and the Semiotics of Rape'. *The Tennessee Williams Annual Review* 10 (2009): 41–72.

—— 'Tennessee Williams and the Southern Dialectic: In Search of Androgyny'. Dissertation, Ball State University, 1993.

Baring, Maurice. 'The Blue Rose'. *The Art of the Story-Teller*. Ed. Marie L. Shedlock. New York: D. Appleton, 1915, 1917: 204–12.

Barnes, Clive. '"Clothes' Needs Some Tailoring'. *New York Post,* 27 March 1980: 1.

'Barton, Lee'. 'Why Do Homosexual Playwrights Hide their Homosexuality?' *New York Times*, 23 January 1972, sec. 2: 1.

Bigsby, Christopher W. E. *A Critical Introduction to Twentieth-Century American Drama*. Vol. II: *Williams, Miller, Albee*. Cambridge: Cambridge University Press, 1984: 15–134.

Bloom, Harold (ed.). *Tennessee Williams*. New York: Chelsea, 1987.

Brustein, Robert. 'Sweet Bird of Success'. *Encounter* 12 (June 1959): 59–60.

Bryer, Jackson. '"Entitled to Write about her Life": Tennessee Williams and F. Scott and Zelda Fitzgerald'. In Voss, *Magical Muse*, 163–77.

Burnett, Frances Hodgson. *The Land of the Blue Flower*. New York: Moffat, Yard, 1909.

Cardullo, Bert. 'The Blue Rose of St Louis: Laura, Romanticism, and *The Glass Menagerie*'. *The Tennessee Williams Annual Review* Premier Issue (1998): 81–92.

Casado, Carmelo Medina. 'Legal Prudery: The Case of *Ulysses*'. *Journal of Modern Literature* 26.1 (Fall 2002): 90–98.

Cocteau, Jean. *The Eagle with Two Heads. Five Plays*. Trans. Carl Wildman. New York: Hill and Wang, 1961: 229–310.

—— Préface. *Les mariés de la Tour Eiffel*. 1921. *Théâtre I*. Paris: Gallimard, 1948.

Crandell, George W. (ed.). *The Critical Response to Tennessee Williams*. Westport, CT: Greenwood Press, 1996.

—— '"I Can't Imagine Tomorrow": Tennessee Williams and the Representations of Time in *Clothes for a Summer Hotel*'. In Kolin, *The Undiscovered Country*, 168–80.

—— *Tennessee Williams: A Descriptive Bibliography*. Pittsburgh: University of Pittsburgh Press, 1995.

Daley, Suzanne. 'Williams Choked on a Bottle Cap'. *New York Times*, 27 February 1983: sec. 1: 1.

Debusscher, Gilbert. 'French Stowaways on an American Milk Train: William, Cocteau and Peyrefitte'. *Modern Drama* 25.3 (1982): 399–408.

—— '*The Gnädiges Fräulein*: Williams's Self-Portrait among the Ruins'. *New Essays on American Drama*. Eds. Gilbert Debusscher and Henry I. Schvey. Amsterdam: Rodopi, 1989: 63–74.

—— '"Minting their Separate Wills": Tennessee Williams and Hart Crane'. *Modern Drama* 26.4 (December 1983): 455–76.

—— '"Where Memory Begins": New Texas Light on *The Glass Menagerie*'. *The Tennessee Williams Annual Review* Premier Issue (1998): 53–62.

Devlin, Albert J. 'The Year 1939: Becoming Tennessee Williams'. In Voss, *Magical Muse*, 35–49.

Donahue, Francis. *The Dramatic World of Tennessee Williams*. New York: Ungar, 1964.

Dorff, Linda. 'Collapsing Resurrection Mythologies: Theatricalist Discourses of Fire and Ash in *Clothes for a Summer Hotel*'. In Gross, *A Casebook*, 153–72.

—— 'Theatricalist Cartoons: Tennessee Williams's Late, "Outrageous" Plays'. *The Tennessee Williams Annual Review* 2 (1999): 13–33.

Durham, Frank. 'Tennessee Williams, Theatre Poet in Prose'. *Modern Critical Interpretations: Tennessee Williams's* The Glass Menagerie. Ed. Harold Bloom. New York: Chelsea House, 1988.

Ellmann, Richard. *James Joyce*. New York: Oxford University Press, 1982.

Falk, Signi Lenea. *Tennessee Williams*. New York: Twayne, 1961.

Frost, Frances. 'The Blue Rose'. *Legends of the United Nations*. New York: McGraw-Hill, 1943.

Fruchon-Toussaint, Catherine. *Tennessee Williams: une vie*. Paris: Éditions Baker Street, 2011.

Gindt, Dirk. 'Tennessee Williams and the Swedish Academy: Why He Never Won the Nobel Prize'. In Kaplan, *Tenn at One Hundred*, 153–67.

—— 'Torn between the "Swedish Sin" and "Homosexual Freemasonry": Tennessee Williams, Sexual Morals and the Closet in 1950's Sweden'. *The Tennessee Williams Annual Review* 11 (2010): 19–39.

Givens, Steve. 'King of the Hill'. *Washington University Magazine* (Summer 1994): 30.

Gross, Robert F. (ed.). *Tennessee Williams: A Casebook*. New York, London: Routledge, 2002.

Gussow, Mel. 'Tennessee Williams on Art and Sex'. *New York Times*, 3 November 1975: 49.

Hale, Allean. 'Early Williams – the Making of a Playwright'. In Roudané, *Cambridge Companion*, 11–28.

—— Introduction. *Fugitive Kind*. New York: New Directions, 2001: xi–xxi.

—— Introduction. *Stairs to the Roof*. New York: New Directions, 2000: ix–xix.

—— 'Tennessee Williams' St Louis Blues'. In Kaplan, *Tenn at One Hundred*, 3–9.

—— 'Three Plays for the Lyric Theatre'. *The Tennessee Williams Annual Review* 7 (2005): 89–103.

—— 'Tom Williams – Proletarian Playwright'. *The Tennessee Williams Annual Review* Premier Issue (1998): 13–22.

Harris, Barbara M. '"It's Another Elvis Sighting, and ... My God ... He's with Tennessee Williams!"'. In Voss, *Magical Muse*, 178–92.

Hayman, Ronald. *Tennessee Williams: Everyone Else Is an Audience*. New Haven and London: Yale University Press, 1993.

Hirsch, Foster. *A Portrait of the Artist: The Plays of Tennessee Williams*. Port Washington, NY: Associated Faculty, 1979.

Holditch, Kenneth. 'Tennessee among the Biographers'. In Kaplan, *Tenn at One Hundred*, 209–19.

——. 'The Last Frontier of Bohemia: Tennessee Williams in New Orleans, 1938–1983'. *Southern Quarterly* 23.2 (Winter 1985): 1–37.

Hofmann, Paul. 'Williams Tells Brother He's Fine; Playwright Phones to Allay Fears, but Doesn't Appear'. *New York Times*, 30 June 1968: 54.

Jackson, Esther M. *The Broken World of Tennessee Williams*. Madison, WI: University of Wisconsin Press, 1966.

Jenckes, Norma. '"Let's Face the Music and Dance": Resurgent Romanticism in Tennessee Williams's *Camino Real* and *Clothes for a Summer Hotel*'. In Kolin, *The Undiscovered Country*, 181–93.

Joyce, James. *Ulysses*. New York: Random House, 1934.

Kalem, T. E. 'The Angel of the Odd'. *Time*, 9 March 1962: 53–60.

—— 'Of Sin and Grace' [Review of *Memoirs*]. *Time*, 1 December 1975: 83–84.

—— 'Theater: Apparitions and Cakewalks'. [Review of *Will Mr. Merriwether Return from Memphis?*] *Time*, 4 February 1980.

Kaplan, David (ed.). *Tenn at One Hundred: The Reputation of Tennessee Williams*. East Brunswick, NJ: Hansen, 2011.

—— *Tennessee Williams in Provincetown*. East Brunswick, NJ: Hansen Publishing, 2007.

Kazan, Elia. *A Life*. New York: Knopf, 1988.

Kenan, Scott. *Walking on Glass: A Memoir of the Later Days of Tennessee Williams*. Amazon Kindle, 2012.

Kerr, Walter. 'A Secret Is Half-Told in Fountains of Words'. *New York Herald Tribune*, 3 April 1955, sec. 4: 1.

—— 'The Stage: "Clothes for a Summer Hotel"'. *New York Times*, 27 March 1980: D 15.

Kolin, Philip C. (ed.). *Confronting Tennessee Williams's* A Streetcar Named Desire*: Essays in Critical Pluralism*. Westport, CT: Greenwood Press, 1993.

—— '"Isolated": Tennessee Williams's First Extant Published Short Story'. *The Tennessee Williams Annual Review* (1998): 33–39.

—— 'The Remarkable Rooming-House of Mme. Le Monde*: Tennessee Williams's Little Shop of Comic Horrors'. *The Tennessee Williams Annual Review* 4 (2001): 39–48.

—— (ed.). *The Tennessee Williams Encyclopedia*. Westport, CT: Greenwood Press, 2004.

—— *Tennessee Williams: A Guide to Research and Performance*. Westport, CT: Greenwood Press, 1998.

—— (ed.). *The Undiscovered Country: The Later Plays of Tennessee Williams*. New York: Peter Lang, 2002.

Kramer, Richard. '"The Sculptural Drama": Tennessee Williams's Plastic Theatre'. *The Tennessee Williams Annual Review* 5 (2002): 1–10.

Kroll, Jack. 'Slender is the Night'. *Newsweek*, 7 April 1980: 95.

Krutch, Joseph Wood. *'Modernism' in Modern Drama*. Ithaca, NY: Cornell University Press, 1953.

Lahr, John. 'The Lady and Tennessee'. In Kaplan, *Tenn at One Hundred*, 211–59.

—— 'Past Imperfect'. *The New Yorker*, 30 April 2012: 76–77.

Leavitt, Richard F. (ed.). *The World of Tennessee Williams*. New York: Putnam's, 1978.

Lehmann-Haupt, Christopher. 'Love Songs of a Crocodile'. *New York Times*, 7 November 1975: 35.

Leverich, Lyle. *Tom: The Unknown Tennessee Williams*. London: Hodder & Stoughton, 1995.

Levin, Harry. Preface. *James Joyce: A Critical Introduction*. 2nd edn. New York: New Directions, 1960: vii–x.

Loomis, Jeffrey B. 'Four Characters in Search of a Company: Williams, Pirandello, and the *Cat on a Hot Tin Roof* Manuscripts'. In Voss, *Magical Muse*, 91–110.

Londré, Felicia Hardison. *'En Avant!* Tennessee Williams between Hyperborea and the Mediterranean'. *Tennessee Williams and Europe: Intercultural Encounters, Transatlantic Exchanges*. Ed. John S. Bak. Amsterdam: Rodopi, forthcoming, 2013.

Mannes, Marya. 'Plea for Fairer Ladies'. *New York Times Magazine*, 29 May 1960: 16, 26.

Maxwell, Gilbert. *Tennessee Williams and Friends*. Cleveland: World, 1965.

Milford, Nancy. *Zelda*. 1970. New York: HarperCollins, 1992.

McCarthy, Mary. 'Oh, Sweet Mystery of Life: *A Streetcar Named Desire*'. *Partisan Review* 15 (March 1948): 357–60.

Moscato, Michael, and Leslie Le Blanc (eds.). *The United States of America v. One Book Entitled Ulysses by James Joyce*. Frederick, MD: University Press of America, 1984.

Moschovakis, Nick, and David Roessel. 'Introduction to "Amor Perdida"'. *Michigan Quarterly Review* 42.3 (Summer 2003): 536–39.

Murphy, Brenda. *Tennessee Williams and Elia Kazan: A Collaboration in the Theatre.* Cambridge: Cambridge University Press, 1992.

Murray, Timothy D. *Evolving Texts: The Writing of Tennessee Williams.* Newark: University of Delaware Library, 1988.

Nathan, George Jean. 'The *Streetcar* Isn't Drawn by Pegasus'. *New York Journal American,* 15 December 1947: 14.

Nelson, Benjamin. *Tennessee Williams: The Man and his Work.* New York: Ivan Obolensky, 1961.

'New Picture' [Review of *Baby Doll*]. *Time,* 24 December 1956: 61.

O'Connor, Jacqueline. 'Moving into the Rooming House: Interiority and Stage Space in Tennessee Williams's *Fugitive Kind* and *Vieux Carré*'. *Southern Quarterly* 42.2 (Winter 2004): 19–36.

——— 'The Strangest Kind of Romance: Tennessee Williams and his Broadway Critics'. In Roudané, *Cambridge Companion,* 255–64.

Pagan, Nicholas. *Rethinking Literary Biography: A Postmodern Approach to Tennessee Williams.* Rutherford: Fairleigh Dickinson University Press, 1993.

Paller, Michael. 'The Couch and Tennessee'. *The Tennessee Williams Annual Review* 3 (2000): 37–55.

——— *Gentlemen Callers: Tennessee Williams, Homosexuality, and Mid-Twentieth-Century Drama.* New York: Palgrave/Macmillan, 2005.

Palmer, R. Barton, and William Robert Bray. *Hollywood's Tennessee: The Williams Films and Postwar America.* Austin, TX: University of Texas Press, 2009.

Parker, Brian. 'The Composition of *The Glass Menagerie*: An Argument for Complexity'. *Modern Drama* 25.3 (September 1982): 409–22.

——— 'A Preliminary Stemma for the Drafts and Revisions of Tennessee Williams's *Cat on a Hot Tin Roof* (1955)'. *Papers of the Bibliographical Society of America* 90.4 (December 1996): 475–96.

Pawley, Thomas D. 'Experimental Theatre Seminar; or the Basic Training of Tennessee Williams: A Memoir'. *Iowa Review* 19.1 (Winter 1989): 65–76.

'People'. *Time,* 13 February 1956.

Porter, Darwin. *Brando Unzipped: A Revisionist and Very Private Look at America's Greatest Actor.* New York: Blood Moon, 2006.

Prosser, William. *The Late Plays of Tennessee Williams.* Lanham, MD: Scarecrow, 2009.

Quinby, Lee. 'Tennessee Williams' Hermaphroditic Symbolism in *The Rose Tattoo, Orpheus Descending, The Night of the Iguana,* and *Kingdom of Earth*'. *Tennessee Williams Newsletter* 1 (Fall 1979): 12–14.

Rader, Dotson. *Tennessee: Cry of the Heart.* Garden City, NY: Doubleday, 1985.

Rasky, Harry. *Tennessee Williams: A Portrait in Laughter and Lamentation.* New York: Dodd, Mead, 1986.

Richardson, Jack. 'Unaffected Recollections: *Memoirs*'. *New York Times,* 2 November 1975: 42.

Robey, Cora. 'Chloroses – Pâles Roses and Pleurosis – Blue Roses'. *Romance Notes* 13 (Winter 1971): 250–51.

Roudané, Matthew C. (ed.). *The Cambridge Companion to Tennessee Williams.* Cambridge: Cambridge University Press, 1997.

Saddik, Annette J. *The Politics of Reputation: The Critical Reception of Tennessee Williams' Later Plays*. Cranbury, NJ: Associated University Press, 1999.

Sandomir, Richard. 'Tennessee Williams: On Age and Annoyance'. *New York Sunday News*, 23 March 1980, Leisure Section: 5, 12.

Savran, David. *Cowboys, Communists, and Queers: The Politics of Masculinity in the Works of Arthur Miller and Tennessee Williams*. Minneapolis: University of Minnesota Press, 1992.

Schvey, Henry I. '"Getting the Colored Lights Going": Expressionism in Tennessee Williams' *A Streetcar Named Desire*'. *Critical Insights: Tennessee Williams*. Ed. Brenda Murphy. Pasadena and Hackensack, NJ: Salem, 2010: 58–79.

Simon, John. 'Damsels Inducing Distress'. *New York* magazine, 7 April 1980: 82, 84.

Single, Lori Leathers. 'Flying the Jolly Rogers: Images of Escape and Selfhood in Tennessee Williams's *The Glass Menagerie*'. *The Tennessee Williams Annual Review* 2 (1999): 69–85.

Smith, Bruce. *Costly Performances: Tennessee Williams: The Last Stage*. New York: Paragon House, 1990.

Smith, William Jay. *My Friend Tom: The Poet–Playwright Tennessee Williams*. Jackson, MS: University Press of Mississippi, 2011.

Smith-Howard, Alycia, and Greta Heintzelman (eds.). *Critical Companion to Tennessee Williams: A Literary Reference to his Life and Work*. New York: Facts On File, 2005.

Spoo, Robert. 'Copyright Protectionism and Its Discontents: The Case of James Joyce's *Ulysses* in America'. *The Yale Law Journal* 108.3 (December 1998): 633–67.

Spoto, Donald. *The Kindness of Strangers: The Life of Tennessee Williams*. New York: Ballantine, 1986.

Stamper, Rexford. '*The Two-Character Play*: Psychic Individuation'. In Tharpe, *A Tribute*, 349–61.

Stanton, Stephen S. 'Some Thoughts about *Steps Must Be* Gentle'. *Tennessee Williams Review* 4.1 (Spring 1983): 48–53.

Steen, Mike. *A Look at Tennessee Williams*. New York: Hawthorn, 1969.

Tharpe, Jac (ed.). *Tennessee Williams: A Tribute*. Jackson, MS: University Press of Mississippi, 1977.

Tischler, Nancy M. *Tennessee Williams: Rebellious Puritan*. New York: Citadel, 1961.

—— 'Tennessee Williams: Vagabond Poet'. *The Tennessee Williams Annual Review* Premier Issue (1998): 73–79.

Tynan, Kenneth. [Review of *Sweet Bird of Youth*]. *The New Yorker*, 21 March 1959: 98.

—— *Right and Left*. London: Longmans, 1967.

—— 'Valentine to Tennessee Williams'. *Mademoiselle*, February 1956: 130–31, 200–203.

Van Antwerp, Margaret A., and Sally Johns (eds.). *Dictionary of Literary Biography, Documentary Series: An Illustrated Chronicle*. Vol. 4: *Tennessee Williams*. Detroit: Gale, 1982–84.

Vannatta, Dennis. *Tennessee Williams: A Study of the Short Fiction*. Boston: Twayne, 1988.

Voss, Ralph F. (ed.). *Magical Muse: Millennial Essays on Tennessee Williams*. Tuscaloosa and London: University of Alabama Press, 2002.

Waters, Arthur B. 'Tennessee Williams: Ten Years Later'. *Theatre Arts*, July 1955: 73.

Weil, Kari. *Androgyny and the Denial of Difference*. Charlottesville and London: University Press of Virginia, 1992.

Whitmore, George. 'George Whitmore interviews Tennessee Williams'. *Gay Sunshine Interviews*. Vol. I. Ed. Winston Leyland. San Francisco: Gay Sunshine, 1978: 310–25.

Williams, Dakin, and Shepherd Mead. *Tennessee Williams: An Intimate Biography*. New York: Arbor, 1983.

Williams, Edwina Dakin, and Lucy Freeman. *Remember Me to Tom*. St Louis: Sunrise, 1963.

Willet, John. *The Theatre of Erwin Piscator: Half a Century of Politics in the Theatre*. London: Methuen, 1978.

Windham, Donald. *Lost Friendships: A Memoir of Truman Capote, Tennessee Williams, and Others*. New York: Morrow, 1985, 1987.

Index

Academy Awards, the, 139, 157
Acapulco, 83–4, 145, 178, 191
Actors Repertory, the, 262
Actors Studio, the, 97, 184
Actors' Lab, the, 120
Adamov, Arthur, 181
Adams, Ansel, 249
Adamson, Eve, 253–4
Adler, Thomas P., xiii, 122, 281, 295, 299
Adventures of Huckleberry Finn, The (Twain), 5
Advocate (journal), 222
Aeneid, The (Virgil), 50
African Queen, The (Huston), 139
Aigle à deux têtes, L' (Cocteau), 121, 195–7, 292–3
Aisne-Marne American Cemetery, the, 15
Albee, Edward, 188, 213
Algonquin Hotel, the, 158
All My Sons (Miller), 120
All Saints College, 9
Alliance Theatre, the, 239
Alouhette, L' (magazine), 29
Alva (OK), 117
Amalfi (Italy), 125, 126
Ambassador Hotel, the, 217
American Academy of Arts and Letters, the, 108, 139, 211, 235
American Conservatory Theater, the (ACT), 232
American Gothic (Wood), 61, 87
American Hospital in Neuilly, the, 124
American in Paris, An (Minnelli), 139
American Prefaces (journal), 29, 38, 44, 61, 271
American Psychiatric Association, the, 159
American Scenes (Kozlenko), 91
American Theater, the, 21, 39
Amsterdam, 11, 15–16

Anderson, Craig, 240, 298
Anderson, Maxwell, 59, 91, 96
Anderson, Mrs E. O., 73, 90
Anderson, Sherwood, 52
Androgyny and the Denial of Difference (Weil), 215
Anna Christie (O'Neill), 45
Answered Prayers (Capote), 235
Anthony Adverse (LeRoy), 46
Antoinette Perry ('Tony') Award, the, 135
Anvil, The (magazine), 28–9, 32, 270
Apollo Theatre, the, 78
Arabian Nights' Entertainments, The (Henry), 38
Arena Theatre, the, 234
Arnold, Matthew, 34
Ash, David, 61
Ashton, Herbert, Jr, 72
Athens, 154, 157
Atkinson, Brooks, 122, 128, 135, 147, 174, 190, 281
Atlanta Constitution (newspaper), 228, 297
Atlantic Monthly (magazine), 217
Auden, W. H., 79, 130, 141, 212, 222
Auld, Linda, xiii
Austen-Riggs Centre, the (MA), 159

Baby Doll (Lavigne), 262
Baden, Michael, 300
Baddeley, Hermione, 194
BAFTA Awards, the, 156
Bak, John S., 260, 270, 280, 290
Baker, Carroll, 156
Balanchine, George, 115
Balch, J. S., 32, 58
Ballad of the Sad Café, The (McCullers), 279–80
Bangkok, 212, 217, 222, 223, 226
Bankhead, Tallulah, 81, 121, 155–6, 194, 199, 280, 288
Bar Bizarre, The (Dakin Williams), 250

314